"There are few authors who can write action sequences . . . the way David Mack does."

"Incredibly powerful, compelling and thought-provoking. . . . Stunning and climactic . . . seat-of-your-pants action-adventure."

"David Mack exhibits superior skill in drawing the reader into the story to such a degree that you have to stop and remember to breathe."

—Jacqueline Bundy, TrekNation.com

"[*A Time to Heal*] is a tightly written, riveting book. A fast read that offers believable intrigue, stunning war descriptions, striking character struggles and nemesis confrontations. If [it] were the score for an opera, it would obviously be the crescendo to the curtain drop."

—Kathy LaFollett, The Lincoln Heights Literary Society

"If you need a story that combines fear, pain, sorrow, suffering, thrills, humor, and an atmosphere awash in raw, intimate emotion and life-or-death tension, Mack is your man."

—Killian Melloy, wigglefish.com

"David Mack clearly has his finger on the pulse of *Star Trek* as we once knew it and as we know it now, elevating him into the top echelon of expert storytellers in both *Star Trek* and in the world of literature. . . . [*A Time to Heal*] could have easily been ripped from today's headlines or the current techno-thriller novels of Tom Clancy."

—Bill Williams, TrekWeb.com

STAR TREK®
VANGUARD

HARBINGER
DAVID MACK

**Based upon STAR TREK®
created by Gene Roddenberry**

POCKET BOOKS
New York   London   Toronto   Sydney   Stars Landing

An *Original* Publication of POCKET BOOKS

 POCKET BOOKS, a division of Simon & Schuster Inc.
1230 Avenue of the Americas, New York, NY 10020

This book is a work of fiction. Names, characters, places and incidents are products of the author's imagination or are used fictitiously. Any resemblance to actual events or locales or persons, living or dead, is entirely coincidental.

 STAR TREK is a Registered Trademark of Paramount Pictures.

This book is published by Pocket Books, a division of Simon & Schuster, Inc., under exclusive license from Paramount Pictures.

ISBN-13: 978-1-4165-0774-1
ISBN-10:   1-4165-0774-4

First Pocket Books paperback edition August 2005

10   9   8   7   6   5   4   3   2   1

POCKET and colophon are registered trademarks of Simon & Schuster, Inc.

Cover art by Doug Drexler; station design by Masao Okazaki; background image courtesy of NASA and the Hubble Heritage Team (STScI/AURA)

Manufactured in the United States of America

For information regarding special discounts for bulk purchases, please contact Simon & Schuster Special Sales at 1-800-456-6798 or business@simonandschuster.com.

We shall not cease from exploration
And the end of all our exploring
Will be to arrive where we started
And know the place for the first time.

—T. S. Eliot, *Little Gidding*

HISTORIAN'S NOTE

Harbinger begins in early 2263, shortly before the promotion of James T. Kirk to captain of the *Enterprise,* and concludes in 2265, between the events of "Where No Man Has Gone Before" and "The Corbomite Maneuver."

2263

PROLOGUE

Commodore Matt Decker wasn't entirely certain what to call the swath of fuzz that currently adorned the lower half of his face. It was too long to be stubble, but far too sparse to be a beard. Scratching it gently during the turbolift ride to the bridge, he found the description he was looking for: It was scruff.

Well, that won't do, he decided. In his opinion, the commanding officer of a starship could be clean-shaven, bearded, or even a bit prickly from time to time. Scruffy, however, was not an option. *Unless it's an intermediate stage on the way to a beard,* he mused. *That would be all right.* Every few months he toyed with the idea of growing a beard. Then he'd note yet another subtle increase in the number of gray follicles populating his chin, and once again the dense bramble of hair would be shorn away until the next piquing of his curiosity.

The hum of the turbolift crested and fell quiet; then the doors swished open. A cascade of gentle synthetic chirps filled the bridge of the *U.S.S. Constellation.* As the burly commodore's first step hit the deck, his deceptively fragile-looking first officer, Commander Hiromi Takeshewada, rose from the center seat and greeted him with a single, graceful nod. He gave her a curt half-nod in return as he strode quickly past the gamma-shift communications officer, whose name once again eluded him, despite his repeated attempts to commit it to memory.

At the science station, Lieutenant Guillermo Masada—whose own neatly trimmed beard Decker struggled not to envy—peered into the sensor hood, which cast a pale blue glow across his brow. The science officer's short ponytail didn't violate any regulations, but it drew a sharp contrast between Masada and the vast majority of Starfleet's close-cropped male officers. Though Decker rarely said so, he often found Starfleet's lockstep mind-set more than a little stultifying.

Takeshewada joined Decker in flanking Masada, who looked up from his sensor readings with an apprehensive side-to-side glance at his superior officers.

"Report," Decker said, cutting straight to business.

Masada reached behind his ear as if to scratch, then gave an almost absentminded tug on his ponytail as he straightened and pivoted toward Decker. "We were running a routine gene-sequence scan on the biosamples from Ravanar IV," he said. "Most were nothing to write home about." He gestured for Takeshewada to look at the sensor data for herself. "Then we found this."

Decker tried to be patient, but at times like this it was hard. "Guillermo, please don't keep me in suspense."

"Sorry, sir. It's a gene sequence unlike anything we've ever seen before. My best guess would be that it has several million chemical base pairs, and it's more complex than simple G-A-T-C. It has molecules we're still trying to identify."

Takeshewada lifted her gaze from the blue-gray sensor

hood. Her already fair complexion looked paler than normal. "That's incredible," she said.

Folding his arms across his chest, Decker said to Masada, "Where did it come from? Some kind of über-life-form?"

"Hardly," the science officer said. "From a simple mold."

"Simple?" Decker shook his head, as much in disbelief as in sheer wonderment at the never-ending tricks the universe had up its proverbial sleeve. "That's a lot of DNA for something I'd scrape off my breakfast. Speaking of which—" He turned toward his yeoman, who happened to be walking past. "Lawford, get me some coffee, will you?"

"Lawford transferred to the *Yorktown* two weeks ago, sir," the yeoman said. "I'm Guthrie."

Decker squinted in disapproval. "And that has precisely *what* to do with my coffee?"

"Nothing, sir."

The commodore pointed the yeoman toward the food slot. "Milk, no sugar."

"I know, sir."

"Thanks, Lawford."

"Guthrie, sir."

"Whatever." Decker turned back toward the science station while the yeoman plodded away, muttering quietly. Returning his attention to Masada, Decker said, "Why would mold need that much genetic information?"

"I don't think it does," Masada said.

Decker was getting annoyed. "That's what I'm saying."

"No, sir," Masada said. "What I mean is, I think only a

very small portion of the genetic string has anything to do with the mold itself. The rest is . . . well, just kind of *there*."

Takeshewada tilted her head in a way that implied she found Masada's answer less than satisfactory. "But what does it do, Guillermo?"

The science officer's eyes widened as his lips tightened into a thin line and his shoulders rounded into a shrug. "No idea. I can tell you that it's big, but other than that . . ." He just shook his head.

"And our tradition of excellence continues," Decker said with a sour inflection. His darkening mood was brightened by the arrival of his coffee. He accepted the mug from Guthrie, then turned immediately back toward Masada. "How soon can you finish some tests and get me a real report?"

"I'm not sure I can," Masada said. "Our lab's good, but it's not *this* good. We're gonna have to send all of this—the samples, the scans, the whole kit and kaboodle—back to Starfleet Command and let them handle it."

Decker's shoulders slumped with disappointment. "Are you serious? We make a once-in-a-lifetime find, and you're telling me we have to punt?"

"I'm afraid so, sir." Masada looked even more disappointed than Decker felt. "With our hardware and manpower, we could spend years on this and not make a dent." Dejected, he added, "It's just too big for us to tackle alone."

With a heavy sigh, Decker resigned himself to the situation. "There's an old saying on Earth," he said as he gave Masada's shoulder a consoling squeeze. "There's no 'I' in 'team.' " Sipping his coffee carefully, he walked down the short stairs to his seat, settled into it with a muffled grunt and a few pops from his aging knees, and pivoted around toward the communications officer. He opened his mouth to issue the order, then remembered that he didn't know what her name was. Glancing at Takeshewada, he gave her a quick nod to carry on.

To the first officer's credit, she knew exactly what Decker needed her to do and covered his lapse seamlessly. "Ensign Ponor, open a secure channel to Starfleet Command," she said. "Prepare to relay information from Lieutenant Masada's station, on his mark." Ponor acknowledged the order, and minutes later Masada finished the data transfer. Takeshewada appeared at Decker's side as he finished his coffee. "Transmission complete, sir. And we have new orders from Starfleet."

"Do tell," Decker said, handing his empty cup to Guthrie, who was breezing past at precisely the right moment to relieve the commodore of his petty burden.

"We've been ordered back to Federation space," Takeshewada said. "To begin patrolling the Klingon border in the Gariman Sector, before putting in for resupply at Deep Space Station K-7."

Decker looked at the mesmerizing drift of warp-distorted stars on the main viewer. "Looks like the Taurus Reach will have to wait for someone else to plant our flag. Helm: Plot a course for Station K-7, and hug the border all the way there."

"Aye, sir," the helmsman said.

It cut against the grain of Decker's nature to turn his back on a mystery such as the meta-genome that Masada had uncovered. Even more difficult was turning away from the exploration of such a vast unknown as the Taurus Reach in favor of a mundane border cruise. But as the starfield on the viewer blurred and shifted, and the *Constellation* turned homeward, he knew that the work he and his crew had begun here, hundreds of light-years from home, was no doubt in very good hands.

2265

1

Captain James T. Kirk walked alone through the crowded, busy corridors of the *Enterprise*. He moved quickly, like a man with a purpose, but the truth was that he had been wandering without a destination for the better part of an hour. Memories of Delta Vega haunted him. Gary Mitchell's eyes, fiercely aglow with the alien power that had corrupted him, refused to stop staring back at Kirk every time he tried to sleep. Night after night, the ghost of Kirk's best friend, dead by his hand, awaited him in his dreams, his spectral stare an inescapable silent reproach.

Even though the power packs Scotty had salvaged from the Delta Vega lithium-cracking station had enabled the *Enterprise*'s warp engines to be restarted, the ship's current top speed was well short of its rated maximum. At their current best possible speed, they were still months from the nearest Federation base. By now Kirk's after-action report—filed via subspace radio—had likely reached Starfleet Command. He did not regret the simple notation he had entered for Mitchell, despite the fact that the man had tried to commandeer the *Enterprise* and had turned his new psionic powers against Kirk. The young captain continued to remind himself that the being who had jeopardized his ship and crew had not been Gary Mitchell—not really. After the *Enterprise*'s failure to breach the energy barrier at the edge of the galaxy, Mitchell—and, later, psychiatrist Dr. Elizabeth Dehner—had been changed by the experience, transformed. Kirk had to believe that the man he had known would not have been capable of such casual cruelty . . . of murder. Instead, he had noted in his log only that Mitchell had died "in the line of duty."

A door opened as Kirk passed by, and the aroma of fresh coffee lured him into the galley. Dr. Mark Piper sat alone at a table, gratefully inhaling wisps of hot vapor snaking upward from his burnished aluminum mug. "Morning, Captain," the grizzled, aging physician said, his voice rough.

The greeting brought Kirk up short. "Is it?" He checked the ship's chronometer, mounted over the galley door.

"It's almost 0100," Piper said. "Technically, it's morning." He sipped carefully at his beverage.

"I guess it is," Kirk said with a wan grin. "Burning the midnight oil?"

"Emergency call," Piper said. "Nothing serious enough to wake you for. But I guess that's not an issue."

Kirk stood in front of the food dispenser, eyeing his choices. "Who was it?"

"Alden," Piper said, then puffed gently on his coffee.

None of the menu choices appealed to Kirk. He sat down across from Piper. "What happened?"

"An accident in engineering." He took another sip, inhaled through gritted teeth, and set down his mug. "Spock's probably writing the report for your morning briefing even as we speak."

"No doubt," Kirk said. His half-Vulcan first officer was nothing if not efficient. However, the same suppression of emotion that enabled Spock to exercise unimpeachable logic in his other official capacity, as ship's science officer, had also led him to urge Kirk to kill Gary Mitchell before his new powers drove him to enslave or exterminate the *Enterprise* crew. Kirk had not heeded Spock's warning, and helmsman Lee Kelso had paid for Kirk's mistake with his life. The captain knew that it was absurd to blame Spock for what happened, or to be angry with him for being so quick to condemn Mitchell to death. Spock's chief duty as first officer was to protect the ship and its crew, even if that meant sacrificing one to save the others.

Knowing those things made Mitchell's death no easier for Kirk to accept, however. He had pulled the trigger and brought a ton of rock down on his friend. No amount of rationalization was going to erase the lingering guilt that had shadowed his every thought since that desperate moment.

After a silent minute, Piper said, "You should eat something."

"I'm not hungry."

"Try getting some sleep, then."

Kirk chuckled ruefully. "Easier said than done."

"On this ship, I guess that's true." Piper grabbed his mug and stood up. "I have to head back to sickbay. Want to stop in and say hi to Alden?"

Before he could accept the invitation, Kirk was cut off by a two-note whistle from the overhead speaker. *"Captain Kirk to the bridge,"* came Spock's voice over the intraship channel.

Stepping away from the table, Kirk thumbed the transmitter switch on a nearby wall panel. "On my way. Kirk out." He closed the channel and looked back at Piper. "Give my best to Alden."

Piper's reply of "Aye, Captain" trailed Kirk as he exited the galley, grateful for something new to think about.

Spock rose from the center seat as Captain Kirk emerged from the turbolift. "Report," the captain said, making a beeline for his chair. He seemed primed to face a crisis that did not exist.

"Receiving an audio-only hail from a Federation outpost, Captain," Spock said, moving to the right of the captain's seat.

Rather than sit, Kirk stood to the left of his chair while he assessed the situation. "Which one?"

"Starbase 47," Spock said, "a Watchtower-class space station, also known as Vanguard."

"Vanguard?" Kirk narrowed his eyes while he pondered that information. Spock had yet to determine what benefit the captain accrued to his concentration by reducing his visual acuity. "I thought that base was years away from being operational."

"Apparently not." Spock added, "They await our reply."

The captain glanced at Spock but said nothing. In one fluid motion he pivoted into his chair and swiveled it toward the communications officer. "Lieutenant Uhura, patch them in."

"Aye, sir," Uhura said. The young woman deftly routed the signal to the bridge's main speakers. "Channel open."

"Starbase 47, this is Captain James T. Kirk of the *Starship Enterprise*. Do you read me?"

"*We read you,* Enterprise," a youthful-sounding female voice said. "*Go ahead.*"

"We require extensive repairs to a number of key

systems. Are you in a position to assist us with maintenance?"

"Affirmative, Captain. Should we clear a berth for you?"

The captain frowned before he answered. "Please."

"Consider it done. What's your ETA?"

Kirk looked to Spock, who answered in a clear baritone, "Six days, three hours, and twenty-four minutes."

"Acknowledged," the female voice said. *"Vanguard out."*

The channel clicked off. Kirk leaned on his elbow and stared hard at the slow drift of starlight across the main viewer. Under his breath he said to Spock, "A fully operational starbase, all the way out here. Must be our lucky day."

Spock sensed the suspicion radiating from his commanding officer. "You seem less than encouraged by the news, Captain."

"How long does it take to build a Watchtower-class station, Spock?"

From memory, Spock said, "On average, four years, nine months—"

"And how long ago was the Vanguard project initiated?"

That required a few moments of thought. "Two years, seven months, and ten days."

The first officer watched the slow curling of Kirk's hand into a fist. "Somebody was in a big hurry to get this station built. With all the saber-rattling the Klingons have been doing, why put a major base this far from the Federation?"

Spock considered the most likely possibilities. "Support for a colonization effort?"

The captain looked unconvinced. "Maybe."

"In the absence of another rationale, it would be the most logical explanation."

"Dig up everything in the databanks on Vanguard," Kirk said. "I want a full briefing before we make port."

2

The sultry jungle night buzzed with the sawing song of nocturnal insects. With a casual sweep of his hand, Cervantes Quinn pulled a long twist of his tangled, bone-white hair from his eyes and tucked it behind his ear. An insidious humidity amplified the post-sundown radiant heat and left Quinn's sweat-sodden clothing clinging like a skin graft with pockets to his thick-middled, past-its-prime body.

He straightened from his crouch and reached into his left pants pocket. Nestled deep inside, under the lockpicking kit, past his last snack stick of meat-flavored synthetic something-or-other, was his flask. As quietly as he was able, he pulled it free, unscrewed the cap, and downed a swig of nameless green liquor. It tasted horrible. He kept it in his flask only because his most frequent employer, an Orion merchant-prince named Ganz, had an irregular habit of demanding that other people pour him impromptu drinks—and then shooting anyone who poured something he didn't like. Ganz liked the green stuff.

Awful as it was, it still constituted a minor improvement over the stale aftertaste of the pseudo-beef snack stick Quinn had devoured an hour ago. He took another swig, then tucked the half-empty flask back into the bottom of his pocket. This stakeout was taking longer than he had expected. He had imagined himself long gone by now, the

pilfered device securely hidden behind the false wall panel
in the cargo bay of his private freighter, the *Rocinante*. Instead, he swatted blindly at the high-pitched mosquitoes
that he could hear dive-bombing his head but couldn't see
unless they passed between him and the lights of the camp
below.

From his vantage point deep in the undergrowth, beyond
the tree line that marked the perimeter of the mining camp,
he saw the prospectors moving from one semipermanent
building to another. Most were winding down for the night,
settling into their bunks, making final trips to the latrine.
Vexing him were the two who continued to sit inside their
Spartan mess hall, playing the most uninspired game of
cards Quinn had ever seen.

He was certain he could beat them handily in just
about any game, from Texas Hold'em to Denobulan Wild-
card. For a moment, he allowed himself to consider
scrapping his mission of covert confiscation in favor of
card-sharking the mining team. Quinn's common sense
awoke from its slumber and reminded him not only that it
would be wrong to cheat honest working folks but that, if
he returned to Vanguard without the sensor screen he'd
been sent to steal, Ganz would garnish his next buffet
with Quinn's viscera.

Patience was not one of Quinn's stronger virtues, but
his impulses were usually kept in check by his healthy
fear of death, injury, and incarceration. Long after he had
become convinced that his knees had fused into position
and would never allow him to straighten again, the last
two miners restacked their cards, snapped an elastic band
around them, and left them on the table as they got up.

They turned out the mess-hall lamp and stepped out the door into the murky spills of weak orange light from lamps strung on drooping wires between their shacks. Despite the multilayered soundscape of the jungle that surrounded Quinn, he heard their every squishing step as they trudged across the muddy dirt road and passed out of sight on the far side of the barracks. Their shadows, long and blurred, fell across another building. Deep, repetitive clomping sounds echoed around the camp as the miners kicked the wet filth from their boots. Finally they entered their barracks, and the door slam-rattled shut behind them.

Batting away lush fronds and dangling loops of thorny vines, Quinn skulked forward toward the camp. An arthritic aching in his knees threatened to slow him down, but he ignored it, lured forward by the promise of an easy night's work. He paused at the edge of the tree line. There was no sign of automated security devices—no cameras, motion detectors, or sentry guns. Not that he had expected any, necessarily, but the presence of the sensor screen in a mining camp had aroused his suspicion. It wasn't the kind of equipment normally found in civilian hands. Ganz hadn't said how he had come to learn of its presence here on Ravanar IV, and Quinn wasn't foolish enough to ask.

He unholstered his stun pistol. The street was empty. In the distance, something shrieked three times in quick succession and something else roared in reply. With his hand resting lightly on the grip of his sidearm, he emerged from the trees and moved in a quick, low jog across the street. The mud under his boots made every step an adventure; it slipped like congealed hydraulic lubricant and stank like the open sewers of Korinar. Several quick steps brought him back into the cover of shadow. He leaned sideways and cast a furtive glance around the corner into the dark, narrow stretch between the barracks and the equipment shed. It was empty, and he stole into it, his feet seeking out the driest—and therefore quietest—patches of ground from stride to stride.

The sensor screen was larger than he had expected. Ganz's drawing of the device had not been to scale, and it had led Quinn to believe that its removal would be as simple as unplugging it and tucking it under one arm. On the contrary, the cylindrical machine was almost as big as Quinn himself, and, if his approximation of its duranium content was on the money, it was at least twice as heavy. He considered stealing one of the miners' cargo pallets, but then he remembered how much noise the lifter would make. *Damn thing'll wake the entire camp,* he groused silently. *This would've been easier if my ship had a transporter.* He had often toyed with the notion of installing one, but his ship's limited power-generation capability meant that to operate a transporter would require sacrificing another system of equal energy level. Unfortunately, the only one that came close was the inertial dampener, and since it was the one thing that prevented routine starflight from turning him into chunky salsa, he was loath to part with it.

An idea occurred to him: *I could just steal the active component and leave the power module. Just take the part that's hard to get.* Examining the device more closely, he realized that the top segment constituted the screen generator, and that once it was separated from the much larger and heavier power supply he would be able to carry it out on his own. He dug into the lower pockets along his pants leg, found the tools he needed, and set to work. Another quick scan registered no sign of power inside the device; it appeared to be inert. That was for the best, in Quinn's opinion. A few simple twists and toggles later, he decoupled its primary power-supply cable.

No sooner had the cable come free than a scramble of data flooded his scanner. Eyeing the readings, he made the belated discovery that the sensor screen had, in fact, been active the entire time he had been here—and, true to its intended function, it had fooled his scanner.

His ears detected the muffled din of an alarm klaxon. Doors banged open against sheet-metal shelter walls. Running footfalls slapped through the mud, converging on his location. Using a sonic screwdriver he'd swiped from a rather daft chap back on Barolia, he torqued off the sensor screen's restraining bolts, wrapped his arms around the screen generator, and hefted it with an agonized grunt. He stumbled backward, tripped over something that he couldn't see in the dark, and dropped the device.

With the unmistakable crack of something breaking, the device struck whatever unseen piece of junk had found its way under Quinn's feet. A sizable chunk of it struck his foot hard enough to launch a string of vulgarities from his mouth. Hopping on his good foot proved an unwise reaction, as he immediately slipped and wound up on his back, in the mud, and looking at a cluster of angry miners at the end of the alley.

"Hey, fellas," he said, flailing in the muck to get himself upright. "I know this looks pretty bad, but—" One of the men drew what Quinn was certain was a Starfleet phaser pistol. Assessing the situation calmly, Quinn ran like hell.

With his arms and legs windmilling as he struggled for traction on the greasy mud, his movement was so clumsy and erratic that the first phaser shot—whose tonal pitch Quinn recognized as level-five heavy stun—narrowly missed him and scorched the wall behind his head. Finding his footing, he sprinted out of the alley on a mad dash for the tree line. As he crossed the street, he heard the group of armed men running up the alley to follow him.

Two more simultaneous phaser shots quickened Quinn's already frantic pace. One sizzled the mud behind his heel; the other passed over his shoulder and crisped its way through the foliage. He plunged straight into the stygian forest, zigzagging through the densely packed trees and ducking through nooses of vine. Blue phaser fire shimmered in the gloom, slicing wildly around his chaotic path.

Where's the damn trail? Seconds seemed stretched by the adrenaline coursing through Quinn's brain. He felt like he'd been running twice as long as necessary to find the path back to his ship. Then he broke free of the jungle's clinging tendrils and stumbled out onto the narrow, dry creek bed he had followed down this side of the hill from his ship. At the time, landing on the other side of the hilltop had seemed clever. Banked in steep, thick cloud cover even at this low elevation, it had enabled him to glide in unseen and unheard.

Now, unfortunately, it meant running for his life uphill.

His pursuers were getting closer. *Time for tricks,* he concluded. Several meters ahead, a sizable boulder offered him some cover. He reached the rock and dove to the ground behind it just before another volley of neon-blue phaser beams lashed across its pitted face. Fumbling through assorted bits of junk in his pockets, he found the detonator. The angry whine of another phaser blast bit off nearly a quarter of one side of the boulder that was shielding him. The odor of scorched carbon and iron reminded him of the stink of an empty pot left on a flame. The crackle of trampled underbrush resumed. They were coming.

He keyed the detonator switch.

Crimson flashes lit up the ink-black night, and a series of tooth-rattling concussive blasts provoked a mighty cacophony of startled noises from spooked animals—followed by the squeak and groan of splintered tree trunks jackknifing and collapsing under their own weight. Alarmed cries of "Fall back!" and "Get down!" mingled with the dull impacts of dozens of high-canopy trees, which dropped in an overlapping pattern carefully planned to foil pursuit. A heavy curtain of smoke obscured his pursuers' line of sight, and the crackle of small fires caused by the diversion covered the sound of his mad dash through the loose secondary-growth brush. He heard someone in the group below, probably the leader, confirm that all his people were okay, then order them back to the camp.

Quinn was glad that no one had been hurt. He had long ago learned the value of simple lies, clear exit strategies, and unexpected diversions. There were few "codes" he actually considered worth living by; most lacked the "moral flexibility" and "ethical adaptability" that he had come to consider indispensable. But the one that he clung to was that no job was worth killing someone over. Sucker-punching them? Sure. Stun them? If need be. But serious harm or killing? That was a line Quinn crossed only in self-defense.

Minutes later, rounding the crest of the hill to its steeper, rockier side, he clambered across loose chunks of flat stone toward the *Rocinante*. Beneath a sloped shale overhang, the ship looked at home in the shadows. Its center fuselage was shaped like a long, thin wedge. Attached to either side were ponderous warp nacelles, bulkier-looking than most and nearly two-thirds as long as the main hull section. Navigational fins, which normally were extended down at a slight angle from the nacelles, were folded upright into their landing configuration. Quinn stepped over the deep gouges the ship's landing gear had cut through the broken rock and dry, granular soil beneath. The entire vessel was dark gray, mottled with slightly lighter-toned splotches where its hull had been crudely patched in one alien shipyard or another over the years. Its four-seat cockpit bay was hidden behind a dark-tinted viewport.

Reaching under his belt, he found the security remote. His fingers were still shaking, from the panic response of almost being shot, as he keyed in the code to open the ventral gangway. The plank separated from the hull and descended with a hydraulic hiss. Plumes of vapor from leaky coolant coils tumbled down like the ghost of a waterfall as he climbed the ramp into his ship. Once inside, he pressed the ramp-closing switch on his way forward to the cockpit. With a sickly gasp and a grinding groan, it lifted shut behind him as he collapsed into his seat.

He was sweating. Trickles of perspiration raced down his face and forearms. Ragged breaths wheezed in and out of him. Catching his haggard reflection in the cockpit windshield, he was dismayed by how cruelly the years had treated him. *Not getting any younger, that's for damn sure,* he admitted to himself. *Runnin' on fumes and luck these days. And I ain't so sure 'bout the luck no more.*

His left hand reached up and started flipping switches to power up the onboard systems, while his right hand worked the controls to energize the impulse drive and warp coils. As an afterthought, he spun his chair half around and turned on the subspace-radio jammer. *Pretty good bet those guys who shot at me are callin' for help.* Temporarily blocking their communications would give Quinn time to leave the system before anyone could come to investigate. He had been cautious about his landing, waiting for six full days after the *Sagittarius* left orbit before he maneuvered his ship out of hiding and dared to set it down so close to the camp. *Still,* he reasoned *no point gettin' careless—well, at least not* more *careless.*

The warp engines were still warming up when the impulse drive indicator light changed to ready. Eager to get off this planet, Quinn keyed the antigrav circuit, retracted the landing gear, and guided the ship forward. As soon as it cleared the shale overhang he angled the nose upward and throttled it out of the atmosphere as quickly as its thrusters could manage.

By the time the *Rocinante* broke orbit, its warp coils had finished their start sequence. Without so much as a look back at the shrinking curve of Ravanar IV, Quinn plotted the longest, most roundabout course back to Vanguard that he could think of, given his current fuel reserves, and made the jump to warp speed. It would be roughly a week before he set foot on the station again. *That should give me enough time to figure out what to tell Ganz,* he figured. *Or else plan a nice funeral.*

Commander Dean Singer looked up as the search party returned to the narrow alley behind the barracks. "Did anyone get a good look at him?" His team responded with dour shakes of their heads. He gave the ruined sensor-screen generator a small kick and sighed. "Great. Just great." Sweeping aside the bulky mining jacket he wore, he plucked his communicator from his belt and lifted the cover plate. It announced the open channel with a double chirp. He set the frequency to the one used by the underground survey team and keyed the transmitter.

The rest of the team milled around looking confused while Singer waited for a response from the research group working underneath the camp, which had never been more than a poor facsimile of a real prospectors' outpost.

Ensign T'Hana answered Singer's message, her uninflected Vulcan voice as bright as a clarion. *"T'Hana here."*

"T'Hana, this is Singer." There was an urgency in his tone. "Is it shut down yet?"

"Not yet, Commander. It will take approximately twenty-one minutes to successfully power down the entire system."

Singer frowned, then resigned himself to circumstances that were beyond his control. "Understood, Ensign. Please expedite the process if the means becomes available."

"Acknowledged, sir."

"Singer out." He flipped his communicator closed with

a slap of his hand. As he bent his arm to put it back on his belt, it beeped twice, signaling an incoming message. With a flick of his wrist he flipped it open. "Singer here."

"Commander, the subspace channel's been restored," said Lieutenant John Ott, the communications officer. *"Opening a secure channel to Vanguard. What do you want to tell them?"*

"Hang on," Singer said. Once again fixing his search party with a fiery glare, he asked, "Can anyone tell me whether the intruder was a Klingon?" Shrugged shoulders and shaking heads accompanied the chorus of mumbled answers. "Miguel, you were the first one into the alley. Can't you tell me anything about him?"

"Not in this light," said Chief Petty Officer Miguel Velez. "I'm pretty sure he had light-colored hair, but I can't really say if it was white, gray, or yellow." No doubt reading the acute disappointment in Singer's expression, he added, "Sorry, sir."

"Not your fault," Singer said. Turning back to his other conversation, he said into the communicator, "Ott, inform T'Prynn we had an intruder, identity unknown. And make sure she understands we need a new sensor screen, on the double."

3

"Bridge to Lieutenant Xiong."

Ming Xiong forced the last of his uniform shirts into his duffel and cinched it shut. He was packed and ready to travel. Reaching to the wall—which was uncomfortably close in the claustrophobic confines of the quarters he shared with the *Sagittarius*'s chief engineer, Master Chief Petty Officer Mike Ilucci—he pressed the intercom switch. "Xiong here."

"It's time, Ming," Captain Nassir said. *"The* Bombay *is standing by to transport."*

"On my way," Xiong said, hefting both straps of his duffel over his shoulder. "Xiong out." He shut off the intercom, made a final survey of his locker to make sure he hadn't forgotten anything, then closed it. Cramped as conditions were aboard the *Archer*-class scout vessel, he was going to miss this ship and its crew. In the two short weeks he had spent with them—the first on his way out to Ravanar IV to examine their initial discovery, and the second now on his return to Vanguard, via painfully indirect routes both times—he had found them to be more relaxed than most of his comrades in Starfleet. As a long-range outrider with just fourteen personnel aboard, it had a close-knit feel that was enhanced by Captain Nassir's easygoing manner.

Unlike most Starfleet crews that Xiong had traveled with, there was little sense of hierarchy among the *Sagittarius* team. The standard duty uniform aboard the ship was a simple green utility jumpsuit without rank insignia or specialist markings, just a patch bearing the name of the ship on the right shoulder and the crewperson's name stitched on the front left chest flap. Though Xiong had at first felt anonymized when he donned an unmarked, borrowed garment, he'd quickly grown accustomed to the less complicated apparel.

The door swished open at his approach, and he shimmied carefully into the corridor, sidestepping with his bulky, heavy duffel toward the aft ladder to the transporter pad. Passing the open galley, he noticed a savory aroma. Ilucci was standing in front of the food slot, holding a plate in one hand and a half-ruptured burrito in the other. Bits of his meal tumbled into his scraggly beard whiskers as he wolfed down his lunch. The heavyset chief engineer struggled to swallow an entire mouthful in one gulp when he saw Xiong; he half-succeeded. Through half a gulletful of semi-masticated food, he asked, "Hey, are you leaving?"

"Yeah, I'm on my way out," Xiong said, pointing aft.

Ilucci dropped the shredded remains of his burrito on his plate and stepped quickly over to Xiong and extended his cheese-and-salsa–covered hand. "Gonna miss ya, buddy." Xiong blinked and felt his mouth pursing as he struggled not to point out the obvious. Looking down, Ilucci realized what the problem was. He wiped his hand broadly across the leg of his jumpsuit, first the palm and then the sides, then extended it once again to Xiong. This time the slim but muscular anthropology-and-archaeology specialist accepted the gesture and shook Ilucci's hand.

"Take care, Master Chief." One of the first things that Xiong had learned after coming aboard the *Sagittarius* was to always refer to Ilucci as "Master Chief." The chief engineer insisted on it. Tellingly, even the commissioned officers respected Ilucci's request and frequently reminded others to do likewise. Ilucci was not a tall man, but his gift for "percussive maintenance" (hitting defective machines until they worked again), his impassioned ranting, and his uncanny ability to start bar fights had long ago earned him the nickname "Mad Man," a moniker that now preceded him by many light-years, no matter how far he traveled.

Clumsily trying to wrap his fingers around the shredded remains of his half-eaten burrito, Ilucci said with an evil grin, "I'll keep the bunk warm for ya."

"Yeah, you do that, Master Chief." One thing Xiong was not going to miss about the *Sagittarius* was "hot-bunking." Because of the ship's acute lack of crew accommodations, only the captain and first officer had private quarters. The other twelve personnel shared four single-bed compartments, sleeping in shifts and taking whichever bunk was empty. As a result, life aboard the scout vessel had a nomadic quality both inside and out. *Strangely apropos,* Xiong mused as he left the galley.

Less than a minute later, he reached the aft ladder. Before he could adjust his duffel for the climb, the mellow-voiced first officer, Commander Clark Terrell, leaned down through the ladderway and extended his hand. "Pass it up to me."

"Thanks," Xiong said, then lifted his bag until Terrell

grasped one of its shoulder straps and hoisted it effort-
lessly up to deck two. Clambering up the wide-planked
ladder, Xiong heard the low hum of a transporter coil en-
ergizing above. He emerged into the transporter bay to
see Captain Nassir standing with Commander Terrell.
The two men were like night and day: Terrell was brown,
beefy, with close-cropped hair; Nassir was slender, pale,
and, like most Deltans, completely bald. A few meters
behind them, science officer Ensign Vanessa Theriault
was adjusting the settings of the transporter panel, seemingly at random. Nodding in her direction, Xiong said
quietly to Nassir and Terrell, "Does she know what she's
doing?"

The two senior officers turned in unison, looked at
Theriault, then looked back at each other. Terrell shrugged
at Xiong. "Probably." Xiong didn't like the sound of that.
He was about to suggest that maybe Ilucci could take over
for the attractive but undeniably kooky young redhead
from the Martian Colonies when Nassir and Terrell both
lost their poker faces and snorted with suppressed laughter. "Relax," Terrell said, patting Xiong's shoulder. "She's
a pro, you're in good hands."

Captain Nassir recovered his composure and took
Xiong aside. "Before you go, there's something I'd like to
give you. A going-away gift, I guess you'd call it." The
captain opened a storage panel along the lower half of the
wall and took out a neatly folded green jumpsuit. It had a
U.S.S. Sagittarius patch on its shoulder, and smelled clean
and freshly sanitized (like everything else on the ship
within reach of Dr. Lisa Babitz, the ship's medical officer).
Xiong's rank insignia and surname were stitched on its

front. "For the next time you visit," Nassir said as he handed it to Xiong, who accepted it abashedly.

"Thank you, sir. It means a lot to me."

Nassir's voice was deep and fatherly. "You're a good officer, Xiong. You've got an explorer's soul. Try not to let it go to waste sitting on that space station."

"I won't, sir. I promise." He shook Nassir's hand.

"You'd better get going. Captain Gannon's a busy woman. Best not to keep her waiting."

"Aye, sir." Tucking his new jumpsuit under his arm, he stepped onto the lone transporter pad. Because the *Sagittarius* was equipped to land on M-Class planets, its one and only transporter was used mostly for emergencies. *Which would explain the thin layer of dust on this thing,* Xiong noted.

The captain stepped behind the control panel with Theriault and keyed a switch. *"Sagittarius* to *Bombay.* One to transport."

"Acknowledged, Sagittarius. *Commence when ready."*

"Safe travels, Mr. Xiong." Turning to Theriault, Nassir said, "Energize." Theriault cast a frozen stare at the controls for a few seconds, then hesitantly reached out for one of the sliders. Nassir gently guided her hand to a different bank of switches. "Begin the dematerialization sequence first," he instructed gently.

Alarmed, Xiong protested to Terrell, "I thought you said she knew what she was doing!"

"It's all relative," Terrell said as the transporter sequence began with a rising whine of sound. The first officer added with a farewell wave, *"Vaya con Dios."*

By the time Xiong realized that he was a live test subject

in Ensign Theriault's transporter-training regimen, he had already rematerialized safely in the far more spacious transporter room of the *U.S.S. Bombay*.

A blue-jumpsuited technician worked behind the transporter console. First officer Commander Vondas Milonakis greeted Xiong as he stepped off the platform.

"Welcome aboard, Ming." The short, balding man grasped Xiong's hand in a firm, radiantly warm handshake. "Good to see you again. How's everybody on the *Sagittarius?*"

"Fine." It wasn't that Xiong disliked Milonakis; he just found it difficult to trust someone who was always so extroverted. Xiong decided that the bold new hue of gold that Starfleet had recently chosen for command officers' jerseys suited Milonakis perfectly.

Giving Xiong's jumpsuit a once-over, Milonakis said, "I see Captain Nassir's still keeping things casual."

Not wanting to prolong the conversation or start an argument, Xiong mumbled a dismissive "Mm-hmm."

"Let's get you some quarters. I think we have a spare bunk on deck five"—he shot a conspiratorial smirk Xiong's way—"if you don't mind sharing the room with a Tellarite."

"Not at all, sir."

"Glad to hear it."

Xiong followed the *Bombay* first officer out the door, then left toward the turbolift. The corridor was busy with personnel moving in quick strides from one task to another. This was the first time Xiong had been aboard the *Miranda*-class starship while it was deployed, but it was just as hectic as he had always expected. Within a few short weeks of his arrival on Starbase 47 it had become obvious that, of the three ships permanently assigned to the station, the *Bombay* was the unsung workhorse—the one that did all the unappreciated labor that enabled the *Sagittarius* to speed away to the edges of known space and the larger, more renowned *U.S.S. Endeavour* to spend its time "showing the flag" and making official first contacts.

As the two men walked, Milonakis made a point of greeting almost every passing member of the *Bombay* crew by his or her given name, reinforcing the first impression he had made upon Xiong weeks earlier—that he was a man who excelled in one-to-one exchanges and could manage dozens of such personal interactions simultaneously. To see him work his way through the lounge on Vanguard, or run into "an old friend" every twenty paces no matter where he was, made it seem as though he very well might know someone on every ship and base in Starfleet.

Milonakis led Xiong into the turbolift, grasped the throttle control, and said, "Deck five." He half-turned toward Xiong. "Bet you'll be glad to get back to Vanguard, eh?"

"Not really."

The first officer nodded once. "Ah, I see. You're a man of action. I can respect that."

More than his assumption of camaraderie, what irked Xiong about the man was that there was no way to take issue with anything he ever said without looking like an ingrate or a misanthrope. Of course, the latter term had been applied to Xiong more than once in the twelve years since he first joined Starfleet, but it was an epithet he was eager to shake off.

"I just like to see things with my own eyes," Xiong said.

"Makes sense."

The turbolift stopped. As the doors opened, however, a woman's voice sounded over the intercom. *"Commander Milonakis, report to the bridge."*

The first officer thumbed a switch on the turbolift control panel. "This is Milonakis. On my way, Captain." He released the switch, looked at Xiong, and pointed down the corridor. "Quartermaster's in five-bravo two-twenty-one. If you need help—"

"I'm fine," Xiong said, stepping past Milonakis and out of the turbolift. "Thank you, sir."

"All right, then." Taking hold of the turbolift throttle once more, Milonakis said to the computer, "Bridge," and the doors hissed shut. From behind them, a deep hum rose and faded in a heartbeat as the turbolift shot up toward deck one.

Xiong's visit to the quartermaster was brief and proceeded strictly by the book. The crew of the *Bombay* was nothing if not efficient. *Of course,* he reflected, *when you're as busy as they are, you have to be.*

Settling into his temporary quarters several minutes later, he felt the low frequency thrumming of the ship's warp engines ramping up to high power. The *Bombay* was accelerating rapidly. Xiong dimmed the lights and dropped with a relieved sigh onto the lower rack of a double bunk. *Seventy-nine hours to Vanguard,* he thought. Folding his arms behind his head, he closed his eyes, heaved a deep sigh, and let himself start to drift off to sleep. *More than enough time to finish my report for Commodore Reyes . . . after a nap.*

The door to his shared quarters opened to admit a

shrilly whistled tune, followed by the person causing it. The overhead lights snapped on to full strength. Peeking through one eyelid, Xiong silently observed the entrance of a young Tellarite officer whose crimson uniform shirt bore the single cuff stripe of a lieutenant. Xiong had never heard a Tellarite whistle before. It seemed louder and more piercing than human whistling. He guessed that it was because of the Tellarites' more robust sinus cavities.

Like a sonic drill, the whistling corkscrewed through Xiong's thoughts. He rolled away from his roommate and pulled his pillow over his head, but still the semi-musical nasal shrieking continued. *He must see me,* Xiong told himself. After six torturous minutes that felt like an hour, he couldn't take it anymore. He rolled over, removed the pillow from his face, and shot a steely glare at the porcine-featured whistler. "What the hell are you doing?"

Recoiling with a surprised expression, the Tellarite said, "I am whistling."

Mustn't lose my temper. Remain calm. "Why?"

"Because I enjoy it. It helps me think."

The irony alone made Xiong clench his jaw. "Would you mind stopping for a while? I need to sleep."

"I'm sorry, I didn't realize it was bothering you." The brawny, black-eyed fellow stepped forward and extended his hand. "Lieutenant Nem chim Loak, impulse drive assistant supervisor."

Xiong shook Loak's large and rough-textured hand. "Ming Xiong."

"Nice to meet you, Ming. Which department are you in?"

"I'm not," Xiong said, already regretting that he'd let the conversation last this long but despairing of a way to end it. "I'm just hitching a ride back to Vanguard."

"Oh—you must be the A&A officer we just picked up from *Sagittarius.*"

"Yeah," he said, choosing to stifle his usual rant about the abbreviation being a misnomer. Though his position was often referred to as "anthropology-and-archaeology officer," it was Xiong's opinion that the job was actually about xenology rather than anthropology. Therefore, he liked to tell people that he should be called the "X-and-A officer." Recently, however, he had been told by more than one person that it was a pretty boring subject for a rant and that he might as well learn to live with the flawed abbreviation.

"So," Loak said, "what were you doing on—"

"It's classified." Just as Xiong had hoped, his comment brought the conversation grinding to an awkward halt. "Anyway, thanks for not whistling. I'm going back to sleep now."

"Um, sure," Loak said. "Do you mind if I read for a while?"

"Be my guest."

Loak grabbed a data display tablet and carried it with him as he climbed into the top bunk. Down below, Xiong rolled over and pulled his pillow back over his head once more. A few deep, measured breaths later, he was almost over the threshold of consciousness, back to sleep.

Then the small room reverberated with Loak's deep, resonant humming. Loud and tuneless, it was enough to prompt Xiong to indulge in homicidal fantasies: *I wonder if*

I can shove this whole pillow through his snout and into his throat.

Xiong stared up at the bunk bottom above him and projected his seething ire toward the drooping bulge caused by the Tellarite lieutenant. Carefully stripping the bilious anger from his voice, he said with poisonous overpoliteness, "Loak?"

The humming paused. From above came Loak's cautious "Yes?"

"Are you familiar with the effects of sleep deprivation on humans?"

"Not exactly, but I—"

"It can cause irrational behavior," Xiong said in a tired monotone that nonetheless conveyed a quiet edge of danger.

"I wasn't aware of—"

"You never know what might make a sleep-deprived human do something insane. A word spoken out of turn . . . a tune taken out of context. Any little thing . . . and a human can just snap."

"I see," Loak said softly. "That's very—"

"Have you ever considered dyeing your hair pink?"

"No," Loak said defensively.

"Are you planning on sleeping any time between now and when we reach Vanguard?"

Suddenly, Loak sounded nervous. "Why do you ask?"

"No reason," Xiong said quietly. "No reason at all." After allowing a few moments for the conversation to sink in, he added, "I'm going back to sleep now."

There was no reply from the top bunk. Not a word, not a whistle, not a single hummed note. Satisfied that he had made his point, Xiong finally relaxed and fell asleep.

He awoke two hours and nine minutes later to the most horrific snoring he'd ever heard in his entire life. The baritone vibrato of Loak's deviated septum shook the bunk frame. Glaring through half-lidded eyes, Xiong reminded himself that, as a guest aboard the *Bombay*, he had the luxury of changing his schedule so that he could sleep while Loak was on duty and simply pass Loak's sleep cycle elsewhere.

I'm still going to dye his hair pink, he decided.

4

Hostile colors coursed through the elite Political Caste-moot SubLink of Tholia. Cacophonous tones of anxiety and dark hues of indignation underscored the collective mind-line of the Ruling Conclave, which reigned supreme over Tholia's Great Castemoot Assembly and the species' telepathic network, the Lattice.

The Federation provokes us, insisted Narskene [The Gold]. *Too long have we left their trespasses unanswered.*

Calming shades of indigo infused the SubLink as Velrene [The Azure] replied, *We have made no claim in that region.* She offered up memories, several hundred generations old, of Castemoot decisions to push Tholia's explorations in every other possible direction but into the Shedai Sector. Dozens of thought-facets twinkled with images of inherited history.

Always have we defended our trailing border, interjected Yazkene [The Emerald], referring to the orientation of Tholia's territory relative to the rotation of the galaxy. *Seventeen previous Castemoots planned to repulse the inevitable Klingon encroachment.* His mind-line darkened with shame. *But when the Federation constructed its starbase, there was no plan. Why were we not poised to retaliate when the Federation came?*

Sonorous chimes heralded the inclusion of Falstrene

[The Gray] into the discussion. *It is pointless to speak of defense unless we commit to colonization. We cannot defend the Shedai Sector from alien incursion unless we occupy it.*

Azrene [The Violet] objected with coruscating anger. *The Laws of the First Assembly forbid it!*

Rolling clamors of dissent propagated laterally and disrupted the Castemoot's already heated deliberation.

The Klingon Empire did not exist when the First Assembly ratified its canon, retorted Radkene [The Sallow]. *The law speaks to the galaxy that was. We must rule in the one that is.*

Eskrene [The Ruby] adjusted her mind-line hue to complement Radkene's. *I concur. Might not the Federation aggrieve the Klingons by impeding their expansion? Our enemies may yet neutralize one another, leaving the Shedai Sector barren once more. Patience is—*

Deafening and blinding, an excruciating thought-pulse ripped through the Political Castemoot. Hues blanched to near-transparency, mind-lines faded, the SubLink faltered. Instinct propelled the conclave participants to escape the SubLink, to retreat into the broader sanctuary of the Tholian Lattice. But there was no peace to be found; a piercing wave of psionic power held the Tholian race in its crushing grip. In a flash, every Tholian mind knew the icy touch of enslavement.

As abruptly as it had come, it ceased.

Echoes of the thought-pulse rocked the Lattice, like the aftershocks that followed quakes in the volcanic Underrock beneath Tholia's three principal continents. Normally, the Ruling Conclave withheld alarming knowledge from the lower echelons of the Lattice-at-large, in the interest of preventing reckless actions by individuals that could bring harm to the rest of the Assembly.

Such discretion had just become impossible.

The Lattice was ringing with terror and incandescent with fury. An ancient and terrible force had seized the Tholians by usurping their most inviolate form of communion. They knew not this power's name, its purpose, or why it had called to them. About it, they knew only two things:

Where it was—and that it must be annihilated, at any cost.

5

Commodore Diego Reyes exited his office and strode across the top level of the operations center of Starbase 47. Even at its least frenetic moments, the nerve center of the enormous facility buzzed with signal chatter and pulsed with foot traffic—yeomen bearing reports and work orders, department chiefs going to or returning from one meeting or another. This morning, service personnel dodged out of Reyes's unswerving path. Technicians tore their eyes from the huge display screens, which wrapped around the top third of the high perimeter wall, to watch the lanky flag officer pass in a swift blur.

Elevated slightly above the chaos was the supervisors' deck, which was situated in the center of the cavernous circular compartment and bounded only by a simple gunmetal-gray railing. The anchoring feature of the platform was an octagonal conference table, into which were set eight situation monitors, each with its own set of controls. Known to the operations staff as "the hub," it was from this compact block of workspace that the bulk of the station's business was managed each day.

Gathered around the hub at 0823, and already deep into the morning staff meeting, were the station's department heads, minus the chief medical officer, who was notorious for shunning such briefings. Commander Jon

Cooper, the station's executive officer, ran the meeting with his trademark low-key aplomb. Lieutenant Judy Dunbar, the senior communications officer, sat with her eyes closed and twirled a curl of her light brown hair around one index finger as she listened and committed the minutes of the meeting to her photographic memory. No one took any notice as Reyes quietly climbed the steps toward the hub.

"Ray," Cooper said to the fleet operations manager, Lieutenant Commander Raymond Cannella, "what's this I'm hearing about a six-hour delay in docking clearance for the *Chichén Itzá?*"

"It's their own fault," said Cannella, a hefty man with a thick, nasal New Jersey accent. "They left Cait two days early but never updated their flight plan. They're lucky we found them a berth at all."

Cooper tilted his head in a half-nod. "Fair enough."

Reyes reached the top of the stairs, and everyone turned at the sound of his approach. Despite his best efforts not to tread with such a heavy step, he found it difficult to muffle his footfalls. The commodore was a big man, tall and broad-shouldered, and his ex-wife had been fond of telling him that his "aura" frequently preceded him, even through a closed door. *Serves me right for marrying a telepath,* he brooded. Lifting his chin in a friendly but curt greeting, he said, "Morning, folks." Overlapping variations of *Good morning, sir* were volleyed back at him. "Mr. Cooper," he continued, "do you mind if I butt in for just a nanosecond?"

"Not at all, sir."

"Thank you." Reyes looked at Vanguard's senior engineering officer, Lieutenant Isaiah Farber. "Mr. Farber, what's topping your priority list these days?"

The heavily muscled Starfleet weight-lifting champion mulled his answer for a moment, then said, "Mostly space-dock systems, sir. We're still fine-tuning the—"

"Because I think that in a claustrophobic environment like ours, it's the little things that raise or lower the bar on our quality of life. Don't you agree?"

A sheepish glance worked its way around the hub, from one officer to another, starting and ending with Farber. He looked up at last and said, "Your food slot's on the fritz again, sir?"

Reyes feigned astonishment. "Amazing, Farber. You must be psychic. Exercise truly broadens the mind, after all."

"I'll have your food slot fixed by 1300."

"Excellent," Reyes said, patting Farber firmly on one beefy shoulder. "God is in the details, Mr. Farber."

"Aye, sir."

Turning his dark gray gaze toward Cooper, Reyes said, "When does the *Bombay* make port?"

"Nine-twenty hours."

"Notify me as soon as they enter spacedock."

"Aye, sir."

"Carry on. My best to Jen and your boy."

"Thank you, sir."

Reyes nodded quickly to the rest of the group, then turned and walked back down the steps. He looked around the ops center, which was packed with computers, commu-nication devices, and gadgets capable of myriad technolog-ical marvels—with the notable exception of being able to produce a cup of coffee. *As frontier hardships go, this is kind of petty,* he admitted to himself. *But if forty years in the service, flag rank, and sector command aren't worth a cup of java, what the hell is?*

He walked into his sparsely furnished office and sat down at his desk. The morning reports and pending orders were all waiting in neatly arranged stacks, courtesy of his alpha-shift yeoman, Toby Greenfield. Although he had expected, upon first meeting her, that her perpetually sunny disposition would grate on his nerves, he had found the opposite to be true. Truth be told, he had to admit that the longer he served with her, the more he grew to appreciate her joie de vivre.

The buzzing of his intercom drew his attention. Recognizing Greenfield's ID code, he opened the channel with a push of his thumb. "Go ahead."

"Captain Desai to see you, sir."

"Give me a moment, then—"

His office door swished open and Captain Rana Desai strode in. The petite, late-thirtyish Indian woman carried a sealed legal folder under her arm. Like many of her contemporaries, Desai wore her raven hair in a stylish but simple bob cut.

Behind her, Yeoman Greenfield stood, looking flustered, in the doorway. She signaled her silent apology to Reyes, then stepped away and let the door close.

Reyes leveled his stare at Desai and said, with monotonal sarcasm, "No, I'm not busy, please come in."

Desai took the folder from under her arm and handed it to Reyes. In a voice that was no less steely for its gentle London accent, she said, "On behalf of the Starfleet Judge

Advocate General, your attempted exercise of eminent domain on Kessik IV is hereby deemed improper, and your petition is rejected."

"Excuse me," Reyes said, his ire rising swiftly. "We laid claim to Kessik IV by the book."

"Maybe you need to read that book again, Commodore," Desai said. "You can't steal a colony from its residents just because you want its dilithium mine."

"First of all," Reyes said, slowly rising from his chair to tower over her, "we're not stealing it, we're buying it. Second, we don't *want* its dilithium mine, we *need* its dilithium mine—it's a matter of military necessity."

She flashed an insincere smirk that bordered on a sneer. "How unfortunate for you that the law wasn't written solely to service your needs."

"Actually," he said, "that's exactly what eminent domain is for. Ambassador Jetanien signed off on this personally."

"Too bad he had no more authority to do this than you did," Desai said. "Eminent-domain law, as written in the Federation Charter, applies strictly to member-worlds of the Federation and unoccupied planets within sovereign UFP territory."

"We planted our flag. That makes Kessik IV our territory."

"If you'd planted your flag *first,* maybe. But the crew of the mining ship *Epimetheus* staked their claim on Kessik IV before Vanguard was even half-built. They have a local government and a solid claim to independence."

Legal semantics irritated Reyes to no end. "They're Federation citizens—the law still applies."

"Not on the frontier, it doesn't," Desai said. "Eminent

domain applies only inside Federation space. And even there, the rights of the state do not trump the rights of the individual, or of free communities on previously unclaimed worlds."

Reyes tossed the folder of legal mumbo jumbo on a stack with a host of other documents he planned to ignore for the foreseeable future. "I like high-minded ideals as much as the next guy, Captain, but I also have to face hard facts: Starfleet needs that dilithium resource. The Federation needs it."

"Then perhaps we should have devoted more time, more ships, and more personnel to securing it before someone with civil rights came along and laid legal claim to it." Abandoning her lecturelike tone, she continued, "As of 0830 today, I have acted on behalf of the JAG office to void the Federation's claim to Kessik IV, and I have countermanded your order to have its residents relocated."

A flare of temper twisted his face into an angry mask. " 'Countermanded'?" In long, ominous strides, he circled his desk toward Desai. Her face betrayed a fleeting sign of fear; then she hardened her features and stood her ground as he harangued her. "Captain, there's one thing we need on the frontier even more than lawyers, and that's a chain of command. You want to challenge me on points of law, fine—but I will not permit you to usurp my authority."

Desai's voice was steady, her gaze unyielding. "I didn't usurp your authority, Commodore—you exceeded it. And it's my job to tell you so." She continued to stare up at him, apparently content to respond to whatever verbal tactic he chose next.

He took the easy way out: "Dismissed."

The dark-skinned lawyer maintained her proud bearing as she acknowledged the command with a nod, turned away, and left his office. Alone once more, he remembered a not terribly clever old joke that suddenly had the ring of truth to it: *What do you call a ship carrying a thousand lawyers into a black hole?*

A good start.

Tim Pennington was still learning the finer points of being a journalist, but after six years as a stringer for the Federation News Service he knew that taking a confrontational attitude with a senior UFP diplomat could be risky.

In particular, it would be exceedingly awkward if an ill-chosen comment were to provoke a heated exchange or angry outburst here, in a public, "outdoor" café on the edge of the plaza for Stars Landing, a crescent-shaped cluster of commercial and—to a lesser extent—civilian-residential buildings that wrapped halfway around the station's central hub. Its architecture, which evoked such natural shapes as shells and honeycombs, was as much a work of art as a marvel of engineering. Some of its structures were nearly twenty stories tall and all but scraped the simulated spring sky of Vanguard's vast habitat shell, which was rich with transplanted flora and teeming with off-duty station personnel and transients. Dozens of people were eating at tables adjacent to Pennington's. Several meters away, two clusters of Starfleet officers had just organized an impromptu game of Frisbee. Without a doubt, this would be a most regrettable place for an argument.

On the other hand, his instincts told him that Ambas-

sador Jetanien was hiding something. He chose his words
with caution.

"I think you're evading the question, Your Excellency."

His thoughts well hidden behind a leathery, unexpres-
sive shell of a face, the alien diplomat chewed another
pickled *keesa* beetle. "Perhaps I was distracted by the fact
that I am eating breakfast. . . . Maybe your question was
poorly worded."

Sickly sweet and pungent odors from Jetanien's insect-
breakfast entrée mingled in Pennington's nose as he leaned
forward and feigned contrition. "May I rephrase?"

"By all means," Jetanien said, spearing another *keesa*
beetle with the two-tined fork clutched in his clawed hand.
His movements were unhurried, graceful. The Rigellian
Chelon was the sort of person who could eat the messiest
meal without making a spot anywhere on his snow-white,
gold-hemmed, satin-textured raiment. Even the headdress
that hung from his gleaming black fez remained pristine.

"Given that the Taurus Reach is so remote from established civilian shipping lanes and Starfleet patrol routes,"
Pennington said, "why has the Federation Council chosen
to devote so many personnel and resources to a mission so
far from home?"

Jetanien chewed slowly. His voluminous, amber-colored
eyes stared past Pennington. *I'll give him credit,* the young
reporter thought. *He certainly knows how to play up a dramatic pause.*

"Exploration has always been the Federation's most
honored endeavor," Jetanien said at last. "The imperative to
make contact with new life-forms and civilizations is the
key to enriching our understanding of the universe, and of

ourselves." Skewering another *keesa* beetle and wrapping it in a twirl of reddish Vulcan seaweed, he concluded, "Our mission requires us to dare the unknown, and few regions within our reach are as unknown—and unclaimed—as the Taurus Reach."

With a sound that Pennington took to be a grunt of self-satisfaction, Jetanien guided another vinegar-scented forkful of his breakfast into his prodigious beak of a mouth.

Suspicion crept into Pennington's tone. "Mr. Ambassador, with all due respect, I received almost the exact same answer from a Starfleet Command press liaison two days ago."

"Really?" Lifting a swan-necked beverage container, Jetanien added, "Imagine that." He downed a generous mouthful of *N'v'aa*, an amazingly sour fruit cocktail that Pennington had sampled the first night he arrived on Vanguard. It was a throat-clenching mistake he had vowed never to repeat. Apparently, only Chelon taste buds found the libation even remotely palatable.

Putting aside the unpleasant memory, Pennington soldiered onward with his impromptu interview. "Is it possible that the Federation's push into the Taurus Reach is part of a broader astropolitical strategy?"

"Could you be more specific, Mr. Pennington?"

"Even a cursory review of regional star maps indicates that the region is bordered almost entirely on one side by the Klingon Empire, and on the other by the Tholian Assembly."

"Quite correct," Jetanien said.

"So what is the Federation's motivation for moving so aggressively into this area?" Pennington clenched his fist as he struggled to make his thoughts coalesce. "The Tholians have consistently pushed the borders of their territory in the opposite direction of the Taurus Reach, but the Klingons are extending their frontier in as many directions as possible. If they expand to the Tholian border, the Federation would be caught in the crossfire of a Klingon-Tholian conflict. Is this station part of an interstellar firewall—a tactic to avert a Klingon-Tholian war and deny the Klingons any more territory on our border?"

Jetanien finished chewing and swallowed with a muffled croaking noise. "A very good question," he said, then picked up his plate and extended it toward Pennington. "Would you care for a *keesa* beetle? They're quite crunchy today."

"Thank you, no."

The ambassador took back his plate. "Suit yourself."

Bland rehearsed answers were all that Pennington had ever heard, from anyone, whenever questions about Vanguard were broached. In press conferences last year on Earth, the president had answered queries about the project with so many euphemisms and empty platitudes that the press corps was surprised he had any rhetoric left for his reelection campaign. Regardless, the questions continued to persist: Why had Vanguard's construction been fast-tracked? Why had three ships of the line been assigned to it on a permanent basis? What made the Taurus Reach a more viable arena for commerce and colonization than the Kalandra Sector, which was so much closer to Federation space?

Pennington had made the interminable journey to Vanguard hoping to find answers to some of those questions.

Instead, he was getting the same talking points as his Earth-assigned colleagues—and, just to make it worse, missing out on the Paris nightlife and press-corps gossip.

Jetanien wolfed down his last few fried beetles. Watching the Chelon diplomat eat, Pennington realized that he had a sudden hankering for waffles. Wondering if the café was still serving breakfast, he turned to summon a waiter.

Before he could shout "Garçon!" a general announcement echoed inside the vast, hollow-doughnut–shaped space of the habitat, emanating from camouflaged speakers and seeming to be everywhere at once. *"Attention, all personnel,"* the feminine voice said in a businesslike tone, *"the* Starship Bombay *is on approach to main spacedock bay two. Alpha-shift maintenance and cargo crews report to bay two for priority operations."*

The message began to repeat as Pennington, suddenly energized, rose from his seat and swiftly gathered his notes off the tabletop. "Mr. Ambassador, will you excuse me? I have a pressing matter to attend to."

Pennington was already several meters away and dodging through the Starfleeters' Frisbee game before he realized he had left without waiting for Jetanien's reply. As he sprinted across the wide-open green, he forgave himself. *Priorities,* he reminded himself as he reached the station core and boarded a turbolift. *You have to have priorities.*

"I don't know what you see in this game," said Jabilo M'Benga.

"Just watch," said his boss, Vanguard's gray-haired, dark-skinned, gravel-voiced chief medical officer, Dr. Ezekiel Fisher.

The two men were alone on the top row of the bleachers beside the athletic field, squinting against simulated sunlight beaming down from an artificial sky. Though the massive inner space was officially designated the "terrestrial enclosure," most of the station's residents called it simply "the park."

M'Benga—a handsome, soft-spoken young attending physician—had been all that Fisher had hoped to find in a successor. His diagnostic skills were second to none, and his bedside manner was personable without being overly familiar. Though he had been on Fisher's staff for a few months, since shortly after Vanguard became operational, M'Benga's quirks and moods remained a mystery to him. The junior physician reminded Fisher at times of a Vulcan; he had served in a Vulcan ward before being assigned to Vanguard, prompting Fisher to wonder if the Vulcans' inimitable stoicism had rubbed off on the young doctor.

In the distance, the skyline of Stars Landing was partly distorted by surface irregularities on the broad central core of the station, which was camouflaged with photosensors that reproduced the images in front of them on massive diodes 180 degrees away, on the other side of the core, to preserve the illusion of an unbroken pastoral vista.

Nestled out of sight, along the gently rising slope that bounded the perimeter of the circular park, were entrances to the station's high-speed maglev tram. The automated people-mover ran a small fleet of trams on two levels, one set in each direction. The system had been designed so that the terminals, which were spaced roughly two hundred meters apart, would each be visited by one tram every two minutes.

A tight cluster of brightly uniformed athletes clashed in a haphazard pile on the grass in front of the bleachers. M'Benga eyed the scrum with detached curiosity. "What did you say this game was called?"

"Rugby."

"And what's the objective?"

"Don't ask so many questions," Fisher said, a hint of his late father's native Tennessee drawl peeking out from behind his words. He gestured to the tray on the bench between them. "Have some chips."

With poise and precision, M'Benga reached out and gingerly plucked a single chip from the plate on the tray, lifted it to his mouth, and ate it without dropping a single crumb.

He reminds me of Noah, Fisher thought, picturing his firstborn son. M'Benga was a bit younger than Noah, and his dark skin was a slightly richer shade of brown, but his and Noah's mannerisms were eerily similar—so precise, so measured. *Is that why I took such a shine to him?*

"Do you think about your next career step?"

M'Benga shrugged. "Now and then."

Stroking the graying whiskers of his goatee, Fisher hesitated to spell out his agenda too bluntly. Decades of experience in Starfleet had taught him that sometimes it was best not to show all of one's cards at the same time. "What do you see for yourself? A few more years and out? Or a future in Starfleet medicine?"

"Definitely a future," M'Benga said, his confidence apparent. "I joined Starfleet for a reason."

"Didn't we all," Fisher said under his breath. More than fifty years of service in Starfleet had left him somewhat world-weary, and he was long past the point of apologizing for it. In his opinion, he had earned the right to grumble a little from time to time. He refocused his thoughts. "If you plan to make a real go of it, the best advice I can give you is this: Learn to see what people don't show you, learn to hear what they don't tell you, and learn to trust your gut."

"Interesting counsel," M'Benga said. "Thank you."

How very Vulcan of you, Fisher mused. "You're welcome."

On the field in front of them, the players wrestled furiously, a writhing pile of color and dirt-flecked sinew. Grunts and groans and agonized shouts were muffled inside the crush of bodies. A pained expression formed on M'Benga's lean, impeccably shaven features as he watched. "I still fail to see the point of this game," he said.

"What's the point of any game?"

After thinking a moment, M'Benga said, "To win."

"Right." Fisher grabbed a small cluster of deep-fried chips and pushed them into his mouth. They were crisp and salty with just a slight tang of vinegar.

"So who are you rooting for?"

"No one," Fisher said. "I just watch."

"You have no interest in the outcome?"

"Not really."

Now young M'Benga looked confused. "Then what do you get out of it?"

"Depends on the game," Fisher said. He wondered if M'Benga would understand his philosophy with regard to competitive sports. "Some games, you admire the skill of certain players or the harmony of a good team. Others, the strategy has a beauty to it. . . . Sometimes, it's enough just to appreciate the struggle."

Nodding, M'Benga said, "You love the effort—regardless of the result."

"Right." Fisher could sense it: *He's catching on.*

"That would be an apt description of the scientific method. Opposed hypotheses vie for evidentiary support—and scientists observe impartially. The result is secondary to the method."

Fisher smiled at the young attending physician. "Not bad. It took my last attending months to work that out."

Gesturing at the quickly intensifying scrum below, M'Benga asked, "Does rugby actually have any rules?"

A wry half-smirk tugged at Fisher's mouth. "Sure," he said. "No autopsy, no foul."

"Angry? No, Your Excellency, I wouldn't say they're angry. I think 'apoplectic' might be a better term."

Senior attaché Anna Sandesjo clutched her briefcase as she trailed close behind Ambassador Jetanien, who swept through the frantic chatter and cluttered work nooks of the Federation Embassy office, grabbing up hard-copy reports from each of the consulate case officers as he went. The towering Chelon diplomat spoke over his shoulder to Sandesjo as he reviewed his daily intelligence updates, one in each scaly, web-fingered manus. "What, exactly, did Ambassador Sesrene say?"

"The translators couldn't parse it," Sandesjo said, taking care not to step on the tail of Jetanien's flowing white coat, which fluttered ethereally behind him as he strode forward. "It was more like a metallic shriek than the chiming tones they usually make. It sounded like he was in pain."

For the sake of brevity, she had substantially understated the situation. Never before had she seen a Tholian become so unhinged without apparent cause. Sesrene's sudden seizure and retreat had alarmed her.

Jetanien stopped her with an upraised hand and loomed over a communications supervisor. "Mr. Stotsky, did you know that the Gallonik III civil war of 2177 was sparked by a single misstatement in its first treaty of global alliance?"

"No, Your Excellency," the supervisor said cautiously, staring up at the enormous Chelon.

"A simple error, really," Jetanien continued, ramping up his well-known dramatic lecturing cadence. "Its articles of territorial sovereignty contained conflicting geographical coordinates for the borders demarcating areas of settlement for its two rival sentient species. Historians chalked it up to a transcription error . . . *after* seven hundred thirty-eight million Gallonikans butchered each other over one of the most picayune clerical blunders in recorded history."

"Tragic, sir," the supervisor said, his voice cowed.

"Indeed, it is. Now imagine how tragic it would be if you actually sent this communiqué to Qo'noS with the modifier *'pu* appended to that ordinarily inoffensive noun. How do you think the chancellor will respond to such a heinous slander against his paternal grandmother? Tell me, Mr. Stotsky, do the Klingons strike you as a species inclined to laugh at our lack of facility with *tlhIngan,* or do you think it more likely they would demand an honor duel, pitting me in mortal combat against the leader of the Klingon Empire?"

"I'll correct the error immediately, Ambassador."

"Thank you," Jetanien said, then resumed walking and tossing words over his shoulder at Sandesjo. "You were saying?"

"Ambassador Sesrene became incoherent for several minutes, then left in a hurry. He hasn't responded to our requests for an update on his status."

"And you didn't see fit to advise me of this last night?"

"Well, it's not as if he declared war," she said.

He reached the door to his private office and turned to face her. "Are you sure? If I sound less than convinced of your analysis, Anna, it's only because I find it refreshingly unburdened by the weight of evidence." Resuming his original course, he stepped toward the door, which opened with a gentle swoosh. She followed him inside.

Sandesjo respected Jetanien's political acumen, and at times she admired his ability to negotiate while under stress. Most of the time, however, she found that working for him was a lot like indentured servitude, with the added insult of knowing the condition was self-inflicted. He could be the grand master of tact and finesse when circumstances demanded it, but with his own staff he demonstrated a penchant for imperiousness.

Jetanien's office was small and densely packed with display screens, all of which faced his simple, curved desk. Every screen snapped to flickering life as he entered, though none made any sound. It was Jetanien's habit, Sandesjo had observed, to raise the volume on a channel only when it had snared his undivided attention.

The ambassador shed his coat, placed it on the ornate coat rack behind his desk, and eased himself down into a half-sitting, half-kneeling position on a piece of furniture custom designed to accommodate such a pose. "Has the Klingon ambassador deigned to join the conversation yet?"

"Not as such," Sandesjo said. She opened her briefcase, removed a Klingon *d'k tahg,* and placed it on the desk. "Ambassador Lugok left this for you."

Jetanien leaned forward and scrutinized the ceremonial dagger. "Left it? Where?"

"In Meyer's leg."

She was surprised that Jetanien hadn't heard about last night's incident in Manón's Cabaret. The brief but profanity-laced altercation between Lugok, the Klingon Empire's most irascible blowhard, and Dietrich Meyer, the Federation Diplomatic Corps's most notorious drunkard, was already well on its way to becoming the stuff of legend.

"I'd express my sympathy for Meyer's pain if I thought he'd actually felt any," Jetanien said. "He'll recover, I presume?"

"Dr. Fisher says he'll be fit for duty by tomorrow."

" 'Fit for duty'? That would be an improvement."

Sandesjo struggled not to roll her eyes. *So much for being diplomatic.* "Regardless, it might be best to assign a new envoy to the Klingon delegation."

Jetanien acknowledged the suggestion with a grunt. "Who do you think Lugok would hate more—Sovik or Karumé?"

"A difficult choice, sir," Sandesjo said. "The Klingons are unlikely to respect Mr. Sovik's logic as much as the Tholians do. Conversely, Ms. Karumé's abrasive negotiating style, despite its resemblance to Klingon manners, might prove inflammatory."

"Your instincts, Anna. Make a snap judgment."

"Sovik's reticence would be seen as weakness by the Klingons. Send them Karumé. They might hate her, but at least they'll understand her."

"Very well," Jetanien said, picking up a sealed envelope from Commodore Reyes's office and slicing it open with the deft pass of a single claw. He plucked the single-page letter from inside and scanned it. "Clear my schedule from 1300 to 1500."

"Yes, sir. Shall I—"

"Notify Ms. Karumé of her new assignment. I want her daily briefing by 1800 hours."

"Of course, sir." Sandesjo didn't know if she was asking unnecessary questions, or if Jetanien made a habit of cutting her off in midsentence as an ongoing cruel jest. "If there's—"

"That's all. Dismissed."

Mustering her willpower, she left Lugok's *d'k tahg* on the desktop instead of wedging it under Jetanien's chin, then exited the ambassador's office.

The walk back to her own miserably cramped, windowless office was brief, but she still managed to be intercepted by five different foreign-service officers with urgent diplomatic crises for Jetanien's attention. It would be up to her to sort the true emergencies from the petty distractions before letting any of these requests reach the ambassador's desk.

She passed through the door into her private workspace and dropped her handful of passed briefings onto her desk. Slumping into her chair, she let her briefcase slip from her hand. It landed on the thinly carpeted floor with a hollow thud. *So much to do,* she realized. Sandesjo's first official item of business, without question, was to inform Akeylah Karumé that she had been named as the new envoy to the Klingon delegation on Starbase 47. Everything else scattered across her desk was, as far as she could determine, tied for second.

All of it, however, would have to wait until she had completed one very important unofficial task.

Sandesjo reached down, picked up her thin, metallic briefcase, and placed it flat on her desktop. Before she opened it, she set its digital lock to a secret combination— one different from the sequence normally used to open it. When she lifted the lid, a false panel opened in the bottom of the case, revealing a compact short-range subspace transmitter. With the flip of a switch, it hummed gently into active mode.

The wait for an acknowledgment was always the most nerve-racking part of filing a report. Until the receiver locked in and finished encrypting the signal, there was an infinitesimal risk that their transmission might be detected and intercepted.

From the receiving end of the audio signal came a guttural voice, which uttered the challenge code-phrase: "bImoHqu'."

It translated roughly as *You look terrible.* Sandesjo resented this cruel joke at her expense, this mockery of the pain and indignity she had endured in order to pass for a human and infiltrate the Federation's diplomatic service. *No time now for hurt feelings,* she reminded herself. She swept her straight, long auburn hair from her eyes. Keying the transmitter, she spoke the prearranged response phrase: *"jIwuQ."*

Translation: *I have a headache.* She vowed that someone in the Empire would pay dearly for these inanities.

"Report," said Turag, the Imperial Intelligence officer embedded with the Klingon delegation aboard Vanguard.

"You're getting a new envoy," Sandesjo said.

"The petaQ'pu *Dietrich is dead, then?"*

"No. Lugok's blade missed the human's femoral artery."

Over the open channel, she heard Turag spit in disgust. *"Sloppy. I would not have missed."*

"And you would have been neutralized." She transferred a data packet to Turag on the subchannel. "I am sending you Envoy Akeylah Karumé's dossier. Lugok will need to see it before Karumé calls on him."

"Understood. What is wrong with the Tholian delegation?"

"Unknown," Sandesjo said. "I will continue to investigate."

"As will we. Qapla', *Lurqal."*

Years of undercover work had left Sandesjo unaccustomed to the sound of her true Klingon name. She masked her unease with a quick farewell. *"Qapla',* Turag."

The channel clicked off. Sandesjo closed her briefcase, confident that, despite the perfect silence of its moving parts, it had reverted already to its disguised form. She tucked it beneath her desk, next to her feet. It was time to get to work.

The slender, leggy young woman reined in a bitter chuckle until it was reduced to a disgruntled huff. *It's always time to get to work when you're a spy.*

6

Tim Pennington collapsed back on his side of the bed. Blissfully spent and aglow with perspiration, he lolled his head to the right and admired Oriana D'Amato's profile. Her wild spill of dark hair, fetchingly tinted with synthetic magenta highlights, obscured her pillow. Both of them heaved heavy breaths. Their chests rose and fell in unison. She turned her head and cast a satiated grin in his direction.

"Welcome back," he said, and they shared a fleeting moment of conspiratorial laughter. Not a word had passed between them in the two hours since she had stepped out of the gangway surrounded by fellow *Bombay* personnel and saw him through the crowd, waiting for her. They had both known with a glance to come directly here, to his Stars Landing apartment, without delay. This was their fourth such liaison in three months—nowhere near frequent enough for Pennington, who had been utterly smitten with her since they met. Easygoing, optimistic, lighthearted . . . everything that made her his opposite had deepened his attraction. Even the contrast of her bright Roman accent and his own Edinburgh brogue—slightly softened after four years in London and six in Paris—excited him.

His fingers traced a gentle line over the alabaster curve of her shoulder and down her arm. "When do you ship out again?"

"Soon," she said, then sighed. "Too soon."

He glanced past her, at the golden yellow miniskirt uniform draped over the chair at his desk. Because Oriana had voiced her lack of enthusiasm for the new women's uniform style when it was first issued, he had suppressed his desire to tell her how amazing she looked wearing it. An hour ago he had considered begging her to leave on the revealing one-piece uniform—or, at the very least, its accompanying knee-high boots—but she had shed them all so quickly once the door closed that he hadn't had the chance. His disappointment was short-lived. *Far be it from me to tell a woman not to disrobe,* he had decided.

Pennington finger-combed a tumbled shock of his short, light-brown hair from his sweaty forehead. "Do you want to have dinner? I could pop over to the café."

Oriana rolled over in his direction, onto her stomach, revealing the perfect slope of her bare back from beneath the silken bedsheets. Planting her elbows on the mattress and her chin in her cupped hands, she teased him with a coquettish batting of her eyelids. "What will you bring me?"

"Name it, my sweet."

She squinted her eyes in mock concentration, as if she were struggling to think of something he would be hard-pressed to find on such a well-provisioned starbase as Vanguard. "Chocolate-covered Kaferian apples?"

"That can be arranged."

Undaunted, she continued. "Deltan champagne."

"Technically, if it doesn't come from the Champagne region of France on Earth—"

"I don't want to have a semantic argument about it," she said. "I just want you to bring me bubbly stuff."

He gave her an obedient nod. "So noted."

With a huge grin, she said, "Brie."

"Now you're just being difficult," he said. "I know for a fact you don't even like Brie. You said it was too bland."

"Good memory," she said. Feigning hurt feelings, she added, "Does that mean you won't bring me some if I ask?"

He smiled wanly. "With or without a pastry shell?"

"A man who knows his cheese," she said approvingly. "How did I get so lucky?"

"I thought I was the lucky one." He sat up and clicked on the bedside lamp so he could look for his pants. As he reached down to pick up his trousers, the station's public-address system squawked from an overhead speaker that was expertly camouflaged in the ceiling.

"Attention all personnel," a female voice said. *"The* Starship Enterprise *is cleared for main spacedock bay three."* Oriana was out of bed and reaching for her uniform while the word *Enterprise* was still echoing in the corridor outside. The announcement continued, *"Support person-nel, all shifts, report for priority operations. All previous work assignments are rescinded pending further notice. Command out."*

After hurriedly pulling on his pants, Pennington turned to see Oriana shimmy into her sheer lower undergarment. "What's going on? What's the hurry?"

"It's the *Enterprise*," Oriana said, flustered. "Dammit." She reached for her one-piece uniform and pulled it on over her head. Her hair, which he had found so attractive when it was splayed across his pillows moments ago, now looked like a frightful mass of tangles, in comparison to the neat beehive currently recommended for female Starfleet officers. She spun and critically eyed her reflection in the mirror over his dresser. "God, I'm a mess."

Pennington plucked his shirt from the desktop where it had been flung in a gesture of wild abandon. He slipped into it with fluid motions that hinted at his many years of training as a long-distance swimmer. "I'm still not getting why—"

"It's Robert's ship," she snapped. "He'll be in port any minute."

The name was a dim memory, known but almost deliberately forgotten. Pennington had pushed it from his thoughts weeks ago, for the sake of convenience. Now it returned with a vengeance: *Her husband.* One leaden moment later, he muttered a heartfelt "Bloody hell."

Her hands were working more quickly than Pennington could follow, curling and twisting and shaping her hair into something that wouldn't betray her most recent recreational activities. "I just can't believe this," she grumbled. "What the hell is the *Enterprise* even doing out here?"

"That's a good question." Pennington started putting on his shoes. "Might be a story in it."

"Lucky you." Oriana turned sideways and peeked at herself out of the corner of her eye, studying her uniform and her hair. "Close enough." She started gathering the loose items of the personal bath kit she had brought with her.

"Leave them," Pennington said. "You can come back for them later."

"Actually, I can't," she said. "At least, I probably won't be able to. The *Enterprise* has been on patrol a long time, so she'll probably be in port for a while."

Pennington understood her point. As long as the *Enterprise* was here, she would have to keep her distance from him and stay close to her husband. "Right," he said. "I see. No problem."

He tried to conceal the wave of bitter disappointment that welled up inside him, but filtering his emotions had never been his strong suit. Oriana stroked his cheek with her palm. His dejection was mirrored in her sorrowful expression. "This is probably all for the best," she said. "Robert was going to come home sooner or later, and your wife will be here in a couple of weeks. . . . It's not like we thought this would last forever."

I'm such a stupid git, Pennington berated himself. *That's exactly what I thought.* "Yes, you're right." It was all he could think to say. He began to feel sick. Then he recognized the sensation: It was the yawning chasm of dread that always preceded the news that he was about to lose someone he loved. *Loved.* The very fact of it was like a cruel joke. It had started out as harmless flirtation, but in swift measure it had turned serious, become tempestuous, and finally had spun out of control. Caught up in the erotic thrill of every illicit moment with Oriana, he had allowed himself to forget about Lora. About his wife.

Oriana finished gathering her things into her overnight bag. Then an idea struck Pennington. "If Robert sees you holding that, won't he realize you were planning on staying somewhere other than the *Bombay?* Won't he ask questions?"

She looked at the bag in her hands. "Damn." Frowning, she handed it to Pennington. "Okay, hang on to it. My friend Katrina will come by later and take it down to my storage locker."

"Sure." He put the bag on the chair beside his dresser, then turned back toward her. "I guess this is goodbye, then."

"It's goodbye for now." She grabbed the waistband of his pants and pulled him to her. Their lips met with practiced ease, and their arms snaked around one another. He lost himself in her hungry, defiant kiss. After several intoxicating seconds she gently nibbled his lower lip. "The *Enterprise* is just passing through," she said, her whisper warm and intimate. *"Bombay* is here to stay." She punctuated her point with a quick flick of her tongue against his. "And I'll be back."

She was out the door before he could bid her farewell.

So much for spending the weekend in bed, he brooded.

"Enterprise, *this is Vanguard control. Prepare to release your navigational systems to our control in twenty seconds."*

"Vanguard, this is *Enterprise*," Kirk said. "Standing by for handoff." No matter how many times James Kirk reminded himself that letting the spacedock team guide his ship into the docking bay was the safest possible option, relinquishing control of his ship never came easy. He sat in his chair on the bridge and leaned forward on his left elbow, the thumb of his closed fist pressed thoughtfully against his lower lip. As the *Enterprise* began its final approach toward the slowly parting docking-bay doors, he took his first good look at the new, pristine gray surface of Starbase 47 on the main viewer.

Vanguard was enormous—no mere G- or K-class station, with a few airlocks, shuttle bays, and spare, utilitarian habitat modules. Nearly a kilometer tall and almost as wide, Watchtower-class space stations were more on the order of small cities. Designed for complete self-sufficiency, they were capable of lending support to colonial operations or serving as home base for missions both exploratory and military, in remote areas where no other Federation support was available. He recalled that, at peak capacity, it would be capable of hosting up to four *Constitution*-class starships in its main spacedock, as many as twelve other large to midsized ships on the spokes of its massive lower docking wheel, and no doubt dozens of smaller craft in the numerous hangar bays along its broad central core.

Emblazoned on opposite sides of the central core and on the top of the primary spacedock—in Arabic numerals almost as tall as the *Enterprise* itself—was the facility's numerical designation, 47, sandwiched between the words STARBASE (above it) and VANGUARD (below). Flanking the name and number were the crimson starburst and banner icons of Starfleet and the United Federation of Planets.

Ensign Varsha Mahtani keyed in a command sequence at the helm. The soft-voiced Indian woman turned toward Kirk and said, "Navigational control transferred, Captain."

"Thank you, Ensign." Kirk glanced over at Spock, who stood at ease next to his science station, watching the image of Vanguard's expansive spacedock swallowing the *Enterprise*. "Thoughts, Mr. Spock?"

"Most impressive," Spock said. "This far from a habitable system and civilized Federation worlds, the acquisition of raw materials for this station's construction must have posed a formidable challenge."

From the other side of the bridge, at the auxiliary engineering station, chief engineer Lieutenant Commander Montgomery Scott turned and leaned on the low railing that ran the circumference of the bridge's upper level. "Aye," he said, joining the conversation. "Movin' that much matériel this far from home this quickly would be a job and a half. Four dozen ships, at least."

"Apparently," Kirk said, "someone thought it was worth it."

Spock descended the short stairs to stand at Kirk's side. He lowered his voice, implying a need for discretion. "This far from Federation territory, a small facility would not be uncommon, as a border outpost. But a facility of this size and complexity . . . implies a mission much larger in scope."

There was no need for Spock to elaborate. Kirk understood his first officer's point: Something important was afoot here on the outskirts of explored space, something so crucial that the Federation was willing to commit itself to the Herculean task of establishing a major starbase that would then be left to fend for itself, come what may.

It was a mystery that now had Kirk's undivided attention.

Reyes strode swiftly through the corridor circling the middle deck of the main spacedock. He was headed to bay two, where the *Bombay* currently was berthed.

The passage bustled with throngs of officers debarking from the *Enterprise* and the *Bombay*. For Reyes, it was easy to tell which crew was which. The *Bombay* personnel had recently received the new Starfleet duty uniforms, which featured more intense primary colors and, for female officers, a one-piece miniskirt. Both the men and women from the *Enterprise* wore the previous generation of shirt-and-trouser uniforms, whose colors were more muted, and lacked the new black collar.

It never ceased to amaze Reyes that, in an organization as large as Starfleet, with all its personnel and its fleets of starships spread across the galaxy, whenever two ships managed to make port at the same time, so many members of their crews seemed to know each other. Already clusters of *Enterprise* crewmen were mingling with *Bombay* officers. Back-slappings and shouted salutations filled the wide, bulkhead-gray corridor with the sounds of joyous reunions, of friends and colleagues and academy cohorts too long separated by the call of duty.

The swelling tide of happy bonhomie brought a broad smile to Reyes's weathered face. It had been a few years since he had commanded a starship, but he remembered well the unique joy that coursed through any vessel at the utterance of two simple words: *Shore leave.*

Reyes recognized the stylishly tousled flaxen hair of the *Bombay*'s commanding officer as she exited the gangway into the corridor. As he approached, he shouted to her. "Hallie!" The attractive, fortyish captain looked around, apparently unable to determine who had called her name. He waved to her, and once again was thankful that his lunar upbringing had made him taller than average for a human. "Captain Gannon!"

This time she saw him. Stepping quickly and with grace, his former first officer from the *Dauntless* slalomed through the moving wall of bodies to join him. He fell into step beside her.

"Commodore," she said brightly. "Good to see you again."

"Likewise, Captain. Everything went smoothly?"

"By the numbers," Gannon said.

"Good, good." He hesitated, telegraphing with silence what he had to say next. "I have some bad news, I'm afraid."

"I figured as much. What can I do for you?"

"Priority signal from Ravanar." The two officers detoured around a large knot of personnel who were moving slowly up the center of the corridor. As they reunited in front of the group, he continued, "We need to get some gear out to them, pronto."

"Not a problem," Gannon said. "Anything else?"

"A few things. You need to pick up a team of dilithium prospectors stuck on Getheon because their warp drive committed seppuku; Lieutenant Commander Stutzman needs to hitch a ride out to the colony on Talagos Prime, so he can rejoin the *Endeavour* when she comes off patrol in a few weeks; and you need to confirm some long-range scans in Sector 116 Theta and update the star maps for a set of grid coordinates that astrocartography will send over in about an hour."

"And make our usual circuit of the homesteader colonies after we do our midsector recon, right?"

"Right, but make the run to Ravanar first."

She seemed to sense the urgency in Reyes's tone. "How soon do you need us to ship out?"

"How soon can you be ready?"

Gannon sighed. "We need repairs and supplies. If I cancel shore leave, and your people move us to the front of the line—"

"It's already done."

Her shoulders hunched into a resigned shrug. "Twenty-four hours?" Reyes's incredulous stare conveyed his disapproval. She revised her estimate. "Sixteen if we push it."

"Do your best," he said.

"Mind if I have lunch first?"

"Eat quickly."

"Do you want to join me?" She gestured out the transparent-aluminum wraparound window, toward the *Enterprise,* which was docked in the next bay, ninety degrees away on Vanguard's main core. "Maybe Captain Pike would—"

"That's Kirk's command now," Reyes said.

"Who?"

"Jim Kirk."

"Never heard of him. What's he like?"

"Don't know," Reyes said. "Haven't met him. Rumor has it he's some kind of young hotshot."

"That's what they used to say about Pike," Gannon said. She looked over at the *Enterprise* again and chuckled. "I can't believe he finally gave her up."

"I know. The *Enterprise* without Pike—it seems like the end of an era." He patted her shoulder then quickened his pace. "Talk to T'Prynn about getting that gear for Ravanar."

"Will do," Gannon said.

Reyes veered off toward a nearby turbolift. Gannon continued along and swiftly vanished into the crowd of red, blue, and gold uniforms swarming through the corridor. Looking out the turbolift door, Reyes eyed the *Enterprise* with quiet admiration. Chris Pike had captained that vessel for two consecutive five-year missions, and he and his crew had distinguished themselves as few others ever had. It was hard for Reyes to imagine someone who could earn greater accolades as a starship commander than Christopher Pike, especially when that officer was as young as Jim Kirk.

Well, someone at Starfleet Command thinks he's qualified, Reyes mused as the turbolift doors hissed closed. *But that's a mighty big ship for a first command. I hope he's up to it.*

Tim Pennington pressed his back into a narrow niche in the wall, not so much to stay clear of the dense pedestrian traffic in the main spacedock corridor as to stay out of sight. Peeking around the corner, he strained to pierce the shifting wall of bodies coursing past him.

Several meters down the corridor, on the opposite side, Oriana waited near the gangway entrance at bay three, where the *Enterprise* was docked. The curvaceous Italian woman paced anxiously, but her face was the epitome of calm. *You'd never guess she's a woman with a secret,* Pennington thought.

Oriana glanced down the gangway, stopped pacing, and waved. All her attention was directed toward Lieutenant Robert D'Amato, who emerged from the gangway and swept her up in a bear hug that lifted her off the deck. He spun her around, a full turn, before planting her back on her feet. Jealousy burned Pennington from within as he watched them kiss. It didn't matter to him that, as the "other man," he had no claim to be jealous of his lover's husband. Feelings were irrational things, immune to logic and reason, and he had never said otherwise.

Fantasies of revealing the affair tempted him, but he knew no good would come of such impulses. As he watched Oriana with Robert, the truth that he had denied for the past several weeks made itself abundantly, brutally clear: She was not going to leave her husband. Robert was her security, her long-term plan, her ace in the hole. Tim was just a luxury, a convenience, a taboo entertainment to be discarded.

They were still kissing. *I should just end it,* he knew. *Walk away. Hang on to my dignity.* As the two lovers pulled apart and began walking down the corridor in his direction, he retreated around the corner and did his best to press himself into the duranium bulkhead. *Dignity? What dignity?*

The D'Amatos passed by him, too wrapped up in the bliss of their reunion to notice him skulking in the half-shadowed corner. For a brief moment, he was grateful to feel invisible, inconsequential. Then relief gave way to shame and resentment.

Before he could savor the maudlin flavor of the moment, his news-service pager vibrated silently on his wrist. An angry sigh flared his nostrils as he raised the device to his eyes and checked the incoming message. It was from his editor.

*Haven't seen a story from you in eight days. Unless
you're dead, file something by tomorrow or we're
giving your column to the new intern.*

—Arlys

*P.S.—Stop filing meals on your expense report.
They're not covered, and you know it.*

He turned off the pager and pulled his sleeve back down
over it. *Time to get back to work,* he told himself. Looking
around at the frenzy of activity produced by having two
starships in port, he knew that there had to be a story waiting to be found.

He would make the usual token gestures of asking the
senior officers for comments, and he would pretend to be
annoyed when they refused to talk. It was all part of the
game. Years of thwarted efforts had taught Pennington that
it was very rare for people in positions of authority to talk
on the record, unless they had an ulterior motive for doing
so. Officers had nothing to gain and everything to lose by
speaking to the press. In Pennington's experience, the only
way to get a quote of value from an officer was to already
know the truth, then make them either confirm it, deny it,
or utter a pathetic "no comment."

His best chance of finding something newsworthy soon
enough to make his deadline was to talk to the people no
one normally paid any attention to. He scanned the crowd
of Starfleet personnel, paying special attention to their
shirt cuffs. He was looking for the ones with no braid
at all.

He was looking for enlisted personnel.

•   •   •

Decorum prohibited Ambassador Jetanien from complaining.

While Lieutenant Xiong sat beside Lieutenant Commander T'Prynn in front of Commodore Reyes's empty desk, Jetanien stood behind them and loomed over the debriefing session. He did it not out of a sense of authority or entitlement, but because he simply could not use the human-friendly chairs, which, even if enlarged for his greater size, were generally unsuited to his less-flexible torso. Forcing himself into a seated position usually resulted in a contortion of his body that was uncomfortable for him and unintentionally amusing for others.

He never complained about the absence of his preferred furniture for waking repose—a forward-sloping seat pad with a counterpoised kneeling pad—because he didn't want to be perceived as the sort of person who always accentuated the negative. In his opinion it was far less inflammatory to simply hold his peace and say that he preferred to stand.

Xiong was in the middle of explaining in exhaustive detail how soil samples had confirmed an age of nearly one hundred thousand years for the recently excavated find on Ravanar IV when Reyes interrupted, "That's all well and good, Lieutenant, but do we know anything *useful* about it?"

The young anthropology-and-archaeology expert glared for a moment, then collected himself. "That depends, I guess, on your definition of 'useful,' sir."

Reyes extended his arms outward as if to embrace the possibilities in his imagination. "What does it do? Who created it? Does it have anything to do with the Taurus Key?"

"It's a bit early to say for sure," Xiong said. "We'd only just started our tests when you summoned me back here."

Reyes winced like a man developing a headache. "Mr. Xiong, please don't tell me I just sent you on a forty-light-year field trip so you could come back here and tell me your results were inconclusive."

"I wouldn't call them 'inconclusive,' sir."

"What would you call them, then?"

Xiong shrugged. "Preliminary."

"I see," Reyes said. He rapped his knuckles on the desktop. "Let's recap, shall we? What's it made of? 'Unknown.' Is it indigenous? 'Unknown.' Does it pose a risk to our research team or this starbase? 'Unknown.' Did I leave anything out?"

Properly chastised, the young lieutenant took a deep breath, then said, "No, sir. That about covers it."

"There was one other development of note," T'Prynn said, making her first comment of the meeting. "After your departure, the research team succeeded in restoring power to one of its isolated components. They were still compiling data when their security was breached, forcing them to suspend operations."

"They activated it?" Xiong was half out of his seat. "When? How? What did it do?"

T'Prynn fixed Xiong with her icy Vulcan stare, which all but bade the high-strung young scientist to be calm. "Only one component was activated, Lieutenant. No effect was immediately apparent." She looked back at Reyes and added, "The more pressing concern is the security breach."

Reyes nodded. "And how much intel do we have on that?"

"Very little," she said. "Sabotage was our initial theory, but witness accounts suggest it was more likely a botched robbery."

Jetanien interjected, "Are we certain it wasn't espionage?"

"Spies observe, Mr. Ambassador," T'Prynn said. "They rarely reveal themselves without good cause. Nothing about this intruder's actions leads me to think he was a professional. In fact, I consider the opposite to be true."

The commodore tapped an index finger against his temple. "Suspects?"

"Nothing actionable," she said. "I will keep you apprised of any new information."

"See that you do." Reyes looked up at Jetanien. "Anything to add, Mr. Ambassador?"

"Only that we need to remain mindful of—"

He was interrupted by a sharp buzz from the commodore's desktop intercom.

Reyes thumbed open the channel. "What?"

The electronically filtered voice of his administrative aide replied, *"Yeoman Greenfield, sir. Captain Kirk of the* Enterprise *is here and wishes to speak with you."*

"Give me a moment to wrap this up, then send him in."

"Aye, sir," Greenfield said, and the intercom clicked off.

Reyes stood up, an action that everyone present had already learned was the commodore's way of signaling that a meeting was over. "My apologies, Mr. Ambassador." To Xiong and T'Prynn he added, "Dismissed."

It's just as well he cut me off, Jetanien decided as he led T'Prynn and Xiong out of the office and down the stairs into the station's busy operations center. *I was ad-libbing, anyway.*

Kirk's brief trip from the *Enterprise* to the operations center of Starbase 47 had only reinforced his perception of the station's enormity. The high-ceilinged corridor outside the gangway ramp had been impressive by itself. Glimpses of the terrestrial enclosure that occupied the upper half of the station's primary hull, above the spacedock, had brought a smile to Kirk's face. The sense of being in the midst of a buzzing hive of carefully coordinated activity was both overwhelming and exhilarating. Of course, none of those things had been the first detail to catch the captain's eye; that honor belonged to the miniskirts. *Someone at Starfleet Command likes me,* he had mused, unable to suppress his appreciative, smirking leer.

He stepped out of the turbolift into the operations center. Its standard duty-shift complement was more than twice as large as his average bridge crew. In the center of it all, standing on a raised platform, watching over the grand circus of quickly changing details, starship traffic, and internal business, was a man not much older than himself. The officer in charge was a pleasant-looking man with a thatch of dark hair; he managed his business with quiet courtesy. Kirk walked past another pair of miniskirted female officers, dodged between two adjacent banks of computers and sensor displays, and approached the platform all but unnoticed. He knocked on the railing post. "Excuse me?"

The officer above him did a small double take, then nodded and smiled. "Hello."

"I'm Captain James T. Kirk, *Starship Enterprise.*"

"Executive officer Jon Cooper," the man on the platform said. "What can I do for you, Captain?"

"I'm looking for Commodore Reyes."

Cooper pointed to a pair of double doors on the opposite side of the room from the turbolift. "His office is over there, sir."

"Thank you." Kirk turned and stepped toward the office.

Cooper called after him. "He's in a meeting, sir."

Kirk turned slowly back toward Cooper. "A meeting."

"Yes, sir. You can check his schedule with his yeoman."

"His yeoman."

Before Kirk could point out that he had no idea which one of the junior officers in this room was the commodore's yeoman, Cooper waved over a chipper young woman with bright, doe-like eyes and an enormous data slate cradled in one arm.

"Toby," Cooper said, "this is Captain James Kirk, of the *Enterprise.* Could you check on the status of the commodore's meeting for him?"

"Of course, sir," she said. She moved to a nearby console, entered her security code, and opened an internal comm channel. Several seconds later, a distinctly annoyed growl of a voice replied over the speaker, *"What?"*

"Yeoman Greenfield, sir. Captain Kirk of the *Enterprise* is here and wishes to speak with you."

"Give me a moment to wrap this up, then send him in."

"Aye, sir," Greenfield said, then clicked off the intercom. She turned to face Kirk. "He—"

"I heard him, Yeoman."

"Yes, sir."

The door to Reyes's office opened. An imposing Chelon in expensive clothing was the first to exit, followed by a young Asian man . . . and one of the most strikingly beautiful Vulcan women Jim Kirk had ever seen. The tips of her pointed ears barely poked out from beneath her long, straight black hair. She met his stare and returned it, without blinking, as she moved gracefully past him, her stride so fluid that she seemed almost to glide. Her statuesque physique and dark intensity captivated Kirk. *She could probably snap me like a twig,* he realized. He was turned half around, still watching her while she watched him back, when Greenfield spoke and broke the spell.

"The commodore will see you now, Captain."

Snapping back into the moment, he reminded himself why he had come here. He nodded to Greenfield, said "Thank you," and walked quickly into Reyes's office. The chirps and chatter of the operations center fell away as the door closed behind him.

Kirk had half-expected to find a lavish office, appointed with extravagances and defined by a huge window on the stars. Instead, he found himself in a moderately sized and extremely Spartan workspace that had no windows—most likely because the operations center was shielded by several layers of reinforced duranium armor plating. The commodore's desk was made of the same blue-gray duranium composite as the walls. There were exactly three chairs (two without armrests in front of the desk, and the commodore's more ergonomic seat behind it), and the room's lone couch looked decidedly unwelcoming.

Much like Commodore Reyes himself.

"Captain," he said, his brow lined with the deep creases of a man who worried for a living. "To what do I owe the pleasure?"

"I was going to ask you the same thing," Kirk said.

"Do tell." Reyes motioned for Kirk to sit.

The captain settled onto one of the chairs. It was even less comfortable than it looked. He fought the urge to fidget. "When we shipped out last year, I never would have expected to return to a starbase this far from home. It's a welcome surprise . . . but still a surprise."

Reyes shrugged. "If you'd rather skip your repairs, we can just pretend you were never here."

Kirk waved away the suggestion. "No, no—we're overdue. It's a good thing we found you when we did." Belatedly, he realized that Reyes's remark had shifted him off his interrogative track. "But that got me to thinking about the old adage: When something seems too good to be true—"

"There was also one about gift horses," Reyes said. "And an old story about a frozen bird that fell in a warm cow pie. But much as I'd love to sit here and trade proverbs with you, Captain, I really don't have the time."

"Permission to speak candidly, sir?"

"Why not? It's bound to happen eventually."

"It seems fairly obvious to me that this station was fast-tracked into service."

"What gave it away? The twenty-four hundred active-duty personnel, or the fact that the spacedock doors open?"

Reining in his simmering temper, Kirk reminded himself that sarcasm was a privilege that belonged only to the highest-ranking officer in any room. "Perhaps a more pertinent question, Commodore, would be, *Why* was Vanguard fast-tracked?"

Heaving a weary sigh, Reyes leaned forward onto his desk. "The same reason any Starfleet project gets the wind at its back. Because someone on the council decided it was important." He picked up a remote from his desk, pointed it at a round-cornered viewscreen on the wall, and clicked the power button. The monitor flickered to life, showing a local astropolitical map. "The red chevron indicates our position. Tell me, Captain—what details on this map jump out at you?"

Either it was a trick question, Kirk knew, or he was being goaded into helping the commodore make his argument. "The borders of the Klingon Empire and the Tholian Assembly."

"So far, so good." Reyes clicked more details into focus. "I presume the green lines and arrows are familiar to you?"

Setting his poker face to "archly bemused," Kirk eyed the map again and said, "Colony ship flight plans."

Click. "And the blue lines and arrows?"

"Trade routes and shipping lanes." Kirk's fist began to clench near his belt. *I should have brought my phaser.*

"And what does all that suggest to you, Captain?"

Have to give him credit, Kirk told himself. *Refuse to give him the obvious answer, and I come off as either an idiot or an insubordinate jerk. Parrot the answer he wants, and I indict my entire line of inquiry as pointless. . . . He's good.*

"A colonization effort," Kirk said, swallowing his pride.

"Precisely," Reyes said. "More than twenty colonies and

half a dozen mining operations have come to the Taurus Reach in the last sixteen months—half of them since this station opened. Our job? Protect them as best we can with what few resources we're given. In other words, standard operating procedure."

"I can't imagine the Klingons or the Tholians have been happy about our move into this region. And I'm sure a starbase on their shared doorstep pleases them even less."

"True," Reyes said. "I'd be lying if I said we didn't ruffle a lot of feathers by building this station. But the alternative would have been much worse."

This time, Kirk really didn't follow. "What alternative?"

"Letting the Klingons expand their reach until they hit the Tholian border. We'd be front row to a war that could last decades; whichever side won, we'd be fenced in, stuck navigating hostile territory in order to explore the galactic rim. . . . We need to keep our options open, for now and for the future."

"With all respect, Commodore, space is three-dimensional, and it's big. Even if the Klingons make a push for the Tholian border, we'd hardly be 'landlocked'—we'd still have options."

"You're talking about taking the long way around," Reyes said. "Away from the galactic plane." He lifted the remote and turned off the screen. "No thank you, Captain. I read the report on your mission to the energy barrier. I'll pass."

Kirk shook his head. "If you think colonizing this region will stop the Klingons from trying to conquer it, you don't know the Klingons."

Reyes's voice became quiet and intense. "The hell I

don't. I was commanding a starship while you were still at the Academy." Regaining his composure, he continued, "You're right about one thing, though. The Klingons will try to take the Taurus Reach. My job is to make sure they don't succeed."

"What about the Tholians? If this turns into a battle on two fronts—"

"It won't," Reyes said. "The Tholians have never shown any interest in this region. They expanded from Tholia in every direction *except* this one. As long as we steer clear of their border, I don't expect any trouble from them."

"And if you're wrong?"

"We'll be sitting on a powder keg."

Kirk frowned. "On that, we agree."

Reyes leaned slowly back in his chair, eyeing Kirk with darkening suspicion. "You think I'm just some paper-pusher, don't you, Kirk?"

"No, sir, of course—"

"Yes, you do," Reyes said, cutting Kirk off. "You think I sit here, safe on a starbase, playing games with people's lives." No longer young or foolish enough to be goaded into embarrassing himself, Kirk stayed quiet. The commodore leaned aggressively forward as he continued, "I take my command just as seriously as you take yours, Kirk. I deal in life and death, war and peace, and everything in between, every day. Bottom line: I make it my business to *know* my business. So, when you walk into my office and presume to give me the third degree with questions I answered to the admiralty months ago, I get the impression you think I'm just some rubber stamp with heavy braid on his cuff."

Choosing his words and his tone with care, Kirk said, "If I offended you, Commodore, please accept my apology. No slight was intended, I assure you."

Reyes gave a small nod of acknowledgment. "Enough said." Turning his chair, he rested one arm on his desktop and glanced sidelong at Kirk. "Anything else I can do for you?"

"Yes, sir," Kirk said, and smirked wryly. "Keep the matches away from the powder keg."

7

Lieutenant Commander Kevin Judge had his hands full. With one word from Captain Gannon, the *Bombay*'s shore leave had been canceled, and repairs that he and his engineering teams had expected to have four days to finish now were being shoehorned into twelve frantic hours.

The gangly chief engineer stalked through main engineering, like a hunting tiger, seeking out whatever was going wrong. He found it, in the form of a well-meaning young ensign who was disassembling the controls for the impulse reactor's primary heat exchanger. "Anderson," Judge said loudly, then coughed. His voice was hoarse from nonstop barking of orders. The rasp of his overtaxed larynx, when added to his already clipped Liverpool accent, made him sound like he had a horrendous cold. He recovered his breath and continued, "Are you mad? Didn't I say to leave the impulse systems until after we leave spacedock?" The ensign rolled her eyes and looked glumly at her half-dismantled pile of hardware. "Put it back together," Judge said.

He dragged himself over to the master engineering console. Planting one hand on its edge, he awkwardly propped himself up while he studied the tall board's blinking status displays. *All bollixed up, as usual,* he grumped, shaking his head. He reached across and thumbed the intercom to the phaser control room. "Castellano, why aren't the phasers back online yet?"

"The plasma relays are still overheating, sir. We had to remove them for recalibration."

Panic and desperation infused the chief engineer's every word. "Castellano, we ship out in less than three hours." He pulled his hand down over his hollow-cheeked face, then roughly scratched his crown of shock-cut hair. "Lock down the phaser capacitors at seventy percent of maximum and fix the plasma relays later."

"Aye, sir. Castellano out."

Another blinking light captured his attention. He opened another intercom channel. "Engineering to ch'Shonnas."

"Go ahead, sir," said Lieutenant Thanashal ch'Shonnas, the ship's darkly reticent Andorian science officer.

"Your status indicator just went red, Shal. What happened?"

"That fix we talked about? Didn't take. All the crystals you sent up were burned out."

"Bloody hell." *Concentrate on my breathing,* Judge told himself. *Unclench fists.* "Hang tight, I'll see what I can do. Engineering out." He flipped a switch and opened a line to the bridge. "Engineering to Commander Milonakis."

"This is Milonakis. What's up, Kevin?"

"Vondy, we're in a bind. We need your magic."

"Name it," Milonakis said.

The chief engineer relaxed a little. Milonakis knew someone on every base and starship in the fleet, and the XO had a particular knack for trading and bartering. If anyone could find what the *Bombay* needed on short notice, it would be him.

"Regulator crystals for the sensor array," Judge said. "All our spares are fried, and our main is cracked. . . . Mayday."

"All right, I'm on it. Milonakis out." The bridge channel clicked off.

For a moment, Judge thought he might have put out the last of the metaphorical fires plaguing his third consecutive shift without a break. Then he turned and found himself chin-to-snout with Lieutenant Loak, one of the more gratingly overeager junior officers on the *Bombay* engineering staff. Something looked different about him.

"Loak, why is your hair pink?"

"Long story, sir."

"No doubt. What's up?"

"Ensign Anderson informs me that you've postponed the repairs to the impulse control," Loak said.

"That's right," Judge said. "You got a beef with that?"

"Certainly not a personal one, Commander," Loak said. "But until we complete these repairs, we will be at less than sixty-three percent efficiency in maneuvers at half-impulse, and strenuous full-impulse maneuvers could overload the system."

"I appreciate that, Loak, really I do. But you might notice we're a little short of manpower down here tonight."

"Sir, we cannot postpone this until after departure. Once the impulse system is engaged, we will be unable to make further repairs to these systems."

"I'm aware of that," Judge said. "I do know how engines work, you know. But we're putting this boat back together with spit and promises right now, so we can ship out on an emergency milk run. We'll be back in six days. Fix it then."

He shooed Loak away as he would a small animal that had overstayed its welcome. "Off you go."

The Tellarite sulked as he stomped away. Judge looked around main engineering. At a monitoring station next to his main console, Engineer Donna Ford was cross-checking the warp power readouts against the rated norms listed on a chart in her hand. Ensign Robertson—whose first name, by coincidence, was also Donna—stood next to her, observing but not doing much else that Judge could see.

"Robertson, what are you doing?"

"Supervising," she said, with a naïveté that Judge found endearing only when he encountered it in attractive young women.

"That's lovely," he said. "Why don't you supervise re-calibrating the alignment of the dilithium crystals? And you can do it yourself, to make sure it's done properly."

She glared at him with wounded pride, then walked toward the main warp reactor. "Yes, sir."

He flashed a reassuring smile at the enlisted woman. "Ford, is it?"

She looked afraid, like a small woodland creature in a spotlight. "Yes, sir."

"Ford, I'd like you to do a favor for me. Find Cargo Chief Hayes and tell him that if he doesn't find our missing duotronic cables, I can't guarantee that his quarters will continue to enjoy the benefits of working lights, ventila-tion, or plumbing."

"Aye, sir," the young woman said, and started toward the turbolift.

"Oh, and Ford? On your way back, stop by the mess hall

and pick me up a spot of tea and some biscuits." Remembering the subtle shades of mistranslation between her American dialect and his own, he shouted out a clarification before the turbolift doors closed. "And by biscuits, I mean cookies!"

A shrill voice came from behind him and cut like a knife. "Cookies? Is junk food all you eat?" Judge turned toward the scolding like a skipper steering his boat into a storm wave. Dr. Hua Sun Lee had snuck up on him to deliver one of her patented harangues. "No wonder you skipped your physical again. With a diet like yours, you must be an infarction waiting to happen."

"I really don't have time for this."

"Five! That's how many times you've made an appointment to take your physical and haven't shown up! Five!" Physically, Dr. Lee was a tiny woman, but she had a temper and a voice that could overpower a charging bull.

Judge handed her his checklist. "It's on my list, Doctor. Unfortunately, so are four dozen other critical items, all of which need to be resolved before we ship out in"—he checked the chronometer—"two hours and fifty-six minutes." Despite his inner voice telling him to remain calm, he felt himself grow more hysterical by the moment. "I've got a mess hall whose food slots haven't been restocked. I have a main sensor array that, for no reason I can possibly fathom, is suddenly blind to the element carbon. My engineering team seems committed to disassembling anything that still works, the cargo chief misplaced all my spare parts, and I haven't slept in over twenty-five hours. I've seen naught but this compartment, the inside of that turbolift, and my own quarters for the past eleven months." His desperation turned to bitter sarcasm. "So I apologize if I've inconvenienced you, Doctor, but, as you might have noticed, I have a few petty details to attend to at the moment."

Dr. Lee frowned up at Judge and shot him the most venomous stink-eye stare he had ever seen. "All I ask is that you cancel appointments you can't keep." She turned, walked a few steps, then spun back. "Tomorrow at 1700 hours?"

His smile wasn't the least bit sincere. "That would be lovely."

"Show up this time."

"Understood."

Lee nodded once, affirming that the discussion was over. She walked away, through a gaggle of junior computer engineers who all were scrambling in a panic toward Judge. "Sir!" shouted Lieutenant Kashuk. "The library computer is offline!"

It was like Judge's worst nightmare during his Academy days. "What? How?"

"We were running a standard optimization cycle after we installed the database upgrade, and—"

"Upgrade? I didn't order any bloody upgrade."

Kashuk and the others traded embarrassed looks. "We downloaded it from Vanguard."

A sick churning feeling spun through Judge's gut. "Tell me you didn't install the Sigma Seven utility with it."

More downcast eyes told him the worst was true: They had tried to load software that hadn't yet been backward-engineered for the *Bombay*'s Mark II computer core. "Let me guess," he said. "It's locked in diagnostic mode and isn't accepting input." Dismayed nods all around. "Unbelievable! Who do you people work for? I thought we were on the same side. Show of hands: How many of you are paid saboteurs?"

"We're sorry, sir," Kashuk said. "We should have read—"

"Forget it," Judge said, slipping into problem-solving mode. "Pull the plug on the main core, interrupt main power and cut off its backup battery, then do a full restart. Go!"

The engineers scurried away to try and repair their mistake before the next one made its entrance. *Best-case scenario,* Judge reasoned, *they might have the computer back up in about two hours . . . which will leave me less than an hour to test the sensors and about a dozen other things.* It took all his willpower and training to stop himself from hyperventilating.

"Mr. Judge," a woman said from behind him.

Well past the point of civility, he snapped, "What?"

Then he turned to see the placid face of Captain Gannon.

"Something wrong, Mr. Judge?"

He brightened his face with a smile whose sincerity was undermined by the anxiety that pinned his eyebrows up around his hairline. "Wrong? What could be wrong?"

"Everything's all right, then?"

"Couldn't be righter." *She's not buying it.*

"Carry on, then." She smiled and continued on her way aft.

"Thank you, Captain." He kept the smile plastered on his face until he was sure that she was not coming back. Sagging with exhaustion and despair against his console, he muttered to himself, "We're so right roundly pooched, it's not even funny."

Tim Pennington lurked in the shadows across from the gangway to the *Enterprise.*

He rechecked his notes while he waited. So far, he'd convinced five lower-decks personnel from the ship to talk with him, either off the record or on the condition of anonymity, about the ship's recent jaunt to the energy barrier at the edge of the galaxy. The mission had failed and resulted in nine deaths. But the true horror, his sources had said, was what transpired later, after the ship began its long journey home.

The first time he heard the story of Gary Mitchell's transformation into a telepathic, telekinetic, homicidal *übermensch,* he had dismissed it as the tall tale of a crewman who had spent too many months on duty without R&R. But the next witness confirmed the report, as did the other three. Aside from expected variances on picayune details, their stories lined up with frightening specificity. If even half what they had told him was the truth, this had the makings of an incredible scoop.

He had multiple firsthand sources; he had been to the station's operations office and received copies of the death certificates for Commander Gary Mitchell and Dr. Elizabeth Dehner; and he had filed a freedom-of-information petition with the station's chief JAG officer, Captain Rana Desai, for copies of Captain Kirk's official after-action reports regarding the deaths of Mitchell and Dehner. Rumor had it that Kirk had listed them as casualties of the failed attempt to breach the energy barrier, when in fact they had been killed under mysterious circumstances on Delta Vega.

From somewhere down the corridor, a turbolift door gasped open. Footfalls echoed brightly and grew louder, sharper, closer. Pennington peeked around the corner. At the first sight of a gold-colored sleeve adorned by two-and-a-half rings of braid, he emerged from hiding. Quickly interposing himself between Kirk and the gangway entrance, he held up his Federation News Service credentials. "Captain, a moment of your time?"

"No," Kirk said. He tried to detour around Pennington, who sidestepped and blocked him again.

"How did Gary Mitchell die, Captain?"

Kirk's expression hardened, and his posture became ramrod-stiff. Anger burned brightly in his eyes. Through a jaw tight with suppressed fury, he said, "In the line of duty."

"*Where* did Mitchell die, Captain?"

"Are you implying something?"

"It's a simple question."

"And you want a simple answer," Kirk said. Pennington nodded. Kirk added, "My answer is in my report. Excuse me." The captain shouldered past Pennington and stepped onto the gangway.

"I've already requested copies of your report," Pennington said. "I'll be interested to see if they match up to the eyewitness accounts I've already compiled."

Kirk stopped. For a moment, Pennington expected the young commanding officer to turn back and prolong the conversation. Instead, without turning around, Kirk resumed walking.

Maybe the witness statements were wrong; perhaps they

were based on hearsay. It was possible that Kirk's official
report would contain no discrepancies at all. But if it did,
his dismissive response was the same as saying "No comment." In the court of public opinion, that would be seen as
suspect at best.

Clicking off his handheld recorder, Pennington decided to head upstairs and ask Captain Desai to expedite
his petition for Kirk's report. If his hunch panned out,
tomorrow's FNS feed would be led by a report with his
byline on it.

Montgomery Scott had just finished a very long double
shift in engineering. The ship had been in dire need of new
power cells for weeks; its warp coils had been overdue for
recalibration. Multiple critical systems throughout the ship
had required swap-outs, or upgrades, or tune-ups. To Scott's
elated satisfaction, Vanguard's spacedock maintenance team
had met all those needs in quick order; he hadn't seen a
starbase so large and well equipped since leaving the core
systems of the Federation. The *Enterprise* still had more
work ahead of it—most notably, a complete refit of its
bridge—but those changes would have to wait until the ship
returned home to Earth.

Taking advantage of a rare free moment in his schedule,
he now was seeking out an item of personal desiderata that
wasn't likely to be available through official channels. A
carefully worded question to his old chum Vondas Milonakis, along with a case of the *Enterprise*'s spare duotronic
cables, had led Scott to the station's lower docking wheel,
where an Orion merchantman known as the *Omari-Ekon*
was berthed.

At the end of a very long, conveyor-like gangway, he saw the closed airlock hatch to the *Omari-Ekon* flanked by a pair of hulking, green-skinned sentinels. Ever the quintessential Scotsman, he walked with unflagging confidence directly toward them.

From either side, each guard grabbed one of his arms, stopping him in midstep and lifting him off the floor. The one with the long, drooping mustache asked in a low hard voice, "Can we help you?"

"Aye, lad. I have a business proposition for your boss."

The guard seemed unconvinced. "Do you even know who my boss is?" Scott winced at the sour stench of the man's breath.

"I'm guessing he's a man who can get things done."

"My employer doesn't like unannounced guests."

"Announce me, then." Scott's biceps were starting to hurt from the two guards' relentless grips.

"Are you carrying any weapons or communications devices?"

"I'm just here as a customer, lad."

"That's not what I asked you."

Scott was growing annoyed. "No, I'm not armed, and I don't have a communicator."

The guards let him down. Mustache, as Scott had decided to refer to the thug in charge, pointed at the wall. "Lean forward and put your hands there."

"Is this really necessary?"

Icy stares and folded arms made clear that it was. He did as he was told. Mustache stood back and watched while the other guard frisked Scott. Several seconds later, having explored areas in which Scott was fairly certain no human

could possibly have concealed anything larger than an in-
grown hair, they allowed him to turn around. "Who shall
we say is here?"

With all the patience and good cheer he could muster, he
said, "My friends call me Scotty."

"Rank, full name, and current assignment."

So much for keeping things cordial, Scott concluded, his
chipper grin turning to a frown. "Lieutenant Commander
Montgomery Scott, chief engineer, *Starship Enterprise.*"

"Hang on." Mustache reached under his jacket and removed a small communicator-type device. He keyed in a
sequence that Scott couldn't see, and spoke quickly in a
low whisper. All the while, he and his compatriot kept a
close watch on Scott, who rocked on his heels, whistled
softly, rolled his eyes from one ceiling pipe fixture to another, and otherwise made a deliberate nuisance of himself,
simply because he could.

Mustache flipped his communicator closed and put it
away. The hatch behind him opened with a grinding scrape.
"Mr. Ganz will see you now."

"Thank ye, lad," Scott said. He walked inside, and the
hatch closed quietly behind him. For a moment, he thought
he was alone in the darkened but immaculate corridor of
the Orion ship.

Then a hand slapped down on his shoulder. He turned to
face a slim man in an exquisitely tailored ash-gray suit and
polished, matching shoes. The man's skin was an unnerving shade of pure coal black, a hue unlike any found in humans; it was glossy, like oil, and it reflected light so well
that Scott could almost see his reflection in the man's high,
broad forehead. His head was shaved, and a tightly twisted

braid of pale violet hair jutted from his narrow chin. "Commander Scott," he said, flashing a smile composed of gleaming black teeth. His flat-black, almond-shaped eyes betrayed no hint of his thoughts. "I'm Zett Nilric. Welcome." Polite as this man was, Scott's intuition warned him that his host was undoubtedly a killer.

"Mr. Nilric, I was—"

"Mr. Zett."

"Sorry," Scott said. "No offense meant."

"None taken," Zett said. "Forgive my interruption. Please continue."

"The bruiser outside said I was to see a Mr. Ganz."

"Yes. He's on the recreation deck. Please follow me."

Zett led Scott a dozen meters or so down the corridor, to a small, exceptionally quiet turbolift. They rode together in silence for several seconds. When the turbolift doors hissed open, a strong, sweet-cherry aroma wafted in from the dim space beyond. No sooner had Scott followed Zett out of the turbolift than he was met by an impenetrable wall of sound, heavy with driving bass and raging with a drone of synthetic chords.

Gauzy, translucent curtains of multicolored fabric were draped in long overlapping swoops, creating a clearly marked path into the heart of this compartment. From the reverberating acoustics and the multiple layers of music, Scott deduced that the space was enormous. Emerging from the maze of curtains, he saw that he was right. Intense shafts of roaming light sliced through the low, smoky haze of narcotic smoke that polluted the air. As his eyes adjusted to the subdued illumination, he observed that the sprawling split-level space occupied most of two upper decks aboard the Orion vessel. Movement from above caught his eye. Looking up, he saw that several sections of the deck overhead had been removed, adding to the impression of an airy, luxuriously open environment.

In every direction something new captured his interest: table after table of different games of chance; exotic women of various humanoid species, either mingling with patrons or dancing around metal poles on raised platforms beneath strobing lights; aliens whose species he had never encountered before; the scent of something tantalizing or something revolting; drinks that bubbled, drinks that frothed, drinks that changed color when they made contact with one's lips. Cloyingly sweet vapors, like honeyed cloves, mingled with the bite of acrid smoke, all of it originating in the countless ornate water pipes—or hookahs, as Scott had learned they were called—that were scattered throughout the room.

Scott felt like a child on Christmas morning.

Zett moved in smooth strides through the maze of gaming tables, which were crowded with loud, staggering, inebriated miners and prospectors. Scott assumed the laborers had come here to squander their earnings and bolster their spirits for another six months of lonely digging on another unnamed rock. Though he hoped he'd be smarter than that with his money, he couldn't really say that he blamed them. Life on the frontier was hard and it was lonely—more for some than for others.

Zett led him aft, to one of two broadly curving staircases that ascended through a crescent-shaped cut to the deck above. The staircase was narrowest at its bottom, and it widened quickly as they climbed. As they passed the middle stair, a lithe, green-skinned Orion woman draped with several carefully overlapped strips of diaphanous Tholian silk stepped between them as she descended. Her very proximity charged the air with erotic energy. Scott's pulse quickened at the scent of her; his eyes were drawn to her dark, voluminous cascade of unkempt curls, her pouting lips and come-hither glance. . . .

Looking at Scott with tired cynicism, Zett said simply, "You couldn't afford her."

"I was just—"

"Not for an hour. Not for half an hour."

"But I wasn't—"

"When you're an admiral, maybe we'll talk."

As the duo reached the top of the stairs, Scott noticed that the music from the lower level faded quickly into ambient background noise. *Acoustic dampeners,* he figured.

Unlike the lower deck of this sprawling private oasis, there were no gaming tables upstairs. In the two rear corners were doors, likely to private offices or residential quarters. The denizens of this deck, Scott noticed, were easily divided into two categories: men and women who exuded the cruel bravado and cold lethality of career criminals and gangsters, and scores of impossibly beautiful, scantily clad men and women whose sole occupation in this environment was painfully obvious.

Zett placed a firm but gentle palm on Scott's back and guided him to stand between a pair of black carved-marble obelisks, in front of a broad dais piled high with cushions and pillows. The dais, Scott noted, was bordered on either side by the two wide gaps for the curving staircases, which nearly met at their apexes, leaving only a narrow strip of floor as an ingress. *Like a moat,* Scott surmised. Around it were more curving draperies. Behind it was an enormous wraparound window framing a broad panorama of the Taurus Reach starscape.

Seated in the center of all this opulence, puffing from a hookah by means of a long ribbed tube with a metallic nozzle, was Ganz, an enormous, thickly muscled, bald green Orion man in a midnight blue caftan. He regarded Scott with caution as he exhaled a plume of earthy-smelling, pale-orange smoke through his broad nose. "Lieutenant Commander Scott," he said, his voice low in both register and volume.

"Scotty, to my friends."

A small crease above the bridge of Ganz's nose wrinkled into a tight knot of suppressed annoyance. "What can I do for you, Commander?"

"I was hoping you could help me procure some special spirits for my private stash on the *Enterprise.*"

Ganz thrust his chin forward as his eyes narrowed. "I'm sorry—did you just say you came here to buy liquor?"

"Aye," Scott said, the minor vibrato in his voice betraying the apprehension he suddenly felt. "But no—"

"You are aware that several establishments on the station serve alcohol?"

"Aye, but not what I'm after. I—"

"If you say you've come looking for *mandisa,* my associate Zett is going to push you out an airlock."

Words logjammed one after another in Scott's throat as he shifted gears in midsentence. He *had* come here hoping to acquire a bottle—or a case—of the rare Orion aphrodisiac, on the assumption that, because they were outside the official borders of the Federation, a loophole might have made it accessible at last. Unfortunately, the stony gaze of the gangster in front of him made it apparent to Scott that he was not the first one to have entertained this notion—nor the first to have dared to bother Ganz with it.

"Of course not," Scott lied, his prevarication as obvious as it was desperate. "In fact, I was going to ask you or your"—he looked around at the coterie of thugs, who were inching closer—"your esteemed colleagues to recommend something exotic."

"Something exotic," Ganz repeated, an evil grin broadening his face. "I think we can accommodate you after all, Commander Scott." He turned and bellowed across the room, "Reke! Come here!" One of Ganz's shabbier-looking henchmen staggered away from his table on the far side of the room. Ganz pointed him back the way he'd come. "Bring the bottle." The bedraggled hoodlum turned, snagged the bottle with a broad sweeping grab, and resumed plodding toward the dais. When he reached Scott's side, Ganz held up his hand, and Reke stopped. Pointing at Scott, Ganz said, "Give him the bottle."

Reke looked at Scott, struggling to focus through eyes dilated with intoxication. Perplexed, he looked down at the bottle in his hand, then glanced pleadingly at Ganz, who scowled back. Cowed, Reke thrust the bottle toward Scott, who took it.

The chief engineer stared at the bottle for a moment, then lifted the cork and sniffed its aggressively pungent contents. "Good God, man, you could strip dilithium with this! What in blazes is it?"

Wobbling on his feet, the henchman belched. Through a thick gurgling croak, he forced out the words "It's green," then he doubled over and vomited on Scott's left boot.

Imagining himself back in Starfleet basic training prior to the start of his academy classes twenty-odd years ago, Scott simply pretended that nothing was amiss. He didn't flinch. His posture remained straight. Eye contact with his host was unbroken. Ganz nodded at him, apparently satisfied with what he had seen. "Enjoy it in good health, Commander."

"I will. Thank you. . . . What do I owe you?"

"Call it a gift," Ganz said. "I don't do business with Starfleeters. Too many . . . complications."

"Right," Scott said. "I see. Mighty generous of you, then."

"You know," Ganz added, "if I was you right now, I'd be—"

"Leaving," Scott said enthusiastically. "A capital idea." Scott lifted his soiled boot free of Reke's mound of ejected stomach contents and shook away the larger chunks. He gestured his farewell to Ganz with the bottle of green mystery booze, then departed without another word to the Orion boss.

Zett was at Scott's back by the time he reached the stairs to the lower level. "I trust you can show yourself out?"

"Aye, count on it."

Despite Scott's assurance, Zett shadowed him all the way to the airlock and escorted him into the corridor beyond. He offered up his unctuous, jet-black grin. "A pleasure."

Scott was halfway down the corridor to the station core before he heard Zett head back inside Ganz's ship. Only as he rounded the corner did Scott permit himself a heavy sigh and an unheard, softly muttered retort of "Wankers."

Rana Desai's feet dragged like leaden weights. Exhaustion had left her feeling like a shell of herself. She had expected to be home more than two hours ago, but a flurry of last-minute work had made this evening into just one more of a long series of painfully late nights in Vanguard's office of the Starfleet Judge Advocate General.

Turning the corner toward her quarters, she imagined the look on her boyfriend's face. She had wanted to let him know about the delay that kept her and two of her lawyers trapped after-hours in the JAG office, but she hadn't been able to steal a private moment to relay the bad news. *He'll understand,* she hoped. *It's the nature of the job. He knows that.*

Her door swished open as she approached, and she entered to a faint aroma of grilled fish. She stopped at the dining table. A pair of still-burning tapers had consumed themselves to within half an inch of their bases. At her place, an immaculate plate was flanked by gleaming silverware. Her water goblet was filled. An open bottle of Jadot Pouilly-Fuisse stood behind her tulip-shaped wineglass.

Reyes stood and stared out the broad window on the far side of the room. He downed the last dregs from the wineglass in his hand, then spoke without turning around. "I started without you."

"So I see." Desai picked up the serving fork and poked the untouched fillet of sea bass, which had long since gone cold, neglected in the middle of the unoccupied table for two. She placed the fork back on the platter, perfectly parallel to the fillet. "Sorry I'm late," she said, pouring herself half a glass of the vintage white wine. "But it's all Pennington's fault."

Reyes continued to gaze out the window. "Mm-hm."

She picked up her glass, circled around the table, and joined him at the window. Trying to read his silences was still a challenge for her, but sensing his moods was getting easier. "What's wrong?"

He looked down into the bottom of his empty glass with a forlorn expression. "Bad news from home."

Placing one hand on his arm, she gently turned him toward her. "What news?"

"My mother." Anguish had recast his normally intense, stoic visage into something tragic. "She's been diagnosed with Meenok's disease."

Desai's voice was a dismayed whisper. "Oh, no. What's the prognosis?"

Reyes's voice cracked and faltered like he was being strangled. "Terminal. A couple months, maybe." He fought to pull in a new breath and exhaled through clenched teeth as he leaned forward and pressed his forehead against the window. "And here I am, at the ass end of the galaxy."

Meenok's disease was a degenerative neurological affliction that continued to haunt the descendants of Earth's first lunar settlers. Its similarity to other, more benign conditions meant that it was almost always misdiagnosed until its final, fatal stages. Victims of Meenok's almost always remained lucid. Unfortunately, its chief symptom during its final stage was gruesome, debilitating pain. Just about the only mitigating factor was that this suffering, though extreme, was brief. So brief, Desai understood, that there was little chance that Reyes could make the journey back to his family's home in New Berlin on Luna before the end came.

A lonesome tear escaped from Reyes's closed eyes. Desai took the empty glass from his hand and set it down on a corner table beside her own. Normally, she found budging him to be like moving a mountain, but tonight Reyes responded to her gentle guidance, like a vessel set adrift. With a gentle nudge, she guided him toward the sofa, eased him down onto it, then settled herself beside him.

"When did you hear the news?"

"About an hour ago. I got the message while I was waiting for you."

Taking one of his large, weathered hands into her own, she said, "Is there anything I can do?"

He shook his head. "Funny thing about life—it sneaks up on you." Squeezing her hands, he continued, "We get over the illusion of our own indestructibility, but we forget that our parents are mortal. Then, one day, one of the people who made you is gone . . . and you realize you're next in line."

"She's not gone yet," Desai said.

"No, not yet. But soon. I recorded a message . . . but it's not the same. It's not like being there." Reyes leaned back and craned his head over the back of the sofa. She watched him study the featureless gray ceiling. He sighed. "I'd always imagined the way she'd smile when I finally told her she was a grandmother. . . . Then I went and married Jeanne and wasted eleven years."

Desai nodded but said nothing; Reyes rarely spoke of his ex-wife, and she had learned that asking him questions

about Jeanne or their marriage or their divorce was strictly
verboten. The real reason for her reticence, however, was
that this was the third time in as many months that Reyes
had made some kind of oblique reference about a desire to
be a father. As enamored as she was of him, she found the
idea of starting a family to be premature. At times like this,
she struggled not to hear her own mother's voice chiding
her: *You're not getting any younger, Rana! A few more
years and you won't be able to have children! What are you
waiting for?*

She pushed her back to the end of the sofa and pulled
Reyes toward her. He leaned back against her torso, and
she began kneading the tension from his shoulders. His
muscles were rock-hard, coiled with the kind of stress
that—according to Rana's father, a doctor—would send a
person to an early grave. Her delicate-looking hands
clenched and pulled at his rocklike trapezius until it slowly
became pliable. Reyes rasped out a half-grunt, half-sigh
that spoke of pain, pleasure, and relief.

Half an hour later, his neck and shoulder muscles once
again feeling like human flesh instead of marble, Reyes
was asleep in Desai's arms. She leaned down and kissed his
deeply creased forehead. Her stomach growled and gurgled
softly from beneath him, but rather than risk waking Reyes
she ignored her hunger and decided to try and get some
sleep instead.

It had been a long day, for both of them.

Human rituals, by definition, were already half-alien to
Spock. Their curious predilection for self-intoxication as a
means of stimulating interpersonal communication only

enhanced Spock's sense of having little in common with the majority of his shipmates on the *Enterprise,* even after being aboard for more than twelve years.

The retirement party for Dr. Piper was to be, Spock had heard chief engineer Scott proclaim, "a ripping good send-off." That, too, confused Spock. Piper was scheduled to remain with the crew until they returned to Earth roughly ten weeks from now, at which time Starfleet Medical and Starfleet Command would assign the *Enterprise* a new ship's surgeon. Celebrating the end of Piper's service while it was still in progress seemed premature, and Spock had said as much to Captain Kirk earlier in the evening, when the ship's senior officers had congregated here in Manón's, a cabaret lounge in Stars Landing.

"Just kick back and enjoy yourself, Mr. Spock," Kirk had said to him. "It's a party. He's earned it. . . . We all have."

Spock was uncertain what, precisely, constituted the value of a party, or against what standard one could be said to have "earned" it as a reward. It was "an intangible fringe benefit of socializing with humans," his former commanding officer, Captain Christopher Pike, had once explained to him. Tonight, however, lacking Mr. Scott's interest in imbibing alcohol, Dr. Piper's yen for telling ribald stories, or the captain's penchant for making impetuous advances toward unfamiliar women, the half-Vulcan officer concluded that "benefit" was not necessarily the word he would have selected for this category of experience. Astrophysicist Sulu and communications officer Uhura, at least, displayed a greater sense of decorum as they sipped at their juice drinks and held themselves at a slight remove from the senior officers' increasingly unfettered revelry.

Clutching his empty glass, Spock got up from his chair. No one else in the group seemed to notice. After moving even a few meters away, he could tell immediately that the *Enterprise* group was currently the loudest one in the nightclub. There was a fairly substantial clamor of over-lapping voices, but Piper's and Scott's guffawing laughs pierced the din. Other tables of Starfleet officers and civilian residents were casting furtive, irritated glances in his shipmates' direction.

There was a line of people three layers deep at the bar. Spock waited his turn, and used the delay to examine the details of the spacious, softly lit club. High ceilings gave it good acoustics, but the dim illumination concealed the room's height, creating a more intimate impression. Squat, movable chairs, ottomans, and tables, combined with over-sized floor cushions, permitted the patrons to group them-selves comfortably in both small and large numbers. Most of the clientele appeared to be well-to-do civilians or com-missioned Starfleet officers. A group of *Bombay* personnel whom Mr. Scott had asked for directions had indicated that Manón's, despite being a privately owned establishment, served as the de facto officers' club on Vanguard. There was a real officers' club on level sixteen, one of them had said, "but no one ever goes there."

He placed his glass gently on the polished stone bartop, just past an imaginary midpoint dividing line. The bar-tender snatched up the glass as he darted over from one side. Eyeing Spock, he deposited the glass—with a dexter-ity that bordered on sleight-of-hand—into a sanitizer. "An-other ice water, friend?"

"Yes, please."

A pleasant, soft purr of a voice turned Spock's head. "Ice water?" An elegantly dressed woman stood beside him with her back to the bar. "I do love a big spender," she added. To the best of his recollection, he had never seen her species before. She was pale and, by most humanoid species' standards, quite aesthetically pleasing. The irises of her large, almond-shaped eyes were vaguely feline and shimmered emerald-green. Her nose was tiny almost to the point of being imperceptible. She wore her multihued hair in an ornately coiffed swirl, like a breaking wave. Her off-the-shoulder dress could at first be mistaken for black, but a closer inspection revealed that it was an intensely saturated purple, like that of the ripest plums. In a very literal sense, she radiated warmth.

"I was not aware that there was any charge for water," he said, resisting the pull his human half felt for the woman.

"Every day I learn something new," the woman said. "I had no idea Vulcans were ignorant of sarcasm."

"Not ignorant, madam. Unfazed."

"Touché," she said. Lifting her chin toward the bartender, she instructed the young man, "Put his water on my tab, Roy."

"Yes, ma'am," the bartender said with a grin.

The lady extended her hand to Spock. He clutched it gingerly between his fingertips, hesitant to grasp it fully because of the potential for unwanted telepathic contact . . . and because of the length and apparent sharpness of her curved fingernails. She shot him an unflinchingly provocative stare and introduced herself. "Manón."

"Spock." He released her hand. "I do not believe I have ever met one of your species before."

"That doesn't surprise me," she said. "Only a few Silgov have traveled this far from the homeworld. Exploration is not what one might call a 'cultural imperative' for my people."

Intrigued, Spock said, "And yourself?"

"Call it wanderlust," she said with a seductive grin.

An excited buzz of discussion rippled through the crowd. Spock turned to see the cause of the sudden hubbub. Crossing the room, from the front entrance to the slightly elevated main stage at the rear of the room, was a tall, young Vulcan woman. He noted that her crimson uniform was of the new miniskirt variety, and that its sleeve cuffs bore the stripes of a lieutenant commander. She ascended the stairs to the stage and seated herself in front of the baby grand piano.

From the corner of his eye, he saw Manón nod to someone. A moment later, a soft spotlight affixed itself to the woman onstage. She sat patiently—waiting, Spock surmised, for the silence that spread quickly across the room. A few dozen people shushed his shipmates at their table. Seconds later the room fell quiet with anticipation.

Manón leaned over and whispered confidentially to Spock, "You're in for a treat. T'Prynn doesn't do this often."

After the briefest hesitation, T'Prynn's fingers danced in a flurry across the keys, building into a classical crescendo that just as quickly melted away into a few slow, melancholy notes that fell like rain. As she segued into a gently flowing jazz measure, Spock marveled at the fluidity of her performance style, which was riddled with breaks, tiny flourishes and hints of influence as disparate as Terran blues and gospel. Even simple measures took on unexpected complexity as she counterpoised mellow bass lines with up-tempo melodies, demonstrating a pianist's natural gift for harboring and reconciling two seemingly contradictory musical ideas at once. Around the room, her audience bobbed in unison, tapped their feet, and seemed to surrender themselves to the unmistakable passion that infused T'Prynn's music.

The tempo increased as she played, subtly at first, then with greater assertiveness after she crossed a musical bridge into a more robust passage of the tune. Then, like turning a corner, she doubled back into quieter territory—only to reverse herself again, leading her performance and the audience into a decidedly muscular, bluesy barnstorm of a run that shook the tables, chairs, and even the bar itself with its simple ferocity. It was several seconds before Spock was able to divert his attention to realize that almost everyone in the room was clapping in tempo with T'Prynn's music, providing her with joyous and completely spontaneous percussion.

A sudden break from the surging of major chords and she was into a series of rapid, virtuoso solos across the right side of the keyboard, each separated by a majestic thumping of the baby grand's lower register keys. Nearly seven minutes after she began, she prolonged the inevitable with a brazen parade of chords punctuated by witty solo asides, and then sailed to a finish with a few graceful—if theatrical—sweepings of her hand across all the white keys from right to left, and a final proud slam of a note.

The room erupted with applause, a standing ovation that was deafening in its exultation. T'Prynn remained seated for a few moments, then she stood and nodded politely to the audience before demurely stepping down off the stage. Spock watched her approach the bar, and he realized that from the moment she had entered the lounge, and even through the duration of her performance, her facial expression had not seemed to change. If one had not seen her hands, she would have appeared to be the very portrait of calm. Her hands, however, had belied her quiet composure, attacking the keys with an intense, ferocious, and sometimes deftly playful quality that Spock could not remember ever seeing in another Vulcan musician. By almost any standard, she had rendered a remarkable performance, but Spock could think of only one adjective that, in his opinion, best described his impression of T'Prynn's musical style: human.

As she neared the bar, the low undercurrent of conversation returned to the nightclub. A handful of patrons stepped away from the counter, ostensibly as a gesture of respect for T'Prynn. She took a freshly vacated seat between Manón and Spock. "Thank you," she said to Manón, "for the use of your piano."

"I should be thanking you for the free entertainment." With a small gesture in Spock's direction, she added, "T'Prynn, this is Mr. Spock."

T'Prynn turned her head and regarded Spock with a neutral expression. "Commander."

"Your performance was impressive," Spock said.

She seemed unmoved by his praise. "Most kind." Lifting her hand, she summoned the bartender. "Green tea, please."

"Where did you study?"

She seemed reluctant to answer, then saw that Manón had already moved away. Looking back at Spock, she said, "Earth."

He hazarded a guess. "At the Academy?"

"During those years, yes. But not at the Academy proper."

"Your interpretation of Gershwin's 'Summertime' was most . . . emphatic."

"It was not my interpretation." The bartender delivered her drink, and she nodded her thanks. "The arrangement was by a twentieth-century jazz pianist named Gene Harris. I merely emulated his approach."

"Regardless, the result was profoundly affecting."

"Are you saying that you felt an emotional response to my music, Mr. Spock?"

"Not at all," he said. "But many in the audience clearly did. Indeed, the profusion of raw emotion in your performance—"

"I permitted myself no such indulgence."

Spock realized that he had misspoken. "Forgive me. I meant no offense. Perhaps it would be more correct for me to speak of the emotional impact of your music."

"Such is in the ear of the listener," T'Prynn said. "Logic would suggest that music is applied mathematics coupled with digital coordination and acoustic manipulation."

His right eyebrow arched with suspicion. "As a fellow-musician, I cannot agree with your definition of music." He noted that she seemed to deliberately break eye contact and turn slightly away from him. He continued, "If your hypothesis is valid, it begs the question, Why have I never heard another Vulcan musician perform in such a style?"

"Perhaps because the majority of them play only for Vulcan listeners," she said. "I doubt that a recital audience in Vulcana Regar would respond to the music I performed tonight with the same approval I received here." She sipped her tea, then added, "Always know your audience."

"There is another possible explanation." He waited until she resumed eye contact with him before he continued. "Perhaps you have found a way to use music as a clever circumvention of the Dictums of Logic."

Now it was her turn to lift an eyebrow at him. "A peculiar notion, Spock. Why would a Vulcan do such a thing?"

He met her stare. "*That* is an interesting question."

"One that I am certain you will ponder in exhaustive detail," she said. "Please share your eventual conclusions with me. I will be most curious to see where your speculations lead." Standing and facing him, she lifted her hand in the Vulcan salute. "Peace and long life, Spock."

Returning the gesture, he said, "Live long and prosper, T'Prynn." He watched her walk away, moving through the crowd with the grace of a dancer. Without succumbing to emotion, he savored the irony that, after all his decades serving aside several perplexing individuals of many different species, he should find a fellow-Vulcan so utterly foreign.

Picking up his ice water and feeling the cool drops of condensation on its exterior trickle over his fingers, he considered that perhaps he had been away from home for too long. Then he thought of his father, Sarek . . . and banished all thought of a homecoming from his mind.

He looked across the room at his laughing, illogical, inscrutably human friends and knew that, as alien as it might once have seemed—and likely would feel again, from time to time—the *Enterprise* was his home.

Though he had nothing to add to their conversation, he returned to the table with his shipmates. Kirk slapped his shoulder. "I saw you chatting up that piano player, Spock. I also saw her leave alone. No sparks?"

"If you are referring to a romantic attraction, Captain, then no. Our conversation was . . . professional in nature."

Kirk didn't look convinced. He smiled at Sulu and Scotty, then said to Spock, "So you're not interested in her, then?"

"Quite the contrary," Spock said. "I found her—and her music—*extremely* interesting."

8

Tim Pennington watched from the observation deck above the Bay Two airlock as the *Starship Bombay* was guided in reverse out the open spacedock doors. It was just after midnight, station time. As he had suspected from the flurry of activity that had surrounded the ship all day long, its three-day shore leave had been canceled, though he did not yet know why.

He felt melancholy. The *Bombay*'s early departure—and the continued presence of the *Enterprise*—had prevented him from bidding farewell to Oriana. She had spent what little free time had remained to her with her husband, Robert.

Adding insult to injury, Robert D'Amato stood only a few meters to Pennington's left, watching the *Bombay*'s departure with a sad but wistful expression. Pennington worked very hard to avoid making even accidental eye contact.

The ship's primary hull cleared the spacedock doors. Now under its own power, it initiated a graceful pivot-and-roll maneuver away from Vanguard, the domes of its warp nacelles glowing brightly. As it slowly accelerated away, the spacedock doors drifted gradually toward each other. A vibration on Pennington's wrist drew his hand to his pager. He pushed back his sleeve and read the incoming message.

It was from his editor—a simple heads-up to say that the story Pennington had filed about the deaths of *Enterprise* officers Mitchell and Dehner had gone live network-wide. Pennington authorized the message's return receipt and pulled his sleeve back over the pager. He smiled to himself as he anticipated the response the story might provoke. *Nothing to do now but wait for it to hit the fan with Kirk,* he mused.

Outside the spacedock doors, the *Bombay* was little more now than a distant speck of shimmering silver-white against the stars. *Godspeed, Oriana. Be safe until we say hello again.*

When he turned to walk away, D'Amato was standing right next to him. "My wife's on the *Bombay,*" the officer said. "First time I've seen her in almost a year, and we got less than six hours together."

"Rotten luck," Pennington said, not quite masking his discomfort over talking to the man he had been cuckolding for three months.

D'Amato nodded. "Life in Starfleet, I guess." He tilted his head in the direction of the departed starship. "Who do you know on the *Bombay?*"

"No one." It was a clumsy, amateurish lie. He realized only after he'd uttered it that he could name at least half a dozen casual acquaintances on the *Miranda*-class vessel. "No one special, anyway," he amended.

"Oh." Robert shrugged. "I just figured because you were watching her ship out—"

"I watch all the Starfleet ships come and go. Kinda goes with the job."

Only now did D'Amato seem to take notice of the laminated FNS credentials strung on a lanyard around Pennington's neck. His tone instantly became one of suspicion. "Journalist, huh?"

"I prefer to think of myself as an investigative reporter."

"What scoop are you hoping for here?"

"You never know."

"Get anything good lately?"

It took all of Pennington's willpower not to blurt out, *Your wife.* "Actually, I just did a story about a pair of suspicious deaths on the *Enterprise.*"

D'Amato's suspicion turned into outright hostility. "Oh, really? And what would you know about it? I didn't see you there." He advanced toward Pennington, who backed up a few steps. "Do you like making up sleaze about good people who died in the line of duty?"

He stopped and let D'Amato come nose-to-nose with him. "Listen up." Pennington poked his index finger into the Starfleet officer's chest. "Don't call my work sleaze. I'm not some hack working for a gossip sheet, I'm a reporter for FNS. I'm a pro. Try reading my story before you bash it."

Tension lingered hot and thick for several moments while the two men stared each other down. D'Amato backed off but kept a cautious eye on Pennington. "Your story better check out," he said. "Or else."

Nothing that Pennington could think to say would sound less than provocative, so he kept quiet and watched

D'Amato walk away. Glancing out into the main space-dock, Pennington noted that the Bay Two doors were once again closed. He thought of Oriana, then about her husband. Confronting him had not been part of Pennington's agenda, and letting the guy have the last word had been particularly galling.

Consolation would come soon enough, Pennington knew: *When he's on his way back to Earth,* he gloated, *and Oriana's back here with me.*

Dr. Mark Piper had expected to find a large, well-supplied infirmary on a station as large as Vanguard. His expectations had been far exceeded when he followed the station map to the medical center to find an entire hospital, still sparkling new and as antiseptic-smelling as a freshly sanitized scalpel. Nestled deep within the station, the heavily shielded complex occupied levels twenty-one through twenty-five, near the core.

The range of its facilities impressed Piper. Vanguard Hospital included a fully staffed emergency room; an infectious-disease ward with an isolation wing; intensive-care units; dozens of specialty units such as pediatrics, obstetrics, physical therapy, and biosynthetics; suites of surgical theaters; a trio of operating rooms that could be reconfigured for various xenophysiologies; eight medical laboratories; a pharmacy; and even a separate dentistry office.

By the time Piper had finished wandering through the multilevel maze of the hospital's many wards and labs and arrived in the waiting room outside CMO Fisher's office, he was, as his father would have said, "plum tuckered out."

Eager to finish his business, he headed for the fanciest-looking door in the room.

From an adjacent office, a young human man wearing a short-sleeved blue physician's tunic called out to Piper before he could knock on Fisher's door. "I'm sorry, sir, Dr. Fisher has left for the day."

"Serves me right for going sight-seeing," Piper said. "I wanted to see what medical miracles had been invented since I last made port. Should've figured he wouldn't wait up for me."

The young doctor had risen from his desk and joined Piper in the waiting room. "Dr. Fisher waits for no man." He offered his hand to Piper. "Jabilo M'Benga."

He shook M'Benga's hand. "Mark Piper, *Enterprise.* Pleased to meet you." Jerking a thumb toward Fisher's office, he added, "Your boss told me he could resupply my sickbay."

"Did he have you submit a requisition?"

"On paper. In triplicate."

M'Benga chortled. "That sounds like Dr. Fisher, all right." He guided Piper to follow him out the door. "If it was approved, it'll be on file in the pharmacy. You'll just need to come down and sign some forms. . . . In triplicate."

"Great," Piper said, walking beside M'Benga into the corridor. "Nothing screams efficiency like red tape."

"New regulations," M'Benga said. "I agree with you, they can be ridiculous. But what can we do? It's this or private practice." He stopped in front of a pair of turbolift doors and pressed the call button.

"Funny you should mention that," Piper said. "That's exactly what I'm doing when I get back to Earth."

Curiosity animated M'Benga's boyish features. "Really? You're not happy aboard the *Enterprise?*"

"My retirement has nothing to do with the *Enterprise*," Piper said. "If you ask me, she's one of the best damned ships in the fleet, and her captain is first-rate."

The turbolift doors opened, and the two physicians stepped inside next to a pair of nurses. M'Benga gave the throttle a twist as the doors closed. "Level twenty-four, pharmacy." The turbolift thrummed as it began its swift, smooth descent.

"So, if it's not the ship or her captain . . . ?"

"I'm just getting old," Piper said. "I've been in uniform a long time, and I've seen a good chunk of today's Federation take shape. . . . I'd like to spend what time I have left thinking about the shape of my own life."

M'Benga nodded. "Yes, I can see how you might feel that way. I imagine one gets a very different perspective on life serving aboard a starship."

"A more claustrophobic one, that's for sure."

As the turbolift shifted to horizontal movement, M'Benga asked, "Do you know yet who'll be taking your place on the *Enterprise?*"

Piper nodded. "A surgeon named McCoy. We already have orders to pick him up at Earth." The turbolift stopped, and Piper followed M'Benga out into the corridor. "As I understand it," Piper continued, "we'll also be replacing a few nurses and a full shift of lab technicians." Keeping an eye on M'Benga's reaction, he added, "I've also heard that Starfleet is planning on adding a few more staff physicians to the *Enterprise* next year." Just as Piper had suspected, M'Benga's attention intensified at the

news. "If you like, I could put in a good word for you before I leave."

M'Benga stopped outside the door to the pharmacy.
"That's very kind of you, Dr. Piper, but I'm not sure the *Enterprise* would have much need of a doctor who served his
internship in a Vulcan medical ward."

The old surgeon couldn't help but laugh. Shaking his
head at M'Benga, he clapped his hand on the young man's
shoulder. "You haven't met our first officer, have you?"

Kirk sat alone in his quarters and read the top news story
on FNS. Every sentence and each new paragraph further
stoked his primal desire to track down reporter Tim Pennington and pummel him, bare-handed, straight into a new
career.

Pennington's feature story was by now distributed
across all of known space, available to billions of people,
and all but certain to cause Kirk no end of trouble. It wasn't
the errors in the story that concerned him; those were few
and relatively inconsequential. In every truly important
sense, the story was factual and accurate. To Kirk's cha-
grin, he also had to admit that it was basically fair.

Anonymous eyewitness statements corroborated one
another's accounts of the bizarre powers Mitchell had displayed during the ship's transit to Delta Vega. The unattributed statements of these alleged witnesses also had
exposed several small but inexplicable discrepancies between Kirk's own official logs, the death certificate filed
by Dr. Piper in the Vanguard operations center, and the account of helm officer Lee Kelso's death on Delta Vega.

Smack-dab in the middle was Kirk's glib verbal evasion:

"My answer is in my report." Opposite the rest of Pennington's story, those six words looked more damning than Kirk could ever have suspected when he'd said them.

The bottom-line conclusion of Pennington's story was simple and to the point: The inconsistencies all pointed to a cover-up. Specifically, Pennington had made a very convincing argument that Kirk had, in fact, personally killed Gary Mitchell and Dr. Elizabeth Dehner. The question that Pennington had left unanswered was whether Kirk's action was justified.

I suppose I should be grateful he cast himself only as my judge and not as my jury and executioner to boot, Kirk brooded. He clicked off the monitor screen, rose from his desk, and collapsed onto his bed. It irked him that members of his crew had spoken without permission to Pennington. Torn between his respect for the freedom of the press and the desire to maintain discipline aboard his ship, he reminded himself that freedoms such as this were what the Federation stood for. He remembered one of the teachings of Captain Friedl Segfrunsdóttir, a professor of Federation Law at the Academy: *It's not enough to stand up for rights and freedoms only when they're convenient. To defend them in principle, defend them in practice, always.*

Kirk had considered those good words to live by then, and he still did now. He resolved not to issue any prohibitions to his crew regarding Pennington, or any other reporter. The story might yet blow over, or it might mushroom into a court-martial. *Damn the consequences,* he decided. *I know what I did, and why I did it. And if I have to answer for that . . . so be it.*

He was about to lower the lights and settle in for a

much-needed night of rest when his door signal buzzed. "Come."

The door swished open. Scotty barreled in, a portable data display clutched in his hand. The look on his face was a mix of horror and righteous rage, and his anger thickened his brogue. "Captain!" He waved the data device at Kirk. "Have ye read this? That daft bugger Pennington's slandered us! Slandered you!"

"Scotty, calm down. It's—"

"—a travesty! That's what it is! I swear to ye, Captain, if I find him, he's goin' head-first into an impulse vent!"

"Mr. Scott, that's not—"

"Of all the bloody nerve! Who does he think he is? And who the bloody hell was he talkin' to? Not my people, I'll tell you that fer nothin' . . ."

As Scotty's tirade continued, Kirk settled into a chair and waited for the chief engineer to pause for breath. Suspecting it might take a while, he made himself comfortable.

9

"Helm, move us into a standard orbit," Captain Gannon said. "Lieutenant Nave, hail the outpost."

Gannon watched the planet's curving line of night slip off of the main viewer as the *Bombay* circuited the upper hemisphere of Ravanar IV. They had made good time, reaching the outpost in less than seventy-eight hours.

Her alpha-shift team was on the bridge. Milonakis drifted from station to station, ever vigilant for potential problems and eager to keep everyone in synch. Lieutenant Oriana D'Amato was at the helm; beside her, navigator Ensign Berry was already hard at work plotting the ship's fastest route to its next urgent task. Lieutenant ch'Shonnas quietly monitored his science display, the cerulean glow from under the sensor hood barely noticeable on his blue Andorian skin.

Lieutenant Susan Nave pivoted away from her communications console. "Captain, we have audio contact with the outpost."

"Patch it through." Gannon turned her eyes upward to help herself focus on the message, tuning out the gentle bleeps and whistles of the bridge's computers at work.

The teasing voice of Commander Dean Singer came through loud and clear. *"Well, well, if it isn't the hardest-working ship in Starfleet."* She could hear his teammates in the background, laughing and making other sounds of relieved jubilation. *"You have our new coffee machine, yes?"*

Coffee machine? Gannon grinned. *His code phrases aren't subtle, but at least they make me laugh.* "Yeah, Dean, we've got your new coffeemaker. You fellas must be pretty surly after a week without your daily java."

"You can say that again."

"It comes with a free pound of whole beans. Do you want the Colombian, the Denevan Mountain Roast, or the—"

"Captain," ch'Shonnas interrupted. "Picking up six signals closing fast." Milonakis dashed toward an auxiliary sensor station. The androgynously beautiful Andorian officer continued, "Traveling in pairs, and converging on our coordinates at high impulse."

"Confirmed," Milonakis said from the opposite side of the bridge. "Boosting power to the sensors."

"Batten down the hatches, Dean," Gannon said. "We've got company. *Bombay* out." With a slashing motion, she signaled Nave to close the channel. "Milonakis, can we identify those ships?"

"Heavy trace elements in their impulse exhaust . . ." He and ch'Shonnas volleyed reports past Gannon, like verbal badminton.

"Local subspace dimpling indicates rapid deceleration from relativistic velocity," ch'Shonnas said.

"Reading unusual energy surges on all six ships . . ."

"Comparing against the databank . . ."

Milonakis looked up, alarmed. "They're Tholian."

Lifting his eyes from his sensors, ch'Shonnas turned toward Gannon. "Confirmed, Captain. Six vessels, Tholian design, on intercept trajectories, and charging weapons."

"Yellow alert, raise shields." She swiveled toward Nave as the warning lights on the walls began to flash. "Hail them." Gannon pondered why a Tholian patrol would be this far from home and why it would act so aggressively. This wasn't Tholian space, and they had never before gone out of their way to pick a fight.

Nave entered the commands and nodded back to Gannon. "Hailing frequencies open."

"Attention, unidentified Tholian vessels. This is Captain Hallie Gannon of the Federation starship *Bombay*. We are here on a peaceful mission of exploration. Please respond."

Anxiety leached the moisture from Gannon's mouth as several seconds dragged on without reply from the Tholians. Once again hunched over his sensor display, ch'Shonnas said, "Captain, the Tholian vessels are slowing to half-impulse, raising shields, and deploying into an attack formation."

"Helm, break orbit, start evasive maneuvers. Get us out of here." The Tholian cruisers took shape on the main viewer. Gannon thumbed the intercom switch on the arm of her chair. "All hands, this is the captain. Red alert! Battle stations!"

My God, Kevin Judge thought. *Has she gone mad?*

Main engineering on the *Bombay* was a madhouse on the best of days. Now the red-alert klaxon was wailing, crimson lights were flashing from every corner and flat surface, and his engineers were scurrying every which way in a frantic race to escape the cold hard fact that they were in the part of the ship that any smart foe would target first and hit the hardest.

He waved down the attention of a team of engineers as they jogged past, each clutching a breathing mask in one hand and a toolkit in the other. "Dump anything noncritical," Judge told them over the din. "Power down secondary systems, route everything to shields, sensors, and tactical!" Working at his master console, he pieced together new circuit paths, desperate to distribute the stress loads that combat-power demands would place on the already sorely overtaxed starship. He felt the impulse engines rumble overhead as the ship broke orbit and accelerated into battle.

The first round of enemy fire slammed into the shields. Warning lights flashed orange, signaling imminent burnouts in the shield generators. "Damage control teams to shield generators one, four, and nine!" Another jarring blow to the shields left Judge clenching his jaw and wincing. Alerts multiplied across his panel.

Shrill whoops and screeches heralded the firing of the *Bombay*'s main phaser banks. Reverberating percussions from the magnetic launchers in the torpedo bay counterpointed the shriek of the secondary phasers kicking in. Power shunts were overheating systemwide as the fire-control center unleashed another volley of torpedoes and followed it with more shots from the main phasers. Judge heard coolant manifolds rupturing two decks above him, but the sudden spike in phaser generator temperatures was all he needed to see. Pointing in the direction of the damage, he shouted to his assistant chief, "McCarthy, get up there and seal that leak!"

From somewhere to his left, someone shouted, "Starboard shields collapsing!" Before he could reconfigure an aft emitter to cover the gap, another voice cried out, "Incoming!"

Judge reached for a breathing mask. "Brace for impact!"

The strike threw everyone portside, like chess pieces swatted from their board by a vengeful god. A deafening explosion compressed the air, which hit with the force of a thunderclap.

Judge peeled his face from the deck to see smoke and fire spreading swiftly across the upper level of main engineering. Firefighters, stunned by the blast, staggered groggily toward the blazes. Events played out in silence before the chief engineer, whose eardrums ached terribly.

Loak, the Tellarite engineer, stood in front of Judge, shouting something. Judge couldn't hear a word the man said. All he could do was shake his head numbly, dazed and deaf. The Tellarite hefted Judge over his shoulder and carried him out of main engineering, following several other engineers as they dashed through narrow channels in the walls of orange fire.

In the corridor, damage-control officers were distributing pressure suits and firefighting equipment. Surrounded by activity, Loak looked like he was talking to a wall. It took Judge a few seconds to realize the junior officer was likely receiving orders from the bridge.

A security officer kneeled down and pressed a breathing mask firmly over Judge's nose and mouth. He pulled greedily at the clean air. Sharp stabs of pain knifed through his ears as they popped, and a muddy facsimile of his old hearing returned. He pulled the mask off his face and pushed himself back onto his feet. From the wall panel, he heard the captain's voice.

"*. . . whatever you have to, just get those shields back.*"

"Aye, Captain," Loak said. "Engineering out."

Judge cornered the younger officer. "Report."

Loak was focused. "Direct hit, main engineering aft. Hull breach, partial pressure loss. Fires on this deck and the two above. Starboard shields down, fire's cutting us off from the damaged generators. We're clearing a path."

"Good work," Judge said, snagging a pressure suit from one of the damage-control personnel. "Suit up and lead us in."

With a proud nod, Loak said, "Aye, sir."

Another round of impacts trembled the ship as Judge shimmied into his insulated pressure suit. "Bloody worthless things," he grumbled.

A cock of his head expressed Loak's confusion. "Sir?"

"Shield generators. They never last more than one hit."

Loak sealed his pressure suit, muffling his reply. "Let's make a better one."

"Ambitious thinking, mate," Judge said. He sealed his suit, picked up his gear, and slapped Loak on the back before pointing to the nearest ladder that would take them to the damaged shield generator. "But one thing at a time, eh?"

Sickbay was empty of patients, and that worried Dr. Lee. She imagined her shipmates wounded or dying in dark, smoke-filled corridors, unable to reach help. Hit after hit pounded the ship, but instead of her triage area filling with wounded personnel, the room remained dark and all but abandoned. One critical system after another shut down as the engineers stole power from throughout the ship to feed its energy-hungry phaser banks. *Wouldn't want to waste power on something frivolous like an operating room,* Lee fumed, saving her darkest sarcasm for later.

It was the isolation of being in sickbay that most troubled her, just as it always had. While other departments remained keenly involved in the struggle to save the ship, the medical staff frequently found itself ignored, taken for granted, left to guess at the cause and meaning of each nerve-racking blast that echoed through the corridors.

Relax, she advised herself. *The battle's less than two minutes old. Maybe it sounds worse than it is.*

Then came the impact that flung her across the room. Meters away, nurses Guerin and Imelio fell together in a heap, and Lee's gray-haired assistant CMO, Dr. Stewart Greisman, sprawled on the floor between a pair of biobeds.

An unfamiliar male voice crackled over the intercom. *"Engineering to sickbay! We've got wounded down here!"*

"On our way!" Lee scrambled back to her feet and reached for a portable medical kit. She looked at her staff. "Come on!" The others hurried to gather surgical tools and medicine while Lee checked her Feinberger to make certain it was in proper working order. Emitting a rapidly oscillating tone, it glowed in the dimming half-light of the suddenly all but powerless sickbay.

More explosions quaked the deck beneath the short, round-faced Korean woman's feet as Greisman led Guerin and Imelio toward her. All three were heavily laden with medical equipment and satchels. "Ready to go, Doctor," Greisman said.

Lee turned toward the door. It swooshed open. She stepped through, her three compatriots right behind her.

"Focus on the ones you can heal quickly," Lee said. "The engineers will need every pair of hands they can get." Greisman and the nurses nodded their understanding. It was the kind of instruction that Lee hated to give; it was essentially an inversion of normal triage priority, whereby the patients who were most gravely injured would be passed over, because they would consume time and resources that could restore several other less seriously wounded personnel to duty. Basically, the more a patient needed their help, the less likely he was to get it.

Of all the types of medicine Lee found herself called upon to provide during her Starfleet service, combat medicine was the only kind that she thought deserved to be called evil.

Kevin Judge staggered out of the fire-filled corridor into main engineering. He pulled off the helmet of his burn-marked pressure suit. It fell to the floor with a hollow thud. Gasping for air, he found it heavy with smoke. Fumes from scorched polymers and vaporized chemicals stung his eyes. He coughed.

"Engineering to bridge," he said.

"Bridge here," Captain Gannon said.

"Starboard shields at half-power, Captain. Best we can do until we put the fires out." Two horrendously loud blasts from the bottom of the ship sent painful vibrations radiating up from the deck, through Judge's body, and into his jaw and inner ear.

"I need more power to tactical, Kevin. Get it from life-support. From the computer. Anything that isn't shields or propulsion, just get it."

"Aye, Captain," he said. "Engineering out." He closed the channel and gulped down another half-poisonous breath. Looking around, he noticed that Ford and Robertson had just extinguished the fire in the back of the main engineering compartment. "Good work, you two," he said. "Grab some tools and follow me."

The two women put aside their firefighting gear and scrambled to gather together a pair of complete toolkits. Judge, meanwhile, twisted his helmet back into place. Robertson and Ford were standing in front of him when he turned around. "Sir," Robertson said, "where are we going?"

"The central Jefferies tube," he said, hefting his own ponderous toolbox. Realizing he would likely dislocate his shoulder before he made it more than a few steps out of the room, he put it back down and rooted around inside for the two items he knew he would need. "We're shunting power mains one and three into the tactical grid."

Ford shot him a worried glance. "One *and* three, sir?"

" 'Sright," he said, plucking a dynospanner from the box.

Anderson piped up, "But that'll shut off life-support."

"Very good, Ensign," Judge said. Digging to the bottom of the cluttered case, he found his plasma cutter.

"Sir, without life-support we'll have less than ten hours of breathable air, and—" The deck lurched as a rough hit battered the ship. The trio landed hard on the floor.

Judge glared at the young enlisted woman. "Ten hours? Try ten minutes. Think short-term, Ford, or you won't have a long term. Grab your tools and let's go."

•　　•　　•

Orders and reports and the chaos of discharged phasers raged around Oriana D'Amato, who was grateful that all she had to do was fly the ship. Captain Gannon was behind her, issuing commands from the center seat. Beside her, Berry was serving as tactical officer, struggling to keep up with overlapping instructions from Gannon and Commander Milonakis.

Gannon's voice snapped, "Evasive, starboard!"

D'Amato accelerated into a looping corkscrew maneuver that almost overwhelmed the inertial dampeners. No matter which way she went, one of the six Tholian cruisers appeared in her path, or another volley of Tholian ordnance cut her off. She had been mostly successful at evading the enemy's attacks, but the hits they had scored had proved to be substantial. "I need covering fire," she said to anyone who was listening.

The response was quick. "Target lock!" Berry said.

Milonakis answered, "Fire!"

Phaser beams slashed across a Tholian cruiser's shields, and a pair of torpedoes knocked it off course, clearing a small gap in their encircling formation. D'Amato piloted the hobbled *Bombay* through the slim passage, only to note that the enemy ships were already regrouped and moving to intercept them again.

"Berry," Gannon said, "plot a warp jump—fast."

Tactics were not exactly D'Amato's specialty, but she knew that the *Bombay*'s best move was to escape. Standing toe-to-toe with six Tholian ships was a losing proposition, and surrender wasn't an option. Despite her limited experience with Tholians, even D'Amato knew that the reclusive aliens were said never to take prisoners. The fact that the enemy vessels were doing everything possible to block the *Bombay*'s retreat seemed to confirm the rumors.

Three Tholian ships streaked past the *Bombay*, zigzagging across its forward quarter. "They did it again," Berry said, pounding his fists on his console full of hastily plotted warp coordinates—now blinking with warning signals. "We're cut off."

At the science station, ch'Shonnas bolted up from his sensor display. "Incoming!"

Milonakis grabbed the railing. "Brace for—"

It felt like the ship rammed into a brick wall. Darkness smothered the bridge. The thuds of tumbling bodies were barely audible beneath an explosive thundercrack, which tore a scream of terror from D'Amato as she was pinned against her helm console. She winced as secondary impacts shook the bridge around her. Eruptions of skin-searing fire and acrid smoke pelted her with incandescent bits of debris.

The seconds it took the emergency lighting to engage were some of the longest D'Amato had ever lived through.

Dim yellowish orange illumination faded up slowly, obscured behind a heavy curtain of thick gray smoke. Ceiling struts hung in twisted bundles, and a load-bearing cross-beam had broken free and smashed through the port-side consoles and railing. Pinned beneath it, lifeless eyes open and staring in D'Amato's direction, was Commander Milonakis.

D'Amato turned her head in the other direction to see that she had escaped a similar fate by less than a meter; Ensign Berry, however, had not been so fortunate. He was skewered to his seat, impaled through his chest by a fallen ceiling strut. D'Amato could only hope his death had been instantaneous.

From behind her came the clatter of wreckage being kicked aside. She turned to see Captain Gannon extricating herself from her chair, which was surrounded by sparking, fallen cables. The captain looked scuffed and had a nasty laceration across her left cheek, just below the eye. The cut bled heavily, sheeting half her face with bright red blood. Without bothering to wipe it away, she stumbled forward to D'Amato. "Report."

"We've lost the starboard warp nacelle, Captain," D'Amato said. Leaning over to check Berry's console, she added, "Shields are gone. Phasers down to quarter power."

Gannon turned toward Nave, who was pulling herself back into her seat at communications. "Nave, did our mayday get out?"

"No, sir," Nave said. "The Tholians are jamming us."

"Prep the log buoy, ten-hour delay."

"Aye, Captain."

Lieutenant ch'Shonnas limped down the stairs from the science station. His right antenna was bent and bruised, and his slender nose now had a sharp break just below its bridge. "The Tholian ships have broken off their attack, Captain," he said.

D'Amato swelled with irrational hope. "They're retreating?"

"Not quite," ch'Shonnas said. "They've regrouped and are bombarding Commander Singer's outpost on Ravanar IV."

"Onscreen," Gannon said.

The science officer reached under Berry's corpse and

switched the main viewer image. The six vessels were now assembled in a tight grouping, firing in unison to deadly effect on the planet surface. Watching the awesome display of firepower was almost hypnotic. As horrified as D'Amato was, she was unable to make herself look away. Then a screech of metal drew her attention to ch'Shonnas, who yanked the fallen metal debris from Berry's chest in a single pull. Free of the strut, Berry's body fell sideways from his chair. With a look of grim sadness, ch'Shonnas dropped the blood-slicked length of duranium to the deck and sat down at the navigator's station.

Gannon stood behind ch'Shonnas and D'Amato and watched the Tholian ships on the screen. "D'Amato, are we still mobile?"

"Barely. Impulse only, and that's spotty."

"Is the warp reactor still online?"

"One-quarter power only, sir."

The captain frowned. She leaned forward and opened an intraship channel. "Bridge to Mr. Judge."

Half out of breath, the chief engineer's voice gasped over the intercom, *"Judge here, Captain."*

"Kevin, I need power, now. Impulse, warp core, batteries—all of it."

"The shield emitters are toast, Captain. I can have partial forward shields in six minutes if we—"

"Forget shields. All power to tactical and impulse."

"I'm sorry? Did you say—"

"There's no time, Kevin. Phasers and propulsion. Now."

D'Amato was certain she heard Judge sigh in resignation.

"Yes, sir," he said. *"Give me sixty seconds. Judge out."*

The channel closed. Gannon leaned forward and rested her hands on ch'Shonnas's and D'Amato's shoulders. "D'Amato, plot a ramming trajectory on the lead Tholian cruiser. Whatever she does, stay with her. Shal, target weapons manually. Hit that lead cruiser with everything you can."

Looking up at the captain, ch'Shonnas said, "Sir, the other ships will—"

"Move to intercept. Yes, I know." Gannon patted ch'Shonnas's shoulder. "I know. Keep your sights on the leader."

Doubt nagged at D'Amato as she laid in the course. "Captain, if we start taking return fire, should I—"

"Hold your course."

The captain didn't need to say any more than that. D'Amato understood, and the shell-shocked glances that passed between herself, ch'Shonnas, and Nave confirmed that they, too, knew that this was going to be the *Bombay*'s last stand. "Aye, Captain. Helm ready."

Eyes fixed on the viewscreen image of the enemy formation, ch'Shonnas locked in his targeting solution. "Weapons ready."

Gannon reached down and opened the intraship channel. "Bridge to Mr. Judge. Report."

"A few more seconds, Captain. We're patching in the emergency batteries now."

Seconds later, ch'Shonnas turned and nodded to Gannon. "Phasers at full, Captain."

Gannon switched channels. "Bridge to torpedo room."

"Torpedo room here," a man's voice said.

"Mr. Vanderhoven, if you lose contact with the bridge,

continue to fire at will. Concentrate your attacks on one enemy vessel at a time."

"Acknowledged."

Closing the channel, Gannon straightened her posture. Blood dripped from her chin and speckled the front of her gold uniform dress. "Helm, all ahead full. Weapons, fire at will."

D'Amato engaged the impulse drive. The *Bombay* lurched forward, then accelerated swiftly on a course straight for the lead Tholian cruiser's center of mass. Luminous blue phaser beams streaked ahead of them, followed moments later by a trio of photon torpedoes. The barrage lit up the normally invisible defensive cocoon of energy that surrounded the vessel, which grew steadily larger on the main viewer. Flickering erratically, its shields dimpled. As the secondary phaser banks hammered them, the dimpling turned to buckling.

The captain pointed at it. "Hit them again!"

"Its wingmen are coming about," ch'Shonnas said, firing another phaser burst.

"Stay on the leader."

On the main viewer, a pair of Tholian ships broke formation and reversed direction, toward the *Bombay*. They accelerated forward, making tempting targets of themselves, no doubt to entice Gannon into dividing her attack. But they also were separating, to either side of the *Bombay*.

"They're flanking us," D'Amato said.

"Steady," Gannon said.

"We're heading into a crossfire."

"Hold your course."

Three more torpedoes streaked away from the *Bombay*

and pummeled the Tholian battle cruiser. Two more of its escorts began breaking formation, pivoting around to face the *Bombay*'s oncoming assault. The first two, meanwhile, closed to optimal firing distance on either side of the Starfleet frigate as ch'Shonnas unleashed another phaser barrage on the lead cruiser.

Warnings blinked on D'Amato's console. She turned toward the captain. "The escorts are locking weapons!" Her hands hovered over the controls, desperate to begin evasive maneuvers.

Gannon's tone was firm. "Hold your course."

The lead cruiser loomed large on the main viewer.

Panic rose in ch'Shonnas's voice. "They're firing!"

"Steady!"

The *Bombay* pitched violently as the Tholian counterattack hit home. Static frizzed across the main viewscreen.

Clutching the back of D'Amato's chair for support, Gannon shouted over the pounding cacophony, "Damage report!"

"Direct hit, port nacelle," ch'Shonnas said.

Nave stood at ch'Shonnas's regular post. Staring into the blue glow of the sensor hood, she called out, "Hull breaches, decks eight through twelve, damage to— More incoming!"

The sound and the shock-tremor were unlike anything D'Amato had ever heard before—crushing booms, hollow crumplings, groans of distressed metal, roars of explosive decompression. She knew, instinctively, that it was the sound of sudden death in space. Her white-knuckled fingers clutched the edge of her helm console, which stuttered between light and darkness.

From belowdecks, the angry screech of phasers and the echoing ring of torpedo launches continued. Even before ch'Shonnas made his report, D'Amato saw the Tholian battle cruiser's shields collapse, and a volley of photon torpedoes slam into it amidships. "Direct hit on the lead cruiser," ch'Shonnas said. "Heavy damage."

"Again," Gannon said, pointing at the crippled enemy ship. Phaser beams sliced through the Tholian vessel, whose image filled the main viewer from edge to edge. "Break off," Gannon said. "Hard to port! Fire aft torpedoes, finish her!"

D'Amato fought with the sluggish, failing helm controls, practically willing the ship to turn as the captain ordered. They had made it two-thirds of the way through the turn when the beleaguered impulse engines began to falter. Then a Tholian plasma torpedo nudged them the rest of the way through the turn and, miraculously, seemed to spur the impulse drive back to full power.

On the edge of the main viewer, D'Amato saw the flash of the cruiser's explosion batter three of its escorts, which now were in a triangular formation and closing fast on the *Bombay*. The captain pointed to the cruiser on the left. "Shal, all fire on that one!" She pointed at the one on the right. "Nave, tractor beam on that one!" D'Amato was about to protest that all power had been diverted to weapons when she recalled that the phaser mains and the tractor-beam emitter shared the same energizer coils.

The auxiliary phaser banks kept the left-side ship engaged while Nave snared the right-hand one with a tractor beam. The young communications officer announced with pride, "Got 'em!"

Gannon glanced at the tactical display between D'Amato

and ch'Shonnas and made a snap decision. "D'Amato, bearing three-five-eight mark eighteen, flank speed!"

More blasts rocked the ship as D'Amato forced the impulse engines to their limits. The Tholian ships seemed slow to respond, likely because they had expected the *Bombay* to make an evasive turn rather than an attack charge. Sensors indicated that the two enemy ships on the *Bombay*'s aft quarter were equally off-balance but swiftly altering course to compensate. The strain on the *Bombay*'s engines was immense; they had been pushed far beyond their rated tolerance even before they started dragging the mass of the snagged Tholian cruiser.

Ahead of them, the cruiser that wasn't bearing the brunt of the *Bombay*'s attack broke away in another attempt at a flanking run. Gannon pointed at it like she was thrusting a sword into an enemy. "Helm, hard to port, ninety-five degrees starboard yaw! Weapons, stay on the second one!"

As she executed the command, D'Amato realized what the captain was doing, and she made small adjustments in the maneuver to maximize its effectiveness. A bone-jarring concussion sent a flash-crack of light and heat rushing into the bridge. Sparks showered down from the rent ceiling. The tactical display hiccuped on and off for a second. When it settled, D'Amato permitted herself a moment of dark satisfaction: They had pulled the Tholian cruiser in their tractor beam into a broadside collision with the one that had just hit their main computer core. Both enemy ships had exploded into a cloud of superheated debris.

"Good work, D'Amato! Hard about!"

D'Amato swung the ship through a 180-degree turn. At the end of it, the cruiser onto which ch'Shonnas was still directing all weapons fire lay halfway between the *Bombay* and the damaged Tholian ship's two reinforcements, which were closing at maximum speed. The battered Tholian cruiser was fleeing the *Bombay,* and its sister ships were moving to defend its retreat.

Gannon seemed hyperalert now. The gleam in her eyes had a feral intensity. "Helm, get in there. Don't let them get away! Weapons, fire all phaser banks!"

For a moment, ch'Shonnas looked like he was going to protest the order, then he triggered a massive phaser onslaught against the escaping vessel. Multiple overlapping beams bombarded the Tholian ship, and its shields flared, then dissipated. A single photon torpedo slammed into its main engine.

Then the two cruisers behind it returned fire at *Bombay.*

The charged-plasma pulses seemed to drift languidly through space, only to speed up at the last second.

D'Amato shut her eyes. The shock of impact opened them again. Light and heat . . . sound and fury . . . the gruesome pantomime of bodies hurled like leaves in a storm. She plunged out of her chair, nauseated by a sudden sensation of weightlessness that just as quickly surrendered to the trauma of brutal deceleration when she hit a bulkhead. Facedown on the deck, she felt a throbbing ache inside her mouth bloom into agonizing pain. She reached up to her lips. Her guttural howls hurled blood and saliva over her fingers. Gingerly reaching past her slashed lower lip, she confirmed that several of her front teeth had been smashed out. Heaving sobs robbed her of breath; tears ran from her eyes.

On the deck next to Berry, ch'Shonnas lay dead, half his beautiful blue face peppered with charred black shrapnel.

Smoke rose from a gaping hole in the navigator's console.

Nave was slumped against a post under the far railing, her face haunted by the same lifeless stare that D'Amato had seen minutes ago on Milonakis.

Captain Gannon crawled across the deck toward the helm console. She pulled herself up like she was scaling a rock face. Inch by inch, fighting for purchase, looking for another handhold. Her strength clearly was waning, but her defiant glare was undimmed. Peeking over the edge of the console, she stretched out her arm, flipped a sequence of switches, activated the tractor beam, this time on the damaged Tholian cruiser. Through the wavy lines and hashing static on the main viewer, D'Amato saw the beam lash out and grab the enemy vessel. Now the captain was reeling it in—and the two undamaged Tholian ships were once again moving to attack position. Gannon reached up and entered another sequence of commands into the console. She turned her head and glared at D'Amato. "Get over here, Lieutenant. I need you."

D'Amato tried to stand, but her legs refused to obey. She followed the captain's example and half-crawled, half-dragged herself across the dusty, debris-covered deck to join her commanding officer at the helm console.

"Computer," the captain said. "Recognize Gannon, Captain Hallie Marie."

"Recognized," came the staticky, distorted reply.

Reacting to Gannon's nod, D'Amato said, "Computer, recognize D'Amato, Junior Lieutenant Oriana."

"Recognized."

"Initiate emergency destruct sequence," Gannon said. "Destruct sequence one, code one, one-D."

"Verified."

"Destruct sequence two," D'Amato said, her voice growing hoarse. "Code one, one-D, two-A."

"Verified."

"Code zero, zero, zero, destruct zero. Thirty seconds."

"Countdown initiated. Thirty . . . twenty-nine . . ."

On the main viewer, the damaged Tholian cruiser struggled to break free of the *Bombay*'s tractor beam.

Gannon's body began to go limp, and her voice softened to a pained whisper. "Don't let them get away," she said . . . then slid down the front of the console and collapsed next to ch'Shonnas, her blank eyes gazing upward.

Alone on the bridge, D'Amato clung to her post, her blood-stickied fingers routing every last drop of power to the wavering tractor beam. The damaged Tholian ship was practically touching the *Bombay*. Only now did D'Amato realize that they hadn't reeled it in; because the *Bombay*'s impulse engines were gone, they had pulled themselves to the enemy vessel, whose two reinforcements now were moving in to retaliate. Just when D'Amato expected the tractor beam to lose hold of the Tholian ship, its power suddenly increased. Someone in engineering had worked one final miracle.

Only a few more seconds, D'Amato knew. *You're not getting away, you* faccia di stronzo!

Firing the *Bombay*'s navigational thrusters at maximum, she forced the trapped Tholian cruiser into a slow roll, turning it instantly into a shield against its allies' counterstrike.

D'Amato had almost had time enough to congratulate herself for her ingenuity when the self-destruct system detonated.

•　　•　　•

Aboard the Tholian battle cruiser *Nov'k Tholis,* Commander Larskene [The Silver] enabled the subspace thoughtwave. Projecting his thought-colors into the Warrior Castemoot SubLink, he petitioned, via the Lattice InterLink, for an audience with the Ruling Conclave of the Political Castemoot. His salutation was met with warm tones of concordance.

The inter-voice of Falstrene [The Gray] echoed across the InterLink, deep with pensive undertones. *Is it done?*

All but the last. Larskene shared facets of memory salvaged from his caste-peers aboard the four destroyed vessels. First was the self-immolation of the Starfleet vessel, along with the *Tik'r Tholis.*

Velrene [The Azure] chimed into the InterLink, coruscating with dismay. *Why was a Federation ship there?*

Defending their outpost. Larskene skipped back along the memory-line to the bombardment of the planet. He highlighted sensing-unit transcriptions of the planet's surface, which showed a humanoid settlement in the exact location of the target.

Crimson agitation swelled in the Ruling Conclave. Angry colors washed down through the thoughtwave InterLink to Larskene. The elite Castemoot's discussion was closed to him. He heard only what they elected to share. The flare of rage in the topmost layer of the Lattice darkened with hues of suspicion and flickered as the collective debated.

Mellisonant tones overlapped as the InterLink reopened, and he was hailed by Azrene [The Violet]. Her soothing thoughtcolors lacked sincerity. *What is the status of the fleet?*

Dozens of points of view coursed upward through the InterLink, projected by Larskene, who had culled them from across the attack fleet's private SubLink as the battle raged. Images overlapped of the lead Tholian cruiser, the *Sek't Tholis,* succumbing to a prolonged barrage by the Federation warship. His own crew offered four distinct perspectives on the enemy's engineered collision of the *Tas'v Tholis* and the *Kil'j Tholis.*

A bland gray hum signaled a momentary muting of the InterLink. Larskene took the opportunity to clarify his mindline and infuse his Lattice-hue with a tint of confidence.

Dulcet tones called him back to loyal attention.

Yazkene [The Emerald] was shrouded in dark colors. *The Federation has come too far to turn back.* His images were simple and direct, the plan of action clear. *When it is done, return to Tholia with the* Vel'j Tholis.

Larskene radiated his understanding in steady pulses. *So shall it be done.*

The InterLink faded as the Ruling Conclave withdrew to its private environs at the Lattice's apex. Larskene's mindline receded along its thought-path, out of the Warrior Castemoot, back into the sanctum of his own being. Before he powered down the thoughtwave transmitter, he sensed the rising tone of patriotism that brightened the Lattice's Sub-Links. Elation was mingled with relief, but a new impulse festered in the collective mind-line of the Tholian Assembly.

For now, the Voice was silent.

But many voices from across the breadth of the Tholian Assembly now were calling for a war to keep it that way.

10

"Mr. Pennington," Reyes had said over the comm, after waking the young reporter from a sound sleep, *"if you want a major news story, get to my office. Now."*

For three months Pennington had been trying to secure a face-to-face interview with the commodore, to no avail. Now that an opportunity had presented itself, he had sprinted from his apartment half-dressed and barely finished pulling himself together by the time he stepped out of the turbolift into the ops center. A tableau of grim faces had put him on notice that the news which awaited him was not likely to be pleasant. Reyes's tight-lipped grimace confirmed it.

He settled into a seat in front of the commodore's desk. His interview recorder, tucked discreetly in his palm, was running. Not wanting to press his luck, he asked no questions.

Reyes didn't look up at him. The older man stared down at a printed report in his hand, which trembled ever so slightly. Teeth clenched lockjaw-tight, he said, "The Federation starship *Bombay* was destroyed with all hands in the line of duty yesterday at 1746 hours, station time."

Pennington stared at him, silent with shock.

There were dozens of questions that he knew he should

be asking, but suddenly he couldn't think of them. All his thoughts logjammed on *her* name: *Oriana*.

One horrific scenario after another played out in the theater of his imagination. Accident? Sabotage? Ambush? As he fought to rein in the mad flurry of half-formed notions running circles in his mind, his journalistic training reasserted itself. "How?"

"That's unclear at the moment," Reyes said. Pennington waited for him to elaborate, but the man had said his piece.

"But you have a hypothesis as to what happened?"

"I have orders to investigate."

"Where was she lost?"

"That's classified."

Pennington saw where this was going. "Her assignment?"

"Classified," Reyes said, his tone regretful.

"Can you at least get me a crew roster?"

Reyes shook his head. "Not until the families are notified, you know that."

"Some scoop," Pennington said, with more bitterness than he had intended. "One of our ships is missing, and so are the details." He pushed his chair back, stood, and switched off the recorder in his hand.

"This was a courtesy, Mr. Pennington," Reyes said. "In an hour I'll be making a general announcement. When I do, you can bet every comm line off this station will be jammed with traffic for the next day. If you want to file this story while it's still yours, I suggest you get a move on."

"Thanks." Pennington walked out and made it most of the way through ops before his false angry glare faltered, threatening to reveal the tears that were welling in his eyes.

He was deeply thankful to reach the turbolift alone. As soon as it had dropped below the upper decks into the sparsely occupied and heavily insulated core section, he halted its descent and let himself sink down to the floor as his sorrow poured out of him. Heaving sobs clogged his sinuses, forcing him to gasp raggedly for air. Tormented wails erupted from deep within him, one after another, for minutes that felt endless.

When, at last, he had exhausted his body's reservoir of tears and rage, he remained seated on the floor of the turbolift, his head atop his knees, his grief-reddened eyes hidden behind his hands. Memories of Oriana's hair, her laugh, her accent . . . they called out to him from the cenotaph of his memories, reminding him that every passing day for the rest of his life would carry him farther from her touch.

A voice from the intercom intruded on his grief.

"Turbolift three-fifteen-alpha passenger, this is the ops center. Are you all right?"

Pennington was glad the person on the other end could only hear him. "Yes," he said. "I'm fine."

"You've been stopped for nine minutes. Are you lost?"

"No." He pulled himself back to his feet and gripped the turbolift throttle. "I'm fine, thank you." Twisting the throttle, he resumed his descent.

"Because if you need directions—"

"Bugger off," Pennington said, ending the conversation.

Thirty seconds later he exited the turbolift and plodded across the empty nighttime park toward his residence tower in Stars Landing. He felt unbearably heavy, too weighty to move, too slow and freighted with despair to continue taking step after step. But he also felt insubstantial, an echo of his former self, a half-faded copy of the man he'd been only minutes earlier, reduced to a lonely pantomime of the life he'd taken for granted.

Time passed in chunks, pieces of it eluding his memory.

He drifted into his apartment, which looked like the heartless gray confines of a prison cell.

Sitting on the edge of the bed, he wondered how he'd got there from the door without walking the space between.

Standing in the lukewarm spray of the shower, he recalled the bed but not his rising; remembered the gaunt stare of his own visage in the bathroom mirror but not turning on the water.

Reading the words he'd just sent to his editor, he couldn't recollect having written them. But there they were:

On stardate 1321.6, the Federation starship
Bombay *was reported lost with all hands while on a classified mission in the Taurus Reach. The* Bombay, *under the command of Captain Hallie Gannon, had been assigned to permanent duty at Starbase 47, under the oversight of Commodore Diego Reyes.*

A complete roster of the Bombay's *crew is being withheld pending Starfleet's official notification of their families. The crew of the* Bombay, *a Miranda-class starship, is estimated to have numbered roughly 220 personnel.*

As of this writing, the specific cause of the Bombay's *destruction has not been made public.*

Pennington grew angrier each time he read it. *Oriana's gone and no one will say how, or where, or who, or why. What the hell is Starfleet hiding?* In Pennington's opinion, the only thing that Starfleet guarded more jealously than its secrets was its pride. *Could it have been crew error? Or did Reyes send them on a suicide mission without telling them?*

The speculation was enough to make him insane with rage. *Someone knows,* he told himself. *Somebody is going to talk, sooner or later. And when they do, I'm going to make certain the truth gets out. . . . I owe her that much.*

Looking around his apartment, he found it difficult to believe that only a few days ago she had been here, or that those few passionate hours had slipped by in such a blur. Then he noticed her small overnight bag still resting on the chair beside his dresser. In the frenzy of activity that had followed the revocation of the *Bombay* crew's shore leave, her friend had never come by to pick it up. His eyes scanned the room, noticing tiny traces of Oriana's past presence everywhere he looked. A decorative hairpin on his nightstand. Bottles of her exotic shampoo and conditioner on his bathroom vanity. One of her earrings on his dresser—which itself had at least one drawer full of her civilian clothes. Strands of her hair in the bedsheets, in the shower stall, on the carpet, on his shirt.

Oh, dear God—if Lora sees this. . . .

Pennington raced to his closet and threw things aside until he found his old duffel bag. He went one square meter at a time, policing up every tiny item that could be linked to Oriana. It all went into the duffel bag, hurled unceremoniously into canvas oblivion. Using the handheld vacuum, he collected up almost all the hair, but he stopped when he got to the bedsheets. Removing the hair would be one thing; washing out the other evidence was a dicier proposition. *Better to dispose of them,* he decided, and stuffed the whole lot, pillowcases and all, into the duffel.

When he was done, he resisted his bitter pangs of guilt.

Rank sentimentalism, he chastised himself. *That's all it is. It's just a bag of junk. It's not her.*

Logic was no match for his mourning heart, still grappling with the utter finality of Oriana's death. His rational mind knew the collection of clothes and toiletries and knickknacks was nothing more than a discreet conglomeration of random items. He knew they had no intrinsic meaning. Peering down into the bag, however, he felt like he was clinging to his last shards of her, the scattered fragments of remembrance. *I know I have to throw it away. But how can I? Would she have done that to me?*

He wondered what trinkets and baubles and mementos Oriana had kept of him. Luckily for her, all those miscellaneous bits of incrimination had been lost along with the *Bombay—*

Oh, bloody hell. He winced as he remembered what she had said to him about her overnight bag, before she left his arms for the last time: "My friend Katrina will come by later and take it down to my storage locker."

The storage locker! She could have anything in there! His mind pinwheeled through worst-case scenarios, all of which had one fact in common: As soon as Oriana's death became official, every last item in her storage locker would be released . . .

. . . to her husband.

Pennington cinched shut the duffel full of Oriana's effects and left his apartment, running to the quartermaster's office.

Kirk rehearsed all the different things he might say, weighed the merits of all the potential opening conversational gambits he might employ. None of them felt right. *There's just no good way to say something like this,* he lamented.

News of the *Bombay*'s destruction had reached him less than ten minutes earlier, courtesy of a private comm from Vanguard's commanding officer. The message had awoken Kirk from a deep sleep. Even to the captain's dream-fogged eyes, Reyes had looked stricken, as if someone had bled him pale.

Without preamble, he'd said to Kirk, "The *Starship Bombay* was destroyed just over eleven hours ago." The commodore had swallowed hard, apparently strained by the effort of keeping his emotions in check. "One of your officers had family on the *Bombay,*" he'd continued. "Lieutenant Oriana D'Amato, helm officer, was married to your senior geologist, Lieutenant Robert D'Amato."

Kirk had thanked Reyes for alerting him before disseminating the news stationwide. Standing in front of the door to D'Amato's quarters, he no longer felt thankful. He dreaded breaking this kind of news. During his years coming up through the ranks, he had dealt more than once with the trauma of losing personnel under his command. His first year in the captain's chair, aboard the *Enterprise,* had only increased that burden. Recording condolences for the families of people like Lee Kelso, or Elizabeth Dehner, or Gary Mitchell, had proved emotionally taxing in the extreme. Until now, however, he'd at least had the buffer of time and distance, and of speaking to people who were, essentially, strangers.

Tonight he would have to look one of his own crewmen in the eye and be the bearer of tragic news. Then he would have to endure the aftermath, whatever it turned out to be. Drawing a deep breath, he calmed himself. *This is my responsibility,* he reminded himself. *D'Amato is one of my crew. If he has to hear this, it should be from me.*

He pressed the door buzzer. And he waited.

Several seconds later the door hissed open, revealing the barefoot D'Amato. His dark blue robe hung open, showing his bare chest and loose, gray pajama pants. Squinting at the light, he sounded as groggy as he looked. "Captain?"

"Mr. D'Amato. Sorry to wake you."

"That's all right, sir. What can I do for you?"

Gesturing through the door, Kirk said, "May I come in?"

D'Amato stepped aside and ushered the captain in. "Of course, sir. My apologies."

"No need." Kirk walked in and stopped in front of a low, padded chair, which faced another one just like it, against the wall on the other side of a low table. As the door closed, D'Amato faded up the lights. Moving to the closer of the two seats, Kirk motioned to D'Amato to take the other one.

With an understandable degree of apprehension, D'Amato settled into the chair. "What brings you here, Captain?"

Words abandoned Kirk for a moment, then he recovered his composure. "I have some bad news," he said. "In a few minutes, Vanguard's CO will be making an announcement, but I wanted you to hear this from me." He paused, drew a small breath, then continued. "Roughly eleven hours ago, your wife's ship, the *Bombay*, was destroyed."

D'Amato's face looked frozen. He didn't blink, he seemed barely even to be breathing. Then his Adam's apple bobbed as he swallowed once, slowly and deliberately. "Lifeboats?"

"They would have radioed for help," Kirk said.

Dismay began to alter D'Amato's features. His brow lifted into a steady crease of alarm, and his eyes grew wide. The tide of his breathing became rapid and shallow, and within seconds he was gasping weakly through his mouth, which drooped open. Turning his head finally enabled him to break eye contact with Kirk. "Was there a planet? Maybe they . . . maybe they beamed down."

"They were bringing supplies to a research outpost. If they were going to beam down, that's where they'd have gone." Before D'Amato could latch on to this fragment of hope, Kirk added, "But Vanguard's lost contact with the outpost, too." D'Amato covered his eyes with one hand. *See no evil*, Kirk thought. *If only it were that easy.* "Is there anyone back home you want me to contact for you?"

Still hiding his eyes, D'Amato shook his head. Inhaling sharply through his gritted teeth left him unable to speak.

Kirk wondered why they didn't teach classes at the Academy about situations like this. *They teach us all about machines and tactics and regulations*, he ruminated. *Would it have hurt to teach us how to talk to people?* He leaned forward. "Whatever you need, just ask. Leave of absence, a transfer planetside—"

"I put in for a transfer last month," D'Amato said, his

voice choking. He lowered his hand from his eyes. "So did Oriana. Home was going to be wherever we ended up." Despondently eyeing his quarters, he added, "Not much point leaving now, I guess. . . . One empty place is pretty much the same as another."

Nodding, Kirk thought of the latest empty space in his own life, the one where his best friend Gary Mitchell used to be.

"I'm sorry, Robert," Kirk said. "Sorry that there's nothing I can say to make this hurt any less, or stop hurting any sooner . . . if it ever does. I can't even say that I know what you're going through, because I don't. But as your captain, and as a friend, I'll be available if you need me, and I'll do whatever I can to help you get through this. I promise."

The gesture of support seemed to draw an even more powerful wave of grief out of D'Amato. As valiantly as he struggled to hang on to his dignity, streams of tears crossed one another's paths as they meandered down his face. "Thanks, Captain."

Kirk reached across the table and offered D'Amato his hand. The geologist reciprocated, and Kirk clasped his hand firmly around D'Amato's, as if they were about to arm-wrestle above the table. "It's going to be okay," Kirk said. "Maybe not any day soon, but someday."

"I know that's true. But it doesn't feel true."

"No, it doesn't." He gave D'Amato's hand a final squeeze, then let go. He couldn't think of anything else to say. To Kirk's relief, before the awkward silence became uncomfortable D'Amato ended the visit with a simple declaration.

"I'd like to be alone now, sir."

• • •

Vanguard, on its best days, wasn't what Cervantes Quinn would call a "festive locale." Naturally, then, he took little note of the dour mood that lay like a shroud over Chief Ivan Vumelko, the Starfleet customs officer who greeted him and the *Rocinante* in its remote, deep-lower-decks hangar bay. It rang of business as usual.

The paunchy, bug-eyed man scribbled glumly on his log sheet. "What's your cargo?"

"Don't have any," Quinn said.

A suspicious stare. "No cargo?" Vumelko eyed the *Rocinante,* then cast his leery gaze back at Quinn. "You left two weeks ago—without any cargo, then, either."

"I went for a joyride." Affecting a deadpan delivery through a mishmash Texas-Alabama-Louisiana drawl wasn't easy, but Quinn made it sound like it was.

"That's a good way to go bankrupt," Vumelko said.

"It's one way. I know quite a few."

"I'll bet you do." Vumelko ducked and walked under the nose of the *Rocinante,* then turned and headed toward the gangway into its aft compartment.

"Hang on, there," Quinn said. "What do you—"

"Snap inspection," he said. "Checking for contraband."

Quinn was going to argue about it, but then he remembered that his cargo hold was emptier than a Tellarite etiquette manual. "Suit yourself," he said. "I'll be in the bar if you need me." He started walking toward the hangar-bay door when it swished open, and a pair of armed Starfleet security guards stepped inside and blocked his exit. He smiled at the two familiar-looking men. "You're slowin' down, gents!" He pointed at the floor behind him, then held up three fingers. "Three whole steps! Time to lay off the Tarkalian ale, Chuck."

"Just sit tight a minute," said Lieutenant Charles.

Tapping his foot with impatience, Quinn counted away the minutes while Vumelko rooted around inside his ship. Amid the shuffle of empty crates and the hydraulic whispers of cargo panels sliding open and shut, a sudden loud crashing of heavy metallic objects echoed inside the ship, accompanied by a rage-inspired string of compoundly modified profanities.

"That's all right," Quinn shouted up the gangway. "Just leave my tools wherever. I'll put 'em away later."

After another minute of foul-mooded grumblings and the occasional *ping* of a kicked tool rebounding off a bulkhead, Vumelko slouched down the gangway, looking more than a little worse for wear. He initialed his inspection form, then handed the clipboard and a stylus to Quinn and pointed to a small box at the bottom. "Sign there."

"I know where to sign." Quinn scrawled his mark on the page, then handed back the form and stylus. "Have a nice day."

On his way up to the park a few minutes later, Quinn was grateful that no one in Starfleet had yet thought of making people sign requisitions to use the turbolifts. He suspected, however, that it would only be a matter of time until that depressing prophecy came to fruition.

Stepping out onto the broad paved walkway that separated the core shaft from the greensward of the terrestrial enclosure, he was taken aback at the absence of . . . well, fun. He had grown accustomed over the past few months to the sound of music from the band shell during the artificial evenings, to the hubbub of competitive sports on the lawns, to the splashing of water in the communal swimming pools.

Tonight, however, a leaden calm lay over the park. Although the synthetic environment lacked wind, Quinn half-expected to see a lonesome tumbleweed roll across the deserted lawn. Alone in the towering vastness of the enclosure, he felt like an insect intruding on the playground of giants. He had planned to stroll across Fontana Meadow—named for the brightly lit jetting fountain plaza in its center—and treat himself to a late-night snack at the outdoor café, but he hesitated when he saw that the fountain was turned off, and the lights in the café were dark.

The obvious sunk in: *Something very bad is going on.* He pressed on into the central zone of Stars Landing and boarded a turbolift. A young woman rode upstairs with him. He smiled at her. She didn't smile back.

The same pervasive mood of gloom greeted him around every corner and on every face. No music issued from Manón's club; conversation in the recreation areas was subdued or nonexistent. People passing by in the hallways seemed to be turned inward.

When he arrived at his usual watering hole for a drink, he understood why. Adorning the huge mirror behind the bar counter was a hand-painted message on the glass—a simple outline of the *Bombay*'s ship emblem with a black band across its center. Above it was the Latin inscription *In Memoriam.* Below it, in capital letters, was stenciled U.S.S. BOMBAY.

"Sweet lord in heaven," he muttered. The sentiment sprang from him without warning, like the shock that had provoked it. Though the ship's crew had been strangers to him, he was overwhelmed by a sudden sense of kinship and bereavement for the fallen Starfleeters.

He sat down at the counter and nodded to the bartender.

"Tequila," he said. "A double."

The bartender eyed a long row of bottles on the shelf behind him, then looked at Quinn. "What kind?"

"Anythin' cheap that ain't green."

Anticipation kindled on his taste buds as the aroma of agave liquor reached his nose. He imagined savoring the sweet and sour notes on the sides of his tongue and the warmth of the alcohol in the back of his throat. Memories of fine tequilas in years gone by were stoked by the promise of a new drink. . . .

A beefy hand clamped down on Quinn's left shoulder and clenched shut like a vise. From his right a slender, glossy black hand gently plucked the double-shot glass of tequila from his grasp. The diabolically polite voice of Zett Nilric was alarmingly close to his ear. "Welcome back, Quinn."

Quinn remained still as Zett's hulking Tarmelite enforcer, Morikmol—whom Quinn had once barely survived describing as a "walking life-support system for a pair of fists"—spun him around on the rotating barstool to face the white-suited thug.

Zett was grinning. That was never a good sign.

"We were beginning to think you weren't coming back," the archly condescending Nalori assassin said.

Fingering the man's lapel, Quinn said, "New suit?"

Morikmol grabbed the back of Quinn's jacket collar and hefted him several centimeters off the floor. Zett lifted the glass in a mocking toast, then downed the double in one gulp. He put the glass back on the bar. "Mr. Ganz is expecting you." Without waiting for Quinn's next retort, the slender man walked toward the exit. The enforcer let go of Quinn, who landed on his feet. The hulking thug gave him a push toward the door. Taking the hint, Quinn squelched his impulse to order another drink.

The *Omari-Ekon*'s gambling deck was just as Quinn had left it a few weeks earlier—noisy and full of losers who had yet to figure out that this house always won. Zett led the way up the curving staircase to Ganz's oasis, and Morikmol followed close behind Quinn, his heavy footsteps sending tremors through the otherwise solid stairs. Knowing the routine by heart, he ambled to his spot between the two obelisks, which he had seen disintegrate a few people over the years, though none so far while the ship was docked at Vanguard.

"Mr. Quinn," Ganz said. "You're late."

Quinn shrugged. "Complications."

The muscular Orion boss took a pull from his hookah nozzle, savored the smoke a moment, then exhaled two thick plumes from his nostrils. He reminded Quinn of a green Brahma bull, except twisted and cruel. The lazy coils of smoke lingered, spreading an odor of burnt cherries with an acrid, metallic bite.

"Complications don't concern me," Ganz said after puffing out his last mouthful of smoke. "My merchandise does."

Though Quinn couldn't see the assassins gathered behind him, he heard the soft rub of several leather holster straps being loosened. He kept his hands steady and open at his sides. "Hence the complication," he said.

He fully expected the next thing he felt would be a pair of disintegrator beams tearing him apart molecule by molecule.

Instead, he watched Ganz formulate a reply. Though he spoke quietly, no one ever missed a word the Orion merchant-prince said. "The explanation you are about to provide had better be phenomenally good."

"The device was too large to move by myself," Quinn began.

"You should have brought help."

"So I separated the valuable part from the worthless part," he continued, ignoring the interruption.

"Clever. Where is it?"

"I tripped and it fell . . ." He mustered all the contrition he was capable of emoting: ". . . and it broke."

Ganz's voice took on a dangerous edge. "You dropped it?"

Behind Quinn the crowd moved closer. The heat of their collective breath and attention was oppressive. He tuned them out. "People were shooting at me."

That seemed to pique Ganz's interest. "Who?"

"Judging by the phasers they were using, I'd say they were Starfleet security."

A nervous susurrus of whispers circled the room in both directions and lapped itself. Ganz passed the moment by taking another long drag off his hookah and blowing a lazy smoke ring in Quinn's direction. "How did they detect you?"

"Cutting the device's power supply tripped an alarm."

Tsk-tsking and waggling his index finger like a re-proachful grandmother, Ganz said, "You should always scan before you cut."

"I did scan," Quinn said. "Nothing showed up—it was a *sensor screen*. Wouldn't be much good if it let you scan it to see if it's on." That got a few stifled chuckles from the crowd.

"True," Ganz said. "Did they identify you?"

"Considering I didn't get arrested when I landed an hour ago, my guess would be no."

Ganz put down his hookah nozzle and sprawled across his mountain of brightly colored cushions until he found a more leisurely pose. "Quinn," he said, shaking his head. "What am I going to do with you? You've put me in quite a bind." Having learned not to put questions to Ganz, Quinn kept his mouth shut and waited for the green man to elaborate. "The sensor screen would have fetched a nice profit on the black market. I already had inquiries from potential buyers." *Oh hell*, Quinn thought. *He's going to make up some insane imaginary number, call it his lost profits, and put me in debt for the rest of my damn life.* Ganz slowly folded the fingers of his right hand, one at a time, beneath his thumb and pressed down until each knuckle made a sat-isfying pop. "But my real disappointment is that I had big plans for that pretty little machine. Plans you just ruined."

"I can't begin to tell you how deeply sorry I am, sir." It was the truth; Quinn couldn't tell him, but only because he wasn't really sorry at all. It was a botched job, part of the game, and everyone knew it. Unfortunately, people at Ganz's level of the game, Quinn had learned, rewrote its rules to suit themselves whenever they saw fit.

This, apparently, was going to be one of those times.

Ganz sat up, stood, and walked slowly toward Quinn. "Let me tell you how you're going to make this right," he said. "You owe me a debt. Not money—a favor. A job to be named later. When I ask it of you, you'll do it, no excuses." He stood mere centimeters away from Quinn, towering over him, his dark eyes glaring down with cruel intensity. "Do we 'reach,' Mr. Quinn?"

"Sure. How can I refuse?"

"You can't." Leaving his warning implied, Ganz turned and padded casually back to his mountain of comfort. Reclining into its lush embrace, he snapped his fingers, and a pair of lissome young women—one human, the other Deltan—sprang to his sides and began doting affectionately and silently on him.

Choking back the bile of his envy, Quinn stood and waited patiently for his dismissal. After a minute or so frolicking with his sylphlike courtesans, Ganz made an exaggerated show of noticing that Quinn was still there. "One last thing," he said. "In case you think you're getting off easy . . . you're not."

Oh, no.

Closing his eyes, Quinn braced himself, and the beating commenced. A sweep kick took his legs out from under him, dropping him on his back. Punches rained down, battering his face and knocking the breath out of him with a few well-placed gut shots. Someone pulled him to his feet and held him steady, but he knew not to say "thank you"; he had taken enough stompings in his life to know they were propping him up only to use him as a punching bag. His vision was hazy and bloodred, so all he saw before each new jab or cross to his head was a dark blur. The hands gripping his arms released him, but he didn't get his hopes up; it just meant whoever had been behind him was moving out of the way, for the assailant who now kicked him in the groin. Nausea swelled inside him, and he dropped to his knees, which probably was very helpful for whoever it was who pistol-whipped him across his temple.

He flopped sideways onto the floor, a thick stream of bloody spittle gushing from his split lip and loosened teeth. Blinking slowly, he fought to see through the heavy swelling around his eye sockets. He recognized the be-spoke white fabric of the pant leg standing in front of him.

Overcoming the hideous pain in the vertebrae of his neck, Quinn turned his head slightly and looked up at Zett. "Nice shoes," he gurgled, causing red-tinged saliva bubbles to froth over the corner of his mouth.

"Thank you," Zett said. Then he pulled back his foot, snapped it forward, and broke two of Quinn's ribs.

"That's enough," Ganz said, and the beating ceased. Morikmol gingerly lifted Quinn's disheveled, sagging bulk into a crude facsimile of a standing position. He turned him toward Ganz, not that Quinn could see the Orion boss—or anything else right now, for that matter. Ganz's foghorn of a voice resonated in the tense hush. "If anyone should ask . . ."

"I slipped in the shower," Quinn said.

"Very good. . . . We'll be in touch."

Borne away in the hands of the Tarmelite, Quinn's exit from Ganz's ship was a swish-pan of blurred vision and an ordeal of pain. The corridor lighting was harsh and bright after the dim, smoky haze of the Orion's lair, but squinting stung his swollen eyes. He was actually grateful when his chin struck the deck back in Vanguard's docking wheel, and he heard footsteps recede back inside the *Omari-Ekon.* The hatch scraped shut. *I'm alone, and I'm still alive,* he realized. It took a few moments for him to believe it. He rolled slowly onto his stomach and drew one shallow breath after another.

He crawled forward. Every muscle and joint burned. When his arms and his legs and his back all finally gave out, he slumped onto the deck for several minutes, then peeked around himself to gauge his progress. To his dismay, he had moved less than twenty meters. Marshaling the atrophied vestiges of his youthful survival instinct, he forced himself to put one hand in front of the other and go on dragging himself forward.

It's a long way to the bar, he told himself. *Keep crawling.*

Diego Reyes gazed out into the endless void beyond the main window in Dr. Fisher's quarters, and he wished for a moment that he could just lose himself in all that comfortingly silent darkness. "It's just been one of those weeks," he said.

Behind him, the doctor sat on his sofa, sipping at the gently spiced, half-decaf coffee he had brewed for the commodore's impromptu, late-evening visit. "Meenok's disease is about as bad as it gets," Fisher said. "I wish I could put a silver lining on your mother's situation, but . . . well, I'm just damn sorry, Diego."

Reyes glanced at Fisher's reflection, half-spectral against

the stars on the other side of the transparent aluminum window. The older man's heavy-lidded eyes projected serenity. It was an emotion that Reyes could only envy this evening.

"I spent the last four days thinking about how awful it must be to get a death sentence like that," Reyes said. "To have a few months to contemplate the end of your life. . . . I just couldn't get my head around it. Then we lost the *Bombay*."

"Two months or two minutes, doesn't make much difference," Fisher said. "No matter how ready we think we are for death, no one's ever ready. Not really."

"Maybe not. But there's a big difference between getting a terminal illness and getting killed in an ambush."

"You sure about that? Are there degrees of dead?"

"I can't take revenge on Meenok's disease. I *can* hunt down the bastards who attacked the *Bombay*."

"Hang on, Diego. You shouldn't jump to conclusions." Over the years, Reyes had learned to heed Dr. Fisher's advice. The old physician, despite being an irascible curmudgeon, was known to dispense some fairly sound philosophy in his spare time. Regardless, tonight his notes of caution sounded naïve.

Reyes's voice simmered with anger. "It was a milk run, Zeke. Simple as it gets. Except they aren't coming back."

Fisher leaned forward with a soft groan of effort and rested his mug on the antique cedar coffee table. "That's the job," the doctor said, the gritty edge of his drawl a bit more pronounced than usual. "Sometimes things go wrong. But it doesn't matter how many times life knocks you down; what matters is how many times you get back up."

"Spare me the pep talk, will you? I know risk is part of the equation," Reyes said, the twin demons of doubt and regret wrestling in his gut. "But the Ravanar system was well charted. No anomalies." In one gulp, he downed the rest of his own mug of black, unsweetened coffee. "If this wasn't an attack, why is my ship missing?"

Fisher folded his hands together. "A lot can happen to a starship, even under the best of circumstances. There's still a lot of things in this galaxy we don't understand."

"Here's what I understand," Reyes said, turning away from the window. "A good ship with a great captain isn't coming home." He stalked into the kitchenette and poured himself another cup of coffee. A faint scent of cinnamon and nutmeg rose on its wisps of steam. "As far as I'm concerned, the only question on the table is, who did it? The Klingons or the Tholians?"

"Why not declare war on both? Could save time later."

Reyes scowled at the doctor as he picked up his mug and gave it a cooling puff of breath. "Ravanar's a long way from the Klingon border, and we've had *Endeavour* patrolling that for a few weeks now. But the Tholians haven't shown any interest in the Taurus Reach, so I can't figure out why they'd do this."

Stroking his goatee, Fisher said, "The Tholians might not have rattled their sabers as loudly as the Klingons, but I'd hardly say they welcomed us with open . . . well, open whatever it is they have." He leaned forward and picked up his mug. "And ever since the Tholian delegation's bizarre collective seizure last week . . . let's just say they've been acting oddly."

Reyes pointed at the coffeepot and cast an inquiring

glance at Fisher, who nodded. The commodore carried the coffeepot over to Fisher and refilled the doctor's mug.

"Thanks," Fisher said.

"*De nada.*" Reyes put the coffeepot back on its warmer pad. He had just taken another modest sip of the warm, soothing beverage when Rana Desai's voice issued from the overhead speaker.

"*Captain Desai to Commodore Reyes.*"

Reyes went to the intercom panel on the wall and thumbed open the channel. "Reyes here. Go ahead, Captain."

In an effort to keep their romantic relationship private, they made a point of hailing each other formally and responding formally when third parties were present—even if, like Fisher, the person already knew about their status as a couple. Though Reyes felt awkward when using ranks to ask Desai over to his quarters for dinner, the strict observance of protocol had already averted a few potential embarrassments for them both.

"*Commodore, I need to meet with you as soon as possible.*"

"Of course, Captain," Reyes said. "Shall I drop by your quarters?" He cast a wry grin at Fisher, who shook his head resignedly.

"*Actually, Commodore, I need to see you in my office.*"

The smirk left Reyes's face.

"Understood," he said, his tone turning serious. "I'll be with you shortly. Reyes out." He moved toward the door.

Fisher followed him and exuded sympathy. "Her office?" He shook his head. "That's not good." At the door, he gave Reyes a firm clasp on the shoulder. "Look on the bright side: If this is trouble, at least the JAG boss is your girlfriend."

"Just what I always wanted," Reyes said with a humorless half-smirk. "A girlfriend who can court-martial me."

Reyes's shout was like a bullhorn. "You're court-martialing me?"

"No. Stop overreacting, Diego." Ensconced behind her office desk, Desai could only hope that Reyes wasn't as angry as he looked. "It's a board of inquiry."

"This is the biggest load of—" Reyes caught himself, then pressed his palm over his sandpaper-stubbled chin and upper lip.

"I don't have a choice," Desai said. "The *Bombay* was lost in the line of duty. There has to be an inquiry."

"Give me a break, Rana." Reyes was pacing now, quickly and with mounting agitation. "This is what you do to a captain who comes home without his ship."

"The inquiry is standard procedure."

"Naming the ship's captain is standard procedure," Reyes shot back. "Not the captain's supervising officer."

She leaned forward and placed her fingertips on the desk. "The Starfleet JAG wants me to depose living witnesses. It's not like you're the only one on the list." His sidelong glance bristled with hostility. She continued, "What did you think I was going to do? Mark the file 'case closed' without doing an investigation? I have my orders."

"History's greatest excuse," Reyes said, rolling his eyes.

"I hope you're not this funny with your judge. You might get that court-martial for contempt."

A retort seemed on the verge of escaping Reyes's mouth,

when he hesitated. His indignation turned to confusion. "I thought you would be the judge."

"No," Desai said. "I can't."

He was staring hard into her eyes. "Why not?"

She looked down and moved a few random items around on her desktop. "I'll be recusing myself."

Reyes's face hardened into a frown. "Because of us."

"Yes," she said. "It would be unethical for me to—"

"You can't do that," Reyes said. "Don't recuse yourself."

"Diego, I have to."

"If you do, you'll have to say why." He shook his head with frustration. "We . . . us . . . our relationship—it'd be *public.*" She wondered if he had any idea how stupid that sounded. "I think that came out wrong," he added.

"You *think?*"

Exasperated and exhausted, he rubbed his eyes. He folded his arms and thought for a few seconds. She kept him in her accusatory glare and waited patiently to see how he planned to dig his way out of this faux pas. "I'm just not ready to add grist to Vanguard's rumor mill," he said. "We're in high-profile jobs. People will talk." He reached down and picked up a large, polished hunk of blue volcanic glass from Desai's desk. "I know that we'd hardly be the first or even the most glamorous couple in the officer corps . . . but I value our privacy."

She couldn't deny that she sympathized with him. Being the topic of lurid gossip was a notion that made her feel ill. And part of the thrill of their romance so far had been in the hiding of it. But this was not about their relationship. "I feel the same way, Diego. But I'd rather recuse myself than give people reason to question my ethics."

Studying the hunk of blue glass in his palm, Reyes drew a long breath then exhaled slowly. He seemed much calmer than he had just minutes earlier. For Desai, one of the most difficult aspects of being romantically involved with him was the volcanic quality of his temperament. His fury could lay dormant for the longest time, then, without warning, *boom.* When he was truly angry, he frightened her a little. At the same time, once he vented his rage, it subsided quickly. Just to complicate the situation further, she was still learning which irritants were most likely to trigger his explosions.

Finally, he broke the tense hush with a dejected-sounding sigh. "I trust you to be a fair and impartial judge, no matter who's standing in front of you."

That makes one of us, Desai reflected.

He put the chunk of glass back on her desk. "Use your best judgment. Let my yeoman know when you need to see me."

Reyes turned toward the door, which hissed open, letting in the soft murmur of whispered conferences between members of her JAG office staff. The commodore walked out without looking back. When the door closed, Desai eased herself into her chair. She imagined what it was going to be like, sitting at a table with her lover, watching him be deposed about his role, however peripheral, in the deaths of more than two hundred Starfleet personnel. *I'm going to hate this case,* she brooded.

On her desk was the report of the loss of the *Starship Bombay.* To her eye, the file looked very, very thin.

Starting tomorrow, she knew, that would change.

•   •   •

Pennington dropped his duffel on the floor. "I need a storage unit," he said to the quartermaster, Senior Chief Petty Officer Sozlok. The dark-furred, vaguely simian-looking noncom seemed in no hurry to service the frantic journalist's request.

Sozlok slid a data sheet on an automated pad across the counter to Pennington. "Fill this out."

The form was long, and it was complicated, and it was everything that Pennington had no time for right now. Keeping up the pretense would be essential, however. "Could you check to see if you have any units large enough to hold a dozen cases of Loperian *reelkot*?"

"Reelkot?" Sozlok looked intrigued. "You'll be needing refrigerated storage, then."

"Yes, exactly." *Why the hell did I say* reelkot? He kicked himself for mentioning something so unusual. This was the kind of visit he would prefer be forgotten. Instead, he'd made it bizarre enough for this guy to tell someone else about it tomorrow over drinks, and interesting enough that it might be repeated.

While he busied himself completing the form, Sozlok clicked through several screens of data, apparently on a search for an available refrigerated storage unit of unusual size. There was no point in falsifying the form, Pennington knew. The noncom would ask for his identification before finishing the rental. For a moment he wondered how he might avoid leaving a trace of his visit, until he remembered that there was nothing inherently suspicious about his actions. *People do this all the time,* he reassured himself. *Nothing to worry about. Calm down.*

A few minutes later, Pennington's form was filled-in,

and Sozlok seemed to have settled on an appropriate unit for him. "Here we go," he said. "Level forty-nine, section three, quad two, unit fourteen-echo."

"Great," Pennington said. As if it were an afterthought, he added, "Do you mind if I check it out before I commit to it? You know—just to make sure."

"Fine by me," Sozlok said.

"Just one thing: I forgot my jacket, and it's going to be colder than hell frozen over in there. Got a spare I could borrow?"

"Probably," said Sozlok, who lumbered away into a back room to scrounge up a loaner coat.

The moment Sozlok was around the corner and his footsteps began to recede, Pennington all but launched himself across the counter, until he was lying on top of it. Reaching over, he turned the noncom's monitor toward himself and started deftly keying commands into its control panel. He knew time was short, but his need was simple: He wanted to know which storage unit belonged to Oriana.

It took only seconds to coax the data from the intuitive interface. Staring at the compartment number, he committed it to memory. During his third pass of mnemonic reinforcement, he heard the growing clap of approaching footfalls. Resetting the interface and turning the monitor back to its prior facing, he slithered in reverse across the countertop and landed softly on his feet. He was standing tall and looking utterly trustworthy as Sozlok returned.

The hirsute alien handed Pennington a bulky, fur-lined parka. "Keep it. It's from lost-and-found."

"Thanks." He slung the coat over his duffel and hefted

both over his shoulder while Sozlok encoded a key card for him.

Handing the card to Pennington, Sozlok said, "This card is single-use only. Go check out the unit. If it's what you want, we'll start an account for you."

"Sounds good." He tucked the key in his pants pocket. "Back in a bit."

"Take your time," Sozlok said, then sighed. "I'm here all night." He wore the fatigued mien of a person trapped in a job he wasn't yet prepared to spurn.

"Hang in there, mate," Pennington said. "Back in a jiff."

Pennington pushed away from the counter and walked away quickly, before he found himself lassoed into another round of depressive banter. Quickening his pace to the turbolift, he told himself for the hundredth time that he wasn't breaking into Oriana's storage unit for selfish reasons. *If her husband found those mementos, it'd be a disaster,* he rationalized. *Bad enough to hear that your wife is dead, but, "Oh, yeah, mate, she was cheating on you, too." That's just beyond the pale.*

Continuing down to the refrigerated-storage area, he kept telling himself that. He expected to believe it any minute now.

An hour. An entire hour.

That's how long it had taken Cervantes Quinn—battered, bloodied, and crawling like a wounded animal—to arrive at a bar that would still let him in to drink. The revulsed stares and the horrified gasps that he'd endured from passers-by hadn't bothered him. Nor had he allowed himself to be upset by the creeping suspicion that more of his blood was soaked into his favorite shirt than was coursing through his veins. He was glad he had saved his ire for this moment.

Hand over hand, with a mighty effort and labored breaths, he lifted himself from the floor and climbed, one exceptionally careful motion at a time, on to the first empty barstool he reached. Sitting upright, he felt the tug of gravity against his body shift. He steadied himself, licked the blood from his own teeth, swallowed, and croaked out a one-word request: "Tequila."

The bartender—a heavy, profusely sweating, and ill-mooded middle-aged Bolian—shot Quinn a disdainful glare. "Got cash?"

It took a few seconds for the question to sink in.

Disgust and indignation lurked behind Quinn's soft tone. "I paid my tab here last month."

"Yeah, I know," the bartender said. "But you also look like you just got rolled. No offense, but you don't strike me as a good credit risk right now."

Quinn dug into his pockets and dredged up one loose bit of currency after another. He piled them haphazardly on the bar. A Federation credit chip, a few Klingon *jiQ,* and half a dozen exotic alien coins lay scrambled together. The bartender scooped them up in a single swipe of his hand and reached for the good Anejo. It splashed into a low glass, the long legs of it clinging to the sides, its sweet aroma pulling Quinn closer, like the ambrosia of Tantalus. The bartender pushed the glass toward him. With aching fingers, Quinn reached for his drink.

A hand clamped on to the collar of his jacket.

He had just long enough to think the word *damn,* but not

long enough to say it, before he was yanked backward off the barstool and dragged toward the doorway—his precious and fully paid-for glass of tequila abandoned on the bar, which grew farther away with each passing moment.

Turning to see who had delivered this injustice upon him for the second time in one evening, he looked into the passionless face of Lieutenant Commander T'Prynn. "Hey," he said, his words slurred by pain and loosened teeth. "I'm not this easy, you know. You have to woo me."

"Be quiet," she said, and he could tell that she meant it. "We are going to speak privately. Until then, I would prefer you did not speak at all."

"Can I at least do my own walking?"

T'Prynn halted, looked him over, and let go of his collar. He collapsed in a heap on the ground.

"Okay," he said. "Dragging's fine."

Breaking into Oriana's storage locker was proving more difficult than Pennington had expected. The dislodged door-control panel dangled from a lone duotronic cable. With sweaty fingers, he guided the lock-picking tools through the bramble of wires, chips, and capacitors. Taking care not to trip the security alarms, he disabled the door's redundant lock mechanisms.

It had been a while since he had needed to call upon these less-than-respectable skills, which he had learned from Unez, his Scoridian journalism mentor in Edinburgh. Working his way through the lock, he thought of an incident several years ago, when Unez had snickered smugly while Pennington fumbled with a simple magnetic bolt on a decrepit old building's service door. As criticism went, it had been decidedly unconstructive, but it was also effective: Pennington had vowed never to suffer that embarrassment again.

The last interlock released with a soft clack.

He picked up his duffel bag and opened the door, which swung outward, expelling a stale gust. The storage unit was about two meters high and as narrow as the door. An overhead light glowed automatically to life, revealing a shallow space. It was only slightly deeper than he could reach without leaning over the frontmost row of stacked plastic containers.

Like a stevedore, he hauled out the boxes and opened each one in turn. Rooting swiftly through their contents, he plucked out items that could link him to Oriana. A photograph of them he had taken with his FNS recorder. Some small handwritten notes of the exceptionally trivial variety—"Stepped out for coffee," or "Missed you this morning," or "Saw these and thought of you"—that he had left for her when their schedules had failed to synchronize as planned. The first bouquet of flowers he had ever given to her, desiccated and bundled in a cone of fragile paper. And, most damning of all, a stack of his passionate letters, which had been instrumental in his courting of her.

He stuffed all of it into his duffel and tied it shut. Slack and half-filled when he'd come here, it now bulged full.

Once all the boxes were resealed and neatly put back in their places, he swung the door closed. It moved slowly, its hydraulic hinges designed to prevent slamming. As it neared the doorjamb it slowed further, inched into place, then suddenly was pulled inward by the magnetic bolts. Whirring and clicking sounds overlapped for a few seconds while the other locking mechanisms automatically secured the heavy gray metal portal.

After repairing the door-lock panel, Pennington hefted the duffel over his shoulder with a grunt of effort and walked slowly away from Oriana's storage unit, in search of a garbage-disposal chute. This entire section of the station smelled mechanical, like hydraulics and ozone. In the rush to make the station operational, some of the less-visible areas, like this one, had been slap-dashed together and still weren't quite up to Starfleet specs. Some of the lights flickered, intercoms crackled and cut out, and the ventilation system rumbled constantly, filling the corridors with a steady flood of dull white noise.

He was grateful for the roar of the air ducts, though, and for his soft-soled shoes, which enabled him to skulk along in near-silence. The last thing he wanted to deal with tonight was running into someone who would ask what he had in the bag.

Roaming for several minutes in an arbitrary left-turn, right-turn search pattern, he paused at every corner, listened for company, and peeked to make certain he wasn't blundering into an unfortunate encounter. He glanced down a short, remote stretch of dimly lit corridor and finally saw a garbage-disposal chute large enough to accommodate his duffel. *Or a body,* his cynical reporter's instincts suggested.

He entered the corridor just as he heard footsteps—and a dry scraping sound—approaching from around the far corner. Ducking quickly back the way he had come, he clutched his duffel, afraid to set it down lest something inside it settle noisily or clank against something else. He concentrated on slowing his breathing, calming himself, remaining still.

Quick footfalls echoed in the corridor, then stopped.

A woman's voice. "This will be a suitable location for our discussion." She spoke with the cold precision of a Vulcan.

"I hope the food's better than the ambience," a man said, in a voice marked by a strangely hard-to-place North American twang. Pennington's curiosity trumped his caution. He slowly leaned sideways and turned his head for a look at the people in the corridor. Lieutenant Commander T'Prynn he knew from her occasional impromptu performances in Manón's. The bruised, bloodied mess of a man sitting on the deck in front of her was someone he had seen around the station but hadn't met.

T'Prynn stood over the man, her posture relaxed, her smoky-sweet voice chillingly emotionless. "Who sent you to Ravanar?"

"Where?"

"Do not make me repeat myself, Quinn."

The man reached up, grabbed a recessed horizontal edge in the middle of the wall and pulled himself back to his feet. "Why ask at all? You talk like you already know the answer."

"It is just as valid to interrogate in order to confirm soft intelligence as it is to obtain fresh data," T'Prynn said. Her head tilted slightly to one side, one eyebrow raised. Her voice remained inhumanly neutral. "You were sent to Ravanar to steal something, correct?"

Smiling, he said, "You have lovely eyebrows."

"You would fit easily down this incinerator chute."

"Whoa!" Quinn held up his hands. "I think you're over-reacting just a little—"

"Your actions led to the loss of a starship and the deaths of hundreds of Starfleet personnel, Mr. Quinn."

Eavesdropping from around the corner, Pennington felt his pulse quicken. In the corridor, Quinn fell silent, his demeanor refashioned from insolent apathy to one of shock and guilt. He ceased struggling in her grasp, and she released him.

Words returned slowly to Quinn. "The *Bombay* . . . ?"

"Yes, Mr. Quinn," T'Prynn said. "The *Bombay* was lost in orbit of Ravanar, destroyed while delivering a replacement for the component you destroyed during your botched robbery."

"The sensor screen," he said, his voice lower than before, making it difficult for Pennington to hear without straining.

"Correct," T'Prynn said.

"You have to believe me, I didn't know it was a Starfleet base. If I'd known, I never would've taken the job."

"So you admit you were hired?"

Quinn froze, looking like a politician who had just made a grievous faux pas in front of a live feed. "I'm not a snitch."

"I would not expect you to be," T'Prynn said. "After all, Mr. Ganz is a notoriously . . ." She studied Quinn's disheveled state, then finished her sentence: *". . . unforgiving* employer."

"Hey, lady, I'm just a simple, legitimate prospector."

She reached forward as if to poke him for emphasis, then lightly touched her fingertip to his collarbone.

He crumpled at her touch, writhing and grimacing in agony. As his knees folded beneath him, she kept her fingertip against him. He flailed desperately to pull her hand away, but seemed unable to bend his arms or turn them enough at the elbow or shoulder to reach T'Prynn's arm. It was one of the most bizarre and intimidating things Pennington had ever seen a Vulcan do.

"The Vulcan martial art of *V'Shan* features a comprehensive study of pressure points and their effect on the central nervous system," T'Prynn said, with not a hint of effort or compassion. "I have no time for your lies, Mr. Quinn. I am well aware of your service to Mr. Ganz as a 'clandestine procurer.' Denying it, while perhaps a useful stratagem in a legal arena, serves only to prolong your current predicament. Do you understand?" Quinn nodded furiously, his jaw clenched too tightly shut for him to answer verbally. T'Prynn withdrew her delicate finger from Quinn's torso. He sagged with relief to the floor. She continued, "I have no use for your apologies, nor am I interested in curtailing your activities." With slow grace she cupped his chin in her palm and turned his gaze upward. "But I do have use for your access to Ganz's organization, and for the places you can go without drawing suspicion or attention."

"Lady, ain't you ever heard the saying 'A man can't serve two masters'?"

"A logical notion," T'Prynn said. "But irrelevant to our conversation."

"I think it's damned relevant." Quinn pushed himself back up the wall, one half-step at a time. "I *have* a boss."

"I prefer to think of myself as your handler."

Lurking beyond the shadowy corner, Pennington shook his head out of pity for Quinn. *Bloody hell, this chap is slow.*

All at once, Quinn caught up with T'Prynn's meaning. "No, no, no, no, no."

"Mr. Quinn, you owe a debt to Starfleet, and to the people whose lives have been lost because of your interference. You compromised a secret listening post, one vital to tracking the movements of Klingon ships in this sector. You can either accept your responsibility to repay this debt through service . . ." Her eyes turned toward the chute to the garbage incinerator.

Quinn responded with a glower of sullen surrender. "Where do we start?"

T'Prynn handed him a Federation credit chip. "Go have your drink. Have several. When I need you, I will tell you."

Pocketing the chip, Quinn shambled away without another word. The Vulcan woman lingered behind for several seconds. Pennington continued to observe her. When she turned in his direction, he retracted his leaning posture to conceal himself. About a minute after Quinn had left, Pennington heard T'Prynn's footfalls growing fainter as she disappeared back into the bowels of the station.

What the hell did I just hear? He dropped his duffel, snatched his data tool from his belt, and hurriedly jotted notes. *Quinn. T'Prynn.* Bombay. *Ravanar. Listening post.* He stared at the words, then added more keywords to his list: *Sensor screen. Ganz. Theft. Extortion. Cover-up.*

It was the sort of lucky break every investigative reporter dreamed of . . . and exactly the kind of sensationalistic story his editor would never run, not without independent confirmation from at least two other sources. *If I could get this guy Quinn to go on the record . . .* Immediately, he scoffed at that idea. *That's a long shot, he has a lot to lose . . . and T'Prynn won't talk. But if* Bombay *shipped top-secret gear to Ravanar, someone in the station's cargo division might be able to confirm that.* He made a note to follow that angle. *It's a start.*

He put away the handheld device and hefted his duffel over his shoulder. A sharp twinge flared in his shoulder socket as he carried the heavy bag to the incinerator chute. Setting it down, he harbored second thoughts. *Maybe I could rent my own storage unit. Just keep all this stuff tucked away. . . .* Then he imagined his own worst-case scenario, a greatly exaggerated report of his demise that would lead to his duffel, full of romantic keepsakes of his dead mistress, being delivered to his wife Lora.

Pennington opened the incinerator chute hatch, picked up the duffel, and pushed it into the dark, vertical channel, which swallowed the bag with ease. He counted off the seconds until he heard the distant metallic echo of an impact, and he said a silent farewell to his mementos of Oriana.

Then he closed the hatch and vowed to learn the whole truth about how she died, and who was to blame.

11

"Would either of you care to explain," Jetanien bellowed, "how I can view this as anything other than an unmitigated disaster?"

Having decided that if he wasn't sleeping tonight then neither would anyone else, Reyes had summoned Jetanien and T'Prynn to his office after returning from his meeting with Desai. He couldn't recall ever having seen the ambassador in such supremely high dudgeon. *"Disaster*'s a strong word," Reyes said. "This is more of a complication."

"Excellent," Jetanien said. "How comforting. Nothing fixes a major security breach like an empty bromide."

"The commodore is correct," T'Prynn said. It annoyed Reyes that even in the middle of the night she still looked crisp, fresh, and alert. "Captain Desai's inquiry, though inconvenient, is hardly an insurmountable difficulty."

Reyes regarded both T'Prynn and Jetanien with the same creased expression of incomprehension. "Why do you two always talk like you're paid by the word?" Neither one reacted visibly to his comment. He continued, "Yes, Ambassador, this is a bad situation. But, as the lady said, we can keep a lid on it."

"It is the nature of legal inquiries to expand," Jetanien said. "The JAG office is not known for conducting superficial investigations. If its questions about the *Bombay*'s mission or the Ravanar colony's true purpose become too pointed—"

"Then we'll know it's time for damage control," Reyes said.

"After they have deposed witnesses and served subpoenas," T'Prynn said, "it might be too late to contain their findings."

"So what are we talking about? Running interference?"

"No, sir," T'Prynn said. "It is too early to resort to counterintelligence tactics. Doing so at this stage might, in fact, create more threads of evidence than it would conceal."

"Point taken. But Captain Desai—" The door signal buzzed once, halting the conversation. Reyes pressed the door-lock release switch on his desk. His auburn-haired gamma-shift yeoman, Midshipman Cadet Suzie Finneran, entered carrying a tray on which rested three beverages: a large mug of sweet coffee, for Reyes, a steaming cup of tea, for T'Prynn; and a misshapen bowl that contained a cloudy broth, which even from across the room stank like a bucket of clams Reyes had once forgotten in the afternoon sun, as a child vacationing on Earth with his parents for the first time. Finneran set the tray on Reyes's desk. The commodore suppressed his urge to dry-heave.

As the yeoman left the office, the stink of Jetanien's soup proved too much for Reyes, who pushed his own coffee aside. He had thought he would need it to stay awake as the wee hours crept inexorably toward the start of alpha shift, but Jetanien's pungent breakfast brew had more kick than smelling salts.

When the door closed, Reyes picked up where he had left off. "Captain Desai could put us in a bind if she presses too hard. Unfortunately, we can't ask her to drop it."

"Agreed," T'Prynn said. "That, too, would draw suspicion."

"We also have to send out a ship to investigate, look for survivors, and survey what's left of the colony," Reyes said. "Standard procedure is to send the closest one. Right now, with the *Endeavour* and the *Sagittarius* still on assignment, that's the *Enterprise,* but I'd rather not bring them into this."

Jetanien lifted his bowl to his beak-shaped jaw, tucked part of it inside his mouth, and savored a loud, guttural slurp. Reyes waited patiently for the diplomat to swallow his gulp. Lowering the bowl from his face, Jetanien looked back at Reyes, then seemed irked to notice T'Prynn watching him, too. "Begging a thousand pardons if I offended your delicate sensibilities."

"I merely was riveted by my anticipation of your next remark," T'Prynn said.

Reyes added, "I'm just impressed you didn't get any on you."

Depositing his bowl brusquely on Reyes's desk, Jetanien seemed to scowl, though not a single feature of his leathery dark green hide shifted in the slightest. *Great,* Reyes grumped to himself. *Just where I wanted that bowl full of sewage—closer to me.*

The ambassador straightened to his full, imposing height. "If the concern is that Captain Desai might unwittingly expose our operation, why not bring her into our inner circle? Surely if she understood the scope of—"

Reyes cut him off. "Because she doesn't have the security clearance," he said. "The only reason Xiong's cleared for this project is because we need him."

Jetanien reached up and clutched the edges of his cassock. "How are we to proceed?" Reyes recognized the clutching gesture as one of Jetanien's more subtle signs of frustration. If and when he learned to recognize a few more of the Chelon's "tells," he planned to invite Jetanien to join him, Fisher, and Cannella for poker some night.

"Depends how vulnerable we are," Reyes said. "What'll Desai find if she digs?"

"Very little," T'Prynn said. "The transmissions between here and the outpost were all well-encrypted. The *Bombay*'s cargo manifests and our bills of lading show no mention of classified technology. And the *Bombay*'s crew had no knowledge of our true mission, and therefore could not have revealed it."

"Vulnerability in the legal sense depends on culpability, Commodore," Jetanien said. "Unless you acted with negligence or malice aforethought, there is no reason to suspect that Captain Desai will have any motive to pursue her inquiry beyond determining the exact cause of the *Bombay*'s destruction."

"That might make its own problems," Reyes said.

"If you are referring to the potential political repercussions," Jetanien said, "leave that to me and my associates. If need be, I can take steps to seal her inquiry's findings for national-security reasons, provided she doesn't uncover anything criminally actionable."

"In other words, as long as I don't give her a reason to court-martial me, you think we can keep this quiet."

"Possibly," Jetanien said. "For now, we should follow established protocols. Send the *Enterprise*."

Reyes turned toward T'Prynn. "You'd concur?"

"It seems the most prudent choice for now, sir."

"All right, then," he said. "We'll have *Enterprise* ferry Xiong to the colony while we ride this one out. Meeting adjourned." His two visitors turned to leave. He tried to take a calming breath and was met by a sulfuric odor. "Your Excellency," he said. Jetanien turned back toward Reyes, who reluctantly picked up the ambassador's clammy, amoeba-shaped bowl of swampwater stew. "Take this with you. . . . Please."

12

Less than an hour after leaving Reyes's office, Jetanien watched Federation Special Envoy Akeylah Karumé guzzle her fourth cup of coffee in two minutes. She was bolstering her courage and sharpening her focus before meeting with the Klingon delegation. The tall, brightly attired human woman preferred the caffeinated beverage be as rich and dark as her own ebony skin tone, and she had sharply refused a yeoman's offer of sugar with the ironically bitter retort, "No, thanks, I'm sweet enough."

Karumé stared at the door to the conference room. Jetanien worried that she might not be ready for the intimidating task of serving as the go-between to the shrewd, aggressive Klingons. "Be careful how you phrase things," he said. "I want to get a sense of what they know about the *Bombay*'s destruction. Do not be put off if they speak rudely to you or make an issue of your sex. Try to draw them out."

She glared at Jetanien while handing her coffee cup to an assistant. "Perhaps you'd like to speak to them yourself, Ambassador?"

"No," he said. "I cannot attend every parley. That is why I have a staff—so that I may delegate. Now, because Lugok saw fit to stab Mr. Meyer, it falls to you to speak for the Federation."

"As you wish," Karumé said. "Give me a moment."

"Whenever you are ready, Ms. Karumé."

She closed her eyes and stood absolutely still, deep in a thought-purging meditation. Because he himself was in no hurry to face Lugok, Jetanien waited in patient silence.

Normally this meeting would have been postponed until a more reasonable hour of the morning, but Jetanien wanted Kirk and the crew of the *Enterprise* to have as much reliable intelligence as possible before they shipped out several hours from now. In any event, he had lately come to realize that the Klingons' schedule was somewhat offset from those of most station residents, which likely made the timing of this hastily convened meeting less of an inconvenience for them than it was for Jetanien and his staff.

"I'm ready now," Karumé said. Three steps toward the door, she halted and looked back at Jetanien, who had followed her. "I thought you said you can't attend every parley."

"I cannot," Jetanien said. "But I plan to attend this one."

Her brow furrowed. "Am I running this meeting, or are you?"

"You are."

"Fine. In that room, don't interrupt me, don't contradict me, and don't undermine my authority as the Federation's interlocutor. If I'm to have credibility with the Klingons, I must have real authority, not just the appearance of it."

"Very sensible," Jetanien said. "Please proceed."

"Follow me," she said, and continued toward the door.

She barged through it. By the time he had stepped into

the room, Karumé was halfway to the conference table.

Lugok, his thick paunch stretching his black-and-gray uniform and metallic sash, rose quickly from his chair. A broad grin lit up his swarthy face. "Ambassador, your concubine is most rude! She doesn't even wait for—" He was silenced by Karumé's backhanded strike to his face, which caught him utterly by surprise and knocked him backward onto the table. Karumé had her hand locked around his throat before he could right himself.

"I'm Federation Envoy Karumé," she said, her voice imperious. "You speak to me. I'm allowing Ambassador Jetanien to observe this meeting, as a courtesy."

Jetanien was about to interject that, as his subordinate, Karumé was in no position to grant or deny him permissions of any kind; then he remembered the promise he had made before walking through the door. He stopped himself before approaching the table, and instead lingered by the wall near the door, watching and listening from a respectful distance.

Recovered from his initial surprise, Lugok reached up, placed his hand over Karumé's, and pried it off his neck.

"You have fire . . . for a human," Lugok said, peeling her fingers loose one at a time. Gripping her wrist, he lifted her right arm over her head. "But your hands are weak."

Undaunted, she smirked at him. "Maybe. But they're quick." A glint of light flashing off metal caught Jetanien's eye, and he realized that in her left hand Karumé held Lugok's *d'k tahg*. She had pressed it, cutting edge first, against the man's crotch. Keeping her eyes on Lugok's face as he looked down at his predicament, she added, "Look familiar?"

Jetanien chastised himself for not even having thought to ask Karumé, before the meeting, whether she was armed.

The other two Klingons in the room—an attaché named Kulor and a bodyguard named Turag—made no move to defend or assist Lugok. Observing the knife poised beneath their boss's genitals, they chuckled cruelly.

No doubt sensing the delicacy of his situation, Lugok resumed eye contact with Karumé, released her hand, and smiled. "An honor to make your acquaintance . . . Envoy Karumé."

Karumé withdrew the blade from the Klingon ambassador's groin, flipped it in her palm, and offered it to him grip-first. "The honor is mine, Ambassador Lugok, son of Breg." He accepted the dagger from her and sheathed it in his boot. She gestured toward the mirror-perfect black table, and the two diplomats sat in adjacent chairs, which they turned to face each other.

Lugok slouched. "Why have you asked for this meeting?"

"Our starship *Bombay* was destroyed yesterday," she said.

"Yes," Lugok said with a grin. "We heard."

"Did you destroy it?"

He laughed. "No, but we applaud those who did."

"Do you know who destroyed our vessel?"

Lugok's amusement turned quickly to boredom. "No."

"Thank you, Ambassador," Karumé said. She stood. "I look forward to our next meeting."

Rising to face her eye-to-eye, Lugok, despite his bulky physique, projected an aura of menace. "As do I," he said.

"Thank you for returning my blade." He marched past her, toward the door on the opposite side of the room from where she and Jetanien had entered. He left in long, fast strides, and his attaché and bodyguard followed close behind him.

The door swished shut a moment later, leaving Karumé and Jetanien alone in the conference room. She turned toward him. "The Klingons didn't destroy the *Bombay.*"

Jetanien was skeptical. "And your basis for this conclusion would be what, exactly, Ms. Karumé?"

"Lugok said so."

"I see," Jetanien said. "Permit me to extend my most humble thanks to you, then, for permitting me to audit this exchange. How else would I have learned that our most aggressive and implacable enemy in known space is also our most credible source of foreign intelligence? Most edifying, Ms. Karumé."

"Klingons take pride in their warmongering," Karumé said. "If they defeated one of our ships in open combat, they'd be crowing about it from one end of the galaxy to the other."

"Unless they plan to destroy Vanguard's starship support in preparation for an assault on the station," Jetanien said. "In that case, better to neutralize our vessels clandestinely, so as to avoid sparking a reprisal before they can capture Vanguard."

Karumé shook her head. "Klingons are cunning, but they're not subtle. When they want to attack, they'll do it in force—and in the open. What happened to the *Bombay* wasn't their style."

"Perhaps." Moving back toward the door he and

Karumé had entered through, he said, "I trust you don't plan to conduct all your parleys at knifepoint?"

"Of course not," she said, following him out. "Lugok won't fall for that twice. I'll have to change tactics next time."

"A phaser, I presume?"

"Cleavage, actually. Emasculation and titillation are oddly connected in the male Klingon psyche."

Where a human might have sighed, Jetanien groaned. "Please don't have an affair with him."

"Wow," she said. "You really *don't* understand Klingon politics, do you?"

Sandesjo sat in the commissary and picked at her breakfast of scrambled eggs, fried potatoes, and toast with jam. Everything about it revulsed her. Its aroma, its color, the fact that cooking had leached all the flavor from it—no one, she was convinced, could ruin a meal like humans. Even their coffee was weak. For the sake of keeping up appearances, however, she made the effort to eat and pretend to enjoy herself. Later, before her work-day overwhelmed her, she would slip away to the lavatory and sneak a couple of *tuQloS* pills to help her body take some sustenance from the human food she was forced to consume.

Most of the seats at her table were empty. The mess halls and commissaries usually were packed in the hours immediately preceding and following the shift changes, and again during the staggered mid-shift lunch breaks. This morning, however, the main commissary on level seventeen was almost deserted. The last time Sandesjo had seen

this many available seats during a prime dining hour was
during the station's first week of operation, when the engineering staff—profoundly irked that their long haul up
from the bowels of the station's power-generation core always left them scrounging for seats and settling for the
least-popular menu items—had sent up a team early, to
fake a radiation leak and clear out the upper-decks personnel, so the engineers could enjoy their choice of entrées in
peace and comfort.

The signal device on her belt beeped. She glanced
down. It was from Turag. The code he'd sent her was an instruction to check in as soon as circumstances allowed.
"Yes, sir," she muttered, figuring that anyone who overheard would assume she had just been summoned by Jetanien. She downed the rest of her coffee in one scalding
gulp, then stood and walked her plate to the return counter,
where she abandoned it still half-full.

Turning toward the door, she collided with Lieutenant
Ming Xiong, the A&A officer who seemed to be invited to
an inordinate number of high-level meetings with Jetanien
and Reyes.

Xiong glanced at the plate Sandesjo had turned in. "Not
hungry this morning?"

"I'm on a diet," Sandesjo said.

"Don't tell me," he said. "The 'drop everything for Ambassador Jetanien' diet?"

She nodded once. "Ah . . . you've heard of it."

"Who hasn't?" He smiled shyly at her and shifted his
weight awkwardly. Breaking eye contact, he glanced away
toward the chow line. Looking back, he said, "Guess I better get on line before Farber eats all the eggs."

"Probably a good idea." She stepped around him. "Enjoy your breakfast, Lieutenant."

"You too," he said, then hastened to correct himself. "I mean, I hope you did, you know, have a nice breakfast."

Tossing her straight, cinnamon-hued hair with a turn of her head, she cast a flirtatious look back over her shoulder at him.

He finished his farewell with a simple, "Have a nice day."

"You too, Xiong." As she left the commissary, she felt him watching her. Despite the brevity of their few meetings, his attraction to her had been clear from the start. *Silly man. He has no idea what he'd be getting himself into.*

Minutes later Sandesjo was sequestered in her office. Her secret communication device opened quietly on her desktop, and Ambassador Lugok's flushed, angry visage filled its screen. His voice was loud enough to crackle the device's speakers with distortion. *"Was your file on Karumé a joke?"*

She turned down the volume on the speaker. "I take it your first meeting did not go well?"

"She nearly cut off my loDmach."

"I warned you she was aggressive," Sandesjo said, an evil gleam lighting up her gaze. "Tell me, did you underestimate her because she was human or because she was a woman?"

Lugok's face bunched with annoyance. *"Don't be stupid, Lurqal. I would never underestimate a woman."*

"Good to know." Chilling her tone, she continued, "My time is short, Ambassador. What can I do for you?"

"What is the Federation doing to learn who destroyed its ship?"

"Enterprise is being readied for departure," Sandesjo said. "Probably within the day."

His brow knitted with confusion. *"Today? There's been no announcement."*

"Starfleet's probably keeping the deployment quiet, but none of the alpha-shift spacedock crew were at breakfast today. They must have been called in during gamma shift."

"Interesting," Lugok said. *"Do you know where the* Bombay *was lost?"*

"Not yet." She transmitted a data file over the secure channel. "I've sent you a list of six star systems that would be worth monitoring during the next few days."

"Your selection criteria?"

"Situated within the range of the *Bombay* at maximum warp for seventy-eight hours, presence of M-Class planets, source of subspace radio traffic within the past three months."

"Very good," Lugok said. *"Let me know if discussions resume with the Tholian envoy."*

"As you command."

They traded valedictions of *Qapla',* then cut the channel.

Sandesjo tucked the closed briefcase device under her desk. She activated her computer, checked her morning schedule, then walked to her door and looked for an aide who would fetch her another cup of watered-down, barely caffeinated Terran swill. It was going to be a long day, and weak human coffee would be better than none.

Her carefully laid plan was derailed by an all too familiar voice of authority. "Ms. Sandesjo," Jetanien said from the doorway, in his favorite tone of arch superiority. "Permit me to thank you for recommending Akeylah Karumé as our new envoy to the Klingon delegation."

"You're welcome," she said. The huge Chelon ignored her.

"Until now, I had been greatly vexed by the problem of how to maintain a political dialogue with the Klingons, while at the same time threatening their chief representative with forced emasculation. Fortunately, Ms. Karumé has adroitly merged these two concepts."

"You must be very proud, sir."

"Exquisitely," he said. "Are you familiar with the Nemite Revolution that occurred two thousand, four hundred and twelve years ago on Tamaros III?"

"If I say yes, will it stop you from lecturing me?"

"It all began when the proconsul to the High Epopt of Tamaros appointed a Yoçarian to serve as the castellan of the capital city . . ."

Steeling herself for a very long history lesson whose only allegorical moral would be another iteration of "Thanks for sending me a maverick," Sandesjo concluded that there wasn't enough coffee in the galaxy to make this job bearable.

"We should have been prepared for this," Councillor Torr said, his tirade inciting a low chorus of grumbles among the rest of the Klingon High Council. The sharp-featured young councillor paced like a chained *targ* in the dimly lit chamber ringed by statues of great warriors of ages past. Chancellor Sturka listened with waning patience as Torr continued. "One of the ships defending Vanguard has been destroyed, yet we are unable to capitalize on this opportunity. Why? Because we have been too cautious in our strategy for seizing the Gonmog Sector."

"Save your propaganda, Torr," Sturka said, his voice worn to a low growl after more than a decade of presiding over this increasingly fractious ruling committee. "They lost one frigate, but another battle cruiser has made port. If anything, Vanguard is better defended than it was before."

"*Enterprise* is there, that's true," said Veselka, a woman whose peculiar charms were matched only by her cunning. "But she made port for repairs, and her captain is untested."

Kulok, the grizzled councillor from Lankal, snorted out a derisive laugh. "Pike, untested? Ridiculous."

"You need stronger *raktajino,* old man," snapped Alakon, a warrior who had risen from commoner origins and earned his place on the council through honorable combat. "Pike commands a fleet now. His old ship is in the hands of a new commander: Kirk."

Argashek grunted and turned toward Grozik and Glazya, his longtime allies on the council. "Kirk? . . . A good Klingon name."

Councillor Narvak interjected, "Just because his name sounds Klingon, it doesn't mean he'll fight like one."

"But it will be fun to see him try," Councillor Molok said, flashing an evil grin that sent creases halfway up the sides of his bald head.

Laughter rocked the hall. Sturka rapped the end of his staff on the cold stone floor. The sharp reports and echoes muzzled the jollity. All eyes turned back to the chancellor, who leaned forward on his throne. "Before we move against Vanguard, we should make certain we know who destroyed their vessel."

"It wasn't us," Glazya said, her wild frazzle of dark hair, her wide eyes, and her upswept eyebrows conveying perfectly her almost feral temperament. "Unless Starfleet blew up its own ship, it had to be the Tholians. After that episode with Ambassador Tolrene here on Qo'noS and Sesrene and his delegation on Vanguard, it's obvious there is something *wrong* with them."

Sturka noted Glazya's point. Tolrene's abrupt seizure and subsequent behavior had been decidedly odd. Reports that the Tholian delegates to Vanguard, Earth, and Qo'noS had suffered the same symptoms at the exact same moment had been even more alarming. It was unclear, though, what had caused the incidents, or why it might provoke the Tholians to start a war.

"The Gonmog Sector is unexplored space," said Councillor Gorkon, a former general who remained the leanest and strongest warrior on the council. Sturka knew that Gorkon could easily defeat him in mortal combat, which is why he had cultivated the former battle-fleet commander as an ally, ever since the day Gorkon had first hinted at his political ambitions. "There are countless unknown threats that could have destroyed the Federation ship," Gorkon continued.

Torr lost his patience. "What difference does it make who destroyed their ship? We should strike before they regroup."

Gorkon turned his forceful gaze against Torr. "Until we know who destroyed the *Bombay,* we won't know whether attacking Vanguard will pit us against one foe or two."

"Facing two foes would only add to our glory," Torr said.

"Only if we win, you ignorant young *jeghta'pu*."

"We have underestimated the Federation in the past," Sturka said. "Not again. Encourage our warriors to boast, it will keep their spirits up. But in here, we face the facts. They have moved many ships and people into the Gonmog Sector—or the 'Taurus Reach,' as they call it. . . . Why?"

"It's obvious," said Councillor Indizar. Slimmer and more feminine-looking than Veselka, she had ascended to the High Council because of her background in covert intelligence. "They fear we will expand our conquests to the Tholian border, leaving them surrounded and unable to grow."

Every councillor nodded in silent agreement—all but one, a heavyset man lurking in the back of the group, half in shadow. Sturka pointed to him. "You have another opinion, Duras?"

Councillor Duras walked forward, stepping into the broad circle of harsh overhead light in front of the chancellor's throne. An acrid, musky odor clung to him like a bad reputation. "The Federation would not risk war on two fronts merely for the possibility of future expansion. A commitment this large can mean only one thing: There is something in the Gonmog Sector that they want. . . . We should learn what it is."

Sturka stroked his bearded chin briefly as he considered Duras's suggestion. "You might be right." He looked up and scanned the faces of the gathered councillors. "It is likely that the Tholians destroyed the Starfleet ship. If so, I look forward to one day facing them in battle. But if other powers are in play in the Gonmog Sector, we must know who they are before our ships cross the border.

"Duras, your suspicion that the Federation has a motive besides expansion . . . interests me. Work with Indizar's people in Imperial Intelligence. If you can show me a plausible alternative motive for the Federation's efforts . . . we'll adjust our strategy and tactics accordingly."

Three successive strikes of Sturka's metal-tipped staff on the stone tile beside his throne signaled that this meeting of the High Council was adjourned. The councillors filed out in a few mumbling clusters, grouped into three rival factions. Keeping them plotting against one another was hard work for Sturka, but it was better than having them plotting against him. Politics was a cutthroat business on any planet, but on Qo'noS the term was always used literally.

Walking quickly back to his chambers, Sturka noticed Gorkon fall into step behind him and his retinue of imperial guards. Sturka nodded to his chief defender, Tegor, to let Gorkon breach the defensive circle. Gorkon slipped inside the perimeter of guards and remained a respectful half-pace behind Sturka. "You know why he wants to investigate the Gonmog Sector," he said. Sturka did not need to ask who Gorkon spoke of. The ex-general's long-festering distrust of Duras made it abundantly clear.

"Of course I do," Sturka said, turning the corner. Outside the narrow slices of window on their right, the sunset washed the First City in soothing crimson hues. "He thinks he'll find something to make himself rich or powerful. Something that can make him chancellor."

"That will be a cold day in *Gre'thor,* my lord."

Sturka imagined his *d'k tahg* sunk deep in Duras's throat. He smiled. "Yes, Gorkon. It certainly will."

13

"Your actions led to the loss of a starship and the deaths of hundreds of Starfleet personnel, Mr. Quinn." T'Prynn's dark and icy declaration burned brightly in Quinn's memory. The burden of his guilt was staggering. *Hundreds of lives,* he told himself. *My fault.* To his own disgust, the only thing he could think of to do about it was order another drink.

He was on his fourth or fifth drink of the evening. In his experience, a well-told series of half-truths, omissions, and exaggerations could postpone most bar tabs for about an hour. Then his excuses for delaying payment would stretch too thin to be credible, and it would be time for him to leave. Somewhere around sixty-five minutes or four drinks into his visits, whichever came first, most barkeeps began to suspect that his tab was going to linger much longer than he himself would. To save everyone the embarrassment and effort of eighty-sixing him, he made a habit of evicting himself before his welcomes had to be officially withdrawn.

Right now his dilemma was that he was uncertain how many drinks he had downed, and his vision was too fisheyed to actually discern the time on his chrono. *Just play it safe,* he coached himself. *Try to sit still. If you don't fall off the stool, they have no reason to throw you out.* The hard part, he knew, would be nursing his drink. Slowing his intake wasn't difficult, but he was unaccustomed to small sips and was more likely to dribble the beverage down his shirt this way.

He had almost concocted a way to ask the bartender for a straw without making himself look stupid when a guest sat down.

Quinn's eyes lazily slid to his left to assess the man. The new guy was human, young, thin, and appallingly handsome in the Federation's currently most-favored, clean-cut way. His clothes were casual but looked and smelled fresh from the laundry. He smiled at Quinn and made a courteous tilt of his head. "Good morning," he said with a mild Scottish accent.

"Maybe it is," Quinn slurred, then he ripped out a baritone belch that tasted of bile and stank of tequila. "Maybe it ain't."

The guy gestured toward the rows of liquor bottles lined up against the wall behind the counter. "Care for a drink, friend?"

Swaying vertiginously on his stool, Quinn shot a glare at the man with the one eye he was able to focus. "My pappy always told me, never trust a stranger who calls you 'friend,' especially if he offers to buy you a drink."

"Did your old man also tell you not to take the drink?"

Quinn held up his glass and called over the bartender. "Another." Jabbing a thumb at the Scotsman, he added, "On him." The visitor nodded his consent, and the bartender began pouring another double shot of tequila. Quinn lolled his head back toward his enabler. "I still don't trust you."

Thrusting out his hand, the guy said, "Tim Pennington."

Seconds passed while Quinn stared at Pennington's hand. Grudgingly, he reached out and shook it. The younger man's hand was smooth and warm, which reminded Quinn that his own hands were not only callused but also clammy from holding condensation-coated cocktail glasses. Fighting back the urge to hiccup, he replied, "Cervantes Quinn."

"A pleasure," Pennington said, then waved down the bartender. "Coffee, please." Noticing the stink-eye Quinn was aiming at him, Pennington amended his order. "Make it Irish."

"You're not quite uptight enough to be Starfleet," Quinn said, studying him. "But you're a bit too scrubbed to be one of Ganz's people."

"Right on the first count," Pennington said. "Though I don't know anyone named Ganz, so you've got me there."

Quinn pounded back what was left of the drink he'd been nursing as the bartender put down the new, free drink from Pennington. Euphoric, soothing warmth spread through his body, starting with every place directly touched by his drink. He sucked in air through numb gums and a dry throat, then mumbled through booze-infused breath, "This guy's either an idiot or the worst liar alive."

Pennington leaned closer, looking aggrieved. "Excuse me?"

"Oh, hell—did I just talk out loud again? I gotta stop doing that." The room's hard edges were beginning to soften, so Quinn took a healthy sip of his new drink.

"Look, I don't know who you think I am—" Pennington paused as the bartender set down his Irish coffee. "But I assure you, I'm not looking to rip you off or jam you up."

He picked up the cup and took a sip. The young man's face obviously wanted to pucker into a knot, but he fought it admirably. Quinn had to respect the effort.

"What's your game, then? You ain't buying me drinks for my personality. Sharp-looking guy like you must be able to rent better friends than me."

"I won't lie to you," Pennington said, then he leaned forward to speak in a more confidential tone. "I'm not really looking to be best buds. Truth be told, I think it's better if most people don't figure on us knowing each other at all."

Quinn glanced down and saw the wedding ring on the guy's left hand, and figured this was all getting a bit too weird. "Hey, pal, I don't mess with married people, on either side, get me? I mean, I'm flattered, really—"

"No no no," Pennington cut in, waving his hands in small frantic circles. "I'm not . . . I mean I don't—that's not what I'm talking about." Collecting himself, he continued, "I'm just looking for information. *Confidential* information."

Numerous possibilities immediately suggested themselves to Quinn. Pennington might be a corporate scout, looking to cut in on Ganz's business. That would give Quinn another buyer, enabling him to negotiate for better prices. Or the young man might be some kind of spy, looking for access or a set of eyes. *Either way, he smells like money.* "What kind of information?"

"Comings and goings," Pennington said with a small shrug. "Unusual details. In particular, any solid leads on things like the loss of the *Bombay*."

Suddenly, the smell that was coming off Pennington

wasn't money but something far less appealing. "How much can you pay?"

"Not much," Pennington said. "This is more about sticking up for the truth."

"Truth can be expensive."

"Look, I'm only a journalist for FNS, but maybe we can—"

"A reporter?" Quinn plastered a dopey grin on his face and slapped his left hand down on Pennington's shoulder. "Hell, son, why didn't you just say so up front? You didn't need to work this hard."

Pennington sighed with relief. "I'm glad to hear—"

Quinn's right uppercut caught the squeaky-clean reporter solidly under his square jaw and lifted his lean, well-toned body a few inches off his barstool. The young man staggered two steps backward, and Quinn lunged forward and finished him with a sloppy but adrenaline-fueled right cross to the side of the head. Pennington collapsed on the floor in a well-dressed and still mostly symmetrical heap.

Weaving like tall grass in a shifting wind, Quinn picked up his drink from the bar, took one step toward the door, and paused above the supine, barely conscious Pennington. "Thanks for the drink. . . . I still don't trust you."

Lurching out the door, Quinn knew he was probably going to feel horribly guilty about this when sobriety returned to him. With that in mind, he set his sights on finding another bar.

Pennington sat on a biobed in the infirmary and massaged his aching jaw, grateful that the damage to his teeth had been limited to a small chip in the enamel of a molar

and a corner broken off one of his upper front incisors—
both easily fixed. He hadn't really expected Quinn to
buddy up to him, or to tell him much of value. But the man
had been stinking drunk, and there had been a slim chance
that the motto *in vino veritas* might once again have proved
its wisdom. *The fact that it didn't work doesn't make it a
bad plan,* Pennington consoled himself.

He looked up from his reflection in the chair's swiveling
mirror and said to Dr. Thelex, the chief of dentistry, "Still
hurts. What can you give me for this?"

"Advice," the gruff Andorian said, his pale eyes peeking
over his narrow, octagonal-frame glasses. "Stay out of bar
fights."

"Anything stronger?"

Dr. Thelex rotated the mirror aside. "You're a pathetic
weakling who should stay out of bar fights."

Great, a dentist with a sense of humor. Pennington's
headache pounded mercilessly as he pushed himself out of
the chair and back on to his feet. "Thanks, Doc."

"All part of the service."

Back to it, then. Pennington walked quickly out of the
dentist's office. He was eager to be out of the medical center entirely. Hospitals were too visceral for Pennington.
Blood and disease, suffering and tragedy . . . the only
places closer to these gruesome facts of mortality were bat-
tlefields, and he made a point of avoiding those, as well.
Some FNS reporters spent their entire careers as war corre-
spondents, warping from one strife-riven world to another,
seeking to put a rational voice on the most irrational, primal form of waste known in the universe. Covering politics
wasn't much better, in Pennington's opinion, but he would

prefer a war of words over a war of attrition any day. History, however, was replete with evidence that the one almost inevitably led to the other, if you waited long enough.

He slipped out the door into the corridor and hurried toward the turbolift. Just after he pressed the call button, a hand slapped down on his shoulder. More than a flinch, he recoiled with frightened surprise.

Behind him, Xiong quickly pulled back his hand and raised both arms to show he meant no harm. Pennington released a lungful of breath that had been trapped by his panic. "Sorry," Xiong said. "Didn't mean to spook you."

"It's okay, Ming. I got decked an hour ago, and I'm a little jumpy."

Xiong lowered his hands. "Are you all right?"

"Yeah, mate, I'm fine. Doc Thelex patched me up, right as rain." The turbolift door opened, revealing an empty car. Pennington stepped inside, and Xiong followed him. "What's got you down here, then?" The doors slid closed. Pennington grabbed the throttle and gave it a twist. "Park level."

Light flashed sideways through narrow vertical panels as the car shot along horizontally toward a free vertical shaft.

"Came looking for you," Xiong said. "Confidentially."

"Always." Three months earlier, after Pennington had begun reporting about events on Vanguard, Xiong had approached him to talk about some off-the-record information. The headstrong A&A officer apparently felt unfairly muzzled with regard to his work in the Taurus Reach, and was looking for a way to force some things into the open. So far his leads had been small and not particularly juicy, but Xiong was privy to certain high-level operations on the station, and he spent a lot of time away on the starships assigned to Vanguard, so there was no telling what he might know.

"I read your piece about the deaths on the *Enterprise*," Xiong said. "I thought you might want to know I've been given orders to ship out with her crew."

"On the salvage mission?" Xiong nodded. The turbolift shifted to a vertical drop as Pennington continued. "When?"

"A few hours from now. They told me to bring a phaser."

"Why? Is there still a problem on the ship?"

Rolling his eyes, Xiong said, "No. For the landing party."

"So the *Bombay* was lost in orbit of a planet?" Again, Xiong nodded but didn't say anything. Pennington had heard T'Prynn say the *Bombay* was lost at Ravanar, but he needed a second source to confirm that fact before he could use it. "Which one?"

"I can't tell you that. Not yet, anyway."

Damn. He pondered mentioning Ravanar and seeing if Xiong would be willing to confirm it, but the A&A officer's cagey behavior felt like a warning not to dig too deeply. Going with his instincts, Pennington moved on. "Do you think the *Bombay* was attacked?"

"I don't know," Xiong said. "And I don't care to guess."

"Fair enough." Watching the level numbers tick by, Pennington noted that their privacy would soon be at an end. *Time for one more question.* "Why is Reyes sending *you?*"

"That's classified," Xiong said. "Look, do you want me to ask around about the Mitchell-Dehner thing while I'm aboard the *Enterprise*? Some of the officers might tell me things they won't tell you."

"Sure, I'd appreciate that," Pennington said. "But I can't use anything you tell me until it's confirmed by another firsthand source. If you find anything really big, remember that I need a reliable source or hard evidence before I can publish."

"I know," Xiong said. The turbolift slowed, then stopped. A hydraulic hiss preceded the opening of the doors, which let out on a wide promenade in the torus-shaped residential tower that circled the core and faced out at the terrestrial enclosure. The two men stepped out of the turbolift. As they walked across the grass and basked in the synthetic solar warmth, Xiong said, "Could you do me a favor while I'm gone?"

Here we go again. Unlike most confidential sources, Xiong had no use for money, and to Pennington's great relief he didn't seem to have any political or personal vendettas to settle. For all the information he provided, Xiong only ever asked for information in return—and always about the same subject.

Pennington grinned. "What do you want to know about her this time?"

"I don't care, anything. Did she have any pets growing up? Where did she go to school? Does she have a favorite flower?"

"Bloody hell," Pennington said. "What am I doing, Ming? Writing her biography?"

"Okay, just the flowers. Find out her favorite flower."

"I'll see what I can do." He began to veer away from Xiong, toward the outdoor café. "This bloody crush of yours had best be worth it, mate, that's all I'm saying."

"It will be," Xiong said, and then he about-faced and headed back toward the turbolift.

Shaking his head, Pennington pulled his data recorder from his belt and jotted another item on his already lengthy to-do list: Anna Sandesjo, favorite flower. He eyed the note. *Poor Ming. Knowing that woman, her favorite flower is poison ivy.*

Xiong made it down the gangway and through the hatch just before the chief petty officer sealed it and signaled all-secure to his deck officer. Passing through the airlock, the A&A officer admired how meticulously the ship was maintained, from its pristine decks to its spotless pressure-hatch mechanisms. *You'd never guess this ship had already seen twenty years of service.*

Adding to the impression of newness were the rich, brightly hued uniforms the *Enterprise* crew had just been issued by Vanguard's quartermaster. Retired now were the muted tones and ribbed turtlenecks of the previous generation of duty apparel; in its place were intense colors, of which the red was the boldest.

The airlock hatch was sealed behind Xiong before he'd made it two steps into the corridor. A Vulcan waited patiently beside the airlock door, standing in classic at-ease posture. "Lieutenant Xiong," he said in a crisp baritone. "Welcome aboard the *Enterprise*. I am Lieutenant Commander Spock, first officer."

"Thank you, sir." Observing the Vulcan's uniform, Xiong endured a moment of cognitive dissonance. "Permission to speak freely, sir?"

"Granted."

Nodding at Spock's bright blue shirt, he said, "I think you might have been issued the wrong color jersey, sir."

"I assure you, Lieutenant, my uniform is correct." Xiong wanted to argue that gold was the preferred color for command officers, but he had already learned better than to argue matters of fact with Vulcans. Perhaps sensing Xiong's unspoken rebuttal, Spock added, "I am also the ship's science officer. . . . I was offered my choice of uniform."

"Interesting choice," Xiong said.

"Perhaps." Spock half-turned while keeping eye contact with Xiong. "Please follow me." With that, he walked away, and Xiong had to step lively to keep pace with the taller man's stride.

"Where are we going, sir?"

"The captain has asked to speak with you."

Figuring that it was probably best not to pester the first officer with too many questions, Xiong kept quiet as he followed him through the corridors. Engineers and mechanics were in and out of wall panels and vestibules, all of them extremely busy but moving at a calm pace and speaking in level tones. The mood aboard the *Enterprise* reminded Xiong of the tenor of life aboard the *Endeavour*, another *Constitution*-class starship; it was efficient, professional, and driven by a quiet pride of purpose.

The turbolift ride to the bridge took longer than Xiong expected. It stopped at nearly every deck. Jumpsuited enlisted technicians got on and off, their hands full of tools and spare parts; male and female officers, all of them looking Starfleet-recruitment-brochure perfect, rode the turbolift while standing ramrod straight. If for nothing else,

Xiong had to admire this crew for its dignity and discipline.

When the doors opened onto the bridge, a small charge of excitement made Xiong draw a short breath. Softly warbling computer tones mingled with the low buzz of overhead power relays. The main viewer showed the core of the station looming large, and the bridge crew was preparing for departure.

"All hatches secure, Captain," said the helmsman. "All systems ready."

"Very good, Mr. Leslie," Kirk said. Turning his chair toward Spock and Xiong, he added, "Status, Mr. Spock?"

"All personnel accounted for, Captain," Spock said. "Essential repairs complete. Ready for service."

"Well done. Lieutenant Uhura, hail Vanguard Control."

"Aye, sir," said the elegant, attractive woman at the communications console. She pressed a few switches, then continued, "I have Vanguard Control on channel one."

"On speaker," Kirk said. Uhura pressed a button then nodded to Kirk, indicating that the frequency was open. "Vanguard, this is *Enterprise,* requesting permission to depart."

"Permission granted, Enterprise. *Standing by to clear moorings on your mark."*

"Helm," Kirk said, "take us out."

"Aye, sir," Leslie said. He patched in his console to the comm channel. "Vanguard, clear moorings in four. Three. Two. One. Mark." Even through several layers of deck plating and dozens of rows of bulkheads, Xiong heard the heavy clunks of Vanguard's mooring clamps releasing the *Enterprise.* "Moorings clear," Leslie said. "Vanguard Control, *Enterprise* is ready to depart spacedock."

"Confirmed, Enterprise," came the well-practiced reply. *"Opening bay doors now. Stand by."*

On the main viewer, the core of the station gradually began to look smaller, as the *Enterprise* reversed away from it, toward the slowly parting spacedock doors.

Kirk swiveled his squarish chair toward Xiong, who had followed Spock down into the lower circle of the bridge. "Mr. Xiong. Welcome aboard."

"Thank you, Captain."

"You're welcome. Now that we've got that out of the way, would you mind telling me what you're doing here?"

"Just following orders, sir."

It was obvious that Kirk didn't care for that answer. "Permit me to rephrase, Lieutenant: Why did Commodore Reyes insist that I take you on our search-and-salvage to Ravanar?"

Xiong sensed that the bridge crew were all eavesdropping intently on his conversation with Kirk. Tuning out distractions, he reminded himself that the key was never to lie, but simply to omit all but the most basic of facts. "I helped set up the outpost on Ravanar, Captain."

"The report from Lieutenant Commander T'Prynn indicated that the prospecting camp was a cover for a listening post."

"Yes, sir."

"But you're an A&A officer."

"I've always considered that designation to be sort of a misnomer, sir. I really deal in xenoanthropology and—"

"My point," Kirk cut in, "is that an A&A officer isn't normally dispatched to set up listening stations."

"That's true, sir."

Kirk's frustration began to seep through the polite ve-
neer of his officer's training. "I know it's *true,* Lieutenant.
What I want to know is why you, an A&A officer, were assigned to help set up the post at Ravanar, and why I'm taking you back there."

"I was available," Xiong said. "And I'm good with
tools."

The voice of Vanguard Control squawked from the overhead speaker. "Enterprise, *you are passing through spacedock doors. Stand by to clear spacedock in twenty seconds.*"

"Acknowledged, Vanguard," Leslie said.

Jabbing one of his seat-arm controls with his thumb,
Kirk said, "Bridge to engineering. Ready for full impulse,
Scotty?"

"*Aye, Captain,*" said a man with a heavy Scottish
brogue. "*Standing by. Just give the word.*"

"Good work," Kirk said. "Bridge out." He closed the
channel and looked back at Xiong. "I don't like secrets on
my ship, Mr. Xiong. My orders are to get you to Ravanar
and send a landing party with you to the surface, and that's
what I'll do. But I'm not going to place my ship or my crew
at risk without a good reason, and if you can't or won't give
me one, their safety comes first. Do I make myself clear?"

"Perfectly, Captain."

"*Enterprise, you have cleared spacedock. Releasing
helm control back to you.*" The gentle curve of Vanguard's
massive top section filled the main viewer past its edges.

"*Enterprise* confirms helm control," Leslie said. "Setting course one-one-nine mark two-six."

"*Confirmed,* Enterprise. *The lane is clear and you are
free to navigate. Safe travels. Vanguard out.*"

"Helm," Kirk said. "All ahead, full impulse. Maximum warp as soon as we clear the shipping lanes."

"Aye, sir," Leslie said, and then he submerged into his duties.

Kirk pulled himself away from running his ship long enough to glance at Xiong and say, "Dismissed."

Walking up the stairs to the turbolift, Xiong was intercepted by Spock, who gave him the boilerplate instructions for getting a berthing assignment from the quartermaster and an ETA of seventy-seven hours to Ravanar. Stepping into the turbolift, he indulged in a moment of cynical optimism. *Seventy-seven hours. . . . If I don't get stuck rooming with another Tellarite, maybe I'll actually get some sleep this time.*

"This board of inquiry is now convened," Desai said, the echo of three sharp double tones from her judge's bell silencing the susurrus of whispers.

She presided from the head of a small table in the middle of a small and sparsely appointed wardroom. A handful of department heads were in attendance, including T'Prynn, who sat alone at the far end of the table. Reyes sat with his JAG defense counsel on Desai's left.

"Lieutenant Moyer," Desai continued, "are you ready to proceed with depositions?"

Holly Moyer, a youthful attorney whom Desai had recruited, represented the JAG Corps. "I am, Captain."

Turning to the opposing counsel, Desai said, "Commander Liverakos, I see you've submitted no requests for deposition interviews. Are you ready to proceed?"

The short, slightly built man frowned. Despite his overall boyish mien, his salt-and-pepper goatee gave him a certain gravitas. "Captain, we move for a postponement of this inquiry, pending the conclusion of the *Enterprise*'s on-site investigation. Any testimony collected prior to that will be merely speculation and hearsay."

"Commander, I've already instructed Lieutenant Moyer to restrict her questions to those establishing the status of the *Starship Bombay* prior to its final departure from this station. As for the *Enterprise*'s investigation . . ." Desai tossed an ephemeral, scathing glance at Reyes. "I was not apprised that such an investigation was under way."

"The *Enterprise* left spacedock forty-two minutes ago," Liverakos said, "en route to the last known location of the *Starship Bombay.*"

"So noted," Desai said. "Regardless, I will be asking Lieutenant Moyer to begin her interviews as soon as possible, in order to complete our review of the *Bombay*'s recent service history. I suspect that we'll have a lot of data to analyze once the *Enterprise* returns and Captain Kirk files his report."

"With all due respect to this board, Captain," Liverakos said, "the recent service history of the *Bombay,* including the logs of her senior officers, are all available by subpoena from the Vanguard operations center. There's no need to conduct face-to-face interviews."

"Your 'respect' is touching, Commander, but I remain the arbiter of whether individual testimony is necessary to a full and proper investigation of this case."

Liverakos opened his satchel and removed a sheaf of paper. Holding it up, he said, "May we confer in private?"

Desai sighed, then got up and motioned to Moyer and

Liverakos to follow her away from the table. The two attorneys joined her in the corner and leaned close to converse sotto voce. Liverakos handed her his stack of paper. "Under Code Five, Section Twelve, Article Four-thirteen of the SCJ, I move for a summary termination of these proceedings."

Moyer stared at him, astonished. "Four-thirteen? Are you kidding? It's the basis for the inquiry."

"It also sets the criteria for determining whether such an inquiry can or should be convened," he said, then listed the actionable causes specified by the *Starfleet Code of Justice:* "Negligence, incompetence, sabotage, and dereliction of duty. You don't have evidence for any one of them."

"Hence we *inquire,* Mr. Liverakos," Desai said. "Which should explain why this is an *inquiry* and not a court-martial."

"It's neither, Captain." His tone remained just civil enough to skirt a contempt charge without stepping over the line. "It's a fishing expedition, and you're using the looser standards of an inquiry to see if you can build a case for a court-martial. If you were conducting a criminal investigation, your witnesses could invoke their rights of silence, counsel, and freedom from self-incrimination. Instead, you're end-running all those protections by holding an 'inquiry' and compelling these people to testify under oath, with little recourse to their rights under the SCJ or the Federation Charter." Handing a copy of his motion to Moyer, he concluded, "In my opinion this inquiry is a civil-liberties violation, and I, for one, consider it a disgrace."

I knew there was a reason I liked this guy, Desai mused as she perused his briefing. It was exactly what she had needed him to do. Her superiors had demanded she hold this inquiry, and it was her duty to carry it out in good faith. However, it was no mistake that she had assigned her best, most aggressive defense attorney to represent Reyes and the crew of Starbase 47. Moyer was a quick-minded, efficient prosecutor, and Desai had needed someone just as talented and driven to oppose her. Liverakos had proved her faith to be well justified.

"A compelling argument, Mr. Liverakos. Let's go back." The trio returned to the table. Desai set down the motion for termination and recomposed her demeanor to address the other officers. "This inquiry is in recess pending review of defense counsel's motion. I'll hear Lieutenant Moyer's rebuttal in my office tomorrow at 1400 hours. Adjourned." She punctuated her declaration with a quick tap of her bell.

The room emptied quickly. Desai gathered her papers into a slim hard-shell case. Moyer and Liverakos paused on their way out to trade quips under their breath. Reyes, Desai noticed, stepped aside with T'Prynn and shared a hushed conversation with her as they exited. Suspicion nagged at Desai's thoughts: Why was the commodore so quick to confer with his intelligence officer? And why had T'Prynn taken such a keen interest in what was likely to be a mundane proceeding?

Desai dismissed both queries. The answer, she decided, was probably quite simple: T'Prynn had needed to make a time-sensitive report to Reyes and so had waited to speak with him as soon as he was free of the protocols of the inquiry. *Occam's razor,* Desai reminded herself. *The simplest answer is usually the best one.* Then her inner voice of experience retorted, *Not for a lawyer, it isn't.*

Walking alone back to her office, she couldn't shake the intuitive hunch that T'Prynn's presence in the wardroom had not been coincidental. There was no empirical evidence to suggest that she had any vested interest in the inquiry's outcome, but something about the quiet intensity of the Vulcan woman's attention to every detail had left a subtle but uneasy impression on Desai. *She wasn't there to see Reyes. She was there to observe the depositions, and not out of idle curiosity.*

As a lawyer, Desai had learned to trust the law, protocol, procedure, and precedents. But before she was a lawyer she had been a detective with the JAG Corps's Criminal Investigation Division, and before that she had started her Starfleet career as a security officer. In the wardroom, Liverakos had spoken dismissively of "mere speculation," but hunches were all about speculation, and being a detective had taught Desai that hunches sometimes took a case farther than evidence.

She had a hunch that T'Prynn—quiet, pretty, "isn't she a great pianist" T'Prynn—was connected to the loss of the *Bombay.*

Believing it was easy. Proving it would be hard.

The best that Desai could hope for was that playing her hunch would do more good than harm. In her experience, the law was a blunt and clumsy instrument with which to seek the truth.

Unfortunately, it was the only one she had.

It would have to do, for now.

Being dragged by my hair across white-hot coals.
Stepping off the turbolift, T'Prynn reflected on her

decades-old training in the disciplines of logic and repeated to herself that pain was only a matter of perception. It could be mastered, it could be channeled, and, even when it could not be eradicated, it could at least be rendered impotent.

A blade piercing my lung.

She knew that her pain was psychosomatic, nothing more than a figment of her imagination. The old Vulcan masters had taught her that there can be no pain if one's mind does not acknowledge it. If one denied it expression, they said, if one could attune oneself to the body's true signals, even the most horrific forms of physical suffering could be quelled from within.

Fingernails gouging a path across my cheek.

Pride and instinct made her hide her agony. She didn't speak of it. Comrades and acquaintances never saw anything amiss, no momentary flickers of discomfort in her eyes, no fleeting twinges or tics to betray her inner torments. Masking distress, whether emotional or physical, was one of the first lessons Vulcan children were taught on their long journey toward mastering the *Kolinahr*—a goal few achieved.

The flashing slice of a lirpa *across my abdomen.*

One step followed another, bringing her at last to the entrance of docking bay ninety-two. The door was locked. She entered her security bypass code, and its two halves parted with a thin pneumatic hiss.

Parked in the middle of the small but austere hangar was Cervantes Quinn's battered old Mancharan starhopper, the *Rocinante*. Quinn was hunched under an open panel in the craft's nose section. Assorted loose parts and tools were scattered like flotsam at his feet. Both his hands were plunged deep inside the ship's inner workings and tinkering loudly with something. T'Prynn's sensitive hearing discerned his every muttered expletive with perfect clarity.

The sharp clacks of her boots on the gunmetal-gray deck echoed loudly in the confined, bare-walled space. Ceasing his labors, Quinn pulled his head out of his ship and looked at T'Prynn, who stalked toward him. "Don't you knock, lady?"

"You said you had information."

"I said I needed to talk to you," Quinn said. He stepped out from beneath his ship and wiped off his hands with a towel looped around his belt. "You got an information leak."

Skull-cracking pressure ballooning behind my eyes.

"Explain," she said, in a tone harsher than what she had intended. When the pain flared, her patience faded and anger proved its power to her, over and over again.

"A reporter," Quinn said. "Name of Pennington. Cornered me in Tom Walker's place, asking about the *Bombay.*"

The splintering break of a knuckle bent backward.

"What did you tell him?"

"Nothing, I left him pickin' up his teeth off the floor."

Emerald hues of panic as his hands grip my throat.

"How much did he seem to know?"

"Hard to say." Quinn walked toward his ship's gangway, kicking a path through his tools, which clanged across the deck. "He didn't ask anything specific."

"I see." That news concerned T'Prynn. A reporter who had no questions, only vague inquiries, usually was waiting for someone to let slip something that confirmed leads already in hand. If Pennington knew as much as she suspected he did, his intrusion into the matter could undo years of careful preparation and jeopardize thousands of lives. "Thank you for bringing this to my attention," she said. "Avoid contact with him in the future."

"Sure," Quinn said, clomping haphazardly up the ramp. "Will do. You got it." He looked disoriented and unstable.

"Do you require medical assistance, Mr. Quinn?"

"Nah," he half-growled. "Just a bucket and some shut-eye."

Not wanting to visualize the rest of Quinn's evening, T'Prynn let herself out and walked back to the turbolift. She turned the throttle grip. "Level twenty-seven, section six."

The coppery tang of my own blood pooling in my mouth.

Fifty-three years had not dimmed the memories. They haunted her, amplified each year by the injustice of being deprived of the purgative release of *Pon farr.* Part of her psyche remained trapped in the final moments of that long-ago death struggle, the moment of her emancipation, the beginning of her bondage to a personal demon more vivid than the pale schemes of the living who surrounded her daily.

Sten's voice, demanding my surrender to his passions.

Her face was a portrait of stoic calm for the handful of engineering technicians who rode with her to level twenty-nine, and for the communications officer who remained on the turbolift after T'Prynn stepped out. Crewmates and strangers passed by her in the corridors, taking no notice of her unhurried pace or her Zen-like countenance. She arrived at her quarters, let the door close behind her, and walked to the center of the room. There, she remained still and allowed her agony to gnaw at her from within. Then she plumbed the crypt of her memory and trained her mind on the one moment that would silence the darker fires of her nature, even if only briefly.

The crack of Sten's neck snapping sideways in my grasp.

For a few moments the primitive part of her *katra* savored that moment. Her conscious mind screamed out with self-loathing—not for having taken Sten's life, but because, even now, decades later, that one instant of manifest rage, sanctified by the *Koon-ut-kal-if-fee*, still gave her a tiny measure of joy. *It was his own fault,* she consoled herself. *He should have let me go when I asked to be released.*

She had never loved Sten. On Vulcan, teaching children to love was considered grossly improper, but every child was taught how to wield the *lirpa* and the *ahn-woon*, and some were instructed in the dancelike martial art of *V'Shan.*

There were many such dichotomies of her upbringing that T'Prynn had never been able to reconcile to her own satisfaction: She had been indoctrinated with pacifism but taught to kill. Her elders had extolled the right of each individual to make their own choices, but they also had expected her to mate with a man who was all but a stranger to her. From the earliest days of her childhood she had sensed that the emotions raging deep inside her were enormously powerful and vital to understanding the true nature of her existence as a Vulcan, yet her people's entire society seemed predicated on the philosophy of suppressing its most profound inner beauties because it feared the ugliness that resided beside them.

All her doubts notwithstanding, T'Prynn had learned

and obeyed, absorbing the tutelage of the Adepts and the stern reprimands of her parents, until she, too, learned to live her life in a state of self-inflicted emotional atrophy.

Then she had seen the lust in Sten's eyes, felt his need to possess her, to smother her, to control her. It was a crude and sickening sensation, and she had obeyed the impulse of her heart. She told Sten to choose another mate and let her go.

Enslaved by his own ardor, he had refused to abandon his claim on T'Prynn. His final demand, before she snapped his fourth vertebra, had been "Submit."

It was a demand now repeated endlessly, in her waking thoughts and in her dreams, by his vengeful *katra*, which he had projected into her undefended mind—and which now lingered in her subconscious, torturing her without mercy, flooding her thoughts with its memories of wounds she inflicted so that they could mingle with the hurts Sten had bestowed upon her.

Submit!

After more than five decades of unrelenting mental strife, T'Prynn's answer remained unchanged.

Never.

14

Kirk sat at the desk in his quarters and reviewed Spock's report of long-range sensor data from the Ravanar system. So far, the information was not promising. There were indications of recent high-energy discharges, which were consistent with the current hypothesis that the *Bombay* had been destroyed. Reinforcing that speculation was the complete absence of signal traffic to or from the system, which implied that there was no one left alive, either in lifeboats or on the planet.

There's always a chance, he reminded himself. *They might be alive but without communications. Until we know otherwise, this remains a rescue mission.*

His door signal buzzed. For a moment he considered making whoever was outside wait while he tossed his damp towel back into his shower nook and swapped his loose civilian shirt for a proper uniform jersey. Then he reconsidered and said, "Come."

The door slid open, and Lieutenant Robert D'Amato stepped inside. "Pardon the interruption, Captain. Is this a bad time?"

"Not at all, Mr. D'Amato. What's on your mind?"

D'Amato took a few moments to choose his words. "I saw that Mr. Spock's roster for the landing party on Ravanar includes Ensign Pawlikowski from earth sciences."

After a brief hesitation, he added, "I also noticed that my name wasn't on the list, sir."

Kirk nodded. "And you feel this was an oversight?"

"I *am* the ship's senior geologist, sir. It should be me."

"You're still on bereavement leave," Kirk said. "For now, Pawlikowski is top of the list for your department."

"Captain, I understand that landing-party assignments are made at Mr. Spock's discretion, but—"

"I selected the landing party, Mr. D'Amato."

Heavy silence followed Kirk's declaration. The thrumming of the *Enterprise*'s engines, straining to maintain maximum warp for an extended run, pulsed through the deck under their feet.

D'Amato seemed to be struggling to restrain a floodtide of temper and grief. "I hereby request permission to return to active duty, and to serve on the landing party at Ravanar."

"Request denied." Kirk walked past D'Amato and tossed his used shower towel into the corner.

"May I ask why, sir?"

"You know why," Kirk said, opening his drawer and removing a clean uniform shirt. "A landing party's no place to work out a personal agenda." He backed off from his reflexive authoritarian mode. "Besides, I think you need to give yourself more time to deal with this. It's been less than three days."

Shaking his head in protest, D'Amato said, "I can be objective, Captain."

"Can you? I'm not so sure."

Pausing to take a calming breath, D'Amato closed his right hand into a fist, which Kirk took as a sign that the man was barely holding himself together. "This isn't about revenge," D'Amato said. "And it's not about some denial fantasy that she's still alive if only I can find her." His jaw trembled as he forced out the words, "I know that she's gone."

"What's it about, then? Proving you're not in pain?"

"No, sir. It's about making this mean something." The shadow of grief darkened D'Amato's face. "I can accept that she died in the line of duty, but not that she died for nothing." Tears of sorrow and anger welled in the corners of his eyes. "Something on that planet was important enough that Oriana and her shipmates were killed for it. I want to know what it was."

Kirk put down his jersey on top of the dresser, then walked slowly back toward D'Amato. "There's nothing wrong with wanting to make sense of tragedy, D'Amato." He placed a hand on the man's shoulder. "But it doesn't always work. I can't promise you that we'll find what you're looking for. Sometimes, the truth is that accidents happen—acts of nature, of random chance, of God, if that's what you want to call it. You want an answer so badly that you might fool yourself into seeing one that's not there."

"No, Captain, I won't." D'Amato straightened his posture, as if he were defying the weight of grief burdening his heart. "I'm a scientist. I have my training, standard protocols, simple rules for reporting only what I can detect, observe, and quantify. You can trust me to do my job, sir . . . to bring you facts, not wish lists. You have my word on that."

The captain considered D'Amato's request. *He is better qualified than Pawlikowski,* Kirk thought. *And the briefing from Xiong suggested we would want an expert in subterranean geology.* Looking back at D'Amato, however, he remained worried about the deep emotional wound the man had just suffered. Letting this man be part of the investigation into whatever events had claimed the life of his wife wasn't against Starfleet regulations, but it felt like a risky decision. *What if I were in his place? Could I put my faith in science? In procedures and protocols and cold, hard facts?* Kirk admitted to himself that he probably couldn't. . . . *But I'm not a scientist.*

"I'll ask Mr. Spock to tell Pawlikowski you'll be taking her place," Kirk said. "Join us in transporter room one tomorrow at seventeen-thirty hours."

With a look of bittersweet gratitude, D'Amato nodded and said, "Thank you, Captain."

"Dismissed." Several minutes after D'Amato had gone, Kirk was still wondering whether he had just made a grievous error in judgment. *I guess I'll find out tomorrow on Ravanar,* he decided, then changed into his uniform shirt and left for the bridge.

With a bucket of ice-cold water and a spin of the hammock, Zett Nilric rousted Cervantes Quinn from a drunken stupor aboard the *Rocinante.* The subsequent, heated exchange of exceedingly vulgar salutations led to Quinn's quick beating by Morikmol, followed by a blurry drag through the corridors of the station. When the haze of Quinn's minor battering began to abate, he blinked and realized that once again he was propped up inside Ganz's dark sanctum on the *Omari-Ekon,* facing the big green Orion himself.

"I have a job for you," Ganz said, reclined on his mountain of rainbow-hued giant pillows.

Acid churned, hot and sour, from Quinn's stomach into the back of his throat. He couldn't tell if the bile was the product of anxiety or of his hangover. With his hoarse croak of a voice, he said, "What kind of job?"

"A delivery," Ganz said. "To the camp on Kessik IV."

"The new dilithium mine?"

Ganz nodded, then surveyed his manicured fingernails. Quinn continued, "What's the cargo?"

"Hardware."

"Hardware?" Quinn had a bad feeling about this. "Are we talking dynospanners, or the kind that'll have Starfleet going up my tailpipe with a tricorder?"

"The kind that repays the debt you owe me," Ganz said.

It's contraband, huh? Whatever. "Where's the pickup?"

Zett cut in, "We're loading your ship now."

"Whoa," Quinn said. "I'm going out hot?"

Ganz leaned forward. "You have a problem with that?"

Quinn understood his situation clearly now: It was a setup. *If I refuse it, he blasts me; if I take the job, I end up in jail.* He sighed. *It ain't subtle, but I guess that's the point.* "No," he said. "No problem."

"Good," Ganz said. "The payment will be raw dilithium crystals, six kilos. Make sure they're pure."

"Right," Quinn said, even though he didn't expect to get past his preflight check with a hold full of illegal cargo. "How do I contact the buyer?"

"Zett'll fill in the blanks before you leave. Which would be right about—"

"Now," Quinn said, "got it. See ya in a few days." *If you visit me in the brig, you green bastard.*

Grateful that he was walking out of Ganz's place this time instead of being dumped out like garbage, Quinn descended the curving stairs two steps at a time and strode across the smoky gaming floor. He shouldered past dense knots of people who crowded around the center stage to ogle the striptease show. As soon as he left the compartment, he sniffed and groaned to realize that the cloying perfume of debauchery clung to his rumpled clothes like a chigger on a bare leg.

He grew angrier by the minute. *If he was gonna kill me, he could have at least been quick about it.* That wasn't how Ganz did business, though. The Orion merchant-prince had a knack for letting others do his dirty work for him.

If Quinn got arrested, he could try to implicate Ganz, but that would lead inevitably to Quinn's "suicide" in the brig. He imagined how some intimidated medic would write up the cause of death: *Subject snapped own neck in fit of depression.* Instead, Quinn would play by the rules, keep his mouth shut, and spend the rest of his natural life in solitary confinement.

Conversely, if Quinn made it to Kessik IV only to be gunned down while delivering a shipment of small arms, Ganz would be light-years away, safely removed from any stain of impropriety. No matter how Quinn looked at the situation, the rules of the game were rigged in Ganz's favor.

In the turbolift, his string of muttered curses bloomed into a shout of frustration. An irrational impulse drove him to kick the wall. Something went *pop* beneath his left kneecap. Hopping on one foot, he fell sideways as the door opened. He landed facedown in front of two young women, who recoiled with disgust, then stepped over him into the turbolift and shared a laugh at his expense as the doors began to close.

Lying on the ground and clutching his knee, Quinn decided—between expletives—that this was shaping up to be one of the worst weeks of his life.

The crawl to the bar seemed mercifully shorter this time.

He was nursing his second double of tequila when he faced facts. *I can't turn down the job. I can't do the job. I can't run.* Circumstances had dealt him a losing hand. Recalling his father's lessons about playing cards for money, he knew what he had to do. *If all the rules work for Ganz, it's time to cheat.*

Swallowing his pride, he made the call.

An hour later, Quinn sat waiting in the meeting place, surrounded by every depressing shade of gray he could have imagined, and a few more to boot. *The brig,* he brooded. *Not my first choice, but I have to admit it's private.*

He had entered through the front door. When the back door opened, he knew it must be T'Prynn. She walked in and was all business. "What is your 'emergency'?"

It confounded him that a woman with a voice so warm could have a heart so cold. "Ganz is setting me up to take a fall."

She arched one eyebrow. "Details."

"His boys are loading my boat with enough guns to buy me twenty years in here."

"So your difficulty is with Vanguard customs?"

"For starters. Knowing Ganz, even if I make the drop, the buyer's got my number."

T'Prynn looked away briefly, thinking. Quinn spent the moment admiring her gentle, innocent-looking profile. *She reminds me of Molly,* he realized. He hadn't seen his third wife since she had tracked him down—on his honeymoon with his fourth wife, Amy—to remind him that their divorce wasn't actually final yet. He shook his head and grinned at the memory of those roof-raising arguments. *It was always something with Molly.*

Turning back in his direction, T'Prynn said, "What is your destination?"

"The dilithium mine on Kessik IV."

She nodded slightly. "Make the delivery."

He blinked. "Maybe I haven't made the situation clear."

"I understand your predicament perfectly. Make the delivery and bring Mr. Ganz his payment." She took a few steps toward the rear door, then paused and looked back. "Our meetings must become far less frequent, Mr. Quinn. Furthermore, in the future they will be set at *my* discretion. Do you understand?"

"Don't call you, you'll call me."

"Precisely. Good night, Mr. Quinn. Safe travels."

She left quickly, without sparing him another word or glance. *Just like Denise,* he reminisced, recalling his first wife with nostalgic fondness. *Yeah, she ditched me with style.*

Swaddled in dark clothes of an exotic alien pedigree, and tucked away in an inconspicuous corner of the enlisted men's club, Tim Pennington sipped slowly at an orange soda.

As usual, he went unnoticed while he listened.

Surreptitiously adjusting the settings on his record-ing device, he aimed it slowly from one table to another, eavesdropping, seeking out tidbits of conversation. Most of what he overheard were run-of-the-mill grumblings—double shifts taken, priority work orders with conflicting needs, broken equipment, and the like. Every now and then, however, he caught something interesting.

"No telling what's even in half those cases," one steve-dore groused to a table full of his comrades. " 'Category-one matériel, handle with care.' That's about all we ever get."

"We loaded one on the *Bombay* last time," another man said.

"I put a ton of C-1s on the *Endeavour* last month," said one woman. "No bills of lading, though."

"There never are," said the first stevedore, and the con-versation veered away once more into generalized com-plaints.

Pennington put away his recorder and slipped out of the bar. He had been hearing this kind of talk ever since he had first arrived on Vanguard. Throughout the lower decks, noncoms and enlisted personnel complained about work orders couched in secrecy, movements of shipping contain-ers whose contents were all but unknown and therefore required the most stringent safety and security precautions, as a safeguard against every imaginable mishap. No one seemed concerned about the insistence on secrecy so much as they were vexed by the labor it added to their daily work schedules.

Riding alone in a turbolift to the cargo levels, he shed his "lurking" disguise, revealing his regular clothes. He tucked the easily compressible alien fabric into his empty satchel and combed his hair briskly with his fingers, shaking out the dry-powder darkening agent he had treated it with. It was a quick change he had practiced for some time, and he now was quite adept at it. Stepping off the turbolift, he orientated himself quickly and walked toward Vanguard's main cargo facility.

Several hatch locks shy of reaching it, he stopped at the security checkpoint. Three red-shirted Starfleet security guards manned this entrance to the cargo warehouse. Each barrel-chested man wore a pistol phaser on his belt. Two stood guard in the corridor, in front of the sealed hatch. The third, ostensibly the one in charge, was inside a phaser-proof booth, monitoring security-camera signals, communications from the station's operations center, and other vital data. All three of them stiffened to alert postures at Pennington's approach.

The guard with the dark crewcut reached for his phaser. "Halt. Identify yourself." His partner, a bald, dark-skinned man, rested his hand on his own weapon.

"Tim Pennington, here to see Chief Langlois."

The one in the booth spoke through an intercom. *"What's your business?"*

"Personal visit," Pennington said. Declaring his profession as a journalist was a surefire way to get himself sent back upstairs in a hurry, and it was for the best if scuttlebutt around the station didn't mention who had received visits from a reporter. He currently enjoyed tremendous freedom of movement around the station, and he didn't want to give Commodore Reyes any reason to revoke that privilege.

"You'll have to wait while we clear that," the booth officer said. Over the open channel, Pennington heard the man hailing Chief Langlois down in the bowels of the cargo facility.

Despite the fact he was hearing it secondhand over the intercom, Langlois's response came through loud and clear: *"Send him down, Wallingford."*

Glowering at Pennington, the security officer in the booth keyed the control and opened the hatch.

Stepping through, Pennington gave the man a jaunty three-finger salute and said, "Thanks, mate."

The corridor on the other side of the hatch was shaped like a long, hexagonal tube. Its far end opened onto a broad walkway, which encircled the top level of the service side of Starbase 47's enormous cargo and maintenance complex. The hum of activity echoed deeply in the yawning, torus-shaped space, which surrounded the energy- and resource-transfer lower section of the station's core. Narrow shafts of bright blue light demarcated zero-g areas, which were designed for quickly shifting certain types of cargo from level to level, but in fact were most often used by the crew for quickly moving themselves between levels.

The cargo warehouse was abuzz with several dozen personnel and multiple cargo-loading vehicles, all of them moving in carefully choreographed patterns, clearing one bay and loading another, checking in one load of supplies while tagging up another to ship out. Supervisors, recognizable by their mustard-colored coverall jumpsuits, tracked each action on small handheld devices and coordinated with the operations center via radio headsets. Small-arms and ordnance handlers wore burgundy jumpsuits, commercial-cargo movers wore olive drab, and the rest of the Starfleet cargo teams wore dark blue.

Pennington rode an empty, open-sided cargo platform down to the bottom level, where he found Chief Petty Officer Elizabeth Langlois snapping out orders quickly, averting logjams and shipping errors. "Blue three-fifteen," she said into her headset mic, "move those prefabs to pallet twenty-two-echo and clear the bay-two platform for red nine-five." She noticed Pennington stepping off the elevator. "Yellow one-baker, this is yellow one-alpha, handing off, confirm." A moment later, apparently having heard the reply she expected over her headset, she lifted the mic away from her face and nodded toward Pennington. "Tim," she said, shaking his hand. "What brings you down to the belly?"

"Checking in," he said with a broad grin. "Everything stacking up okay down here?"

"Can't complain," she said, leading him out of the way of a fast-moving cargo loader. "Trying to load up the *Meriden* for another colony run tomorrow." They stepped inside her cramped but immaculate office, which sat in a nook of the central core. She flumped into her swiveling, rolling chair. "Someone on gamma shift lost a power generator marked for the Trinay III outpost, and we get to pick up the pieces."

Pennington leaned sideways in the open doorway. "Another fun-filled day of opportunity and adventure, right?"

"Something like that," she said. A series of orange lights started to blink on the situation monitor above her desk. She sighed and got back up. "Look, thanks for the drop-in, but we're busting down here today, and I really need to get back to it."

"Right, sure," Pennington said as he followed her back out into the frantic rush of activity on the main floor. "Before I go, can you maybe fill in the blanks for me on a thing or two? Off the record, of course."

"Depends," Langlois said. "What's on your mind?"

"C-1 cargo," he said. "Do you move a lot of it here?"

"Hang on," she said. Flipping her headset mic back down to her face, she keyed the transmitter on her belt. "Yellow one-alpha, checking in. Fred, what the hell are you doing up there? . . . Well, you've got a red-green overlap on platform four. Fix it." Covering the mic with her hand, she looked back at Pennington. "I can't talk about C-1s, Tim, you know that."

"Come on, Elizabeth, I'm not looking for details. No names, no dates. Just general, deep background, right?"

"Just a sec." Down came the headset again. "Fred, I swear to God, if you don't make red nine-five secure that pallet, you'll be on solid-waste detail for the rest of your hitch, *capisce?*" She looked back at Tim. "What kind of background?"

"A general comparison," he said. "Do you see more C-1s here than you did on your last posting? Does Vanguard move more C-1 cargo than other starbases?"

"We move a lot," she said. "But that's all I can tell you."

"Isn't that odd, for a colony-support mission profile?"

"Step left," she said, and he did as he was told. A large

pallet loaded with photon torpedoes floated past, driven by a silent antigrav skiff. "We're multimission-capable, just like every starbase. Colonization, exploration, combat-operations support. . . . Goes with the territory."

"Right," Pennington said. "Thanks for your time, I'll clear out and let you work." He dodged under a crane-lifted shipping container and bounded back onto the elevator platform.

As he keyed in the command for the top level, Langlois called out, "Just so you know . . . yes, it's odd."

It began to rise, lifting him away from her. He shouted back down, "But what does it mean?" She shrugged her shoulders.

Ascending out of the "belly" of the station, Pennington was no closer to the truth than he had been before his visit. He had confirmed only that Starfleet was keeping some details about its mission a secret; such a weak lead wasn't even worth a cup of coffee, never mind a feature headline on FNS.

Patience, he admonished himself. *Someone on this station knows about the sensor screen and wants to talk. I* will *find that person.* He knew it might take days, weeks, or a hell of a lot longer than that. Keeping promises had not been his strong suit of late. He resolved that this one would be different. *I'll find the truth, Oriana,* he vowed. *For you.*

Reyes waited patiently after pressing the door signal for the second time in a minute. He felt exposed and transparent standing in the corridor, even though no one had passed by him while he had been waiting. The potential for embarrassment was more than sufficient to leave his face flushed with warmth.

When the door finally slid open, he didn't get quite the greeting he expected. Desai was wrapped in a pale blue bathrobe and toweling her short, dark hair. She looked up at him with a befuddled expression and resorted to their public formality. "Commodore?"

"I always thought that was just a saying," he said, pointing at her wet hair. " 'Not tonight, I'm washing my hair.' "

"I haven't used that one on you yet," she said. "I'm saving it for a special occasion."

"I see." He peeked over her shoulder into her dim quarters. "Am I early?"

Her eyebrows lifted in surprise. "For what?"

He heard footsteps getting nearer. Edging forward, he said, "Mind if I come in?"

She halted his progress with a palm against his chest. "What are you doing here, Commodore?"

Keenly aware of whoever was approaching, he lowered his voice. "Isn't it your turn to make dinner?"

That seemed to amuse Desai. "I don't think so."

Gesturing toward the sound of looming footfalls, he said with naked urgency, "Rana, please." Rolling her eyes, she stepped aside and waved him in. He made it through the door, which closed before the passerby reached the corner. "Is this some lawyer technicality because we didn't get to eat last time? Because I ought to get credit for making that dinner, even if we didn't eat it."

Desai walked back toward her bathroom. "It's not like that," she said. "It's much simpler, actually."

"Really?" Reyes never ceased to be amazed by her ability to confuse him then make him feel like it was his own fault by telling him that her convoluted mind games were "simple."

She continued her end of the conversation from the bathroom, her voice pitched upward with its increased volume. "Legal ethics, Commodore. I presume you've heard of them?"

Mentally jumping ahead three steps in the conversation, Reyes growled with frustration. "You've got to be kidding me! You can't see me socially because of the damned inquiry?"

"You're quick, sir. I like that in a witness."

"This isn't funny, Rana." She glared out the bathroom door at him. He corrected himself. "Sorry: It's not funny, *Your Honor.*" She returned to brushing her hair.

"You're right," she said. "It's not. Technically, this is an ex parte discussion. It would probably be best if you left."

He stood, stunned and quiet, for several seconds. He waited for the punch line, or the wry grin that would let him off the hook. Moments later he realized that he was waiting in vain.

"Great jumpin' jehoshaphat, you're serious."

Desai emerged from the bathroom clad in her bright gold miniskirt uniform. Striking a pose with one hand planted on the curve of her hip, she fixed him with a stare that under any other circumstances he would have described as being of the come-hither variety. She smirked. "Don't let the hemline fool you, sir. I'm all business. Now, get out."

"Yes, ma'am," he said, an eye-rolling grimace conveying his profound disappointment in this unexpected change of plans. She walked behind him to the door. *Probably to make sure I really leave,* he mused. The door hissed open. He paused on the threshold and turned to face her one more time. "Y'know, you're cute when you're ethical."

With her fingertips against his chest, she gave him a playful nudge past the doorjamb. "Good night, sir." She backed away from the door, which closed. Though Reyes knew he was probably only imagining it, he was almost certain he heard her laughing on the other side. Mustering his pride, he ambled away to see if Fisher, Cannella, and the rest of the usual suspects were up for a few hands of seven-card stud at Manón's.

"Vanguard Control/*Rocinante*. Requesting departure clearance, bay ninety-two."

The reply of the flight-control officer, or FCO, was distorted by the thrice-rewired speaker on Quinn's cockpit dashboard. "*Rocinante*/*Control. Submit your flight plan and stand by for preflight check.*"

"Acknowledged, Vanguard. Transmitting flight plan."

Outside in the hangar bay, the door to the corridor opened. Chief Ivan Vumelko, the same grouchy customs inspector who had knocked Quinn's tools all over the hold a few days ago, was back to see him off on another trip. Trailed by a pair of Starfleet security guards, Vumelko marched directly up to the nose of the *Rocinante* and slapped his palm on the side of the wedgelike forward fuselage. "Open her up, Quinn. Snap inspection."

Damn. Quinn unlocked the gangway and lowered it. *Figured there was a fifty-fifty chance T'Prynn might've had my back on this one. Just don't panic.* Reaching up to a vestigial coolant pipe for a handhold, he lifted his maladroit bulk out of the pilot's chair and walked back into the hold to meet his guests, who were already ascending the gangway. "Morning, boys."

"Stow it, Quinn." Vumelko keyed his headset transmitter. "Control/Vumelko. Bay ninety-two, starting spot check." Aiming his tricorder at one shielded cargo container then another, he said, "What's in the boxes, Quinn?"

"Hardware," Quinn said. "Stem bolts, dynospanners, sonic screwdrivers, gravitic calipers—"

"That's nice, shut up." Vumelko pointed at one of the crates and looked at the two guards. "Open it."

Play it cool. There was always a chance that Vumelko would be repulsed by the smell of oiled machine parts and, in a sudden and uncharacteristic moment of inattention, forget to rescan the crate's contents once the sensor-scrambling box was open. The chemical odor of silicate lubricant and freshly cut metal filled the cargo hold as the lid came free. Vumelko pointed his tricorder into the box and ran a standard molecular scan.

I'm dead.

Turning off the tricorder, Vumelko motioned to the two guards. "Close it up." He turned toward Quinn, who slouched, preferring to be led away with a whimper rather than a bang. Vumelko extended his hand. "Your pass-chip, Mr. Quinn." With a glum frown, Quinn surrendered the chip, without which he couldn't legally import or export cargo from Federation ports. Vumelko inserted it into a slot on his tricorder, entered a few commands, then removed the chip.

He handed it back to Quinn. "Good luck in the hardware business. Try not to screw yourself." Vumelko keyed his mic as he led the two security guards down the gangway. "Control/Vumelko. Bay ninety-two, clear for departure."

Despite being numb with shock and weak with adrenaline trembles, Quinn closed the gangway hatch and returned to the cockpit. The voice of Vanguard Control crackled over his speaker once more. "Rocinante/*Vanguard Control. Flight plan cleared, preflight check complete. Hangar bay door opening. Stand by.*"

"Control/*Rocinante*. Acknowledged." With a deep hum of magnetic gears, the hangar-bay door crept upward, revealing a rectangular patch of nebula-clouded starfield. The stars drifted slowly from left to right in the frame of the hangar entrance, owing to the slow rotation of the starbase itself.

Rocinante's fusion drive turned over with a satisfying roar that sent a shudder through the deck and up Quinn's spine. Taking off was his favorite part of any journey. Landing was always a crapshoot. So far his luck had held, but he'd lost count of how many times he had welded the *Rocinante*'s struts back together after one of his trademark rough homecomings.

Throttling the small ship forward, he refused to believe he had actually made it past a customs check with a cargo hold full of weapons. It began to sink in only after he had safely warped away. But even as he gave belated thanks to T'Prynn for helping him evade arrest on Vanguard, he knew that escaping Ganz's trap on Kessik IV would be his own problem to deal with. *One crisis at a time,* he told himself. *One crisis at a time.*

15

Kirk watched the main viewer, mesmerized by the enormous chunks of gray debris tumbling erratically in orbit over Ravanar IV. Leslie swiveled his chair away from the helm. "This is as close as we can get for now, sir. Any closer and we risk a collision."

"Understood," Kirk said. Such a collision posed no real danger to the *Enterprise*, thanks to its shields; the real concern in this case was that valuable forensic evidence regarding the destruction of the *Bombay* might be lost or compromised if proper precautions weren't taken. The captain turned his chair toward the port-side engineering station. "Mr. Scott, begin recovery at your discretion."

"Aye, sir." The chief engineer turned his full attention back to his console as he initiated the piece-by-piece salvage of the orbiting wreckage.

On the opposite side of the bridge, Spock—who Kirk was still not accustomed to seeing in a blue sciences uniform—peered down into the sensor hood and called out relevant information as it became known to him. "Debris density suggests three principal groupings," he said. "Dispersal patterns are consistent with two major detonations . . ." He looked up and added, "And a collision."

The comment turned heads all around the bridge, from Scott and Leslie to Kirk and Uhura. At an aft sensor station, the visiting Lieutenant Xiong appeared equally intrigued. "Interesting," he said. Kirk got the distinct impression that Xiong was imitating Spock, perhaps unintentionally. "Do we have enough data to speculate which parties were involved?"

"Scanning for trace elements," Spock said. "High levels of carbon, methane, sulfur . . . and crystalline silicon."

Scotty interjected, "Tractoring in a big piece of somethin' now, Captain—and it doesn't look like it came from one of ours." He squinted at the main viewer as a small chunk of twisted metal grew larger on the screen. "Judging by the look of that armor layer, I'd say it's Tholian."

Spock straightened and faced Kirk. "I concur, Captain. Scans are consistent with known Tholian composites. Based on the volume of debris. and the configuration of its largest pieces, I estimate that we are looking at the remains of four Tholian heavy cruisers mixed with the wreckage of the *Starship Bombay*."

"Four cruisers," Kirk said, now awed by the story he imagined must lurk in these scattered, scorched fragments. "That must have been quite a battle."

Looking at the main viewer, Spock added, "I will submit a more detailed report after we complete our scans and conduct a forensic investigation of the recovered debris. However, one last item seems worth noting." He reached down and patched in an enlarged view of a mangled wedge of the *Bombay*'s saucer section. "The close proximity of debris from the Tholian cruiser and the *Bombay*, combined with the fact that the *Bombay*'s selfdestruct package has been detonated, suggests that Captain Gannon's final tactic was to sacrifice her ship—

and destroy another of her attackers at the same time."

At the Academy, Kirk had heard cadets from less gender-egalitarian colonies and civilizations scoff at the idea of women commanding starships. (Though, to be fair, a few cadets from matriarchal worlds had felt the same way about men in the center seat. He considered both prejudices equally narrow-minded.) *If only those people could see how Hallie Gannon met her enemy,* he reflected with grim pride. *You can't argue with bravery like this.*

"Good work, Spock. Have Scotty and his team continue analyzing the ship debris. I want a scan for life signs at the outpost on the surface as soon as possible."

"Already done, Captain." The Vulcan officer held his unblinking gaze for a moment. Kirk felt his jaw clench as Spock continued in his stately monotone, "No life signs on the surface. The outpost is gone."

At the aft station, Xiong sprang from his chair. "Gone?" Everyone looked at him, and he recoiled at the sudden surplus of attention. Walking down into the center of the bridge, he continued, "Commander, can you elaborate? What kind of structural damage are we dealing with?"

"Quite literally, Lieutenant, the outpost is gone. Its coordinates are now the epicenter of a sizable crater."

Cutting in, Kirk said, "Spock, are we certain there are no survivors? Could they have moved out of the blast range?"

Calm as ever, Spock said without inflection, "Negative. Every living thing on Ravanar IV has been exterminated. . . . This planet has been sterilized."

Sterilized. A chill of horror crept down Kirk's spine.

"Cancel the landing party," he said. "As soon as we police up the debris, we—"

"We still have to go down there," Xiong said urgently.

"That would be most illogical, Lieutenant," Spock said. "The listening post is completely eradicated. There is no hope of a successful rescue or salvage operation."

"It wasn't a listening post," Xiong said.

Abrupt revelations, in Kirk's experience, rarely preceded good news. "Go on," he said to Xiong.

"It was an underground excavation, an archaeological dig. At least, it was, until we found an artifact we couldn't identify. That's when we brought in the Starfleet Corps of Engineers."

"The listening post," Kirk said, piecing this together in his head, "was really an S.C.E. team."

"Right," Xiong said.

"Here to study an artifact—which you found."

"Yes, sir."

Kirk glanced briefly at Spock, if only to avoid burning a hole through Xiong with his glare of anger. "I don't recall seeing this in your report, Lieutenant."

"I'm sorry, Captain, it was classified. Commodore Reyes's orders. I know it isn't likely that anything is left of the dig, but I have to see for myself. Please, sir."

Attempting to put a label on his reaction to this sudden snippet of information followed immediately by a request, Kirk decided that "conflicted" would be an understatement. He was not in the habit of rewarding junior officers for withholding vital, mission-related information. On the other hand, he had been itching to know what was so important to the Federation that it built a starbase as large as

Vanguard this far beyond its established border. If the excavation on Ravanar IV had been important enough for Commodore Reyes to classify it and order Xiong to lie about his mission objectives, then there was a good chance that the site below was connected to the bigger picture of Starfleet's push into the Taurus Reach.

Kirk rose from his chair, snapping orders even before his feet touched the deck. "Mr. Spock, assemble the landing party. Scotty, you have the conn." Staring hard at Xiong, he added, "Lieutenant, if you have anything else to tell me—"

"I'll know when I see the site, Captain. Until then, I have to ask you to trust me, as one Starfleet officer to another."

For some men, that would not have been enough. But for Jim Kirk, that was the most solemn vow there was.

He gestured toward the turbolift, where Spock stood waiting. "Let's go, Lieutenant."

The siren song of the transporter effect diminished as the final shimmering, golden speckles faded from Ming Xiong's sight.

His peripheral vision was hindered by the narrow visor of his metallic-red flex-fiber radiation suit. *I hate these things,* he brooded. Ever since childhood he had despised enclosed spaces. The misery of being sealed up in radiation gear was sometimes mitigated by the view outside. Today, however, the view of Ravanar IV offered no solace—only a smudged sky of churning ash clouds and a broad vista of barren, smoldering dirt that stretched away toward some nearby hills and a distant horizon.

To look around at the rest of the landing party, Xiong had to turn his entire torso. On his left, Spock circled the group, following some readings from his tricorder. Walking close behind him was security guard Luke Patterson. Turning the other way, Xiong saw *Enterprise* senior geologist Lieutenant Robert D'Amato take some readings with his tricorder. Security guard Scott Danes waited patiently a few meters away.

Kirk stood next to Xiong. *"This used to be a jungle,"* the captain said, his dismay evident despite his voice being filtered through the radiation suits' shared comm channel.

Pointing down a slope of smoking ash and pulverized rock into a smoke-shrouded valley, Spock said, *"The outpost was down there, Captain."*

Acting on a single nod from Kirk, Danes and Patterson moved quickly down the slope, ahead of the rest of the landing party. Patterson tested the ground as they went, checking for bad footing or other hazards. Danes observed the surrounding desolation for any sign of company and occasionally looked back to make certain the rest of the group was all right. When they were about halfway down the slope, Kirk followed in their steps, and the rest of the team took his cue and followed him.

Tromping down the slope, Xiong struggled to pierce the dusty gloom below and locate the concealed entrance to the underground excavation. Descending into the smothering blanket of smoke, visibility decreased rapidly, until Kirk, just a few meters in front of Xiong, was only a hazy silhouette against the gray twilight. The rest of the landing party was little more than dim shadows, their labored breathing a low rasp over the suit comms. Jagged chunks of red-hot rock littered their path.

"We should reach the remains of the outpost any minute," Xiong said, more to reassure himself than to edify the others.

"There are no remains to find, Lieutenant," Spock said.

"We don't know that, sir. There might be——"

"We are now more than fifty meters below the recorded ground level of the outpost," Spock said. *"Logic suggests that the attack which destroyed the base was sufficiently powerful to expose the excavation below."*

Adding insult to injury, D'Amato quipped, *"So much for Xiong's artifacts."*

"That's enough, Lieutenant," Kirk said. *"Mr. Xiong, you know what we're looking for better than my security guards do. Take point and lead us in."*

"Aye, sir." Xiong quickened his pace down the slope and soon edged in front of Danes and Patterson. Staring down at the tiny fragments of charred rock and powdery dust under his boots, he tried to discern any sign of the catacombs he and the others had navigated when they first discovered this place. Every new step hammered home the grim realization that there was probably nothing left of the greatest archaeological discovery of the century except for memories and ashes.

Then it took shape in the dreary dimness—the outline of an enormous but disjointed mass of rubble. Xiong remembered first seeing it whole; it had been a truly unsettling experience. Now, beholding it shattered and collapsed, his initial fear of the artifact was transformed into anger at its loss. Its four evenly spaced external supports, which rose up and curved inward, towered nearly thirty meters over-head. The circular platform at which they had intersected had been obliterated, and the clawlike hemisphere it had supported had fallen onto its mirror-image counterpart below, yielding a disturbing, saw-tooth arrangement of shattered black volcanic glass. The lower hemisphere sat at the top of a gradual incline whose surface was rife with grotesque, semi-organic, semi-mechanical shapes and pro-trusions. Even in its current debased condition, the artifact continued to evoke in Xiong a sense of palpable menace.

The landing party regrouped around Xiong and stared at the ruins of the artifact. Danes and Patterson gazed upward in amazement. D'Amato scanned it with his tricorder. Arching his right eyebrow, Spock said, *"Fascinating."*

"Xiong," Kirk said, never taking his eyes off the alien structure. *"What is it?"*

"We don't know, sir." Noting the irritated look on Kirk's face, he added quickly, "We were just starting our research when someone knocked out our sensor screen."

Kirk took a few steps up the low incline, then stopped. *"What kind of research?"*

"Everything," Xiong said. "Materials analysis, reverse engineering, cultural profiling. The S.C.E. had more than a dozen people down here."

D'Amato looked up from his scanning, alarmed. *"Captain, I've got readings below the ruins—complex structures, definitely artificial."*

Kirk looked at his first officer. *"Spock?"*

Activating his tricorder, Spock quickly performed his own scan. *"A power-distribution system, Captain,"* he said. *"A primary tap appears to have been physically severed seventy-one-point-two meters away, bearing three-one-five."* He turned off the tricorder and slung it back at his side as he finished. *"The artifact appears to have been powered by a remote source. Readings indicate that it was capable of harnessing a vast amount of energy."*

Kirk once again focused on Xiong. *"What was the S.C.E. doing before the outpost was attacked?"*

"The next item on the agenda when I left was to try and restore power to a few isolated components. That's why they had the sensor screen—to prevent their work from drawing attention."

Kneeling down amid the twisting biomechanoid tendrils that covered the slope, D'Amato pressed his gloved hand against it. He seemed entranced by its dark coils and dust-shrouded patches of perfectly smooth, opaque black glass. *"Xiong, how many of these structures have been found?"*

"This is the only one," Xiong said, then added, "That I know of."

Kirk glanced at Spock then asked Xiong suspiciously, *"When did you find it?"* Xiong noticed that Spock and Kirk both were listening attentively for his answer.

"A few months ago, shortly before Vanguard was declared fully operational. Why?"

Spock said to Kirk, *"Then this find could not have been the impetus for Starfleet's push into the Taurus Reach. Construction of the station began nearly two years prior to this excavation."*

Nodding, Kirk took another look around the dustblown jumble of ancient debris. *"What brought you out here in the first place, Lieutenant? Without a working starbase for support, this is a long way to go on a hunch."*

"I'm sorry, sir, but—"

"—*but that's classified*," Kirk interrupted. "*Of course it is.*" He turned his back on Xiong. "*D'Amato, finish your scans of the structure and verify your readings with Mr. Spock. Patterson, Danes, help Mr. D'Amato collect any samples he might need for analysis.*"

Everyone snapped into action and conversation ceased.

Regret nagged at Xiong as he wandered around the base of the ruins. He hated keeping information from fellow Starfleet officers, regardless of the orders he had been given. A truly staggering discovery had inspired the Federation's exploration and colonization of the Taurus Reach, but in Xiong's opinion whoever was making the "big picture" decisions about this mission was going about it all wrong. *All they care about is gaining an advantage, getting one up on the Klingons or the Tholians. Why is it always about keeping secrets? If only they'd let the scientists handle diplomacy instead of the politicians, maybe we could stop trying to make weapons out of everything.*

When he had expressed such sentiments to his father years ago, the "old man" had laughed at him and labeled him a "deluded peacenik." On the day that a shuttle came to take Xiong from his home in Kunming, China, to Starfleet Academy in San Francisco, his father stopped laughing at him . . . or speaking to him. "How ashamed you must be," Xiong had shouted as the old man walked away from him. "You wanted an architect and you got me." Now, more than twelve years later, Xiong was hundreds of light-years away, marveling at an ancient majesty that was abandoned before modern humans even existed . . . and still his rage refused to die.

An earsplitting whine cut the air.

Kirk bellowed, *"Fall back! Everybody out!"*

The first explosion tore Danes in half.

Xiong sprinted back toward the rest of the landing party.

Billows of red-orange fire jetted out of cracks in the artifact. Detonations erupted inside its interlocked hemispheres. Shrapnel rocketed in all directions. A blazing-hot fragment struck Xiong behind his right knee, buckling his leg. He fell face-first at the bottom of the slope and howled in agony. Unable to roll over, he twisted his torso and reached instinctively for the bloody tatters of his knee.

Blasts shattered the bases of the four towering supports. Xiong stared up in mute horror as the closest one fell toward him, in what seemed like surreal slow motion. Panic froze him in place. Paralyzed, he watched the gargantuan, curving rib of black stone rush down at him.

Someone's arms wrapped around his chest. His feet dragged through the dust as he was pulled backward, each bump and jostle sending sharp stabs of pain into his knee. The falling support crashed to the ground and broke into millions of pieces. The impact displaced a wall of air, knocking Xiong and his rescuer away in a flurry of stone fragments. Its crashdown was followed by three others, all of which boomed like thunder. Dark plumes of roiling dust and smoke mushroomed up, completely obscuring all visibility for several seconds.

When the smoke cleared, Xiong turned to see who had just saved his life. Lying behind him, his own radiation suit torn in several places by hunks of shrapnel, was Captain Kirk. Barely visible behind him, sprawled in the dust and still-smoldering debris, were Spock, D'Amato, and Patterson. Waved over by Kirk, Patterson limped to Xiong and saw his mangled knee. Without saying a word, Patterson tore off a section of his own damaged suit and began tying a tourniquet above Xiong's knee.

"Spock," Kirk said, sounding winded, *"report."*

The first officer reached for his tricorder, only to discover it was no longer on his belt. D'Amato nudged Spock's shoulder and handed him his own tricorder. Spock activated it and made a quick scan. *"Proximity fuses. Traces of enriched sultritium . . . high concentrations of triceron and thracium."* He deactivated the tricorder. *"Demolitions, Captain. Tholian-made."*

Using the control pad on the wrist of his radiation suit, the captain opened the surface-to-ship channel. *"Kirk to Enterprise."*

"Scott here, Captain."

"Five to beam up."

Scott clearly knew something had gone wrong. *"Five, sir?"*

"We'll need a recovery team for Ensign Danes's body."

Dismayed, Scott replied, *"Aye, sir. I'll see to it. Stand by for transport."*

Patterson finished tying the tourniquet on Xiong's leg. Xiong nodded his thanks to the security guard.

Waiting in shocked silence for beam-out, Xiong listened to a gust of wind shriek around the landing party. The lower half of his right leg was growing numb. Looking around at his comrades, guilt swelled inside him. *I brought them down here.* He glanced at the glowing-hot pile of smashed rock where the artifact used to be, and thought of the boyish young security guard who had just died there.

He died because of me. For my mission. For a handful of secrets I never wanted.

He felt the immobilizing embrace of the transporter beam. As the dematerialization sequence energized with a musical ringing of white noise, Xiong imagined Captain Kirk writing a letter to Ensign Danes's family, telling them that he didn't know what their son had died for.

Not good enough, Xiong decided. *Not even close.*

Kirk sat on the edge of the biobed and pulled on a fresh shirt his yeoman had brought from his quarters. Spock, D'Amato, and Patterson were with him in sickbay, each of them confined by Dr. Piper to their own biobed. The monitors over their heads reported their pulse rates with softly throbbing *bum-bump* biofeedback tones.

A blond nurse had tended their minor injuries while Dr. Piper performed an emergency surgical repair of Xiong's knee. At first the doctor had opined that he might need to amputate Xiong's leg above the knee and replace it with a biosynthetic. Kirk hoped, for Xiong's sake, that Piper was wrong.

A brief, three-note whistle preceded an intraship hail. *"Bridge to Captain Kirk,"* Scott said over the sickbay speaker.

Rising from the biobed, Kirk walked to the wall panel and opened a two-way channel. "Kirk here."

"Recovery team is back aboard, sir. Mission accomplished."

Kirk appreciated the chief engineer's discretion in leaving certain details unsaid. "Thank you, Mr. Scott. What's the status of our salvage operation?"

"*We'll have everything aboard in about six hours, sir.*"

"Any sign of the *Bombay*'s log buoy?"

"*Aye,*" Scott said. "*We've got a lock on it. It's next on our list.*"

"Good work," Kirk said. "Notify Mr. Spock as soon as it's aboard."

"*Will do, sir.*"

"Kirk out." He thumbed off the comm switch, then heard a door slide open behind him. He turned to see Xiong hobble out of the recovery room. The lieutenant's sweatpants looked amusingly lopsided, with the right leg sliced off above the knee to reveal the servo-enhanced brace that supported his nearly mummified knee. "Mr. Xiong. Still in one piece, I see."

"Thanks to you, Captain." One halting step at a time, Xiong moved to the biobed on which a fresh blue uniform shirt and his gear—which amounted to a communicator and a tricorder—were neatly arranged and awaiting his return.

Dr. Piper emerged from the recovery room carrying a small plastic container with a prescription label. He handed it to Xiong. "Take one of these at night before you go to sleep. It'll reduce the pain and swelling and speed up the healing."

"Thank you, Doctor." Xiong placed the prescription bottle on top of the shirt, then folded the garment in half over it. He stared down at his things for a moment, his fists clenching on the edges of his shirt.

Kirk recognized the younger man's look of self-blame, that haunted expression of anger turned inward. He had seen it on his own face eight years ago, after his moment of fearful hesitation on Tycho IV led to the deaths of nearly two hundred of his *Farragut* shipmates, including his commanding officer, Captain Garrovick.

"Captain," Xiong said, "I just want to say . . ."

Kirk took advantage of Xiong's pause. "Is this an apology, Lieutenant?"

"Kind of, sir, yes."

"Keep it. You have nothing to be sorry for." Seeing that Xiong was gearing up to protest, Kirk continued, "What happened down there wasn't your responsibility, it was mine. I ordered the landing party, I led the mission. You made a convincing case for inspecting the site, but I made the decision to go. My command, my crewman, my responsibility. Clear?"

Xiong didn't look as if he believed it—not that Kirk had really expected him to—but he nodded and said, "Yes, sir."

"All right, then. Go back to your quarters and get some rest. We'll be back at Vanguard in a few days."

Xiong lowered his voice to a conspiratorial whisper. "There's something else I need to tell you, Captain." Looking up with hardening resolve, he added, "Something important."

The intensity of Xiong's demeanor commanded Kirk's full attention. In the same hushed tone, he said, "About what, Lieutenant?"

"I want to tell you why Starfleet is out here," Xiong whispered. "And why one of your men died today. . . . You saved my life, Captain. The least I owe you is the truth."

16

Anzarosh, Kessik IV's shabby spaceport town, was one of the most depressing places Cervantes Quinn had ever visited.

Hands tucked inside the warm pockets of his greatcoat, he leaned against the forward landing strut of the *Rocinante*. The slow-burning cigar clenched between his teeth was half-gone. It sizzled as he took another puff. Lethargic coils of grayish smoke snaked away and lingered in the dank predawn air. Overhead, the landing pit yawned open to a dismal patch of gray sky. A faint mist of chilly rain drizzled down.

Just as Quinn had expected, Ganz's client had arranged for him to put down in the most remote, decrepit docking pit possible. Its amenities consisted of tangled fuel lines, a burgled maintenance locker, and rust. The whitewashed concrete floor was spiderwebbed from edge to edge with deep cracks. It was the kind of place to leave a body if you wanted to be sure it wouldn't be found anytime soon.

Arranged in four neat rows, halfway between the small freighter and the wide hydraulic doors that led to an underground freight-rail loading platform, were the twenty-four cargo crates Quinn had smuggled off Vanguard.

The doors opened. Broon, an unkempt bear of a man, lumbered in, his open trenchcoat fluttering behind him like a battle flag. He was followed by an entourage of ten surly-looking lowlifes, all of whom came carrying disruptor rifles.

Quinn slowly removed his right hand from its pocket, tucked back his coat, and rested his hand on the stun pistol he had strapped on for just such an occasion. "You're late."

"And you're an idiot," Broon said, his voice a guttural rasp. His men fanned out in a semicircle and surrounded Quinn.

With a nonchalant sideways puff of cherry-scented smoke, Quinn said, "I was smart enough to get this far."

"If you had any brains, you wouldn't have come at all."

On the edge of his vision, Quinn caught the silhouettes of snipers inching along the top edge of the docking pit. "What? And miss out on all this?" His hand closed slowly over the grip of his pistol. "Do you want your guns or not?"

"Oh, we'll take the shipment, Mr. Quinn," Broon said. His men began raising their weapons in Quinn's direction.

"Not until you pay for it," Quinn said. "My employer told me to bring back six kilos of pure dilithium." He ignored the malicious chuckling that spread like a virus between the gunmen.

Broon smirked. "I think you've misunderstood the nature of this transaction, Mr. Quinn. That cargo is not our purchase—it's our reward."

"No, I understand perfectly," Quinn said. "If I got busted on Vanguard, Ganz would've whacked me in the brig. If I made it here, you'd kill me and take the guns." Cautiously, he pulled his left hand out of its pocket. "I'm changing the deal." He held up his left hand to reveal a small, rapidly blinking device. His thumb kept a small red switch on its side pressed in. "Dead-man switch. One kilo of ultritium in each case. I let go of this without keying off those detonators, anybody inside half a klick's gonna have a real bad day. *Comprende?*"

No longer smirking, Broon made a slow, cautious gesture to his men to lower their weapons. He kept his eyes on Quinn the entire time. "We don't have the dilithium," Broon said. "It wasn't part of our deal."

"Make me an offer," Quinn said, inching his pistol from its holster. "Make this trip worth my time."

"First we need to set terms," Broon said. "How is this going to go?"

Quinn tried to keep tabs on where all of Broon's men were. A few had slipped behind his ship, maybe hoping to tackle him and seize the dead-man switch. He pivoted slowly to keep them at bay. "You're gonna find some way to pay for these guns," Quinn said. "Then you're gonna put the payment on my ship, and I'm gonna leave." He noted the snipers adjusting their aim. "As soon as I'm clear of the docking pit, I'll key off the detonators."

"Ridiculous," Broon said. "As soon as you're clear, you'll blow us to bits."

Shaking his head, Quinn said, "No, 'cause my boss is your insurance. If I kill you, he kills me. My way, we both live."

"Until Ganz sees you alive," Broon said. "Then I'm a dead man." He looked at his men. "We all are."

A puff of cigar smoke passed through Quinn's best *trust me* grin. "Not if you make good by paying for the guns," he said. "Call it a show of good faith."

"Orions don't believe in good faith," Broon said. "They

believe in contracts and revenge. My contract is to kill you."

"And mine's to sell you a bunch of guns. I prefer mine."

Broon glowered at Quinn for a long moment, then walked slowly toward the rows of crates. "An impasse," he said. "That's what we have." Resting his hands on top of a crate, he continued, "Unless, of course, one of us backs down." He looked over his shoulder at Quinn. "I have to wonder . . . where would a fringe-prospecting loser like you get his hands on twenty-four kilos of ultritium?" Caressing the edge and corners of the lid, he added, "You wouldn't just make that up, would you?" His hands cupped the flip-latches of the crate lid. "No, of course not. That would be stupid. Suicidal, even."

Quinn aimed his pistol at Broon. The gunmen on every side of him lifted their own weapons back into firing positions.

"Don't open that crate," Quinn said. The pistol quaked slightly in his hand.

"Or what, Mr. Quinn? You'll stun me?" He flipped the latches open. "Why not just blow me up?"

"Don't make me tell you again," Quinn said. "Seal those latches and step back."

Broon left one hand gripping the handle of the lid as he turned to face Quinn. "Ganz told me you were a lousy poker player, Quinn. You don't know how to bluff." He flipped open the lid—revealing a circular disk of weapons-grade ultritium secured to its underside, as well as the blinking detonator affixed to its center. His jaw dropped in horror.

Quinn shouted, "Are you crazy? You could've set it off!" Broon didn't respond, he just stood and stared at the munitions charge half a meter from his face. "Close that lid *very gently,*" Quinn said. "And the rest of you—put down your damn guns." At first only a few of Broon's men laid down their weapons, but within seconds they all did. "Slide 'em toward me," he said, making certain to hold his dead-man switch high over his head for all to see. Looking back at Broon, he saw the big man easing the lid closed with almost comical slowness. "That's it," Quinn said to him, "nice and—"

The detonator fell off the ultritium charge. Then the munition fell from the lid, revealing itself as a hollow fake.

Damn cheap glue, Quinn fumed.

Broon reached for a pistol tucked into his belt. "Kill—"

Quinn's first shot knocked Broon backward over the crate. Dodging for cover under the wing of his ship, he managed to take down a gunman who was reaching for his rifle. *Only nine to go,* Quinn thought. He hoped for a quick demise. On every side, he heard Broon's men scooping up their rifles. He wedged himself inside the port-side landing strut, hoping it might limit to six the number of people who were about to kill him.

He closed his eyes and fired blind. Multiple screeching rifle shots overlapped all around him. Half a second later, he was the only one firing. He took his finger off the trigger and opened his eyes.

All the gunmen lay stunned. Quinn looked at his stun pistol, then at the unconscious men. *Did I do that?* He looked again and realized that whatever weapon or weapons had incapacitated Broon's thugs, it hadn't been his crude sidearm. Letting his pistol lead the way, he crept away from the landing strut. At the edge of the wing he remembered the snipers. Peeking upward, he saw no sign of them. *What the hell?* Skulking around the gunmen, he stopped when he reached Broon, who looked up at him through glazed eyes that betrayed a grudging respect. "Snipers . . ." he croaked. "Very clever." A gurgling noise rattled inside the man's throat; then he passed out.

Surrounded by artfully wrought violence, Quinn realized what had happened; there was only one "logical" explanation.

T'Prynn.

A crueller man might have laughed.

A more noble man might have felt ashamed.

Quinn bound and gagged Broon and his gunmen, collected their weapons, loaded his crates back on to the *Rocinante,* and went in search of another buyer for his cargo.

Kirk was unaccustomed to having so many people on his bridge when there wasn't a crisis. The *Enterprise* was en route back to Vanguard under routine conditions, but in the twenty-five hours since Xiong had divulged the classified details of his mission, Spock, Piper, and Scotty had been engrossed in fevered research of the data stored on Xiong's tricorder. Spock and Piper had busied themselves at science station one, while Xiong and Scotty had been working at the station right next to them. For Scotty and Piper, the yeomen hadn't been able to fetch coffee fast enough this evening.

Patiently waiting in the center seat, signing off on fuel-consumption reports and sipping long-since-cold coffee, Kirk had yet to hear a single report from anyone that explained what Xiong had revealed. Noting the hour,

Kirk was about to turn in for the night when Spock called to him. "Captain."

He joined Spock and Piper. The first officer looked no worse for his efforts, but the long hours had taken a terrible toll on the old physician. Kirk said, "What have you got?"

One of the overhead displays switched to a complex helical design composed of multitudes of colors. "The biological samples recovered by the *Constellation* crew included a unique and complex genetic material, Captain," Spock said. "A team at Starfleet Research and Development has since named that gene sequence the Taurus Meta-Genome."

"It's like our DNA," Piper said, "but a lot more complicated."

"How much more?" Kirk's real concern remained unvoiced: *Complicated like warp-geometry calculus, or like Gary Mitchell on Delta Vega?*

Enlarging the image on the overhead, Spock said, "The Taurus Meta-Genome contains a staggering quantity of raw information, encoded in a biochemical matrix. Compared with all currently known humanoid genetic material, it is more complex by several orders of magnitude." Kirk did a double take, then looked again at the image with a new wonder and respect. Spock added, "Its value to science is potentially incalculable."

"Coming from you, Mr. Spock, that means something." Kirk looked at Piper. "Where did it come from?"

Piper pointed at a notation in fine print at the bottom of the screen. "Ravanar IV, Captain. A survey team scraped it up with a simple mold. They didn't know what they had until the *Constellation* was long gone from the system."

Now Kirk had heard everything. "Mold?"

"Only the first six base-pairs seem directly related to the mold," Piper said, pointing to the relevant molecules. "The next five pairs seem like barrier proteins, designed to keep the mold's genetic data separate from the rest of the sequence."

"So the mold is only a carrier?"

"Precisely, Captain," Spock said. "There is also a repeating sequence, which might serve to prevent errors in replication. I have never seen such symmetry in a genome before. If I were to offer an educated guess, I would say that it was artificially engineered."

Genetic engineering. Even the mention of it recalled for Kirk ethics lessons from Starfleet Academy on the evils of bioengineering for "eugenic" purposes. Despite his reasonable certainty that humanity's failed efforts in that field were unrelated to what he was seeing here, a chill shook him. He put aside his gut reaction. "Is this a blueprint for a life-form?"

"Unlikely, sir," Piper said. "Not unless it's the size of a small moon. I think Mr. Spock hit the nail on the head when he said it looked like information storage. I'd say it's raw data."

The imprecision of it frustrated Kirk. "For what?"

Piper and Spock both wore poker faces. Finally, the first officer simply said, "Unknown."

Seeking a new avenue of inquiry, Kirk said to Xiong, "This is why you were on Ravanar?"

Xiong looked up from his work at the adjacent station. "Yes, sir. I went in with the *Sagittarius* crew on an early mapping assignment."

"And that's when you found the artifact?"

"To make a long story short, yes."

"There's more on that, Captain," Scott said. "Look here." The entire group crowded around the second science station as Scott transferred his work to the overhead screen. Wireframe models were superimposed on virtual models of the intact artifact Xiong had discovered underground. "With the kind of power this thing must have had, its range would have been tremendous."

Once again, the expertise of Kirk's senior officers left him feeling half a step behind. "Its range, Mr. Scott? Range for what?"

Scott sounded shocked that he had to explain himself. "Broadcast, sir." Waving toward the image on the screen, he continued, "I didn't see it until Lieutenant Xiong showed me the whole works in one piece just now. Then it hit me—it looked like an oversized subspace relay coil." Punching a few keys, he added some schematic data as an additional overlay. "These are the systems D'Amato scanned beneath the thing, before it blew up. You can gussy it up all you like, but the laws of physics don't change. *That* is a subspace transmitter."

It was Xiong's turn to let his jaw hang open while he stared at the chief engineer's work. "Commander Scott," he said, "what would be the effective range of such a transmitter?"

"That size?" Scotty shrugged. "Huge, lad. If I had the time, maybe I could do the math and—"

"Approximately two hundred eleven point six light-years," Spock said. "Assuming a power source sufficient to accelerate the coil's primary oscillator to full velocity."

Xiong looked at Kirk like a child pleading for Christmas

gifts. "Captain, could we check the databanks for any unexplored M-Class or formerly M-Class planets within that radius of Ravanar IV? It might help direct the search for more artifacts or other samples of the meta-genome."

Kirk nodded his assent to Spock, who leaned over the sensor hood and patched in to the ship's computer library.

"Searching," Spock said over the gentle hum and whir of the computer. "Several such planets are within the specified area." He routed the data to the overhead, replacing the genome information with a star map.

Xiong studied it quickly, eyes darting from one highlighted name to another. "There," he said, pointing. "Erilon."

Calling up supplemental data, Spock read aloud, "Class-P, glaciated. No sign of intelligent life detected by remote survey probes. Believed to have been Class-M until approximately twenty-nine thousand years ago, when the companion of its primary star diminished in magnitude."

"It's near the Klingon border, right along the *Endeavour*'s patrol route," Xiong said. "We could ask them—"

"Lieutenant," Kirk said, cutting him off. "I'm not about to send another Federation starship on a wild-goose chase to a dead block of ice based on your hunch." Gesturing at the star map, he continued, "There are dozens of candidates, and no reason to think that one's a better bet than the others."

"True," Xiong said, "but it's the only one on the list that has a Starfleet ship passing within one-point-five lightyears in the next five days. Might as well start there."

Before Kirk could rebut Xiong, Spock chimed in. "Logical."

"Fine," Kirk said. "Will the *Endeavour* crew know what they're looking for?"

"They'll know," Xiong said. "We should notify them on a coded frequency."

"Very well. Mr. Scott, Dr. Piper, continue your analysis and contact me if you learn anything new." Kirk walked toward the turbolift. "Lieutenant Uhura, please help Mr. Xiong send a priority coded signal to the *Starship Endeavour*." The turbolift door opened and Kirk stepped inside. "Mr. Spock, you have the conn."

The doors closed as Kirk gripped the turbolift throttle. Watching the deck lights blur past, he grinned at the realization that he and Commodore Reyes would have much more to talk about at their next meeting than at their first. *This time,* Kirk promised himself, *I'm getting some real answers out of him.*

Lieutenant Moyer sat with her hands folded on the wardroom table and hurled questions at Commodore Reyes. He did his level best not to get out of his chair and strangle her. "Would you describe the workload of the *Bombay* crew as excessive?"

"No," Reyes said, then heeded his counsel's advice not to elaborate unless instructed to do so. It was the fourth day since Desai had overruled Liverakos's motion to terminate the inquiry, and Reyes's first day being deposed.

Moyer reviewed her notes. "How many separate action items did you assign to the *Bombay* on an average cruise?"

"The number varied." *The literal truth and no more. Next.*

A predatory gleam seemed to brighten the prosecutor's face. "On her last cruise, scheduled for a fifteen-day duration, you assigned the *Bombay* nine mission objectives in six star systems. Matériel transport to outposts on Ravanar and Getheon, colony visits to Talagos Prime, Jemonon, and Kilosa. An officer transfer to the *Starship Endeavour*. A reconnaissance assignment. Two star-mapping assignments. Was this level of activity typical aboard the *Bombay* since she was placed under your supervision?"

"No," Reyes said. His throbbing pulse was giving him a headache, and his ears felt as though they must be glowing red. Just for practice, he smiled calmly at Moyer.

"Was the usual workload greater than what I've just described, or lesser?"

"Greater," Reyes said.

His answer sent her scrolling through her notes. "Two days ago, fleet operations manager Raymond Cannella said that, quote, 'The *Bombay* was our workhorse. She picked up all the slack.' End quote. Yesterday, Vanguard executive officer Jonathan Cooper told this board that, quote, 'No matter how much we asked Captain Gannon to do, she always got it done.' End quote. In light of these statements, Commodore, do you think that it's possible that the *Bombay* was overburdened?"

Defense attorney Liverakos raised his hand slightly from the table, which Reyes took as his cue not to answer. "Objection," Liverakos said. "Calls for speculation, and seeks to ask my client to potentially indict himself."

"Sustained," Desai said from the head of the table.

Moyer didn't seem the least bit fazed, and continued as if nothing had happened. "Commodore Reyes, could some of the tasks you assigned to the *Bombay* on her last cruise have been assigned to either the *Sagittarius* or the *Endeavour?*"

"Not likely, no."

"Why not?" The department heads in attendance all leaned forward to catch every nuance of his response.

Damn, an essay question. "Because their mission profiles are radically different. They aren't suited for full-time support operations. *Bombay* was."

"The *Endeavour* is a *Constitution*-class vessel, is it not?"

He could already see where Moyer was going, and he pitied her. It would be a long way for her to go to end up back where she started, but he played along, a polite captive to the legal process. "That's right."

"Aren't starships of that class frequently called upon to carry colony supplies, transport critical components, and make new star surveys?"

"Yes."

"So why haven't you assigned some of that workload to the *Endeavour* in the months since it was detailed to your command? According to Vanguard's operations records, every grid-check and regular colony tour for the past four months was conducted by the *Bombay*. What made the *Endeavour* exempt from these duties?"

"The fact that I needed her on a long-term patrol of the Klingon border," Reyes said. "The *Endeavour* might be able to handle cargo delivery as well as the *Bombay* did, but the *Bombay* wouldn't have provided the same level of deterrent to the Klingons as a *Constitution*-class starship."

"I see." Moyer nodded and made a notation on a small pad in front of her. "Surely, the *Sagittarius* could have made the occasional colony tour? Or handled the rush shipment of emergency supplies?"

He wondered if Moyer was making asinine assertions simply to fuel his temper and draw him out. If so, he would have to congratulate her later. "The *Sagittarius* has other assignments better-suited to her design and crew, Lieutenant. She's an *Archer*-class scout vessel. She's made to go very far, very fast, and not be noticed. She goes to the edge of nowhere and peeks behind the curtains. Her hold is barely large enough to carry her own mission supplies, never mind regular cargo deliveries. Using it for colony runs would be a waste."

"And the loss of the *Bombay* wasn't a waste, Commodore?"

"No, Lieutenant. When a Starfleet ship and her crew are lost in the line of duty, it is *never* a waste, only a tragedy."

She paused to digest that. "Of course, Commodore. Your Honor, I request that my last question be struck from the record."

"So ordered," Desai said.

Moyer took a breath, reviewed her notes again, then recovered her composure and resumed eye contact with Reyes. "Let's discuss the periodic maintenance and supply of the *Bombay* in the weeks leading up to its loss in action, and in the hours immediately preceding its final departure from the station."

"Very well," Reyes said, his own anger now subsided.

"Subpoenas to this station's operations center yielded more than sixty unfulfilled requisitions from the *Bombay* for spare parts, replacement tools, and backup components."

She handed a data slate to Reyes that displayed a menu of the unfulfilled requisitions, then continued.

"Unfulfilled requisitions for similar matériel filed during the same period by the starships *Endeavour* and *Sagittarius* totaled only fourteen—combined. Six from the *Endeavour*, eight from the *Sagittarius*."

Another slate was pushed in front of Reyes.

"Why do you think there is such a pronounced variance in these totals, Commodore?"

For the first time since his midshipman days, he felt dumbfounded. "Well, the *Endeavour* is a younger ship than the *Bombay* was. Almost ten years younger. . . . The *Sagittarius?* Well, she's almost brand-new. And small. Easier to maintain."

Moyer scrolled through her own slate.

"Your records also demonstrate a sharp discrepancy in the total number of hours these three vessels logged in spacedock receiving scheduled maintenance to critical systems." She retrieved a thick binder of printed records. "During the past one hundred days, the *Starship Endeavour* received more than four hundred sixteen hours of maintenance and repair by Vanguard personnel. The *Sagittarius* received two hundred fifty-one hours of service. The *Bombay?* A measly one hundred four hours."

The binder hit the table in front of Reyes with a slap.

"Explain this to me, sir," Moyer said. *"Bombay* needed ten times more matériel than the *Endeavour,* but got only one-quarter as much time in your spacedock. Why?"

Fighting to muzzle his own temper, he concentrated on unclenching his jaw first and on breathing second. He cast an angry glance at his defense counsel, then permitted himself a fleeting glare at Desai. Finally, from beneath a creased brow, he answered, "I don't know."

An hour ago, he had dismissed this inquiry as a waste of time. Now he asked himself if Moyer was right. *Did I send them out too soon? Were they not ready? Did I push too hard?*

Moyer made another small mark in her notes and carried on. "Let's talk now about this morning's report via subspace from the *Enterprise,* and whether better tactical procedures on Vanguard might have prevented the ambush of the *Bombay.*"

"Objection," Liverakos said. "Such an inquiry would risk exposing classified tactical information and methods that are vital to the defense of this station, and to the security of the Federation."

"Overruled," Desai said. "I'm not going to let you shut down an entire avenue of questioning, Counselor. You may object to the discussion of specific technologies, policies, and methods as necessary. Lieutenant Moyer, please continue."

Reyes knew that, like any good lawyer, Moyer clearly sensed that she had opened a gap in the information barrier, and would relentlessly exploit it until all his picayune missteps and misjudgments were laid bare and daisy-chained into a litany of failure, incompetence, and negligence. He resolved to remember Liverakos's instruction to keep his answers as monosyllabic as possible, and to just get to the end of the deposition without incriminating himself.

Then it would be time to find a way to stop this witch hunt before it derailed the entire mission and truly made the deaths of Captain Gannon and her crew a waste after all.

17

It was far too early in the morning, Reyes had slept much too little the previous night, and the coffee was barely strong enough to merit the name. Despite the carefully balanced climate controls inside the starbase, he felt the same rising wall of pressure in his sinuses that he had felt on landing missions just before storms broke. Leaning forward in his chair, he rested his elbows on his desk, cupped his face in his hands, and exhaled a long, tired breath that was heavy with frustration.

The other four people in his office waited patiently for his moment of dismayed fatigue to pass.

Captain Kirk and Lieutenant Xiong occupied the chairs in front of his desk. Standing against opposite walls, flanking the two seated officers like rooks at either end of a chessboard, were Jetanien and T'Prynn.

Reyes spent a few seconds massaging the bone around his eye socket. It ached deeply. "Lieutenant," he said at last, "what part of 'classified' did you not understand?"

"I presume that's a rhetorical question, sir?"

"Do you think humor is your best tactic here, son?" Taking the commodore's meaning perfectly, Xiong said nothing.

"It's not his fault," Kirk said. "I gave him no choice."

"That's very noble of you, Captain," Reyes said. "It's

also a complete load of crap." Kirk clearly meant to press his case, but Reyes kept going. "He could have briefed you in private, or told you only about the artifact. Instead he gave you—and most of your senior officers—the entire history of the project."

"True," Kirk said. "And my officers gave you one of the best leads you've had on this project since it started."

"Also true," Reyes said, though it galled him to admit it. He glared again at Xiong. "And completely irrelevant."

Kirk stood, apparently for no other reason than dramatic effect. "So what now?" He paused behind his chair and leaned on the back of it. "Unbreak the egg?" Talking and walking, he took a few steps toward T'Prynn. "Court-martial a young officer who only wanted to share what he thought was vital information?" Circling around toward Jetanien, he continued, "Ask Starfleet to relieve me of command?" He saved his big finish for his last turn, back toward Reyes. "Or maybe shanghai my ship and crew into your service?"

"None of the above," Reyes said.

Xiong looked relieved. Kirk looked surprised.

Moving away from the wall to loom over Reyes's desk, Jetanien entered the conversation. "A court-martial, though it would be an eminently appropriate remedy for Lieutenant Xiong, is not a viable response at this time." Spreading his arms in a gesture of acceptance, he added, "Let us just say it would be an exceedingly delicate matter to argue under the rules of Starfleet jurisprudence."

"You mean it'd be an embarrassment," Kirk said cynically.

"No, Captain," T'Prynn said, still content to remain at a

slight remove from the discussion. "It would be a national-security disaster for the Federation."

"Which naturally brings us back to the topic that initially brought us here," Jetanien said. "The attack on the *Bombay.* Since our earliest scout flights pushed into this region, there have been rumblings of discontent from the Tholian Assembly and the Klingon Empire. Although a major initiative such as Operation Vanguard cannot help but provoke the ire of our rivals, one of our chief priorities is the avoidance of hostilities—at any cost."

Tapping two fingers on the cover of Kirk's report, Reyes said, "Are your people *sure* it was the Tholians who destroyed her? Because I can't work with educated guesses and maybes."

"We're sure," Kirk said. "My chief engineer confirmed that the wreckage of four Tholian cruisers was mixed with the debris from the *Bombay.* And the data on the log buoy indicates that just prior to their attack, they had detected six Tholian ships closing on attack vectors. The evidence is solid."

"Good," Reyes said. For a moment, he allowed himself to be impressed by the fact that Hallie Gannon had taken out four enemy ships; then he had to remind himself that she and her crew were still dead.

Like an angry dog pulling at its leash, Kirk seemed eager to spring back into action. "What's our response?"

"Your response," Reyes said, "is to go back to the *Enterprise,* purge all data regarding the Ravanar mission and Operation Vanguard from your databanks, and never talk about any of this with anyone ever again. I'm granting you and your men retroactive security clearance so I won't have to string up Mr. Xiong by his thumbs, but he'll be spending the next few months serving the most horrible duty assignments I can find."

"Let me rephrase," Kirk said. "What response will you be recommending to Starfleet and the Federation Council?"

Jetanien interposed himself subtly between Kirk and Reyes. "We will consider a variety of appropriate courses of action, Captain. Our current circumstances afford us a significant degree of latitude in our decision-making."

Kirk wasn't a tall man to begin with, but standing in the shadow of Jetanien's massive bulk exaggerated that fact. What he lacked in height, however, he clearly made up for with tenacity. "That sounds like a very diplomatic way of saying we're not going to do anything."

"My interpretation might differ from yours," Jetanien said.

His face reddening with indignation, Kirk shouldered past Jetanien and leaned halfway across Reyes's desk. "Don't tell me we're going to bury this. The Tholians ambushed a Starfleet vessel. They killed more than two hundred men and women." He pounded his fist on the desktop. "It was an act of war!"

"A full-scale conflict with the Tholian Assembly would compromise our mission in the Taurus Reach," Jetanien said. "We have to weigh the costs of the *Bombay*'s loss against—"

Kirk raged at Jetanien, "Weigh the costs?" Glowering at Reyes, he said, "He's talking about politics—I'm talking about justice!"

"You're done talking, Captain," Reyes said. "You ship

out in three days. I suggest you use that time to work on your temper. Dismissed."

The fair-haired young captain straightened his posture into one of proud defiance. He looked down at Lieutenant Xiong. "You deserve better. Push for the court-martial." Turning on his heel, Kirk walked in smooth, confident strides toward the door.

As it opened, T'Prynn spoke, halting him at the threshold. "I know you think justice was betrayed here, Captain." He cast an angry look over his shoulder at her. She added, "But believe me when I tell you that justice has a *very* long memory."

Kirk said nothing more. He walked out and the door closed behind him.

Reyes concealed his annoyance as Xiong struggled not to make eye contact with anyone else in the room, even though everyone was now looking directly at him. "So how 'bout it, Lieutenant? You want to push for that court-martial?"

"No, sir."

"Smart boy. Dismissed."

Xiong snapped out of his seat and was gone from the office before the order was ten seconds old.

The commodore shook his head and frowned. "Best field archaeologist in Starfleet. And the biggest pain in the ass."

"With great talent often comes great impudence," Jetanien said.

"You're just making that up," Reyes said.

"I was wondering how long it would take before you finally caught me." Shifting his mood back to the serious, he continued, "This sudden increase in hostilities by the Tholians places us in a dangerous bind, Commodore. If the details of this attack reach the Federation Council, they will almost certainly insist on declaring war against the Tholian Assembly. Once we are so engaged, our forces will be unable to secure the Klingon border, and the Klingons are practically guaranteed to seize the opportunity to push into the Taurus Reach. If we permit this attack to take us to battle on one front, we will inevitably face a war on both fronts—and that is a war we cannot win."

"I'm not thinking that far ahead," Reyes said. "Right now I'm worried about the board of inquiry; it's starting to feel like it's being run by the Salem judiciary. If the JAG office files enough subpoenas, somebody'll say something they shouldn't. And once it's out—well, that'll be that."

Jetanien folded the claws of his hands together in a slow, pensive gesture. "I might be able to open a discreet dialogue with one of Captain Desai's superiors. Someone who could quash her inquiry."

"That'll just make her more suspicious," Reyes said. He sighed. "If I could just bring her into the loop, explain the mission to her, I know she'd find a way to shut it down, subtle or not."

In a tone that implied it was painfully obvious, Jetanien asked, "Why not just grant her security clearance, then?"

"I gave clearance to Kirk and his men because I had to," Reyes said. "It was that or court-martial Xiong and lose our best hope of piecing all this together. I'd have a harder time justifying a breach for a JAG officer."

"Not necessarily," Jetanien said. "The risk is the same,

only the circumstances are different. The admiralty would understand, I am certain."

"I'm guessing you've never met the admiralty," Reyes said.

"I sponsored several of their commissions," Jetanien said.

Reyes grimaced. "Well, that explains quite a bit."

"Gentlemen," T'Prynn said with a lilt that sounded suspiciously teasing to Reyes's ears. "This situation is not as intractable as you seem to think. There are . . . *discreet* options."

The Chelon ambassador turned his body to look at T'Prynn. Reyes reclined his chair and folded his hands on his lap. "I presume," the commodore said, "that you have a proposition?"

She arched a single, thin eyebrow. "Indeed."

For several hours, on the far side of a semiopaque security curtain that had been erected in the main spacedock hangar, a team of stevedores had been off-loading from the *Enterprise* mangled piles of metal, and shipping containers packed tight with small debris. One load at a time, it was all being transferred into Vanguard's repair and salvage bay.

Isolated on the observation deck, watching the dim outlines of the activity from afar, was Tim Pennington. He leaned against the cold, floor-to-ceiling transparent aluminum barrier. He pressed his forehead against it, and the empty compartment behind him fell away from his thoughts as he watched the final, tragic homecoming of the *U.S.S. Bombay*.

For the past three months, word of the *Bombay*'s return

to Vanguard had been cause for celebration. This morning there had been no cheerful reveille to herald its approach. Federation banners throughout the station remained at half-mast, and more than a few Starfleet personnel had bucked the regulations and worn black armbands of mourning when on duty in more remote areas of the station, away from the eyes of supervisors. Pennington had mistakenly thought the period of mourning passed after the first few days, but news that *Bombay*'s remains had come home had reopened this fresh emotional wound.

He had intended to write an exposé. Tell everyone why the ship had been lost in action. Secure justice for Oriana and her shipmates. He had overheard T'Prynn speaking about the listening post on Ravanar, about the sensor screen damaged by an inept thief, but he had no hard evidence, no witnesses he could trust not to recant. He had been reading smuggled transcripts of the Starfleet JAG's board of inquiry about the loss of the *Bombay*. The thrust seemed to be toward blaming Reyes and the Vanguard staff for over-working the ship and failing to provide it with proper maintenance. He had considered sharing his leads with the prosecutor, but he changed his mind when he realized that his complete lack of evidence would make his tip even more useless to her in court than it was to him in print.

Desperate to vent his pent-up emotions, he'd written a memorial instead, culled from the personal recollections and anecdotes he'd been inundated with while devoutly pursuing some unnamed and elusive secret. His personal contributions, about Oriana, had been altered enough to protect their privacy—and to prevent her husband from learning of their affair. He'd read his own memoirs and cringed at how maudlin and banal they seemed. Yet those were the ones that his editor, Arlys, confessed had made her weep for the lost men and women of the *Bombay.* "You put faces on them, Tim," she'd written in reply to his submission.

His mirage-like, long-faced reflection looked back at him from the transparent aluminum. Over the past few days he'd had time to think, and to recant the convenient lie he had been telling himself. *I didn't scrub every trace of Oriana from my life to protect her husband's feelings. Telling myself it was for his benefit was just an excuse.*

Down in the docking bay, the off-loading was complete. The *Enterprise* slowly shut its scalloped aft hangar doors, and a team of zero-g workers in lightweight EVA gear retracted the gauzy privacy screen that had been obscuring the view. With the transfer finished, Pennington saw no point in prolonging his vigil. He pressed his right hand against the barrier, and his throat tightened with grief. *Welcome home, Oriana.*

The first clue that word of his dustup on Kessik IV had reached Vanguard before Quinn did was the cordial nods of greeting he received from Ganz's two hulking doormen. Normally when Ganz entered the Orion's ship of sybaritic delights, the two bouncers either watched him suspiciously or, on their more extroverted days, sneered slightly in his direction. Until today, however, a courteous welcome had never been on the menu.

Strolling through the gambling parlor on the lower deck, Quinn sensed people noticing him, heard his name bandied about under the music. For a few seconds, he felt like a celebrity. Being just a little bit famous excited him—until he thought about it for a few moments too long. *All these people know who I am, and they know what happened on Kessik IV. . . . All these strangers.* His exhilaration turned to a feeling of violation.

Midway between the roulette wheel and the card tables, Zett intercepted him. On this occasion, the slender Nalori killer was decked out in a light-khaki casual suit. He made a point of invading Quinn's personal space. "Welcome back," he said loudly, over the music. "Mr. Ganz has been expecting you."

"I never pictured you as the earth-tones type," Quinn said.

"Mr. Quinn, I am in no mood to carry you up those stairs. Please do not force me to break your legs."

"Can't keep him waiting, can we?" Quinn made a sweeping arm gesture toward the stairs. "Lead on."

The march up the stairs seemed, in Quinn's estimation, to lack the pall of dread that had marred his previous visits. Then he realized that he might have allowed T'Prynn's interventions on the Kessik IV job to make him overconfident; he had no reason to think he was still enjoying her protection. *On the other hand, if I'm worth that much to her, she'd be a fool to let me walk in here without taking some kind of precaution.* It was a comforting thought. Ignoring the prudent inner voice that told him not to count on it, he clung to his new cocky attitude and followed Zett up the stairs to the "sweet spot" in front of Ganz's two disintegrator obelisks. Immediately, Quinn noticed that the usual inward push of gawkers was not in evidence. The coterie of retainers seemed to be keeping their distance today.

Lounging on his scatter of bright pillows, Ganz enjoyed a long, deep pull from his hookah. The air on the quiet upper level was dense with grayish violet pipe haze. Opening his eyes, Ganz smirked at Quinn. "Heard you had some trouble."

"I don't have your dilithium," Quinn said.

Ganz's voice was quiet, deep, and dangerous. "Why not?"

"I made your delivery to Broon. He didn't want it."

"Is that a fact."

"Yeah," Quinn said, "but don't worry." Using an old sleight-of-hand trick his uncle had taught him, Quinn produced a Federation credit chip from his right palm. He snapped his fingers and flicked it forward, onto the floor directly in front of Ganz's bare green feet. "I got you a better deal."

Ganz sat up, leaned forward, and plucked the chip off the floor. Holding it between his thick fingers, he stared at it for a moment. Then he looked at Quinn . . . and stood. Walking toward Quinn, Ganz's every step projected strength and power. Lying down he merely seemed bulky; on his feet, in motion, the rippling movement of his muscles became much more apparent. He was heavyset in his torso, but not in a way that suggested softness; the added mass only made him more imposing.

The Orion merchant-prince's chin was level with Quinn's eyes. He spoke very quietly, but the deep register of his voice was such that Quinn felt every word tremble the air around him. "You know I sent you there to die, right?"

If street-fighting as a boy had taught Quinn anything,

it was when not to blink or back down. "Yeah, I figured."

"But you came back anyway."

"You told me to sell your cargo," Quinn said, quiet bravado masking the sick swirl of fear that was turning his guts to mud. "I sold it. Money from the job is yours. Deal's a deal."

"Good answer," Ganz said. "I don't know how you made it back here alive. I don't even know how you got that hardware through Starfleet customs. I don't want to know." Leaning down, he filled Quinn's ear with the most unnerving whisper he had ever heard. "But either you're smarter than you look, or you've got powerful friends. Either way . . . you just made yourself useful." Ganz withdrew and backed up half a step. "Come back in a few days," he said. "I might have some work for you." The Orion turned and walked back toward his mountain of pillows.

Taking that as his cue to leave, Quinn ambled casually away and descended the stairs like a man with nothing to fear. Less than halfway down, Zett was once again at his shoulder. "You're probably feeling proud of yourself," the Nalori said.

Quinn made a point of eyeing Zett's suit again. "Have you considered patterns? Solids are very last year."

"You should have killed Broon and his men when you had the chance," Zett said.

"I don't kill unless I have to," Quinn said. "And I've yet to see a profit that was worth a man's life."

"That's because you live small and have no imagination," Zett said. "You humiliated Broon then sold guns to his rival. He'll send people after you. Assassins. There'll be nowhere you can go that he won't find you."

"You're wrong," Quinn said, bounding off the stairs and onto the gaming floor. "I have a *very* rich imagination."

Zett sneered. "Your insolent japes won't save you when Broon's men come calling."

"No, but they'll make my death eminently quotable." They passed a man who was facedown on the cards table, weeping into an empty stretch of felt where his chips used to be. Quinn adroitly snagged the man's untouched cocktail, which even from more than a meter away Quinn's nose knew contained tequila. He sipped as he stepped inside the turbolift. Making a broad shoulder-roll that sloshed booze on Zett's perfect tan shoes, Quinn added, "Why're you so worked up? Afraid I'm gunning for your job?"

"You could not do my job," Zett said.

"Yeah, I hear being head waiter is hard work." He guzzled the last of the booze and lobbed the empty glass at Zett. "Think fast." The man reflexively caught it in one perfectly manicured hand. "Good catch," Quinn said. As the lift door closed, he snuck in one last gibe: "Table four needs menus."

The muffled crash of the thrown glass against the other side of the closed turbolift door brought a malicious smirk to Quinn's face. Exiting through the airlock a minute later, he looked up at the two doormen, nodded his farewell, and received two polite nods in return. Sauntering away, he fished a cigar from his inside coat pocket, then found his lighter and ignited it. A thick plume of smoke lingered around him as he made the long walk back to the upper levels. *I'm forty-nine, four times divorced, and one mistake away from waking up dead. But I'm still breathing, so here's to me.*

Several minutes later, he was ambling through the middle of Stars Landing. He ducked down a shortcut, a long and narrow sliver of space between two buildings. He was almost at the end when a large humanoid silhouette blocked his path. A stray shaft of light glinted off the man's pistol, which was steadily leveled in Quinn's direction. He considered turning tail and making a run for it, but it was a skinny straightaway with no cover and no doors. *I'll never make it,* he knew. *Damn, and this was a good cigar.*

Quinn straightened his posture and chose to meet death with his eyes open. He put his cigar in his mouth and braced himself.

The gunman tensed, as if he had suffered a full-body muscle cramp. His knees wobbled, he crumpled downward, and then he fell on his face with a dull thud—revealing a tall and slender feminine silhouette behind him, one hand still extended to where the man's shoulder had been. The woman stepped over the fallen assassin and strode forward, elegant and purposeful.

Grinning broadly, Quinn took another puff of his cigar.

T'Prynn emerged from the anonymity of shadow and looked at him with the most intense and beguiling dark eyes he had ever seen. "I have need of your services," she said. "Come with me."

Tim Pennington stepped through the door into his apartment. The sight of his wife smiling at him scared him half to death.

"Hi, honey! Surprise!" She stood in the middle of the living room, holding an ugly knickknack in one hand and his favorite pint glass in the other. Dozens of tiny bits of her tourist-trap junk from around the galaxy now littered his once-pristine shelves and tables. He stared at her, expressionless, like a man fresh from a difficult session at the dentist.

"Lora," he said, shocked into a monotone. "You're here."

"I got a spot on an earlier transport," she said, then tossed her bit of junk and his pint glass on the sofa and flung herself on top of him. Draping her arms over his shoulders and behind his neck, she said with a lascivious grin, "I insisted."

His smile looked and even felt genuinely happy. It was a reflex. "And how could they say no, right?"

"Exactly," Lora said. She kissed him, hard and hungry, with a passion that he was sure would swallow him whole unless he pulled back. He fought the urge and threw himself into the moment. The hesitation in his actions felt obvious to him, and he expected to be taken to task for it any second now. Instead, Lora broke away first, did a small pirouette, and laughed. "I saw a lot of cute little shops along the boulevards when I was coming in," she said. "Restaurants, too. Want to get dinner?"

"I'm not really hungry," he said, his melancholy slowly rising to the fore despite his conscious effort to suppress it.

"Quick, call security," she said. "Someone must've stolen your stomach. You're *always* hungry." She shrugged. "Later, then. Whenever you like." She began moving around the room, rearranging all her little bits of junk in ways that subtly eclipsed what few personal items he had chosen to adorn his living room shelves and tables with. It was as if he suddenly didn't exist in the apartment he'd occupied alone for more than three months. "You've certainly settled in," she said. Obliviously shifting and moving his life around, she prattled on, "If I know you, you've already got your routine all worked out. Up early, swimming laps, then somewhere obscure for a café con leche. A hard day chatting people up and trying to trick your editor into reimbursing your dinner checks." She stopped messing with his things long enough to cast a playful, simmering glance in his direction. "Am I right?"

"Pretty much," he said with a faltering grin. It felt like a ghastly bore that despite four months away from her he was as stale and predictable as ever. The mystery that came with novelty had long since worn off their relationship. He resented that he was an utterly known quantity to her, hated that she simply knew the minutiae of his life without having to ask. Then he remembered Oriana and savored a bittersweet taste of smug revenge.

He hadn't meant to lose himself to his dark mood so deeply. Lora's tone became concerned. "What's wrong? Are you upset?"

"Yes, actually," he said. Even knowing what she would ask next, he didn't elaborate, preferring to make her draw him out.

"About what, sweetheart?"

"The *Bombay,*" he said. "I just finished a memorial piece, full of stories from people who lost friends or family. I've been working on it ever since the news first came in. . . . I guess it just got under my skin, is all."

"Objectivity was never your strong suit, was it?" She moved close to him and stroked her fingertips through his hair. "You always get too close to your stories and get all wrapped up."

"Yeah," he said, his voice barely more than a quiet hush of breath. "You know me." His eyes closed as if magnetically sealed. Something inside him just didn't want to look into Lora's eyes right now. He swallowed hard. "I always get too close. And that's how people get hurt."

Sequestered in the unlit cargo hold of the *Rocinante*, T'Prynn handed Quinn a palm-sized data card. "Take this to residential compartment 2842," she said. "Hide it somewhere easily described, then send an anonymous message to Tim Pennington with instructions on how to find it."

Quinn held the data card between his thumb and forefinger. He regarded it with quiet suspicion. "Why?"

A decades-old memory of the blunt end of a *lirpa* rattling her jaw colored her words with aggression. "Excuse me?"

"This ain't what I signed on for," he said. "You said you needed me to get around on planets you can't go to. You didn't say anything about me being your delivery boy."

"I said I would contact you when I had use for you."

"What is this? A joke? Drop a data card? Make an anonymous tip? You could do all this yourself."

"Yes, I could." She suppressed Sten's *katra* memory of her elbow shattering the bridge of his nose, while waiting for Quinn to reason out the subtext of her statement.

"You're making me do this just to prove that you can."

"Correct."

"Just showing me who's boss."

She arched one eyebrow at him. "Indeed."

He thrust the data card back at her. "What if I say no?"

"Then next time I will let the bounty hunter shoot you."

He stuffed the data card in his coat pocket. "Right. Where'd you say this thing's goin'?"

Sleep eluded Pennington.

Beside him, Lora was deep into a REM phase and sprawled over more than two-thirds of his bed. Inspired by their prolonged separation, she had been unwilling to take "no" for an answer when she had pounced on him. The mood had felt awkward and empty to Pennington; he'd felt like a person whose between-meal snackings had left him with no appetite when dinner came. All the same, he had gone through the motions, indulging her with the pleasures he knew she preferred. Emotion might have betrayed him, but muscle memory had remained true.

That was two hours ago.

The ceiling was painted with dappled light filtered through the boughs of trees outside the bedroom window. He had always been fond of the old-fashioned–looking sodium lamps that ringed Fontana Meadow. Tonight, their dusky orange glow mingled with organically shaped shadows to resemble golden camouflage.

He rolled to his left, away from Lora.

With slow, cautious motions he rotated his pillow in search of a spot of refreshing coolness.

A slow, deep breath felt good, but he was no less awake at the end of it than he had been at the start.

It was 0338, a time that his father had always described as seeming "less real" than other parts of the day. A dark Limbo betwixt the late night and the dawn, it was like a No Man's Land for the ordinary soul. More and more lately, however, Pennington had found himself stalking leads and drafting stories here in the wee hours.

Soundless and discreet, his pager blinked with a soft green light that indicated he had a new message. Grateful for any excuse to slip out of bed, he scooped up the small device, pushed aside the sheets, and stole away to the living room, where he sank heavily onto the sofa with a huff of breath and checked the message on his pager.

No source ID, he noticed. *Odd.* Anonymous messages were not difficult to send via the service he used, but few reliable sources ever took that precaution. Information was all well and good, but it was generally not safe to take anonymous sources "at their word." His editor almost always insisted on either two credible corroborating sources, or lots of rock-solid evidence.

He opened the message and at first didn't know what it was.

It read, simply:

Compartment 2842. Behind the bedroom ventilation grate.

Without exception, it was the vaguest lead he had ever been offered. *What are they trying to lead me to? A body? A safety violation?* He was ashamed to admit that the sheer mystery of it actually intrigued him. Running off in the middle of the night to pursue something this flimsy was absurd.

From the bedroom, Lora began to make a bizarre wheezing-warbling sound. Pennington asked himself whether he would prefer to go back inside and lie down next to his wife until the faux sunrise, or slip out of the apartment to see what this idiotic tip was all about.

He got up and started looking for his shoes.

•   •   •

Zett walked three steps behind Qoheela, a beefy Tarascan hit man. Morikmol had found Qoheela lying facedown in a narrow alley near Quinn's favorite drinking establishment. On Ganz's orders, Qoheela had been escorted onto the *Omari-Ekon*. Qoheela's plodding footfalls trembled the staircase as he crested its top steps. Moving quickly, Zett passed the bulbous-eyed amphibian and guided him toward the spot between the twin black obelisks.

Standing and clearly in a foul mood, Ganz glared at Qoheela from beneath a furrowed brow. "You're one of Broon's men."

"That's right," the Tarascan said, his voice translated by a device beneath his tapirlike snout, which waggled as he spoke.

"Who said you have Vanguard privileges?"

"It's a public facility," Qoheela said snidely.

Stepping lightly, Zett positioned himself just behind Qoheela's left flank.

Ganz's indignant expression never wavered. "I don't like complications on my turf," he said.

"Your deal went bad," Qoheela said. "Broon put a contract on Quinn. End of story."

"I'll tell you when the story ends," Ganz said. As he lifted his hand to give the signal to disintegrate the Tarascan, Qoheela struck out to either side with his richly muscled arms and hit each obelisk hard enough to crack both bases and tilt them apart. Sparks fountained from the breaks in the stone.

Qoheela lifted his foot to step forward toward Ganz.

Zett's fist struck the Tarascan on his spine, just above

the pelvic assembly. A sharp, wet snap of shattered bone was heard by everyone in the room. Qoheela stopped in midstep, then slumped. Zett drew his short, curved *yosa* blade. Before Qoheela's knees touched the deck, Zett circled him in a dancelike motion and executed a perfect slash across the creature's jugular. Black blood jetted out in a fan-shaped spray, just missing Zett, who twirled away. By the time the slender, well-dressed Nalori had finished his well-rehearsed *chom* pattern, Qoheela had pitched forward. He was now exactly as Morikmol had found him, only dead. A pool of Qoheela's jet ichor spread swiftly around him on the pristine deck.

One of Ganz's more attentive retainers offered Zett a clean towel for his *yosa*. He accepted it and wiped the blade clean. Handing back the sullied linen, he was offered another, this time dampened with warm water, for his hands. A retainer held his weapon while a young woman draped the damp cloth over his hands. He cleaned them, digit by digit, with the care of a surgeon.

Morikmol and another large specimen of useful muscle wrapped Qoheela's corpse in an old rug and ported it away to be immersed in liquid nitrogen until it crumbled into a pile of brittle, grayish dust. Zulo, the resident "cleaner," was already pouring a small jar of chemicals on the blood puddle to break it down at the molecular level and evaporate it. Within minutes, Zett knew, the floor in front of Ganz would be pristine once more. Only the leaning, splintered obelisks remained amiss. *No doubt Ganz will have those replaced by the end of the week,* Zett figured.

Killing the Tarascan had been a necessity of protocol. Though Zett had no objection to the idea of someone tak-

ing a disruptor to Cervantes Quinn, there was still a right
way and a wrong way to do things. Sending an assassin
into Ganz's "home base" without first asking his permission had definitely been the wrong way for Broon to proceed. And had Qoheela known what was good for him, he
would have taken the painless death of the disintegrator
rather than the bloody end Zett had dealt him.

Zett had no regrets save one: That it couldn't have been
Quinn's throat that his *yosa* opened. Picturing Quinn's violent demise, he smirked. *Someday,* he consoled himself.
Sooner or later that half-wit will stop being useful. He rested
his hand on the grip of his blade. *Please let it be sooner.*

Compartment 2842 was an as-yet unassigned Starfleet
residential cabin. Most of the section in which it was located
appeared to be vacant. Pennington hadn't needed any special tricks to gain entry. Whoever had been here before him
had left the door unlocked. It swished open, revealing nothing but darkness. Pennington reached in, fumbled around,
and turned on the light.

It was a shell of a room. No furniture, just a thin layer of
ugly carpeting and institutional-looking blue-gray bulkheads that were desperately in need of some artful touches.
He stepped inside, wary of a trap. Listening for company,
he heard only the ventilation system, low and muffled. Inside the compartment the air was stale, and Pennington surmised that the ventilation for these quarters probably hadn't
been activated yet.

Eager to get in and out of the compartment quickly, he
moved into the bedroom and looked around for the ventilation grate. He found it along the top edge of the wall, near

the low ceiling. Testing the grate, he felt that it was loose.
He pulled it free and reached behind it. Probing gingerly
with his fingers, he easily found something small lying on
the bottom of the ventilation duct. Removing it, he saw it
was a standard-issue data card.

He looked up and around, listening again to make sure
he was alone and that no one had snuck into the compartment in the few moments he had spent searching. Returning to the card in his hand, he pulled his data recorder
from his belt and inserted the card. A menu appeared on
his device's screen.

The volume of information on the card was amazing.
Skimming its contents, he realized that it contained sensor
logs, audio files of intercepted Starfleet comm traffic, official Starfleet documents, and a timeline of events . . . all of
it related to the destruction of the *Starship Bombay* in orbit
of Ravanar IV.

It can't be.

Common sense told him to get out of there and find a
safe place to review the contents of the data card.

Adrenaline and his instincts as a reporter told him no
one would come looking for it—or him—here, so he might
as well see what he had right now.

Minutes sped past as he raced through one document
after another. Logs detailed the ambush of the *Bombay*
and the Ravanar colony by six Tholian battle cruisers.
Even a requisition order for the sensor screen, authorized
by Commodore Reyes and classified by order of Lieutenant Commander T'Prynn, was included in the support-
ing documentation. Searching quickly, he found the work
order for the shipment of the sensor screen, and saw that it

had been carried out by a Starfleet cargo chief named Is-rael Medina. The same man had also been responsible for checking in the recovered debris and log buoy of the *Bombay*—as well as captured wreckage from four of the six Tholian ships.

Medina, Pennington repeated to himself, memorizing the name. *Israel Medina. If I can find him, get him to corroborate the sensor screen and Tholian ship debris, and authenticate the* Bombay*'s log buoy data . . .*

Pennington knew exactly what it would mean.

The biggest story of his career.

War with the Tholian Assembly.

And justice for Oriana and more than 220 other people who died in the Tholian sneak attack.

It was time to find Chief Petty Officer Israel Medina.

Ezekiel Fisher lumbered toward the front door of his quarters, fumbling with the belt of his bathrobe. Bad enough it was dark, but his eyes were crusty with sleep and some damned fool was sounding his door buzzer for the fourth time in a row. "I'm comin'," he said with a hoarse croak of a voice. "Hold your horses."

He opened the door. Standing on the other side, looking pale and shell-shocked, was Diego Reyes. "She's dead," he said.

"Hang on," Fisher said, instantly sharpening to waking alertness. "Who's dead?"

"My mother," Reyes said, his eyes averted from Fisher, staring instead at some far-off point that seemed to be beneath the floor. "Just got the message."

"But they said she had months—"

"They were wrong," Reyes said. He sounded hollow. "It was more advanced than they thought. . . . It just ate her alive."

"Dear God," Fisher said. He was about to invite Reyes in, then hesitated. "Diego, I'm not saying you have to go, but why come to me?" The old doctor leaned forward to try and snag some eye contact. "It's Rana you should be talking to."

Reyes shook his head. "Can't right now."

"What? Because of all that legal mumbo jumbo she gave you the other night?" Fisher frowned. "To hell with that."

"Bad timing," Reyes said. "That's all."

"Be that as it may, she can do a lot more for you right now than I can."

"Honestly, Zeke," Reyes said as tears welled in his eyes, "I don't think there's much anyone can do for me right now."

In the space of just a few seconds Fisher could see that his friend was on the verge of emotionally unraveling. He reached out and grasped Reyes's shoulder and gently led him inside. "Then I guess you better come in and let me pour you a drink." Reyes drifted forward. Fisher steered the man to a seat, then moved off to find his stash of good single-malt scotch.

Sitting quietly, Reyes rubbed the wetness from his eyes, which now were brightly bloodshot. Fisher poured two doubles of twenty-five-year-old Macallan, then carried the bottle and two glasses to the coffee table. He set one in front of Reyes, who reached out and picked it up, then the doctor sat down across from his visitor.

Reyes sipped the drink, then stared forlornly into its amber depths. "What now?"

"Sit and drink," Fisher said. Then he added, "Slowly."

"That's it? No words of wisdom or comfort?"

Fisher shrugged. "What do you want me to say, Diego?" He took another sip of scotch. "When Hannah passed away a few years ago, a lot of people tried to say things they thought would help. 'At least you had forty-nine great years together,' or, 'She was lucky to have had a husband like you.' I figured out nothing anybody says makes it better. Nothing makes it hurt less. Nothing makes the person you loved any less gone." He made a small tilting gesture with his glass. "The best thing anybody did for me was sit and share a drink and just not say anything at all."

"That was me," Reyes said.

"I know."

"I didn't say anything because I didn't know *what* to say."

"It was the right choice. Now shut up and sip your drink."

The better part of an hour crept by while they nursed their scotch in silence. Finally, Reyes muttered quietly, "I wish I could be with Rana right now."

Realizing that he had no sage commentary on that subject, either, Fisher uncorked the Macallan and poured them each another double.

Working from the information on the data card, Pennington had determined that every entry by Chief Petty Officer Medina was made during gamma shift, and that he appeared to be responsible for loading and unloading operations in salvage bay four. Putting those two details together, Pennington reasoned that if he made it down to salvage bay four before the shift change at 0800, he should be able to find Chief Medina.

As he approached the entrance to the salvage bay, the door swished open and a distinctly metallic odor flooded out. Ozone and acetylene exhaust were thick in the air.

Stepping inside, he saw that the place was packed from floor to ceiling with shipping containers, broken machines, bins of spare parts, and open-top crates of scrap metal. Somewhere in the distance, probably on the far side of the cavernous compartment, he heard the soft hum and whine of an antigrav load lifter. As in so many other areas of the starbase, the lighting was uniformly bright and flat.

He felt like a rat in a maze as he wandered into the monotonous grid of stacked and ordered crates and bins. His footsteps echoed and reechoed, announcing his presence more clearly than he would have preferred. At each intersection he glanced to either side, seeking some sign of another sentient presence. He walked for more than two minutes before a man with a cargo tracker appeared from around a corner two intersections ahead. Pennington waved to the olive-skinned man, who wore the blue coverall jumpsuit of a Starfleet cargo handler. Within a few paces' distance, he noticed that the man's jumpsuit was partially unzipped to midchest, and the top of it had folded over, partly obscuring the name stenciled over the cargo handler's left chest pocket. Only the last four letters were visible: DINA. *Close enough,* he decided. "Chief Medina?"

The man had a slight Spanish accent. "Who wants to know?"

"My name's Tim Pennington," he said. Laying his cards on the table, he added, "I'm with the Federation News Service."

Medina looked at Pennington as if he had just said he

had the plague. It was a reaction to which Pennington had become accustomed. Leaning slightly away, he said, "What do you want?"

"I just need to ask you a few questions," Pennington said. "It can be off the record, no names. I'm not looking to put you on the spot here."

The man was becoming more apprehensive. "About what?"

"I just need you to look at some orders that have your name on them," Pennington said. "Cargo transfers, matériel receipts." He reached into his coat pocket and retrieved printouts of the official documents he had seen on the data card. Handing them to Medina, he said, "Have you seen these before?"

Waving his hands, Medina stepped back. "No, not here." He looked around nervously, then grabbed Pennington's coat sleeve and pulled him down one of the side lanes, then into a shadowy nook between two large shipping containers. Safely under cover, he plucked the papers from Pennington's hand. "Where'd you get these?"

"That's not important."

"Yes, it is." Medina flipped from one page to the next, growing more agitated as he went. "This is all classified."

"I have other sources," Pennington said.

"Then why do you need me?"

"Because I never trust just one source." Tugging on the pages, he added, "Sources lie. Documents can be faked."

The dismay on Medina's face grew more obvious. His voice diminished to a horrified whisper. "Not this time," he said. "These are my work orders."

Lowering his own voice, Pennington said, "So you did

load a sensor screen on the *Starship Bombay*?" Medina nodded. "And you off-loaded the *Bombay*'s log buoy from the *Enterprise*?"

"*Sí*," Medina said.

"Was its data intact?"

Again Medina nodded quickly. "Lieutenant Commander T'Prynn and Lieutenant Farber recovered its memory core as soon as we brought it aboard."

"The logs said the *Bombay* was attacked by six Tholian cruisers, and your cargo receipt says you transferred wreckage from Tholian hulls into the salvage bay."

"*Sí*," Medina said. "It's all with the forensic team now." Pennington jotted notes in his recorder. Medina watched him and looked very nervous. "You can't use my name."

"I don't have to," Pennington said. "You're a confidential source. Federation law says I don't have to reveal your identity to anyone, no matter what."

"You're sure?"

"I'm positive." He switched off his recorder and tucked it safely away inside his coat. "Thanks, Chief. I owe you."

Pennington slipped away and walked quickly for the nearest exit. The urge to run, to sprint, was bursting inside him. He felt history waiting for him, he heard Truth and Justice summoning him back to his computer terminal. It took all his discipline to preserve a façade of calm as he made the long trek back to his quarters.

It was the greatest feeling he knew.

He had a story to write.

18

Every new sentence that Commodore Reyes read added to his furor. Filed just over a day earlier, it was the lead story on the Federation News Service's afternoon feed, and apparently every other major news service had picked up the story with the FNS attribution: "The Ambush of the *U.S.S. Bombay*," by Tim Pennington, FNS Correspondent, Starbase 47.

Jetanien paced back and forth in Reyes's office, reading the same report off a small handheld device. The Chelon's tired groans occurred almost synchronously with Reyes's, leading the commodore to conclude that they were on the verge of a collective apoplexy.

His desk intercom buzzed, and Yeoman Greenfield said, *"Lieutenant Commander T'Prynn is here, sir."*

"Send her in!"

The door opened and T'Prynn entered, looking crisp and unruffled and all but perfect in her pale, graceful way. As soon as the door closed, Reyes's harangue began.

"I thought you were going to put a lid on this!"

Jetanien joined the dressing-down. "This is a complete fiasco, Commander. We are poised on the brink of war!"

Without breaking her stride, she continued walking until she was directly in front of Reyes's desk. "The situation is under control," she said.

Reyes held up his copy of Pennington's feature story. "You call this 'control'? This cocky little newshound has names, dates, sensor logs that prove that the Tholians destroyed the ship . . . is there something I'm missing, Commander? Because it looks to me like the worms are out of the can here."

Behind T'Prynn, Jetanien stormed up and loomed over her, bellowing down at her like a father castigating an unruly child. "Billions of lives are in jeopardy because of this lapse! The Federation Council is already speaking of war against the Tholian Assembly, and Ambassador Sesrene has severed diplomatic relations as a result. Our entire mission could be over in a matter of hours unless we—"

"—remain calm, Ambassador," T'Prynn interrupted, in her softest dulcet tone. "Unless we remain calm. Which I urge you both to do now."

"Give me one good reason to trust you," Reyes said.

The communicator on T'Prynn's belt beeped twice. She unclipped it and flipped it open. "T'Prynn here."

"Commander, this is Captain Desai. I'm in the residence of reporter Tim Pennington, in Stars Landing. Could you join me here as soon as possible, please?"

"On my way, Captain. T'Prynn out." She closed her communicator and secured it back on her belt. Looking at Reyes, she said, "You should trust me because I am about to make one of your problems go away." Glancing at Jetanien, she added, "And the other will soon follow."

Desai stood in Tim Pennington's discombobulated living room. In her hand was a tricorder. On its screen was the list of contents encoded on the data card that her security detail had found in Pennington's possession. Her first glance at the card's trove of information had provoked waves of professional envy; this was exactly the kind of evidence that Lieutenant Moyer had been fighting to obtain for the board of inquiry. Her second review of the data had caused a different reaction.

Pennington and his wife, Lora Brummer, were under guard in the bedroom while half a dozen security guards tore up the rest of their home. Desai had been almost irritated by the smug way Pennington had accepted the search warrant and admitted her and the guards; he seemed to regard the entire proceeding as just another ho-hum detail of his profession and evinced no concern for the fact that his exposé might hurl the Federation into a war for which it was not ready.

T'Prynn walked through the open front door. She surveyed the damage, then stepped over a toppled chair to join Desai. "How may I be of service, Captain?"

She handed T'Prynn her tricorder. Keeping her voice down, she said, "We found this data in Mr. Pennington's possession."

The Vulcan woman clicked and scrolled quickly through the information on the data card. "Interesting," she said softly.

"He refuses to say how he acquired it," Desai said. "It occurred to me that there are very few people on Vanguard who can access this kind of intelligence." Reaching over the top of the tricorder, Desai tapped in a few simple commands, calling up some new highlighted data. "So I searched the information on the card for leads to its source. I found this." She waited several seconds while T'Prynn looked at the highlighted name on the shipping order: Israel Medina. "I ordered him brought to my office for questioning. Of course, I probably don't need to tell *you* how *that* worked out."

"No, of course not." T'Prynn handed the tricorder back to Desai. *"I* cannot compel *you* to do anything, Captain."

"I'm going to ask you a simple question, Commander, and I am *ordering* you to answer me truthfully. Was the outpost on Ravanar IV part of an ongoing Starfleet Intelligence operation?"

Though Desai was unable to quantify how T'Prynn's mien had altered, it unequivocally just had. T'Prynn's dark eyes took on a smoldering quality. "Ask Israel Medina," she said. On that note, she turned, walked away, and was gone.

Ask Israel Medina. Desai smirked ruefully and shook her head. *If only it were that simple.* She clapped her hands twice, and the security guards gathered around and gave her their full attention. "We're finished here," she said. "Release Mr. Pennington and his wife." She ejected the data card from the tricorder. "Let him know I'll be keeping this. As a souvenir."

Zeke Fisher sat alone in his office. The monitor on his desk was showing Tim Pennington's FNS report about the ambush of the *Bombay*. Fisher had watched just enough of it to get the gist, then he'd muted the audio so he could think.

His door signal sounded. "Come in," he said. The door opened and Dr. M'Benga walked in, looking energetic and textbook-perfect. He was carrying a data slate. Fisher projected a fatherly smile toward him. "Jabilo, what can I do for you?"

"Good morning, Doctor," M'Benga said, looking suddenly a bit nervous, like a student facing the principal. He motioned toward the chairs in front of Fisher's desk. "May I sit down?"

"Be my guest." Fisher leaned back and relaxed as M'Benga sat down. "What's on your mind?"

"I need to ask a favor," M'Benga said.

Pointing at the slate, Fisher guessed, "You need a consult?"

M'Benga handed the device across the desk to Fisher. "No, your signature." Fisher glanced at the display and recognized the open document before M'Benga added, "For my transfer application."

Fisher scrolled through the completed application. "Starship duty?" He looked up at M'Benga, his surprise transmuting to resentment. "Jabilo, I groomed you to run a state-of-the-art hospital, and you want to be a sawbones on a starship?"

"It's not about Vanguard Hospital," M'Benga said. "This is a terrific facility. It's just that I joined Starfleet to see new worlds and meet new species. And I feel like that would be easier to do on a starship assigned to frontier duty."

Holding up the slate, Fisher said, "You know it can take months for Starfleet to process these? Or longer?"

"All the more reason not to wait," M'Benga said.

The weathered CMO shook his head in dismay. His carefully laid plans for retirement were unraveling, and there was nothing he could do about it. He opened his desk drawer and searched for a stylus. "A damn shame," he mumbled. Snatching the stylus from the jumble of clutter, he reviewed the transfer request, signed it, then handed back the slate.

M'Benga accepted it with a humble nod. "Thank you, Doctor." He stood up to leave.

"Promise me one thing," Fisher said. M'Benga stopped and looked back. Fisher continued, "When the rest of the galaxy all starts to look the same, come back here so I can retire."

"Fair enough," M'Benga said with a half-grin.

Fisher shooed the younger physician away. "Go on."

Left alone with his disappointment, Fisher checked the calendar. He was unsurprised to find that it was, in fact, a Monday.

Kirk sat at the small monitor in his quarters, reviewing Tim Pennington's story about the ambush of the *Bombay*. His dinner of lamb stew and sautéed green beans sat untouched on the desk. Spock stood behind the captain, watching over his shoulder.

"His command of the facts is impressive," Kirk said.

"Indeed."

Arriving at the end of the article, Kirk swiveled his chair to face Spock. "The fallout from this won't be pretty."

"I suspect that will prove to be an understatement."

Feeling lost in his own thoughts, Kirk stood and paced away from the desk, exhaling his anger in a low huff. "What the hell is Pennington thinking? Is he *trying* to start a war?"

"If I understood you correctly, Captain, you yourself

advocated just such an action scarcely forty-eight hours ago."

An angry glare was Kirk's instinctual response. He forced himself to shed it and calm his temper. "I've had time to think since then. Time to consider . . . another point of view." He leaned against the hexagonal-pattern screen that divided his quarters into a sleeping area and a dining area and workspace. "What do we really know about the Tholians, Spock? They're nothing like us. Not humanoid, not interested in the same kinds of planets. Maybe there's more we don't understand about them. . . . Just because we weren't aware of any Tholian claims in this sector doesn't mean there aren't any. Maybe we didn't think our actions were provocative, but who knows how it looked to them?" He shook his head, unhappy with playing the part of devil's advocate but nonetheless appreciating the importance of doing so. "How do we know that we aren't the aggressors here? What if we cast the first stone, without even realizing it?"

"All valid lines of inquiry, Captain," Spock said. "However, it is likely that the Federation Council will focus instead on one incontrovertible fact: That the Tholians destroyed the *Bombay*. In light of Mr. Pennington's article, they will not be able to ignore it."

Suspicions and doubts pushed themselves front and center in Kirk's thoughts. He walked back to the desk and skimmed the article again. "How did Pennington get all this information?"

"Presumably, he had a confidential source."

"It would have to be someone fairly high in the chain of command to get him this much information," Kirk said.

"A logical assumption."

"But Reyes runs a tight ship, one of the tightest I've seen. I don't think his officers would talk to a reporter, on or off the record." Kirk narrowed his eyes as he stared at the screen. "Lower-decks personnel wouldn't have this kind of access."

"Perhaps Pennington himself has means we are not aware of."

"No," Kirk said, shaking his head. "He's a competent reporter, the Gary Mitchell piece proved that. But to get a break like this . . . it's almost impossible. Look here, in paragraph seven—he's quoting information that would have to have come from *our* duty logs. Pennington's good, but he's not *that* good, Spock. . . . Something's wrong with this picture."

"Your hypothesis suggests three likely scenarios, Captain. First, that there is a security leak in the command staff of Starbase 47. Second, that an enlisted crewman or non-commissioned officer gained access to classified data for the purpose of relaying it to Mr. Pennington. Or third, that Mr. Pennington himself has the requisite skills to penetrate Starfleet security protocols."

"None of which'll make me rest any easier tonight." Kirk clicked off the monitor. "Start encrypting all communications with Vanguard. That includes routine operations. And put a hold on all personal transmissions by the crew until we're safely out of the base's monitoring range tomorrow night."

"Yes, Captain."

"Dismissed."

Spock left quickly, no doubt on his way to the bridge to

relieve Scotty at the conn and implement the new security protocols.

Alone in his quarters, Kirk continued to ponder the security leak aboard Vanguard. Determining who had provided Pennington with such sensitive information would likely be a nigh-impossible task. Figuring out what other secrets might have been compromised by the leak would be even more difficult. But one other question, perhaps the least knowable of them all, was the one that haunted Kirk the most profoundly.

Why?

Reyes steeled himself for another miserable day of depositions. He and his department heads filed into the wardroom, their already grim moods further darkened by the morning news feeds about the *Bombay*. Rumors of war had already made the rounds of the starbase and were well on their way to a second circuit, freshly embellished with new exaggerations.

Desai and the two JAG lawyers, Liverakos and Moyer, entered through a separate door at the back of the room and quickly took their seats. No sooner had everyone settled into their seats than Desai double-tapped the judge's bell on the polished-wood table three times. "This board of inquiry is hereby reconvened," she said. For the past several days, she had ended her opening remarks there, preferring to allow the attorneys to take over. Today, she continued, "Because of new evidence made known to this board, evidence that suggests the loss of the *Bombay* was the result of a carefully premeditated sneak attack by forces of the Tholian Assembly, it is the summary ruling of this board that

Captain Gannon and her crew are absolved of any wrong-doing.

"Furthermore, this board also finds insufficient evidence to warrant further deposition of the *Bombay*'s supervising flag officer, or the command and support staff of Starbase 47.

"All records of these proceedings are hereby ordered sealed and classified by order of the Starfleet Judge Advocate General. These proceedings are closed. We are adjourned."

She tapped her bell once, collected her papers, rose from the table, and exited so quickly that her gold dress uniform resembled, to Reyes's eyes, little more than a blur. Moyer and Liverakos followed her out, exchanging confused shrugs and bewildered stares as they went. As the door closed behind them, Reyes and his department heads remained seated at the table, all of them stunned into silence.

Finally, it was fleet operations manager Ray Cannella who made the remark that needed to be said.

"Who wants to get lunch?"

Heads turned as Pennington walked past one of the outdoor cafés of Stars Landing. Affecting a nonchalant demeanor, he secretly basked in the sudden embrace of notoriety. He tried not to be too proud of his "accomplishment." If his story had the impact that he expected it to, then war between the Federation and the Tholian Assembly likely was not far off. Dark days would soon come to Vanguard, and to countless other places.

But the Truth is served, he reminded himself. *Justice for the* Bombay. *And for Oriana.*

Back in his apartment, Lora was still fuming about the late-morning search and interrogation by the Starfleet JAG office, but he had been expecting it. In fact, for the sense of vindication it offered him, he had welcomed it. Being despised was acceptable as long as he wasn't being ignored.

Getting closer to the café, the inviting aroma of espresso and pastry drew him in. He had all but surrendered himself to the anticipation of a latte and a beignet when his FNS pager buzzed softly on his wrist. The message on it was very brief: *Real Time*. It was the instruction his editor used when she wanted him to make contact via accelerated subspace radio. This far from Earth, even FTL communications normally lagged by as much as a full day. To maintain a real-time channel across such a vast distance required enormous amounts of power, and for most civilians it was prohibitively expensive.

Forcing away thoughts of the latte and pastry that would have to wait until later, he made his way up to the starbase's communications office. The small but technology-packed facility buzzed with countless overlapping audio feeds from around the galaxy. A bank of monitors on a far wall flickered with activity. Pennington held up his FNS credentials for Ensign Mugavero, the liaison officer on duty. "I have a request for a real-time channel to Earth," he said.

The blue-shirted young man led Pennington into a private room and entered the FNS code into a computer terminal. Moments later, the FNS icon appeared on the screen.

Mugavero motioned for the reporter to have a seat. "Here you go. It'll take a few seconds to connect, but once it does you should be in real-time contact."

Pennington sat down. "Thank you." The ensign left the room and closed the soundproof door behind him. A few seconds passed while Pennington pondered what Arlys could be so eager to tell him. An award? A promotion? An invitation to serve as the Paris correspondent? *After breaking this story for them, it's the least they could do.*

Arlys Warfield's image flickered onto the screen. A stern-jawed woman with a steel-gray brush cut, her fiery glare was said to be capable of breaking people's will, and her bullhorn of a voice could clear a path on any urban thoroughfare in the Federation in seconds flat. During the brief time that Tim had worked for her in the Paris office, he had overheard one of her senior editors remark that her last name was Warfield because a warpath simply wasn't wide enough to grant passage to her rage.

She reached forward, apparently adjusting the picture on her own monitor. *"Tim, is that you?"*

"Yes, Arlys, I'm here—in real time."

"Ah, there you are," she said. Her tone became venomous. *"You* idiot."

"Excuse me?"

"You blithering Edinburgh blockhead."

"Arlys, I'm sensing you're not entirely happy." Despite the staticky subspace feed, he now noticed that she looked even more disheveled and fatigued than was normal.

"Do you have any idea how many hornets you stirred up? How much trouble we're in?"

"We knew we'd be ruffling feathers," he said. "You said—"

"Forget what I said. That was when I trusted you."

"Now hang on, there's no—"

"How credible were your sources?"

"First-rate," he said, suddenly very defensive. "I heard it from a command-level source, found a stack of corroborating evidence, then I got *that* vouched for by someone directly involved."

"Well, check your syndicated feeds, because you've been duped," Arlys said. *"We all have."*

Sweat dampened his collar. His pulse throbbed uncomfortably in his temples. "Duped? . . . I don't understand."

Arlys massaged her forehead. Her expression was one of deep pain. *"Tim, how did you find that amazing evidence of yours?"*

He recoiled from the question. "It . . ." Suddenly, he felt very foolish explaining it. "It was an anonymous tip."

"An anonymous tip," she parroted. She threw a murderous glare at him from across the light-years. *"Wonderful."*

He wasn't sure he wanted to know the answer to his next question, but he had to ask anyway. "What was wrong with it?"

"Everything, for God's sake!" She flipped through the stack of papers on her desk, crumpling them and flinging them away as she ranted. *"Chronological inconsistencies in the sensor logs, fake security codes— Dammit, Tim, the logs from the* Enterprise *were signed by an officer who wasn't even alive when those reports were filed! You've got comm-traffic recordings on channels our own signals team confirms were clear. This isn't evidence— it's fiction!"*

Shock was setting in. "But I got it confirmed. . . ."

"According to Starfleet, you got snookered. And according to me, you just got fired."

It took a few seconds for those last few words to become real for Pennington. "No, Arlys, please, you can't . . . you—"

"Your unpaid expenses are being sent back to you, we're not covering them," she said. *"You can still submit stories as a stringer if you want, but I'd stick to canned releases for a while if I were you."*

"Arlys, wait, we can—"

"You're fired." She switched off the channel without even adding *Good luck* or *Take care*. The FNS icon flashed briefly on the screen, which then went dark. Pennington slumped forward and let his head thump against the offline monitor.

This isn't happening. This can't be happening.

It wasn't long before he was hyperventilating. He stretched the collar of his shirt away from his chest and pulled it up over his nose. Taking long, deep breaths and exhaling heavily, he calmed himself by degrees. Bile crept up his esophagus. His stomach heaved. *So this is what total failure feels like.*

Reason reasserted itself momentarily. He powered up the monitor in front of him and patched in to Vanguard's internal directory. Selecting "M," he scrolled quickly down to Israel Medina's name in the crew roster.

It wasn't there. There was no entry between "Medeira, Specialist Roderigo," and "Meeker, Ensign Rory."

Oh, bloody hell, no.

The entire distance between the communications office and salvage bay four blurred past the sprinting reporter.

He bounded into the salvage bay, which was busy with second-shift activity. An antigrav load lifter nearly clipped him at the knees until a sharp-eyed crewman whistled shrilly behind Pennington's ear and waved him out of the way. The first person whom Pennington was able to flag down and corner long enough to swap two words was a frazzled-looking young woman who had "MALIK, K." stenciled on the front of her coveralls.

"Crewman Malik, can you help me please?"

She looked at him with the pity one would expect for a lost child. He hadn't realized how desperate he sounded. "What's wrong, sir?"

"I'm trying to find Chief Medina," he said.

She shook her head and leaned closer, as if she had misheard him the first time. "Who?"

"Chief Israel Medina, the gamma-shift cargo supervisor."

Malik shrugged. "Never heard of him, sir. Our gamma-shift supervisor's Master Chief Shalas." She pointed down the long aisle of shipping containers at an Andorian woman in a red Starfleet uniform shirt. "That's her down there. She's covering beta shift today."

Pennington backed away slowly toward the exit, no longer caring whether he blundered into the path of some large, dangerous machine. It hardly mattered anymore, one way or another. *A quick death might be preferable,* he decided.

As meaningless as such concepts as "day" and "night" were in deep space, as far as local time aboard Vanguard was concerned it was the middle of the night. Naturally, it was now, during the sleep cycles of the majority of the Diplomatic Corps staff, that Tholian Ambassador Sesrene had elected to call a meeting with Envoy Sovik, who, in turn, had woken Ambassador Jetanien, who then roused Anna Sandesjo and brought her down here for no good reason except perhaps to fetch the Chelon a bowl of his offensive-smelling broth.

Sesrene, true to character, treaded the fine line that separated curt from rude. *"Your government has recanted its call for war."* He spoke through the room's universal translator. The metallic screech of his true voice was muffled but still audible from inside his envirosuit. *"We have no further business."*

Sandesjo remained a short distance behind Jetanien and Sovik, who stood at the meeting room table across from the Tholian delegation, which was composed of Sesrene and his attachés, Pozrene and Tashrene. Lifting a hand to stifle whatever reply Sovik had been formulating, Jetanien said to Sesrene, "Quite the contrary. We remain concerned about your health. This is the first we've seen of your delegation since your . . . *episode* a few weeks ago. Are you well? Do you require any medical assistance? Or adjustments to your living quarters?"

Sesrene reached out and initiated a touch-telepathy link with his attachés, a practice that Sandesjo had found odd until she realized that it was not all that different from humanoids conferring in whispers. Until their conference was concluded, there would be nothing to do but wait in patient silence.

The three Tholians were all bundled in their golden-hued envirosuits, about which Jetanien had prattled on during the long walk from his office. Composed of Tholian silk, the envirosuits were surprisingly lightweight and flexible around the Tholians' crystalline, arthropod bodies. No warmer than room temperature on their exterior, their interiors sustained a combination of intense heat and crushingly dense corrosive gas—a Class-N environment that was duplicated in their quarantined residential suites. What little of their heads was visible through their translucent faceplates suggested that their species exhibited a wide variety of colorations. With their multilimbed physiques, Tholians reminded Sandesjo of the venomous *ghewpu'tlh* that populated some of the darker, untamed forests on Qo'noS. Being in the same room with them made her deeply curious as to how one of these exotic-looking *novpu* would fare in single combat against a Klingon warrior.

Finally, the touch-telepathy link was broken, and Sesrene's eyespots brightened slightly as he said, *"A temporary affliction. It is of no further concern."*

"We are greatly relieved to hear that, Your Excellency," Sovik said with a small nod.

"We have no more business with you at this time," Sesrene said. He turned away from the table, and his attachés moved in synch with him.

"Ambassador," Jetanien said, his voice suddenly large enough to fill the room with its deep, booming resonance. Sesrene paused then turned very slowly back toward Jetanien, who continued, "Though our council has chosen the path of peace, do not be misled into thinking that we are fools. We know full well that your forces attacked and destroyed our vessel at Ravanar. Starfleet will watch your borders far more closely from now on. . . . We won't be taken by surprise again."

The implied threat seemed to hold Sesrene and Jetanien

in place, like the opposing poles of a magnet, filling the room with an undercurrent of violent reprisal.

Then Sesrene ended the discussion.

"Neither will we."

In unison, the Tholian delegation left the room, moving with almost mechanical precision. Once they were gone, Jetanien turned away and exited through a different door, saying nothing but clearly expecting Sovik and Sandesjo to follow him.

The Chelon didn't speak until the three of them were in a turbolift on their way back upstairs. "That was not good," he said. Then, to Sandesjo's amazement, he said nothing more. Even after they returned to the deserted Federation Embassy office, he had nothing to add to his statement in the turbolift.

As the ambassador marched toward his office, Sandesjo said to his retreating back, "Should I postpone your morning meetings?" For once, Jetanien neither interrupted nor answered her. He went into his private office and closed the door, which emitted a soft double-beep to indicate that he had locked it.

She and Sovik looked at each other. He raised one eyebrow. She shrugged. He departed, and she made the long, lonely walk back to her private quarters.

The repetitive grind of long days, which by now had blurred together, left Sandesjo enervated. Filing a report with Turag would no doubt be a tedious matter, and it was one that she would prefer to put off until morning. Unfortunately, she knew that he would be livid if she waited that long to brief him.

She locked her door, then unlocked her slim briefcase

and opened it on her dining table. *I hate the waiting,* she fumed, as the device established its encrypted subspace link. *It takes too long. Sooner or later, someone will notice.*

"bImoHqu'," came the challenge-phrase.

In a glum monotone she answered, *"jIwuQ."*

Turag's harshly shadowed face replaced the Klingon trefoil emblem. He grinned. *"Another late night, Lurqal?"*

"Don't call me by my true name, you *yIntagh,*" she said. "I don't like being reminded."

"Spare me your tale of woe. Report."

"Jetanien told Sesrene that the Federation knows the Tholians destroyed the *Bombay.* Both sides seem ready for war."

"Then why aren't they at war?"

"Clearly, Jetanien and his peers have a larger objective—one that war does not serve."

"If the Federation is unprepared to make war to hold its ground in the Gonmog Sector, we might find it easier to stake a claim here than we thought."

"Perhaps." She transmitted to Turag an image she had clandestinely recorded during the meeting between Jetanien and Sesrene. "In any event, Sesrene and the other Tholians appear to have recovered."

"Any word yet on what caused their seizures?"

She shook her head. "None."

"Jay'va," Turag muttered. *"If we could find the source, we could use it against them. It would be a great help when it comes time to conquer them."*

"I will keep that in mind," Sandesjo said.

From the other end of the conversation, Sandesjo heard

the beeping of a comm signal. *"Lugok demands an update,"* Turag said. *"I must go. Qapla'."*

"Qapla'," she said, then shut down the channel as quickly as possible. She had just locked her briefcase when the door to her quarters opened without warning.

Standing in Sandesjo's doorway, shadowed by backlighting from the corridor, was Lieutenant Commander T'Prynn.

"Good evening, Miss Sandesjo."

She nodded politely, but her throat tightened. "Commander."

T'Prynn walked in uninvited. The door closed behind her. Standing in front of Sandesjo, she drummed her fingertips once on the closed lid of the briefcase. "Working late?"

"Just finished," she said.

"Good." Moving with exaggerated slowness as if to prolong the moment, T'Prynn circled the table, trailing her right index finger along its edge. Her fingernail left a subtle gouge in the table's varnish. "Then I am free to take my time."

Sandesjo was convinced that T'Prynn's dark brown eyes were staring clean through her pseudo-identity. The lithe Vulcan woman, who was slightly taller than Sandesjo to begin with, took advantage of the fact that the younger woman was seated and loomed over her. "Some things are best done by degrees," T'Prynn said. "Do you concur?"

Sandesjo stared back with equal intensity. "Absolutely."

T'Prynn's hand shot forward and grasped a fistful of Sandesjo's auburn hair. Sandesjo grabbed T'Prynn's arm and dug her fingernails into the skin. Twisting Sandesjo's hair as she pulled, T'Prynn yanked her, shrieking, from her chair and slammed her, back-first, against the wall.

The Vulcan woman's kiss was rough and hungry. Sandesjo reveled in it until their lips parted. They both breathed heavily and eyed each other through chaotic locks of ferally tousled hair. Sandesjo gasped for breath through a delighted smile. "You're early, my love."

Saying nothing, T'Prynn gave Sandesjo's hair another hard, aphrodisiacal twist and kissed her again. Blissfully surrendered into her lover's embrace, Sandesjo savored the irony that not only had she forsaken Klingon tradition for the touch of other women, but that of all the women she might have loved she had lost her heart to a Vulcan.

Breaking free of the devouring kiss, T'Prynn tugged on Sandesjo's sleeve and, moving with the languid grace of a slow-dancing flame, led her toward the bedroom.

The inevitable, eternal reproach of her ancestors haunted Sandesjo's thoughts: *They will never let me enter* Sto-Vo-Kor. Sinking onto the bed beside T'Prynn, however, she decided that the dishonor of her next life would be a small price to pay for such a love in this one.

Hours later, Pennington returned home to his cluttered, search-tossed apartment and glowering wife. After drowning his sorrows in the pub nearest his apartment, a bout of the spins and an episode of public vomiting had left him with no choice but to call it a night.

Eyeing his miserable state, Lora sneered and said, "I see you're taking the phrase 'filthy, stinking drunk' literally."

He wanted to act aloof, but tears rolled freely from his eyes as he slurred out, " 'Sbeen a miserable damn day."

"Oh, I see," she said. "You have some sob story that explains why I haven't seen or heard from you for twelve hours?"

"Liars!" He stumbled against the coffee table and kicked it over, impervious to pain for the moment. "I wanted truth with a capital 'T' and got crap." As he staggered slowly to his liquor cabinet, his vision softened but his righteous anger didn't. "Set me up, the bastards. Data card, Medina, all of it, just a sham." He yanked open the cabinet door and fumbled to grab the whiskey.

Lora tried to steal the bottle from his hands. He refused to let go. "Put that down," she said. "You're drunk."

"Am I?" With a violent tug, he pulled the bottle free of her hands. "Have you got physical evidence? A second witness?"

"What in God's name are you going on about, Tim?"

The cork of the whiskey bottle came free with a delightful, hollow-sounding *foop*. He swigged a hefty mouthful and didn't bother to sleeve the excess from his chin afterward. "I lost my damn job! They fired me. . . . Jesus, don't you read the news?"

"This is about your *Bombay* story?"

"That's what I always liked about you, Lora—you're *quick*."

She threw up her arms and stormed away from him, seeking the safety of a little distance. "Well, *excuse me* if I find you a little hard to follow when you come home a drunken mess."

"They buried the whole thing," he said, falling backward onto the couch. He grunted heavily on impact. "FNS denied the story." He put the bottle to his lips and upended it, dumping a solid double down his throat. Seconds later, he felt sick. "And those bastards at the Federation Council . . . said they can't go to war 'cause all the evidence is fake. Fake! Are they kidding?" He fumbled the bottle and spilled half its contents into his lap. He rubbed his face vigorously. It was numb to his touch. "Is this right? The goddamned Tholians killed her, but Starfleet does nothing! Is that fair? Am I supposed to call this justice?"

Lora folded her arms. *"Who* did they kill?"

"What do you mean, *who* . . . ? They killed the whole damn crew, two hundred people, the team on the planet—"

"You said they killed *her.*"

Paralysis set in instantly. He grappled with his whiskey-fogged short-term memory, trying to replay his own words of a few seconds earlier. The warmth of the booze departed his face, which he felt turning cold and gray with dread. A shiver of guilty horror trembled his entire body.

His wife glared at him with a hatred like ice.

"What was her name?"

He had rehearsed a thousand lies in case this day ever came. Telling stories fleshed out with fine details was his stock-in-trade. He dealt by day in facts and obstinate truths, which had only given him a better appreciation for what they sounded like. Inventing a clever but unimpeachably simple cover story had been easier than he had expected. All that remained now was to let the story work its wonders.

Instead, his mouth blurted out "Oriana."

Lora's fury dissolved into agony, then she screamed with rage as she hurled her knickknacks at him, one after another. A porcelain rabbit pelted the top of his head. He yelped in pain as the horn of a pewter unicorn impaled his thigh. Pennington fell to the floor and retreated into a fetal curl behind the overturned coffee table as his wife continued her barrage.

When it finally ceased, he opened his eyes to find her sitting cross-legged on the other side of the room, weeping angrily into her palms. "You bastard," she said between distraught whimpers. "Damn you."

He was still too shell-shocked to leave the protective cover of the coffee table. "Lora," he began, "I . . . I just—"

"Shut up, Tim. Just shut up." She thrust her hands away from her face, revealing her tear-streaked makeup and swollen eyes. "I'm done talking to you. Get out."

"It's my apartment," he said.

"You found another bed before, you can do it again. Get out."

Pennington crawled first on to the couch, then he pushed himself back to a standing position from there. He picked up his bottle of whiskey, which lay on its side on the sofa. Inspecting it close up, he realized it was empty. He cast a bitter glare at Lora, then he turned and hurled the empty bottle into the bedroom. It shattered on the wall above the bed, sprinkling the sheets with countless shards of glass.

"Sleep well," he said, then staggered out of his home with no other place to go. Walking away from his front door, he grew more aware with every step that because of one critical mistake, the life he had known was gone—his reputation, his career, his marriage . . . and then he realized, with the perfect clarity of the damned, who he had to thank for his current circumstances.

Time for a little talk, he decided. *Face-to-face this time.*

19

Lieutenant Uhura read through the results of her work one additional time. Soft synthetic tones signaled incoming transmissions and completed computer functions. The *Enterprise*'s computer had been working overtime comparing Tim Pennington's allegedly fraudulent evidence with the *Enterprise*'s own databank records regarding the destruction of the *Bombay*, and with its copy of the recordings on the *Bombay*'s emergency buoy. A gentle whirring emanated from the console in front of her, caused by fans that were cooling some of the more sensitive circuits in the delicate duotronic system.

She locked the latest results of her studies on the screen beside her work panel, then swiveled her chair toward the first officer, who was conferring quietly with Captain Kirk at the science station. "Captain? Mr. Spock? I've completed my analysis."

The two men needed no further prompting. They halted their conversation and joined her at her station. Kirk leaned forward, his hand on the back of her chair, while Spock stood tall behind him, hands folded behind his back. Before the change to the new uniforms, Uhura would not have paid much attention to the captain's proximity, but the high cut of her miniskirt made her a bit self-conscious. Tugging it down, she corrected her posture and turned her chair demurely away from the captain.

Kirk said, "Report, Lieutenant."

"It's just as you suspected, Captain." She pointed at some highlighted items on her screen. "The documentation itself is fake, but much of its content was accurate." Switching the screen to a specific example, she continued, "For instance, the intercepted comm traffic that shows military activity by the Tholians is genuine, but Pennington's source put it on the wrong frequency." Another screen of information appeared at her touch. "His lead about the *Bombay* transporting a sensor screen to the outpost on Ravanar IV was correct, and the documents that supported it were in authentic Starfleet formats, but the names of supervising officers on the forms were obviously wrong."

"A logical tactic—if the forger wanted the documents to be easily discredited," Spock said.

Uhura wasn't following Spock's reasoning. "But if the goal was to discredit them, why fill them with real intelligence?"

"Guilt by association," Kirk said.

"Precisely, Captain," Spock said. Looking back at Uhura, he continued, "Discrediting the documents was not the goal, Lieutenant. Using the documents to discredit the truth they contained was the objective."

Uhura looked at the data again, and this time she was appalled. "Then whoever did this had access to all the real intelligence data," she said.

Spock nodded. "A logical deduction."

"In other words, Starfleet created this fraud," Uhura said.

Kirk straightened his posture. "I believe the preferred term is 'disinformation campaign.' "

"Sir," Uhura said, turning her chair toward Kirk, "this 'disinformation campaign' smeared the reputation of a civilian reporter. Shouldn't we do something to correct that?"

The captain seemed reluctant to answer her. He looked at Spock, who arched an eyebrow, then said to Uhura, "There is nothing we can do, Lieutenant."

"I don't understand," Uhura said. "We have the evidence. We know that it's real, that his facts were *essentially* true even if the fine print was wrong. Why can't we—"

"Because it would be a court-martial offense," Kirk said.

Uhura stared in shock at Kirk, then she looked to Spock for a second opinion. He lifted one eyebrow and said, "The captain is correct. Commodore Reyes ordered us to purge our databanks of all information regarding our mission to Ravanar IV. We can not use this information to exonerate Mr. Pennington in the court of public opinion . . . no matter how unfairly we know he was treated."

Shaking her head, Uhura said, "That's not justice."

"No, Lieutenant," Kirk said, "it's not. But as someone recently told me, justice has a long memory. . . . And something tells me it won't forget about Mr. Pennington any time soon."

Absorbed in his handwritten notes for his speech at the *Bombay* memorial, which was scheduled for the following morning, Reyes walked into his quarters and heard the door close behind him—taking with it most of his reading light.

His quarters were almost completely dark. Looking around, he saw that the only source of illumination in the main room was a lone candle on his dining table. It cast a soft ring of golden radiance over a small circle of serving plates and bowls, all filled with food. Seated at the table was Rana Desai. She greeted him with a tiny wave of her hand. "I made dinner."

Reyes joined her at the table and set down his notes beside his place setting. He hesitated to sit down. "Everything looks wonderful," he said. "What's the occasion?"

"It was my turn," Desai said.

He nodded and sat down. "The chicken smells great," he said, even though he wasn't hungry.

"Tandoori," she said. "My mother's recipe."

Sorrow fell across Reyes's face like a curtain. His head suddenly felt heavy, and his chin drooped toward his chest.

Desai was out of her chair and at his side immediately.

"Diego, I'm so sorry, I didn't mean to . . ." Her apology trailed off as she gently coiled her arms around Reyes's head and embraced him to her. "Zeke told me what happened. Why didn't you come to me?"

"Because I'm stubborn," he said.

"It was because of the inquiry, wasn't it?"

"Yes."

She kissed the top of his head tenderly, a gesture he knew was one of sympathy. "You're a stupid, stupid man sometimes."

"I know."

She turned his chin upward so that he was looking her in the eye. "How are you holding up?"

"I'm functioning," he said. "But I'm not happy about it."

"You should take some time off. Go back to Luna and see your family. I'm sure they'd love to see you."

"Some of them, maybe," Reyes said. Noting her stare of gentle reproach, he added, "It's eight weeks there and eight weeks back. Starfleet's not going to grant me a four-month bereavement leave. . . . I asked."

Stroking her fingers through the gray brush-cut behind his receding hairline, Desai said, "I'm sorry, Diego."

"Nothing to be done about it." He added with a rueful grin, "I knew space was a big place when I took this job."

"It just seems unfair, is all," she said.

"Sure it is—but what isn't?" Reyes reached forward and picked up the bottle of wine on the table. He examined the label. "The '51 Brunello Riserva," he said. "Very nice."

"It was that or the Chateauneuf-du-Pape '41," Desai said. "But I figured with tandoori chicken—"

"You made the right choice." He untangled her arms from his neck and gently kissed the palm of her left hand. "And so did I, when I fell for you."

She perched on his left thigh, half-lit in the candlelight. "Does thinking about her make it better or worse?"

"I'm not sure." Reaching his arms around her, he began tearing the foil off the bottle of wine. "Right now, the hurt doesn't change much, whether I'm thinking about it or not. At this point, I have to make an effort not to think about her, if that's what you're asking."

"I was just wondering if focusing on good memories might help." Lowering her head, she shook it in denial. "That's foolish, I guess. Ignore me, I'm just a lawyer—I don't know what I'm talking about."

"Thinking good thoughts probably can't be any worse than beating myself up for not being there," he said. "Hand me the bottle opener?" Desai leaned over and grabbed the small air-needle cork remover, then handed it to Reyes, who pushed it through the cork and began carefully pumping air into the tiny pocket of space beneath it. "It's funny, but ever since I learned Mom was sick, I've been fixated on a Spanish lullaby she used to sing to me when I was a boy." The cork popped free. He set it aside and gestured to Desai to snag a pair of glasses. "She only kind of sung it—her voice when she was putting me to bed was half a whisper. I don't even remember the words anymore . . . just the sound of it. A song sung just for me."

"Do you even remember what it was called?"

"No idea," Reyes said. "Mom used to talk about teaching it to Jeanne, but somehow there was just never time."

"Well, you were only married to her for eleven years," Desai teased. "You think these things happen overnight?"

"I think Mom was just waiting for me and Jeanne to have kids. If Jeanne had gotten pregnant, I think she and Mom would've found the time." At the mention of children and pregnancy, Reyes noticed that Desai looked away, subtly distancing herself from the topic. He wondered if there was something in Desai's past that made it a sore point. Closing the subject, he said, "Anyway, I doubt my father would know what the song was. He was never much for sentimentalism."

Desai put the two glasses within easy reach. One at a time, he tipped each glass at a slight angle and filled its lower third with the deep-crimson, complexly aromatic Montalcino. He handed one glass to Desai and lifted the other for a toast. "To those who are gone but never forgotten." Their glasses clinked with a delicate chiming sound, and he savored the layers of flavor in the wine. Desai finished her sip first, then reached down and picked up his notes for the memorial address.

"For tomorrow?"

"Yeah," he said. "I presided over a couple funerals aboard the *Dauntless,*" he said, "but paying respects for an entire ship and her crew . . . that's a duty I haven't had before."

She put down his notes. "I'm sure you'll do fine."

"It's not my speech I'm worried about," he said. "Tomorrow I'm going to say a lot of high-minded things about courage, and justice, and why we're all out here risking our lives. It's going to be inspiring, if I say so myself." He took another long sip of his wine. "I just want to convince myself it's as true as I'm saying it is."

Desai kissed him tenderly on the lips, then touched her forehead to his. "You will," she said. "You made a believer out of me, and I'm a lawyer—I don't trust anybody."

Tim Pennington wasn't sober yet. It had been nearly four hours since he was evicted from his own apartment. The warm numbness of his buzz had passed, however, leaving behind only severe halitosis and the woozy feeling of walking on rubber legs.

He lingered on Fontana Meadow, listening to the gurgling of the fountain and wallowing in the solitude. Then the dome of artificial sky rapidly brightened with a new ersatz dawn. Alpha shift would start soon. Station personnel would report to their regular duty stations.

That's my cue. He headed for the turbolift.

Minutes later he stepped off on to level five, near the station core. He found the office he was looking for, then sequestered himself in a small maintenance nook a few meters away. Standing with his back to the wall, he faced the door and waited, taking shallow breaths and listening for footsteps.

Precisely fifteen seconds before 0800, he heard the crisp clack of boot heels on metal deck flooring. He held his breath.

T'Prynn arrived at the door and entered a security code on the digital keypad next to it. The door opened. She stepped halfway in, then paused in the doorway. With her back still turned to him, she said, "Are you coming in, Mr. Pennington?"

So much for the element of surprise.

Prying himself out of his corner, he plodded toward her office. She stepped in and waited on the other side of the door until he was close enough for the sensor to hold it for him. He hesitated, then dragged himself inside.

Even before the door closed, the heavier gravity pulled his feet to the deck. Dry heat attacked his skin like a hydrophage. The inside of her office was mostly dark, just a few spills of red light on the walls and a harsh white overhead above her desk. Like many other Vulcans whose rank afforded them such privileges, T'Prynn had altered the environmental settings of her personal workspace and, Pennington assumed, her living quarters to emulate the climate and gravity of her native Vulcan.

It took him a few moments to acclimate himself to the new conditions. T'Prynn used the time to take a seat behind her austere, curved desk. She sat in a relaxed pose, resting her arms at her sides. Aloof and apparently unfazed by his impromptu appearance on her doorstep, her voice was as seductively husky as it was cold. "To what do I owe the pleasure of your visit?"

"I came to say . . . 'Congratulations.' "

One eyebrow lifted, turning her mien curious. "For what?"

"Don't be so modest," he said, laying bare his sarcasm. "Taking all that real intelligence and dressing it up to look fake? That was brilliant." Without betraying any reaction, she got up from her chair. He pressed on. "Reeling me in with the anonymous tip? Nice touch." T'Prynn unlocked a wall panel for a narrow storage compartment as Pennington's rant gained momentum. "Oh, but your masterpiece— your pièce de résistance—had to be making up an entire person to vouch for all those lies, so that I'd have someone to trust." She glanced at him as she opened the panel. His spiel built toward a crescendo. "What utter genius! Sending me a walking, breathing, flesh-and-blood lie to convince me that all the other lies are true . . . I confess, Commander, my hat's off to—"

She pulled a familiar-looking duffel bag from the storage nook and tossed it in a clanking heap at Pennington's feet. "One of the facts of life aboard a brand-new starbase," she said, walking back to her desk, "is that not all the onboard systems are fully functional right away. Like the garbage incinerators, for instance."

Sheer surprise, the impact of the unexpected, silenced Pennington for a moment. He stared at the duffel, memories of Oriana's life and death flooding back into the forefront of his thoughts. When he looked up at T'Prynn, she was as neutral in her expression as ever, but he thought he could almost detect a small hint of smug self-satisfaction in her demeanor.

Disgust grew inside him, like a dark bloom opening on a moonless night. "So what?" Not seeing any reaction on her part, he shook his head at her, chuckled grimly, almost pitied her. "Is this some kind of threat? Play ball or you'll tell my wife about Oriana? Stop making trouble or you'll smear my good name?" He stepped over the bag and walked forward, one unusually heavy, ponderous step at a time. "Well, guess what. Lora knows already. She left me. And my reputation? You already did a number on that, thanks a lot." He planted his knuckles on her desk and leaned forward. "You've got nothing on me. Not a damn thing. I'm down, but I'm not done. . . . I'll be watching you."

He straightened his posture, never breaking eye contact with her. She remained as stoic and unblinking as ever. He wondered if she had even paid attention to a single word he said. *It's like talking to a bloody mannequin.*

Pennington walked away from her, picked up the duffel, and headed for the door. Just before entering the range of the sensor that would open it for him, he looked back. "I'm your worst nightmare, Commander—a Scot with nothing left to lose."

"My *nightmares* are worse than you could ever imagine," T'Prynn said sharply. Before he could inquire about this abrupt sundering of her emotional control, she bolted from her chair and turned her back on him. "Good day, Mr. Pennington."

Sensing the deadly seriousness of her dismissal, he left without pressing her patience further. Back in the corridor, he sighed with relief as gravity gave up some of its dominion over him, and the relatively cool air suddenly leached sweat from his overheated, overdried skin.

He wondered where to go next. Lora would still be packing, so returning home was out of the question for now. Then he remembered the *Bombay* memorial scheduled at 1100. It would be newsworthy, and if he left now he would be able to stake out a prime spot from which to listen, and record the event, and begin compiling his first non-FNS, purely freelance submission in several years.

It wouldn't be much; it might not merit anything more than an unattributed two-line blurb at the end of a text feed. Earning his way back to credibility, back to being a headline reporter whose name was worth more than a punch line for a joke, would be a long and tedious journey. The pessimist in him asked how it could be worth such a struggle to rebuild his career when it would always carry this blemish of failure.

Then he faced his only other option: Quit and admit defeat.

Not bloody likely.

He stepped into the turbolift and decided to stop at the café before the memorial. If he really was going to start his career over again, he would need caffeine—and lots of it. Descending toward the terrestrial enclosure, words he had uttered defiantly to T'Prynn returned to him, this time as a solemn pledge that he made to himself:

I'm down, but I'm not done.

20

The door signal buzzed as Reyes was making a final check of his dress-uniform decorations. "Come in." He heard the swish of the door opening as he adjusted the overly tight jacket.

Out of the corner of his eye, he caught the unmistakable, ponderous shape of Ambassador Jetanien. The Chelon diplomat turned his body one way then the other before he saw Reyes in the small alcove beside the door. "Are you ready to go?"

"Pretty much." Reyes gave a last, ineffectual finger-combing to his thinning, dark gray hair. He stepped toward Jetanien, fully intending to lead the Ambassador out, but instead he came to a halt a few meters shy of the door.

Jetanien sounded concerned. "Something wrong?"

It was likely intended as a superficial query, along the lines of *How are you?*, but Reyes considered it carefully for several seconds. "Not exactly wrong," he said finally, "but definitely on my mind." Reyes interpreted Jetanien's patient silence to mean that the Chelon was willing to hear him out. "A lot of hard questions got asked during the *Bombay* inquiry," he said. "I got blindsided a few times, too. Now I wonder if maybe I deserved it."

Folding his claws together at his waist, Jetanien asked, "How so?"

"The maintenance schedules . . . the matériel shortages. I put Hallie and her crew through the wringer, month after month, without a break. She never complained, so I figured everything was fine. But that was just Hallie's way— she'd never make a fuss. She was always ready to make the best of a bad situation and give you a smile and say, 'No problem.' "

Bowing slightly forward, into what seemed to be a pensive stance, Jetanien made a few low clicking sounds before he spoke. "Do you think that if the *Bombay* had been better maintained that it might have prevailed against the Tholian ambush?"

"No. . . . They were outnumbered, outgunned. It's a miracle she put up as good a fight as she did."

"Then it is not worth castigating yourself over," Jetanien said. "Perhaps the deficiencies in the *Bombay*'s maintenance and supply were material factors in its loss at Ravanar—but it is just as likely that they were not."

"Maybe," Reyes said, "but I need to know. If simple mistakes got that ship destroyed—"

Jetanien interrupted, "Are we now to hold ourselves to an impossible standard? We are engaged in a long-term operation that is almost certain to claim more lives before it is done. Mistakes will be made—some by you, some by me, and more by countless others known and unknown to us. We are not infallible; neither are we omniscient or omnipotent."

"But we drive ourselves as though we are," Reyes said. "And we push others along with us . . . maybe too far."

"Just as Captain Gannon pushed herself and her crew," Jetanien countered. "They accepted the dangers of this mission, just as we did, because they knew that something greater than ourselves is at stake. It is the calculus of the few versus the many, Commodore—and you know as well as I that we have come too far to succumb now to doubt or indecision."

"That still doesn't answer the only question that really matters to me," Reyes said. "All I want to know is whether I was responsible for what happened to Hallie and her crew."

"Yes, you were," Jetanien said. The brusqueness of the statement caught Reyes off guard. Then the Chelon added, "You were their commanding officer—that makes you responsible for everything they did, and for the fate that they met. Does that make you culpable? No. . . . What's done is done, Commodore. No one is asking you to take the blame." Jetanien stepped toward the door, which slid open. He gestured toward it. "We're asking you to help us find a glimmer of hope in this tragedy. We're asking you to lead."

Reyes nodded slowly and walked toward the door. As he passed the ambassador, he said quietly, "Thank you, Jetanien."

Jetanien made his hushed reply as he followed Reyes into the corridor. "You're welcome, Diego."

Reyes didn't visit the terrestrial enclosure very often. Official duties kept him inside his office or the operations center most of the time; occasionally, he saw the inside of a meeting room or made a late-night visit to Zeke or Rana's quarters. Standing beside the spare, small podium, waiting for executive officer Cooper to introduce him, Reyes was overwhelmed by how large Vanguard's "park" really was.

Seated on the bleachers that surrounded the athletic fields, and gathered on the sloping lawn behind the bleachers, were several hundred station personnel and civilian residents who had turned out to hear his memorial address this morning. At the back of the crowd was Lugok, the portly Klingon envoy.

Standing together in the front row before the podium were the senior members of the clergy who resided on the station: Father McKee from the nondenominational Christian chapel; Rabbi Geller; Imam al-Jazaar; Brother Sihanouk from the Buddhist temple; Zharran sh'Rassa, from the Andorian *eresh'tha;* and Gom glasch Moar, the resident Tellarite *throg,* or "sin eater."

Speaking to large groups was one of the few things that still made Reyes sick to his stomach with anxiety. He took a slow, deep breath and checked for the fifty-third time that his notes were still secure in his hand.

Less than a minute before 1100, Commander Cooper emerged from the standing crowd around the podium, nodded to Reyes, and walked up the three stairs onto the raised platform. He moved to the lectern, switched on a small microphone sensor, and cleared his throat. "Good morning. Please rise." The crowd rose from its seats or from the lawn. The Starfleet personnel in the audience stood at attention, and a respectful hush settled over the throng. Cooper nodded to Reyes, then looked back at the crowd. "Please welcome Commodore Reyes."

Polite, muted applause greeted Reyes as he ascended the stairs. Cooper yielded the lectern to him then stepped off the podium, leaving Reyes as the sole focus of attention. Reyes glanced at his first note card, then wondered why he had brought them; he was too nervous to make sense of what he had written. He turned the cards facedown on the lectern, drew a breath, and looked out at the small sea of faces that surrounded him.

"Thank you Commander Cooper," he began. "Fellow Starfleet officers; enlisted personnel; civilian residents; and honored guests; thank you for being here this morning.

"Today, I stand with you in grief. I mourn with you. Like many of you . . . perhaps all of you . . . I lost someone I knew aboard the *Bombay*. . . . A friend. . . . For five years, before she was the *Bombay*'s CO, Hallie Gannon was my first officer aboard the *Starship Dauntless*. From her first day aboard she was everything a captain could ask for in a number one; tireless, efficient, always ready to take on one more job. When she took command of the *Bombay*, I knew her crew had scored a lucky break.

"Last week, they lost their lives serving one another, serving Starfleet, and serving the Federation. History will remember them as heroes. But I'm sure that many of you will remember them first as friends, and as loved ones. Some of you served with them on other ships, some of you attended Starfleet Academy or basic training together. You knew them in ways that others throughout the Federation could not. Feel honored that you had that chance, even though the pain you feel for their loss is heartbreaking.

"I wish I could undo it, but I can't. . . . My words must pale when compared to the tragedy that took their lives, shrink when measured against the vast emptiness their deaths have left in our lives. Some of us are in denial; we can't believe they're gone. Some of us are raging and desperate to strike back at someone, anyone, just so we can feel like we're doing something to balance the scales.

"Our anger is justified, but we must not let it consume us. We must not let our sorrow be turned to hatred. Justice is not vengeance, even if some want to believe otherwise. At times like this, it's vital that we embrace the better angels of our nature, no matter how hard it is.

"We also can't let our loss paralyze us. Among the obligations of all those who wear the Starfleet uniform, one of the most sacred is our duty to one another. It is a commitment that does not end with the loss of one life, or one ship. The best way for us to honor the sacrifice of Captain Gannon and her crew is to continue their work, to finish what they started, and to make sure they didn't die in vain.

"There's a poem, 'The Young Dead Soldiers,' by Archibald MacLeish of Earth, that honors those who've died in the service of their people. Speaking for the fallen, he wrote: 'Our deaths are not ours; they are yours; they will mean what you make of them.'

"That's as true today as when he wrote it, more than three centuries ago. When Starfleet personnel give their lives in the line of duty, they know that it will fall to history—to the living—to judge whether their sacrifices were made in vain, or for a greater good and a better future.

"Ultimately, the value of their lives depends upon how we honor them, and upon how faithfully we continue the work that they began.

"Captain Gannon and her crew gave us their deaths; let us give them their meaning—of peace and wisdom, of service and freedom, of courage and hope."

Reyes paused. Reverent silence surrounded him like a bulwark. Scanning the crowd, he saw faces streaked with tears, heads bowed in grief, friends and shipmates clinging to one another for emotional support. "When I was a boy on Luna, my father and I planted a tree to honor my grandfather when he passed away." He turned his head and looked toward Stars Landing and the far side of the enclosure. "In honor of the *Bombay* and her crew, a tree is being planted right now on Fontana Meadow—a Denevan dogwood. With its year-round flowers and solid roots, it's a reminder of the lesson of the Psalms—that the life of a good person is like a tree whose leaf does not wither.

"Trees take a long time to grow, and wounds take a long time to heal. But it's time for us to begin. Great labors await us, but so do great wonders. Captain Gannon and her crew are taken from us, but our lives will be their legacy.

"Thank you."

He gathered up his note cards and left the podium to strong applause. As soon as he had cleared the stairs, Commander Cooper was back at the lectern, providing instructions for those who wished to follow the clergy to religious memorials scheduled for 1200, and explaining how to find the grief counselors' offices in Vanguard Hospital.

Lost in his own thoughts, Reyes didn't see Kirk until the young CO intercepted him on the edge of the dispersing crowd.

"Commodore," Kirk said, falling into step beside him.

Reyes nodded politely. "Captain."

"Good speech," Kirk said.

"Thank you."

"I'm curious," Kirk said. "That part about some of us wanting to strike back at anyone . . . was that meant just for me?"

"Not *just* you, no." The two officers stepped onto a flat, moving walkway that would carry them to a bank of turbolifts along the station's core. "You aren't the only one who feels a sense of duty to Starfleet personnel lost in action."

"I didn't think that I was," Kirk said. "But if you're worried that I'm going to do something rash, you needn't be. I'm still a Starfleet officer. Duty comes first, always."

"I'm glad to hear that," Reyes said. "And for what it's worth, you did inspire at least one part of my speech."

"Dare I ask?"

"The part about making certain they didn't die in vain." Reyes lowered his voice. "You and your crew did good work on Ravanar IV. How your chief engineer solved a riddle that's baffled an entire team of R&D engineers for two years, I'll never know . . . but I'm glad you came along when you did. Hallie and her crew are going to be missed around here, but thanks to you and your crew, their sacrifices weren't empty ones. They owe you a debt of gratitude, Kirk . . . and so do I."

Kirk extended his hand to Reyes. "It's an honor just to serve, Commodore."

Shaking Kirk's hand, Reyes nodded with respect. "Likewise, Captain. Likewise."

Cervantes Quinn strolled past the athletic fields. Reyes's speech had just ended. The crowd was beginning to disperse into clusters, which wandered off in seemingly random directions. Quinn was looking for Tim Pennington, who he knew would come here to listen to the memorial address if not to report on it.

From the moment Pennington's story had broken on FNS, Quinn had known that the data card he had planted and directed Pennington to find had been instrumental in exposing the truth of the *Bombay*'s destruction. When the story unraveled the following day, however, he had realized only then that he had been an unwitting accomplice to the ruination of Pennington himself.

Though the litany of Quinn's criminal misdeeds would have filled a book, the one principle that he clung to was that he never deliberately hurt anyone just to make a profit. Stealing a man's property from a warehouse was one thing; violating that man's home was going too far. Scamming a man who had decided to play cards was to be expected; cheating an honest man who never asked for trouble was just plain wrong.

He had thought he was passing information to Pennington, doing the young reporter a favor. Instead, he'd handed the man the professional equivalent of hemlock.

Pennington was sitting on the top row of the bleachers closest to the podium. He looked terrible; his hair was unwashed, stubble peppered his cheeks and chin, and his clothes were wrinkled and stained. *Poor bastard,* Quinn thought, *he looks as bad as I do.*

Quinn climbed the bleachers to the top row and walked toward Pennington, who was busy composing text on his handheld recording device. The younger man looked up at Quinn as he sat down next to him. Pennington's face registered recognition first, followed by dread.

"Sorry I sucker-punched you the other day," Quinn said.

Still wary, Pennington pretended to resume working on his recorder. "No worries."

Unsure how to proceed, Quinn watched the crowd for a moment, then said, "How 'bout we do this over?"

"Do what over?"

Quinn held out his hand to Pennington. "Cervantes Quinn—have rustbucket, will travel."

Cautiously, as if he might be reaching toward a live wire, Pennington reached over and grasped Quinn's hand. "Tim Pennington, public laughingstock."

"Glad to meet you." Quinn reached inside his coat and produced a flask. He unscrewed the cap, downed a swig of booze, then offered it to Pennington. "Care for a drink?"

Pennington gave the flask a suspicious look. "What is it?"

"Green and foul."

He took the flask from Quinn's hand. "Sounds perfect." He helped himself to a long pull from the flask, then handed it back. "Thanks."

"Don't mention it."

While Quinn took another nip of the sour green stuff, Pennington put away his recording device. "I can't place your accent," the young man said. "Where are you from?"

Quinn sleeved a small dribble from his chin. "All over."

"No," Pennington said, "I meant, what's your ancestry?"

"Oh," Quinn said, making a large nod of comprehension. "I'm a drunkard."

"A citizen of the galaxy, then."

"Precisely."

Pennington's cynicism reasserted itself. "So what's this all about? What do you want?"

Quinn shrugged. "Like I said, I felt bad."

"About punching me in the bar."

"Yeah, that's right."

The reporter shook his head. "That's pretty thin, mate."

"Take it or leave it," Quinn said.

Pennington pondered that. "What's in it for me?"

"I travel a lot," Quinn said. "Here and there, wherever. You can tag along, if you don't mind tight quarters. Get out and see the galaxy a little. Who knows? You might learn something."

Nodding, Pennington volleyed back, "What's in it for you?"

"Someone to play cards with on long hauls." Looking around at the now-empty bleachers and increasingly empty athletic fields, he added, "Unless you think your legion of friends and adoring fans wouldn't approve."

"All right, I'll take it," Pennington said, then plucked the flask from Quinn's hand and took another drink. The alcohol made his voice sound choked-off as he tried to pass the flask back to Quinn. "Cheers, mate."

"Finish it," Quinn said. "We'll get more later."

Pennington knocked back the last of the green hooch in the flask and winced. Quinn didn't know what the young reporter had done to deserve what T'Prynn did to his career, or even if he had deserved it at all. What he did know was that the next time someone came looking to take a cheap shot at Pennington, he would be there to make sure they didn't get the chance.

I helped wreck this guy's life, Quinn brooded behind his crooked smile. *But I swear to God, I'm gonna help him fix it.*

Though Manón's Cabaret would not officially open for a few more hours, its proprietress kindly admitted T'Prynn shortly after the end of Commodore Reyes's address at the memorial. Taking her place at the piano, T'Prynn closed her eyes and railed against the *katra* of Sten, whose voice jabbed at her conscious and subconscious mind with his endless calls for her submission.

Never.

Her fingers found the right keys purely by muscle memory. Improvised notes of a somber tone flowed from her mind to her hands, giving vent to her sorrow. Her face remained stoic as she wept in chords and melodies, grieving in slow progressions of D-minor. By an infinitesimal degree, the psycho-emotional pressure battering her brittle mental shields abated, and for a brief time Sten's harassing voice fell silent.

A key change helped her find a roundabout passage into Paul Tillotson's moody instrumental "Morphine." It didn't bother her to play without an audience; their applause was of no interest to her. She didn't play for them.

Minutes passed as she savored every subtle riff and turn in the centuries-old composition. She was uncertain which she admired more, its emotional complexity or its mathematical subtlety. As with most enduring musical forms, she concluded that the two were, in fact, inalienable.

She finished the song and reveled in the silence.

"Most skillfully executed," Spock said.

T'Prynn opened her eyes and turned her head. The first officer of the *Enterprise* stood at ease in front of the stage. His long face was stern and unyielding, in the finest Vulcan tradition. She nodded to him. "Most kind, Spock." With a focus on embodying calm in her every word and gesture, she slowly rose from the bench, closed the keyboard cover, and stepped off the low stage. "Manón usually brings me tea after I play. Would you care to join me?"

"My visit will be brief," Spock said. "I must return to the *Enterprise*. We leave within the hour."

"I understand." She gestured to a nearby table. "Sit down."

The two Vulcans took seats opposite each other. Manón emerged from the kitchen carrying a tray, on which rested a china teapot, two cups, and spoons. The supernaturally radiant woman set down the beverages on the table, between Spock and T'Prynn, then left the room without saying anything.

T'Prynn poured herself a small cup of steaming-hot green tea. Still holding the pot, she cast an inquiring look at Spock. He declined with a small gesture of his hand. She set down the teapot. "Share your thoughts, Spock."

"You are most proficient in your art," he said. "Though I suspect few Vulcans would approve of your techniques."

"Do you disapprove, Spock?"

"I seek to understand."

Holding her cup in both hands, she sipped her tea. Its gentle bitterness was tempered with jasmine and peppermint. "It would be a privilege to share my art with you."

He lifted his chin, betraying a small glimmer of pride. "I think that our styles would not be compatible."

Despite her struggle for control, her left eyebrow lifted, betraying her annoyance. "Double-entendres do not become you, Spock. Speak plainly."

"The public disgrace of reporter Tim Pennington," he said. "Evidence suggests it was your doing."

"Evidence can suggest many things."

"I submit that it is now you who is not speaking plainly."

T'Prynn set down her teacup. "For the sake of discussion, let us proceed on the assumption that Mr. Pennington's disgrace was deliberately engineered. Does that offend you, Spock?"

"I find lying offensive," Spock said. "In particular when its effect is to inflict harm."

"What if its primary effect is to avert violence, or even a war? Does the pursuit of a noble aim make some lies permissible, even if collateral damage occurs as a result?"

"Morality is not necessarily logical," Spock said. "But logic's foundation is truthfulness. A lie is its antithesis."

"Your analysis is narrow, Spock," she said. "Under the correct circumstances, if enough lives—or perhaps the right lives—were at stake, you would understand the logical rationale for the tactical use of falsehood." She picked up her teacup. "But you are young. Time is an excellent teacher."

"You are not that much older than I am—T'Prynn, daughter of Sivok and L'Nel."

Hearing her parents' names gave her pause. Obviously, Spock had researched her past history and was attempting to provoke her, though to what end she wasn't certain. Setting down her tea once more, she maintained eye contact with the half-Vulcan man. "I am more than twice your age, Spock—son of Sarek and Amanda."

A handful of dirt flung into my eyes.

She tensed as Sten's *katra* took advantage of her agitation to reassert its assault on her psyche. A non-Vulcan would not have detected the microexpressions that played across her features in moments like these. She hoped that Spock, being half-human, would lack the insight to notice.

Concern hardened his features. "Your mind is troubled."

"It is a private matter."

I swing the rock and feel his pain as it gouges his chin.

"I know that you have not returned to Vulcan for fifty-three years," Spock said. "You live in exile. Why?"

"Self-exile," she said.

"You were pledged to Sten, son of—"

"I know his name."

Sten's hands lock around my throat. I tighten my neck muscles to prevent him from crushing my trachea.

"You slew him in the *Koon-ut-kal-if-fee.*"

"Yes," T'Prynn said softly.

"Is that why you do not return?"

"No."

Spock pondered that. "Please tell me why you choose exile."

"I prefer not to."

"As you wish," he said, and rose from his chair. "Thank you for the music and the offer of tea." He walked toward the exit.

Sten's agony is mine as the blade of my lirpa *slams down on his foot, severing most of his toes.*

T'Prynn called out, in a voice just shy of a shout, "Spock."

He stopped and turned back toward her.

Mustering her courage, she said simply, "I am a *val'reth.*"

His curiosity visibly aroused, Spock lifted one eyebrow. He returned to her side and lowered his voice to a confidential hush. Like most Vulcans, he respected the delicacy of these matters. "You host another's *katra* against your will?" She nodded, once, very slowly, and Spock understood. "Sten."

"Yes. He forced himself into my mind as I killed him."

"Logical," Spock said. "Death was imminent, and you had physical contact because of the *koon-ut-kal-if-fee*."

"Indeed," T'Prynn said. "Though I suspect his motives were driven more by spite than by logic."

"You climbed the steps of Mount Seleya?"

"I did," she said. "I passed through the Hall of Ancient Thought. But when the priestess tried to claim Sten's *katra* . . . he would not leave."

"It is not logical," Spock said, clearly surprised.

"It is when one considers Sten's principal objective at the time of death—to force me into submission. He projected his *katra* into me not for return to his ancestors, but to continue the fight until I surrender."

"Is there nothing that can be done?"

"The Adepts consulted the ancient texts and melded with me far too many times for my comfort," she confessed. "The consensus was always the same: They cannot force Sten's *katra* from me without destroying it . . . and my own *katra*, as well."

Spock nodded gravely. Apparently, he understood the dire consequences of *katra* possession as well as she did. Until she was rid of Sten's *katra*, she could not enjoy the release of *Pon farr*, would be denied the serenity of *Kolinahr*, and could not be assured that her own *katra* would find rest with those of her ancestors. In effect, she was condemned to do battle for her mind and soul every day, until

her will faltered or Sten finally abandoned his mad onslaught.

"May I be of aid or comfort, T'Prynn?"

"No, Spock. This affliction is mine alone. But I thank
you for your kind offer."

He held up his hand in the Vulcan salute.

"Live long and prosper, T'Prynn."

She stood and returned the salute.

"Peace and long life, Spock."

She watched him leave, then she reached for her tea.

The bones of my hand splinter beneath Sten's heel.

The teacup fell from her hand and smashed on the floor.

T'Prynn walked back onstage, sat down at the piano,
and lifted the cover from the keys.

Sten's *katra* raged inside her. *Submit!*

She raised her hands, then brought them down for a
booming, low-C crescendo. *Never!*

"Ready to clear moorings, Captain," Leslie said.

"Thank you, Mr. Leslie," Kirk said. "Initiate departure
sequence."

"Vanguard Control," Leslie said. "*Enterprise* is ready to
depart spacedock."

"*Confirmed,* Enterprise. *We'll lead you out. Opening
bay doors. Stand by.*"

Though Kirk could not pinpoint any one detail or other
that made the difference, he could tell his ship was back in
prime condition just by the way it felt and sounded around
him. The steady, low vibrato of the impulse engines in the
deck, the fine-tuned pitch of systems operating in harmony . . . the *Enterprise* was herself again, thanks to hours

of labor by Scotty, his engineers, and the Vanguard space-dock team.

In a matter of weeks the *Enterprise* and her crew would be home, back in the heart of the Federation. From there, the rest of the galaxy lay open before them, ripe for exploration and discovery. Worlds and civilizations unmet by humanity called to Kirk like a siren's song; he was old enough now to have put aside childish desires, but he remained young enough at heart to smile with the excitement of facing the new and unknown.

"Enterprise, *you are clearing spacedock doors. Stand by for helm control in thirty seconds.*"

On the main viewer, the docking clamps and airlock port of Vanguard's core slowly receded as the *Enterprise* was guided out of spacedock by Vanguard's navigational system. Kirk settled into his chair and checked a refueling report his yeoman handed to him. He had just finished and handed it back when the turbolift door opened, and Spock stepped onto the bridge. The first officer moved directly to Kirk's side.

"Welcome back, Mr. Spock," Kirk said. "We almost left without you." In a more confidential tone, he added, "Did you finish your business on Vanguard?"

"Not entirely," Spock said. "Unfortunately, there is nothing more that I can do at this time."

"I see," Kirk said.

On the main viewer, the upper hull of Vanguard loomed large as *Enterprise* cleared the spacedock doors.

"Enterprise, *we're releasing helm control now. The lane is clear and you are free to navigate. . . . Godspeed,* Enterprise. *Vanguard out.*"

"Helm control confirmed," Leslie said. "Course, Captain?"

Kirk nodded at the screen. "Earth, Mr. Leslie. Warp six."

"Aye, sir."

As Vanguard shrank into the distance and the *Enterprise* turned toward the curtain of stars, Kirk looked at Spock. "I'm sorry you didn't find what you were looking for, but for what it's worth, I think we'll be back here again."

"Agreed," Spock said, as the *Enterprise* jumped to warp.

Bundled in a bulky maroon jacket and thick gloves, Ensign Stephen Klisiewicz, science officer of the *Starship Endeavour*, could barely see the tricorder in his hand, never mind work its small controls. His parka hood was cinched tight to keep his ears warm, but that precaution, coupled with the shrieking arctic wind, made it almost impossible to hear the device's high-pitched oscillations as it scanned the surrounding terrain.

Dimly lit by the light of a white-dwarf sun, the rest of the landing party had fanned out and moved away from the towering glacier of dark-blue ice that held Klisiewicz's attention. Getting a clear reading from inside the frozen mass was proving troublesome, and he couldn't tell whether the problem was trace elements in the water, radioactive interference from the bedrock beneath it, or a complete malfunction of his tricorder.

Commander Atish Khatami, the *Endeavor*'s first officer, tromped toward him, the wide ovals of her snowshoes leaving behind distinctive waffle-tread prints in the formerly pristine snow. Shrouded in cold-weather gear, she looked identical right now to the rest of the landing party, except for the white rank insignia that circled the cuffs of her jacket sleeves. "Klisiewicz," she said. "We're not reading anything over here. I think we should beam over to the next survey point."

"Can I have another minute, Commander? I might have something, if I can just break through the interference."

"Make it quick," Khatami said. She unclipped her communicator from the broad utility belt around her waist. It flipped open with a distinctive triple chirp. Adjusting its gain, she spoke into it, "Khatami to *Endeavour*."

Captain Zhao Sheng answered. "Endeavour *here. Go ahead.*"

"Our sweep's mostly finished; we're waiting on Klisiewicz to finish scanning the galaxy's largest ice cube. Anything new and exciting up there?"

"*Actually, yes,*" Zhao said. "*The* Sagittarius *just reported that its long-range sensors picked up subspace signal traffic inside the Taurus Reach. Looks like we might have some first-contact missions ahead of us.*"

Klisiewicz and Khatami turned toward each other. Even though neither one could see the other's face under the breathing masks and goggles, Klisiewicz was certain they were both smiling the same goofy grin. *First contact! That's the whole reason we're here!*

"That's great news, sir," Khatami said.

"*I agree,*" Zhao said. "*And with the* Exeter *relieving us on border patrol, I'd like to get back to making those missions happen. How long until your survey's done?*"

Khatami and the rest of the landing party—which consisted of chief engineer Bersh glov Mog; Ensign Bonnie Malmat, senior geologist; and security guards Jeanne La Sala and Paul McGibbon—gathered around Ensign

Klisiewicz. Noting the general mood of impatience pressing in on him, he shouted over the wind, "Hang on, I've got an idea." On a hunch, he resorted to a simpler scanning protocol and made another attempt to pierce the interference. Like a Rorschach blot, an image appeared on his tricorder screen.

"Commander," he said. "You'd better look at this."

The first officer carefully sidled up to him, her snowshoes overlapping his own in an awkward jumble. He shifted his posture to let her look at his tricorder display. She stared at it for several moments, but he knew not to interrupt her chain of thought. Khatami was one of the smartest officers Klisiewicz had ever met; he knew that if she had any questions, she'd ask.

"Question," she said. "Is that the same configuration?"

"Affirmative," he said. "But bigger. A lot bigger."

"How far down is it?"

"Almost a hundred meters," Klisiewicz said.

Khatami waved over Malmat and showed her the tricorder data. "Does that look like a natural formation to you?"

Craning her neck and leaning forward to see the tricorder, Malmat said, "No. Too symmetrical. It's definitely synthetic, Commander."

The entire landing party stared up at the sapphire-tinted glacier as if it were about to lash out at them. Above it, the silvery sky was streaked with bruised pink clouds that were dimming with the encroaching dusk. Wind yowled furiously around the Starfleet team, whipping snow-devils into frenzied dances. Khatami turned toward Mog. "How long to excavate it?"

Folding his arms, the Tellarite chief engineer gave

the glacier a long look, then said, "About thirty seconds."

Panic was not a normal reaction for Klisiewicz, but he knew right away what his friend was about to propose. "No! It's too—"

"Get behind that bluff," Mog said, then flipped open his communicator. "Mog to *Endeavour*. Arm phaser banks one and two and stand by to receive my firing solution."

Khatami and the rest of the group were already jogging in comical snowshoed strides toward the bluff while Mog and Klisiewicz bickered at the base of the glacier. "Mog, don't be crazy! You could damage it! What if it has defenses? What if—"

"Relax, Steve," Mog said. "I know what I'm doing."

"At least use the tricorder to calculate the—"

"Don't need it." He lifted his goggles and squinted at the glacier; then he lowered his breathing mask and grinned at Klisiewicz. "Take cover. I'll be right behind you."

Convinced that logic wasn't going to win the day with the headstrong Tellarite, Klisiewicz scrambled across the snow plain toward the rocky bluff where the rest of the landing party had already ducked and covered. Watching his enormous snowshoes flopping clumsily with each step, he felt like a sprinting circus clown.

A few meters shy of the bluff, Mog ran past him. "Step it up, kid, or you'll get a tan you'll never forget!"

They leaped together over the bluff into the protective shadows on the far side. Half a breath later, the wind was outscreamed by the whine of a phaser strike as bright as the dawn.

Klisiewicz shut his eyes and covered his ears until it was over. It seemed to him like a lot longer than thirty seconds.

Finally, the screeching of the phasers ceased, leaving only the banshee moan of a freezing gale.

Peeking over the edge of the bluff, Khatami muttered something in Farsi that the wind drowned out. In staggered motions, the landing party got to its feet and looked out toward where the glacier had been only seconds before.

Some of the ice that had been vaporized was flurrying back down around the landing party as snow. Most of it, however, had escaped into the atmosphere as heated gas and likely would not recondense for several hours. A relatively small amount had been left behind as liquid water that pooled in the fresh, three-hundred-meter-deep crater in the ground. The phasers had bored through the ice and scoured down to bare stone, revealing a massive rock basin.

Dominating that basin was a structure unlike anything else Klisiewicz had ever seen. Composed of a gleaming black substance that resembled both glass and stone, its overall affect was insectoid and sinister. The largest component was an open dome. It consisted of four massive legs, evenly spaced, broad and thick at their bases and tapering at their apexes, which were joined by a sturdy disk-shaped structure. The disk itself formed the apex of a truncated, conical claw that was suspended above its mirror image, which was recessed into a broad, sloping circular dais half the circumference of the open dome. Biomechanical tubing and components snaked like varicose veins across the structure's every surface. It was several hundred meters in diameter, more than two hundred meters tall, and even from more than a hundred meters away it radiated a tangible aura of power.

Klisiewicz activated his tricorder and pointed it into

the basin. "I'm getting bioreadings in the meltwater, Commander."

"Probably just bacteria released by the thermal effects," Khatami said.

"Maybe," Klisiewicz said. Removing the sample rod from his tricorder, he kneeled down, tapped through the crust of ice that was swiftly knitting itself across a freshly melted puddle near the crater's edge, and scooped up a few droplets of water. Inserting the rod back into the tricorder, he ran a detailed chemical analysis. The results confirmed his suspicions. He offered the tricorder to Khatami. "Recognize it?"

She didn't have to answer. Her silence as she gave him back the tricorder was confirmation enough that she knew the Taurus Meta-Genome when she saw it. She flipped open her communicator. "Khatami to *Endeavour*."

"*Go ahead,*" Captain Zhao said.

"Captain, we . . . Ensign Klisiewicz has made a remarkable discovery, sir. He's found an alien structure in need of further analysis, and . . . life signs, sir."

"*What kind of life signs, Khatami?*"

"Type-V," she said, using the code for the meta-genome.

After a brief delay, Zhao said, "*Acknowledged. Prepare to beam up. We'll notify Vanguard to send in the specialists. . . . And tell Klisiewicz I said 'nice work.' Zhao out.*"

Staring down into the basin, Klisiewicz shook with the raw thrill of discovery. The tip from Xiong had been a long shot, but it had paid off. Unlike the Ravanar artifact, this one appeared to be intact. There was no telling what clues it might yield in Starfleet's search for the secrets of its creation.

More important, Klisiewicz knew, finding another sample of the meta-genome on a world that also housed another of these majestic machines was unlikely to be a coincidence. Klisiewicz was certain that when they compared notes, Xiong would agree that the meta-genome and the massive artifacts must somehow be connected. Klisiewicz didn't know yet what that connection might be, but looking down at the glistening obsidian structure below, he was certain that he had just taken the first step toward deciphering a map written on the stars.

A smirk tugged at the corner of his mouth.

Here we come.

EPILOGUE

Scorching wind ripped across a blackened plain on Ravanar IV. Gargantuan stratocumulus mountains of dust, blasted high into the atmosphere, blotted out the starlight, turning the night into a pitch-black inferno of howling sandstorms.

The Shedai Wanderer moved through the lightless maelstrom, guided by memories that refused to die. *There was life here,* she recollected. *Brief . . . fragile . . . but it was here.*

It was too soon, she knew, for this world to have run its course. It should have had billions of years left to it. The Shedai would not have chosen it otherwise. *Someone laid waste to this orb with malicious intent.* Arriving at the sandswept ruins of the Conduit, she intuited who was to blame for this horror.

Once more they wreak their havoc upon us.

Eons had passed in blessed silence. Left to bury themselves in their own ashes, most of the Shedai had been content to let the past claim them, satisfied to slumber until time unmade them with the slow inevitability of entropy. A few who could not abandon their legions of helpless "flickers of life" to the arbitrary designs of the universe had remained awake these many millennia, perhaps entertaining some forlorn hope of finding new hosts for the Conduits, and of elevating the Shedai once more to their past glory.

Until the song of the Conduit roused her a day-moment ago, the Shedai Wanderer had given up such ambitions; she had been embraced by the blissful darkness of oblivion. Wrenching herself back into the light, the heat, the torment of mere being, was an indignity that stoked her fury. The song of the Conduit had brought her up from the bedrock, out of the cold sanctuary of her grave, into this fiery desert wrought by fear and hatred.

She picked through needle-like fragments of the Conduit's explosively shattered black stoneglass. *Our legacy has become a target.* The Wanderer cast her fury upward, toward the obscured heavens, imagining who would be so brazen as to risk awakening the wrath of the Shedai. *Only a great power would dare such a reprisal.*

She clutched the razor-sharp black shard, paying it no heed as it sliced through her flesh; she knew the wound would heal in moments.

They will come for us next, she concluded.

I must awaken the others.

The saga of
STAR TREK VANGUARD
will continue

GUIDE TO PRINCIPAL CHARACTERS

COMMODORE DIEGO REYES
(COMMANDING OFFICER)

A fifty-something human officer of Chilean ancestry, born and raised in the Lunar settlement of New Berlin, Reyes is a rough-hewn but amiable CO, with an appreciation for irony and dark humor. As a thirty-year Starfleet veteran, he's experienced enough not to be easily surprised, but he's still intrigued by the unknown and the mysteries of the universe. His command style is smooth and decisive, seldom hesitant, and can come in quick bursts.

Despite his friendly disposition, he maintains more emotional distance from his crew than most *Star Trek* COs we've seen. He hides his strongest feelings, is stoic about pain, and limits his mirth to a lockjawed grin. Part of Reyes's closed-off manner is the result of his bitter divorce from his ex-wife, Jeanne, which has made it difficult for him to trust anyone or form close relationships. Though he won't admit it aloud (and maybe not even to himself), he really wishes he had children.

Reyes is one of the four people on the station aware of the secret aspect of the Federation's mission into the Taurus Reach. The others are T'Prynn, Jetanien, and Xiong.

LIEUTENANT COMMANDER T'PRYNN
(INTELLIGENCE OFFICER)

A relatively young (seventies) Vulcan, T'Prynn keeps a
low profile aboard the station, specializing in information
gathering and analysis, threat assessment, and, when necessary, covert ops. Her wit is dry, her sarcasm sharp, her
voice smoky-sweet. Off duty, T'Prynn sometimes plays
piano in the starbase cabaret. In contrast to her cool behavior, her music is passionate and eloquent. Her performances lead some of her associates to wonder if it's her
way of circumventing her people's strict dictums of logic
in order to express her turbulent inner state of mind. Like
many other Vulcans, during childhood she was pledged to
a mate, Sten. Upon reaching adulthood, she spurned him.
Unwilling to release her, Sten invoked the *kal-if-fee*. But
instead of selecting a champion to fight on her behalf, she
herself faced Sten in ritual combat and slew him to win
her independence. The unexpected consequences of that
act have tormented her ever since.

AMBASSADOR JETANIEN
(SENIOR FEDERATION DIPLOMAT)

On permanent assignment to the Federation Embassy on
Starbase 47, Jetanien supervises a small staff of envoys,
attachés, and aides to deal with the full spectrum of diplomatic issues that come up in the Taurus Reach. Jetanien is
a wise and learned statesman with a firm belief in the

ideals of the United Federation of Planets, a wry sense of humor, and an appreciation for unpredictable twists of diplomacy. When the need arises, he can be a passionate orator and a tough negotiator. His knowledge of history is detailed and highly nuanced. His role is to expand Federation control in the region through political alliance and expansion of colonial holdings.

Jetanien is a Rigellian Chelon, a species glimpsed among the background aliens during *Star Trek: The Motion Picture*. The Chelon are amphibious bipeds, tall, broad, with a tough armored hide where their turtle-like ancestors once had a carapace. Their skin tones range from greenish to blue and yellow, and, rarely, black. Their eyes are large and see well in darkness. Their clawed digits are long, webbed, and nimble. They live much longer than humans, and reach maturity more slowly (thirty years).

LIEUTENANT MING XIONG
(ARCHAEOLOGY & ANTHROPOLOGY OFFICER)

Xiong is not just a brilliant researcher. He is trained in a variety of skills, including piloting, general engineering, and operations in extreme environments. Despite his skills, however, he's not likely to advance in rank. He has a lot of suppressed anger and can be hostile toward authority figures. He says things in meetings that he shouldn't. He's young enough (thirty-one) to be an idealist and old enough to be disappointed by the galaxy's cynicism. His superiors respect his talents but worry that his volatility will embarrass them, spark a war, or be aimed at them. Because of Xiong's expertise and security clearance regarding the Taurus Reach mystery, Reyes cuts Xiong a lot more slack than he does to other officers—but there is a limit.

What really bothers Xiong is that he wants more openness in the exploration of the Taurus Reach mystery; he sees a chance for the open exchange of scientific ideas to build bridges to other civilizations, like the Klingons and the Tholians, but he's been ordered to keep his findings quiet. As long as he plays by the rules, he'll continue serving detached duty aboard the three starships assigned to Vanguard's command. Like many idealists before him, he rails against injustice and defends underdogs, even when it puts the Federation in politically awkward binds. Experience has not yet dimmed his belief in justice; Xiong joined Starfleet not just to see the galaxy, but to help it.

DR. EZEKIEL FISHER
(CHIEF MEDICAL OFFICER)

Called "Zeke" by those closest to him, Fisher is the "old man" among the crew: Been around, seen it all, and he is wise enough to know there's no perfect solution to any problem; there are only solutions with degrees of imperfection. He knows that Starfleet and the Federation have their flaws, as does every species and political system, and he isn't afraid to tell it like it is. He has little patience for pretense and usually sees right through people's façades. Fisher is in his eighties, and after more than fifty years "in the service" is weary of Starfleet life. He plans to retire in a few years and return home to Mars. While he works as CMO on Starbase Vanguard, he's training his replacement, attending physician Dr. Jabilo M'Benga.

Fisher's wife, Hannah, passed away of natural causes a few years ago; his sons Ely and Noah live far away, on Deneva and Alpha Centauri. Neither followed him into medicine, unlike his daughter, Jane, who runs a family practice back on Mars. All three of his children have kids of their own.

CAPTAIN RANA DESAI
(JAG OFFICER)

In her late thirties, Desai is a specialist in interstellar law. A talented investigator and trial lawyer, she has a mind like a steel trap. Though she's quick to pounce when regulations are being bent too far, she also understands that the unpredictable nature of life on the frontier requires a certain flexibility. Also, this is new territory, with rules of its own: It's her job to figure out what those rules are as Starfleet probes deeper into the Taurus Reach, and what they might mean for the Federation. It's also her responsibility to make sure their people understand and respect that as much as they adhere to Federation law or Starfleet regs. Given the complex issues that often come up, this can be a difficult balancing act. Though she and Reyes share deep convictions about duty, law, and justice, they often disagree on how best to serve these ideals.

TIM PENNINGTON
(JOURNALIST)

Frontier correspondent for the Federation News Service,
Scotland-born Tim Pennington is a smart, young (twenty-
seven), brash, and persistent all-around-pain-in-the-ass journalist covering the Federation's activities in Starbase 47's
particular corner of the galaxy. Pennington (for whom the
Pennington School of *Deep Space Nine* fame will one day be
named) is *Vanguard*'s twist on *Star Trek*'s traditional "out-
sider" character. He is the voice of the common man among
the Starfleet officers, diplomats, and hostile aliens, questioning everything from the point of view of the "little guy."

Pennington is a thoughtful man, and he chooses his
words carefully. He views the power players on the station
as obstacles to "the truth," and he bends the law as far as he
can to get information, access, and evidence. Pennington
strives to remain objective, but he knows that truly objective reporting means more than parroting both sides of a
polarizing issue. He is shrewd and insightful, and he understands people as well as he does politics. His greatest struggle is to maintain the same high standards of ethics in his
personal life as he does in the professional arena.

CERVANTES QUINN
(TRADER)

Like Harcourt Fenton Mudd and Cyrano Jones, Cervantes
Quinn is a solitary, semi-legit soldier of fortune always try-

ing to stay one step ahead of Starfleet, but usually he's in way over his head. He owns the *Rocinante*, a small cargo ship for hire. He traffics in goods both legal and not, does some prospecting and some smuggling, gets into lots of trouble, and commits the occasional good deed. Quinn always expects the worst while hoping for the best. He's been married four times, each experience worse than the last—but still he hears love's siren call. He's been arrested more times than he can count, but never convicted, and so he continues to tempt fate. He is a provocateur; he loves to sow chaos, then sit back and watch the fun. He cracks wise, is a master of ironic understatement, and loves to push people's buttons. He plays all sides against one another and, if all else fails, he's pretty good at throwing sucker punches. He's not without a conscience, though; he won't knowingly let someone be hurt by his schemes, and he won't profit from others' suffering.

ANNA SANDESJO/LURQAL
(FEDERATION DIPLOMATIC ATTACHÉ/KLINGON SPY)

Senior diplomatic attaché Anna Sandesjo looks human, but she is in fact an agent of Klingon Imperial Intelligence. She has infiltrated Starbase 47's diplomatic team in order to provide the Empire with information about the Federation's true intentions in the Taurus Reach. To that end, Sandesjo listens, watches, collects data, and reports regularly.

Sandesjo's original name is Lurqal. She uses a subspace transmitter concealed under a false panel in her briefcase to report regularly to another Klingon covert operative, Turag, who is part of the Klingon delegation to Vanguard. She also has infrequent contact with Klingon envoy Lugok. Sandesjo is stronger than she looks; after all, she is a Klingon. But she is not by nature a warrior. She is from a caste of political and scientific elites, not of a noble house but not a commoner—more from the landed-gentry class.

GANZ
(MERCHANT-PRINCE)

An Orion, Ganz is a self-styled mogul, the type of merchant-prince glimpsed during one of Pike's illusions in "The Cage." He has been lured by the Federation's interest in the Taurus Reach into seeking new markets for his illicit trade, which ranges from narcotic substances to weapons smuggling and sexual commerce. As a general rule, he forbids his employees from doing business with Starfleet personnel.

Ganz is honorable, to a point; reneging on deals is bad for business. He is utterly ruthless and not above using intimidation or outright violence to get his way. Regardless, he knows his limitations; he won't let his people pick fights with Starfleet or openly antagonize the Federation. He conducts his business for the most part aboard a large, lavish yacht docked at Vanguard.

ACKNOWLEDGMENTS

First, I need to thank my lovely and patient wife, Kara, who for the second year in a row was forced to cope with my near-total absence from her life during the holiday season. Instead of helping her trim the Christmas tree, I hid away in my home office struggling to string words together.

My greatest thanks, however, go to my editor, Marco Palmieri, who in the spring of 2004, shortly after I had turned in the manuscript for my previous novel, *A Time to Heal,* asked me if I would be interested in writing the first volume of a brand-new *Star Trek* book series. There are several such series these days, so new ones don't get created that often. Being asked to help nurture a brand-new series concept into existence is a tremendous privilege, which makes Marco's invitation a remarkable show of faith. I am honored that I was the one he chose.

Inspiration, though sometimes a solitary gift, was, in the case of *Harbinger,* the product of a fruitful collaboration. Much of the vision for what lay inside the station was provided by designer Masao Okazaki; his enthusiasm and genuine passion for this project helped clarify my own ideas during the writing of the manuscript. Likewise, my gratitude goes out to Doug Drexler, who rendered Masao's designs into one of the most gorgeous covers yet to grace my words. Furthermore, the counsel and creative suggestions of Paula Block and John Van Citters of Paramount Licensing were invaluable. Their keen instincts for storytelling, coupled with their oracular knowledge of the minutiae of this broad shared universe, helped bring the "big picture" of the *Star Trek Vanguard* saga into sharp focus.

This book required me to spend a lot more time writing from inside a Vulcan's head than I had ever attempted before, and fellow-author Susan Shwartz, who has collaborated with Josepha Sherman on some of the most acclaimed Vulcan-themed books in *Star Trek* history, very generously provided me with guidance and a sounding board as I developed the backstory for the character of T'Prynn.

Author and editor extraordinaire Keith R. A. DeCandido once again proved himself a valuable resource and a good friend, from the earliest days of developing the *Star Trek Vanguard* series bible to helping me reason out some of my plot conundrums.

To the Malibuvians . . . you know who you are. Just keep on being your crazy selves.

To my agent, Lucienne: Thank you for making sure I got paid for this.

To my wonderful parents, David and Yvonne, thank you for a lifetime of encouragement. I could not have become what I am without your love and unswerving confidence.

I also owe a debt of gratitude to the many fine teachers who inspired me to chase my dreams: Kenneth Beals; Carolyn Bruneau; William Rathbun; Charles F. Rockey, Sr.; Bruce Geisler; and D. B. Gilles. You all fanned the creative spark until it grew into a flame. Thank you.

He currently is working on an original novel and developing new *Star Trek* book ideas.

A graduate of NYU's renowned film school, Mack has been to every Rush concert tour since 1982. He currently resides in New York City with his wife, Kara.

ABOUT THE AUTHOR

DAVID MACK is a writer whose work spans multiple media. With writing partner John J. Ordover, he co-wrote the *Star Trek: Deep Space Nine* episode "Starship Down" and the story treatment for the *Star Trek: Deep Space Nine* episode "It's Only a Paper Moon." Mack and Ordover also penned the four-issue *Star Trek: Deep Space Nine/Star Trek: The Next Generation* crossover comic-book mini-series "Divided We Fall" for WildStorm Comics. With Keith R. A. DeCandido, Mack co-wrote the *Star Trek: S.C.E.* eBook novella *Invincible,* currently available in paperback as part of the collection *Star Trek: S.C.E. Book Two—Miracle Workers.*

Mack's solo writing for *Star Trek* includes the trade paperback *The Starfleet Survival Guide* and the best-selling, critically acclaimed two-part eBook novel *Star Trek: S.C.E.—Wildfire* (reprinted in the paperback compilation *Star Trek: S.C.E. Book Six—Wildfire*). His other credits include "Waiting for G'Doh, or, How I Learned to Stop Moving and Hate People," a short story for the *Star Trek: New Frontier* anthology *No Limits;* S.C.E. eBook #40, *Failsafe;* the short story "Twilight's Wrath," for the *Star Trek* anthology *Tales of the Dominion War;* the *Star Trek: The Next Generation* duology *A Time to Kill* and *A Time to Heal;* S.C.E. eBook #49, *Small World;* and *Star Trek Vanguard: Harbinger.*

Of course, there would be no *Star Trek Vanguard* without the original, classic *Star Trek,* and for that I thank Gene Roddenberry and all the talented writers, actors, and production personnel who helped bring that show to life.

Lastly, just a trivial note: For those of you reading this who live on what society thinks of as a "normal" schedule, I would just like you to know that you were probably asleep when the bulk of this book was written. Owing to circumstances beyond my control, most of my work on *Harbinger* took place between 11 p.m. and 4 a.m. U.S. Eastern Time. Right now, for instance, it's 4:23 a.m. Unfortunately for me, I also have a full-time job to go to during regular business hours, so you can see why this writing schedule proved to be ever-so-slightly problematic. . . .